John Saeki runs the graphics desk in the Hong Kong office of the international newswire Agence France-Presse. He spends his working days writing, designing and editing maps, charts and information graphics on world news. When he is not composing explainers and factfiles on spy scandals, refugee crises and wildlife, he likes to explore the historical trails and villages of Hong Kong. And when he is not doing that, he might well be writing songs about the scandals of the territory and the hopes and aspirations of its people. He has lived in Hong Kong for 17 years and, together with his wife Catherine, is raising a family in the strange, mixed-up place he calls home.

The Tiger Hunters of Tai O

John Saeki

BLACKSMITH BOOKS

The Tiger Hunters of Tai O
ISBN 978-988-77927-1-0

Copyright © 2017 John Saeki

Published by Blacksmith Books
Unit 26, 19/F, Block B, Wah Lok Industrial Centre,
37-41 Shan Mei Street, Fo Tan, Hong Kong
Tel: (+852) 2877 7899
www.blacksmithbooks.com

Edited by Grahame Collins
First printing 2017

Supported by

香港藝術發展局
Hong Kong Arts Development Council

Hong Kong Arts Development Council fully supports freedom of
artistic expression. The views and opinions expressed in this project do
not represent the stand of the Council.

CONTENTS

1   Ghost Riders 7

2   You Ain't Nothing but a Hound Dog. 30

3   Fever 50

4   Night in Tunisia. 77

5   Mac the Knife 106

6   Rags to Riches 131

7   The Lion Sleeps Tonight 146

8   Great Balls of Fire 182

9   Seven Lonely Days. 201

10   Bye Bye Blackbird 224

11   Ring of Fire 264

12   In Other Words 283

I

GHOST RIDERS

"Call me Ishmael!" the salt-encrusted mariner barked out as he opened the door to his old friend. He was standing in front of Captain Robert Falkirk, in the doorway of his creaking beach hut at Pui O, on Hong Kong's remote Lantau Island. The constant, uneven sound of waves engulfed Ishmael's home, his life and his soul.

"What brings you here, Captain?" he said as he embraced his former comrade-in-arms.

"Police work, of course," Falkirk replied with a big grin.

"Since when did Pui O get annexed by the Tai O constabulary?"

Falkirk was a day's hike outside of his beat.

"I was over in Mui Wo fetching supplies," he said, proudly holding up a new hunting rifle.

"What do you need that for?" Ishmael asked, intrigued and anticipating.

"The Beast of Tai O is back, my friend, and this time we're going to get him."

"Well, you'd better come in for a drink then, and tell me how we're going to do that."

"Do you have any news for me, Ishmael?"

Ishmael nearly blurted out that he had seen the Mongoose earlier in the day, but something made him hold back.

"It's a full moon. The horseshoe crabs are back," he said instead.

"Splendid. Are we firing up the coals?"

They took a walk along the beach to the shore where the alien-like sea creatures congregated every year.

Ishmael noticed the silhouette of a ship on the horizon, travelling south. He had a good idea who would be on it, but he ignored it and looked down. He picked up a hefty crab. "She'll do," he said.

"Funny looking buggers eh?" Falkirk noted.

"The stuff of nightmares, like monsters of the deep. Harmless though. We're the monsters, Falkirk, as you well know."

"Yes, I often wonder if the Beast of Tai O was in fact a man."

"I doubt it, we're more prolific. It was only one or two a year that went missing. War made the Beast look like a kitten."

"Aye, that's hard to deny," he conceded.

Mui Mui took the crab from Ishmael and washed its arachnid form under their pump outside the hut. She walked so well on her wooden stump that most people failed to notice she only had one leg.

"Not bad," she said, casting her expert appraisal at its hard greenish-grey shell, remembering a blood-splattered Japanese army helmet she had put a hole into.

"Who's manning the fort?" Ishmael asked.

"Simon Lee's running the show, with his pal Jagan."

"Lee? Jack White's secret love-child?"

"The very same. Likely into the fifth beer of their shift by now, listening to that god-awful American radio of theirs and talking the usual gibberish."

"What are ghost riders?" Sergeant Jagan Singh wondered back at the fort, swirling the beer around in his tin mug.

Deputy Inspector Simon Lee listened carefully to the wailing tune with its galloping rhythm.

"Horsemen, I'd imagine, galloping across the skies," he offered.

"They sound heroic, don't they?" Jagan said, trying to catch the words of the scratchy tune that came piping through the speaker on the police radio.

"They probably think for themselves, say what they think, and go where they like."

"I like the sound of that. Freedom."

"Yeah. I think it's a good position to be in. I might quit the marine police and see if I can apply for a job as a ghost rider," Simon said, peering through the reception room window, looking for the moon over the harbour.

"I'm not sure if there are any posts in the colonial administration for ghost riders," Singh said, opening the fifth bottle of the night.

Simon found the moonlight reflected in the water and followed it back, catching a glimpse of the source just before a cloud wrapped it up.

"No? Maybe, at some wild frontier post, a long way from the peacocks in Central?" Simon suggested.

"Well, that would be right here then. We're about as far away as you can get from the peacocks. This is the Wild West of Hong Kong, Simon, isn't that why the peacocks sent you here?"

"Oh yes, I forgot."

"You never forget."

"This beer is good."

"It's good."

"Hang on a minute, listen. They sound heroic, but it's the opposite. They're trapped, Jagan."

> *"If you wanna save your soul from hell a ridin' on our range. Then cowboy change your way today or with us you will ride. Tryin' to catch the devil's herd across these endless skies."*

Simon spoke along to the music. "It's a warning, Jagan, that's what it is. Get out before it's too late."

"I still think they sound heroic," Jagan decided.

"The American radio plays some great music, even if they talk a huge amount of tosh in between," Simon said after another swig of beer.

"Yes, interesting that such a fanatical race can create such great music."

"They're not a race, you know."

"You know what I mean."

"Not one bit. I never know what you mean. What do you mean by fanatical?"

"Fanatical self-belief. Fanatical self-righteousness."

It was Jagan who had found a way to use the police radio to tune in to American military broadcasts during their long night shifts. Not every constable approved of it, but when he was on duty with Simon Lee he knew that they would be tuning in, while the rest of the garrison slept or got drunk in the village.

Nothing major had happened on the night watch for a while. There was of course a wildness there that made life unpredictable, but for weeks at a time the place was simply a backwater, its lifeblood slowly seeping out as the fisheries declined and the salt pans shrivelled under the burning south China sun. During those times of quiet the night watch was a pleasure, usually enhanced by beers that the duty constables put on order with the day patrols. Most of the day boys were happy to supply, collecting 10 cents of "tea money" for every bottle delivered.

The quiet time would lull them into an illusion of calm. They all knew it was an illusion, but they were young and every day was a new universe that was potentially easy to cruise through, offering new pleasures and new hopes. Each day that passed from the last major incident made the new peaceful world they had woken up in seem more real, all the less likely to be shattered by some rude intrusion.

The "intrusion" could be anything from a sinking refugee boat from which they rescued terrified children, a gunfight between rival fishermen or Triads, or political agitators hacking at each other while shouting

Nationalist or Communist slogans. Or it could be a lone murder victim dumped after some disastrous domestic dispute, the cause of which would never be known outside the family of those involved – secret clan history that would be whispered through the ages, never to be exposed as fact or history.

Pirate and bandit attacks were dropping in frequency by the 1950s but they still posed a threat. This quiet backwater required regular armed patrols equipped with sub-machine guns, rifles, hand grenades and mortars. The foot patrols around the district were so heavily armed the locals called them "Pangolins." Not the most aggressive of mammals, but a strange and ridiculous creature fortified by armoured plating. The "intrusions" were not as infrequent as the young officers tended to think after a couple of days of quiet, especially after their fifth beer when the American Forces Radio filled their heads with fantastic landscapes and heroic horsemen.

They were in Tai O, on the south-western tip of Lantau Island, and therefore the very edge of the British Crown Colony of Hong Kong. Standing on the end of the police pier you can almost cast a fishing line into Chinese waters, certainly watch pink dolphins flit from one side of the border to the other with no regard for man-made boundaries that only exist on maps and in the minds of men. The place had been inhabited by fisherfolk and salt farmers for centuries and was an important Guangdong province trading post well before British merchants started eyeing up the China trade in Canton. Wandering Portuguese had beaten the Brits there by two centuries, leaving behind the Fan Gwai Tong hamlet named for "gwai" or "ghosts" – in other words, foreigners. By the time the British eventually assumed power in the area, fishing and salt production provided the largest income. A long shallow bay set up perfect salt-drying beds, protected by a unique seawall that had been built in the time of the Qianlong emperor some 200 years earlier. Salt connected Tai O to Imperial China, then to war-torn China, and continued to tie it to Communist China. It also taught

Tai O smugglers to work under the radar of imperial tax-collectors, Japanese military blockades, and embargo enforcers during the Korean War, when contraband continued shifting all around southern Chinese ports.

Along with the rest of Lantau Island, Tai O had remained outside of British control until British territory was extended by the addition of the New Territories in 1898. In 1902, the new overlords quickly established a police post at the far south-western reach of the colony – for its strategic position to guard an imperial frontline, not to police the population that for centuries had more or less been self-governing.

While the sea hemmed in Tai O on its western side, its other three sides were blocked off by mountains that were mainly left wild and forested, but also hosted an unusually high number of monasteries and nunneries. There was no surfaced road connection to Tai O, with buses only reaching the nearby Sham Wat road where sturdy sedan-girls waited to carry the wealthier passengers on their shoulders over a rugged mountain trail to the village. The nearest sizeable settlements were Tung Chung in one direction, where a Qing-dynasty fort and a dozen growling curs guarded village houses, and Mui Wo in another direction, a day's hike away, and the main port back to Hong Kong Island – and therefore back to civilisation as far as all gweilo 'ghost persons' and government employees were concerned. For many in Central and Kowloon, Lantau Island as a whole was the epitome of the rural, distant and untamed outpost. There were no proper roads, no hospitals, not even a restaurant. Instead there were pythons, leopard cats and wild boar. The fact that the same beasts could be found on Hong Kong Island made no difference. Lantau was the feral place. There were strange religious people in the mountains, Christians at the Trappist Monastery at least, the rest of them mumbo-jumbo-uttering oriental mystics. Other than that, peasant farmers eked out a subsistence existence inland, while fishermen and pirates worked the waters, the shoreline and the islands. Clans lived secretively behind high walls housing God knows how many people and how many guns. And for those who had even heard of Tai O and its sea-gypsies, the stilt-village at the end of Lantau Island was way beyond the pale, a dark and chaotic portal to ancient and alien lifeforms. It was a place of smugglers, illegal immigrants and mud-skippers.

Some in Central saw the Tai O Police Station, at this far-flung edge of the colony, as a ship without a rudder. The rudder was broken, or at least, it was drunk. The broken rudder was Captain Robert Falkirk, an undisputed war hero. Not only had he escaped from Stanley Prison during the brutal Japanese occupation, but he had stayed with guerrilla forces in south China, helping to coordinate other escapees through sweltering rainforests and up over the mountain gorges onto the Tibetan plateau, and down the other side of the Himalayas. He did this journey about 10 times, they said, fighting all the way. Each time he got to the safety of British India he would turn around and go back to south China to guide the next lot of desperate escapees. He fought the Japanese, he fought confused footsoldiers of both the Nationalist and Communist China, he fought bandits, mercenaries, mutineers, snakes, bears and wild cats. He killed a tiger in Yunnan province, they said. Falkirk could not be faulted.

So when he demanded to command Tai O, no one had the confidence to point out that a man of his age and habits should probably be kept to a desk job on Hollywood Road, where he could at least be picked up whenever he fell into the gutter on his way home from a heavy night in an opium den. But Tai O was where he wanted to go – not because he wanted to be out of sight, because he honestly couldn't have cared less what people saw him do, but because he wanted fresh-faced commanders and superiors and their uppity juniors to be out of his sight. Or as he put it himself in his application, "I'll be damned if I have to see you jumped-up bastards from Eton trying to run this fucking shithole for the short few years that remain of my life."

Thus he commanded Tai O, the legendary guerrilla, the reclusive curmudgeon. His style was laissez-faire, just like Hong Kong. The less the better. He didn't care about the formalities or the pretensions of the younger officers; he didn't like most of them in any case. What he liked was opium and beer and women. But any new police who took the old man's disdain for colonial pomp as evidence that he had given up on life made a big mistake. Under the hedonism and his dislike for the minions of empire, Falkirk had a fierce sense of morality that some would say was tyrannical. In the few hours a day that he was sober he could flash an angry edict of righteousness that would trample all over the bureaucratic and ineffective efforts of his underlings, and solve a problem that had been brewing for weeks – though just as often it would solve nothing. He hated the kleptoparasites who joined the force to rob the weak. He had a reputation for dispatching fatal dismissals to bullies and thieving underlings, and there was a long line of superiors who had been sent packing back to the comforts of Central after impotent attempts to rein in the wild old goat.

But as recruits got used to the rhythm of the station, they learned to weave around Falkirk's seemingly unpredictable and volatile outbursts. Some held him in awe, some were sympathetic to an old hero they recognised to be lonely and disillusioned. Others were less respectful, thinking he was over the hill. Still others dismissed him as a madman, and some despised him altogether. Those who had joined the police because they saw it as the most powerful Triad force in the territory mostly learned to duck under Falkirk's random swings of rage, though every now and then the Captain hooked a fatal blow. The overall effect was that in practice, as Falkirk's enemies loved to hammer home the point, Tai O Police Station was a rudderless ship for much of the time, though sometimes the rudder would violently swing into action and lurch the vessel into uncharted territory.

Jagan and Simon both liked Falkirk in their own ways. Jagan's respect leaned towards awe. He often retold the stories of Falkirk's guerrilla exploits. These stories had a tendency to become more incredible as the years went by. When the war had ended, the official version of

Falkirk's epic trips from south China to Hong Kong told of three or four repeated journeys, certainly enough for the Captain to justifiably earn his hero status. By the early 1950s the number was around eight, hitting double digits by the mid-50s, which is also around the time when the tiger killing had solidified into historical fact. This happened with no help from Falkirk, whose reputation only grew by the fact that no-one had heard him speak about his own actions during the war. Jagan was personally responsible for some of the exaggeration, but it wasn't just him. The phenomenon was Hong Kong-wide and was fuelled by friends and enemies alike.

Simon was less reverential. He suspected that some of the stories were tall. He noticed they got taller with every telling. He had heard the tallest of the tales among the fishermen and the salt-farmers who credited Falkirk with a godlike status and nicknamed him "Old Typhoon." What Simon related to more readily was the manner in which Falkirk dismissed police higher-ups to their face. Drunk or sober, Falkirk had nothing to fear from the bureaucratic types in the upper echelons, and Simon wanted to have that magic, wherever it was that Falkirk got it from. Simon recalled the time dysentery was sweeping through an old warehouse, where about 500 refugees who had arrived in two drifting fishing boats were being held while the authorities tried to work out what to do with them. Falkirk was shouting down the radio: "We need a doctor right now, and basic medical equipment, or else you are going to kill these people."

"There's nothing we can do, Falkirk, you saw the message from Central. We're not a welfare agency, old boy."

"Sod you. I am personally taking the police launch to Cheung Chau, and I'm going to put a doctor on the boat, and he is going to come here."

"I order you to stay where you are. Repeat. Stay where you are."

"Is that your order? Here is what you can do with it: Shove it up your arse. Repeat, shove it up your arse."

Simon dreamed of having conversations like that, but he knew it wasn't his style.

Simon Lee was born a mongrel bastard in Kennedy Town to 22-year-old Lee Ka-yee, the niece of a renowned dai pai dong and bar owner, Lee Kwok-hung. It was 1932 and uninhibited racism was the norm in polite society. His 25-year-old British father, Jack White, was in no position to acknowledge him. Jack had been in the Hong Kong Police Force for just three years when Ka-yee – or Peggy as he decided to call her – announced she was pregnant. It had all started with the reputation for Kwok-hung's noodles. The dai pai dong became a favourite after-hours drinking spot for lower-ranking European policemen, and the owner's niece Ka-yee became a serious talking point among the lonely single men that served the empire, pounding the streets of its Chinese colony. Soon Ka-yee became known as Peggy – or as "Jack's girl" – to all the regulars at the bar. Jack had courted Peggy relentlessly to win her over his rivals. He used all his reckless courage, charm and warmth to seduce her, promising her the world tomorrow while making her believe she was queen today. When she announced she was pregnant he was struck by a bolt of fear. He knew he had made a mistake. He recognised mistakes. He had made them before in Holmfirth, Yorkshire, where he had left a four-year-old son and two-year-old daughter with a woman he knew he would never return to. It was unthinkable for him to marry Peggy, but he vowed he would make sure she had what she needed, and he vowed to be a father to this child of his, as best he could. There was no public acknowledgement that Simon was Jack's son, but close friends – and some enemies – knew the situation.

Peggy and Simon lived with Uncle Kwok-hung, a pragmatic man who had always loved his niece and didn't judge her for her mistake. Jack visited every leave day and gave Simon all the time he could. He wanted Simon to know his father. He had already made a mistake in

Yorkshire, and now it was time to do it right, even if that was basically an impossibility in the colony at that time.

As Simon grew bigger there were hikes, trips to the races, deep sea fishing expeditions. Sometimes Peggy joined them, sometimes she left them to it. As Jack always said to Peggy, in the 'real world' she was his wife. By the eve of the Japanese invasion, nine-year-old Simon had already experienced rural beats with his dad, having been taken on as a coolie, often with one or two other ragamuffin mates from the narrow lanes of Western District. Simon never questioned his relationship with his dad. To him it was normal that dad didn't actually live with them and Uncle Kwok-hung, but that he would appear every few days, sometimes just for dinner with Peggy and beers with Uncle. Then he would be there again on his days off, for dim sum breakfast in the morning and some expedition with Simon in the afternoon. If Jack had two days off in a row he would normally stay with them. One day a kindly Western missionary gave Simon a blessing and sympathised with him, saying it must be a terrible hardship to grow up without a father. Simon was horrified at the thought and emphatically agreed with the devout man. Yes, it must be awful, he said.

Then the Japanese forced their way into the colony in a firestorm of bullets and bombs. Jack told Peggy to keep her head down and keep their son close by at all times. He gave her all the cash he had and joined the volunteers to man the Wanchai Gap. He was in a small band that were pushed back to the Repulse Bay Hotel before they finally saw the futility of their stand and surrendered. Jack didn't survive the expatriate prison camp at Stanley. He was caught trying to escape, and was held in solitary confinement for two years until he died of tuberculosis a week before the end of the war.

After the war, 13-year-old Simon, known locally as "Little Mixed Blood", and his 34-year-old mother were working their shift at Uncle Kwok-hung's dai pai dong when a British woman walked in, took one look at Simon and burst into tears. "Here he is, Trevor, no mistaking him, I can see Jack's eyes looking back at me," she said to the man who followed after her. Peggy was protective of Simon, shooing him to the kitchen.

"You must be Peggy," the woman said. Peggy looked back at her and she too saw Jack's eyes. She burst into tears.

"I'm Nancy, Jack's sister."

Nancy's husband Trevor had heard about Jack's love-child along the police gossip lines, but he wasn't a talker, he had no stomach for gossip. He more or less accepted the stories but never confronted his brother-in-law and colleague about them. Jack's sister Nancy was a nurse at Queen Mary Hospital. She and her husband were also interned at Stanley, along with their 17-year-old daughter Helen who died of influenza after just one year, leaving them heartbroken. They saw little of Jack in solitary until the guards realised he would die, and they allowed Nancy some time with her brother. That's when Jack told her about Simon and Peggy and begged her to promise she would look out for them.

After several visits to the noodle shop, Nancy and Trevor persuaded Peggy and Simon to move in with them. Officially they were servants, but behind the closed doors they were a family, united by the huge losses of a father, husband and brother whose bid for freedom ultimately killed him, and of a daughter, cousin and niece who never had the chance to reach adulthood.

For all that, it was never a joyless household. Trevor MacPherson was always ready to get his accordion out to sing his drinking songs for family and friends. Nancy never tired of telling tales of calamity from Queen Mary's, which often had tragic endings; and yet she had a way of telling them, sympathetic to the people involved, never missing the opportunity to describe the comic side of a burst appendix or to ridicule the arrogance of a fresh medical graduate straight off the boat from the London School of Medicine. Peggy always had the gossip on the people in the street. They weren't far from her uncle's place, still in Kennedy Town, so she knew most of the Chinese in the neighbourhood, and through the servants' network she knew far more about the expat households than any of them would have guessed.

When Simon was 16, Trevor signed him up with the Police Cadets. It wasn't a career that he was hell-bent on, but he did want to please his uncle. Trevor, for his part, had misgivings. There was corruption in the force, but it was a time of rebuilding after the catastrophic war years. There was a chance, thought Trevor, who had a tendency to be over-optimistic, that those crucial years could see the rebirth of a new, vibrant force, one that would be committed to serving the community, one in which a young man could build a career he would be proud of. He had no idea then how deep the corruption would set in over the following two decades.

Simon was a steady, stoical cadet. He liked the physical work, he found the written stuff straightforward. The camaraderie was tolerable, there were always one or two allies to be found. He was at first surprised that the casual everyday racism of the streets he grew up in was imported whole and institutionalised in the police force. It was something that Trevor hadn't warned him about, because in 30 years of singing, skipping and laughing through the force, he had never noticed that he was part of an institution that was built firmly on the principles of a racially-segregated world order. To put it simply, racism was a core principle of the British Empire and all the institutions that served it.

Until Simon joined the force, Trevor always believed it was equally fair to European, Indian and Chinese alike. Of course, wages differed and roles were divided, but it was all done perfectly fairly, he thought, until he started to witness his own nephew held back by barriers he had never imagined. The racism was set in black and white on paper, in the money they earned, the rooms they slept in, the tasks assigned. But more insidious was the unwritten racism in the failure to recognise a colleague, the curt dismissal, the snide comments and the sniggering laughter. Such were the daily experiences of all in the force, except the minority of well-kept European officers who thought life and everything was all a jolly good laugh; especially the new recruits of Simon's age, who were too young to experience being at the other end of that, when the Japanese turned the Asian world order on its head for a few years. Simon of course had special privileges as mixed-blood, and as the nephew of respected veteran Trevor MacPherson, but that only kept him in a state of limbo: half native, half colonial, neither one nor the other. He was used to it, and Trevor, with his eyes beginning to open, was frequently surprised at how easily Simon laughed it off. Trevor's last act with the police force before retiring was to make sure that Simon got onto a full European officer's contract. It wasn't an easy thing to arrange, but the six-and-a-half-foot rugby union fullback was awfully persuasive once he got a bee in his bonnet.

"I think Falkirk is a ghost rider," Jagan said.

"Trapped?"

"No, the heroic variety, free to think, speak, go where he likes."

"Well, he is half myth in any case."

"What do you mean, half myth?"

"The tall stories, Jagan."

"They are true, Simon, you've heard them as many times as I have."

"I don't go around collecting them like you do, or adding to their height."

"Nonsense old boy, you need more beer."

"Yup. I need more beer, if you're about to start the old legends again."

"Listen, do you know that Falkirk killed a tiger?"

"Yes, I've heard that story a few times, usually from you."

"Well yeah, I know. But did you know that there are rumours that the Beast of Tai O is back?"

"Is that a fact?"

"No it's a rumour, like I said."

"I mean is it a fact that there are rumours that the tiger's been seen again?"

"Yes, the rumour is a fact."

The moon was out again, casting light across the bay. Its pale blue glow illuminated a junk. Simon caught a glimpse of people on the vessel, more than usual for that time of night. A Nationalist flag at the front. Trouble? He lazily wondered.

He came back to Jagan's tiger. "So it is true?"

"Well, it's only a rumour. A rumour is only as good as its source, right?"

"Who did you hear it from?"

"Blind Wang."

"Blind Wang? He hasn't seen anything since the Japs gouged his eyes out."

"Yes but he's a reliable witness. He believes that it's that first one from back in July, returning."

"Well, the first was only a rumour in any case. So basically we are piling one speculation on top of another."

"Hold on a minute Simon, what's the chance that two different tigers have been on Lantau in a year? It must have been the same one. The Beast of Tai O."

"Or none."

"The law of averages would suggest that at least one of the rumours could have been right."

"You're clearly insane. Going by rumour it's possible that a tiger was seen in the last year, or there could have been two, or the same one was seen twice, or no-one saw anything at all."

"Exactly. It's very interesting."

Simon shook his head. The shadows on the junk had looked quite animated, but it was out of sight now.

"Anyway, I know for a fact that the last tiger in Hong Kong was killed at Stanley Prison in 1942. My uncle Trevor told me. My dad was one of the poor chaps assigned to guard against it at night, because it had been prowling near the camp bungalows for a few nights. It had killed one of the guards."

"I know, an Indian."

"Really? Anyway my dad was armed to the teeth – with a gong and a brush. He's lucky he survived the watch, though he didn't survive the camp. They got the tiger in the end. Trevor took me to a temple in Stanley when I was 15. The skin was stretched above the altar. A big beast, I can tell you."

"Yes, I know the story. Ask any of your Indian colleagues, we all know the story because we were the big heroes. Not only was one of us killed, but it was an Indian policeman who killed the tiger. With one shot to the brain, as the ravenous beast charged."

"So there you go then, you know as well as I do that the last tiger was shot in '42."

"Do I have to spell it out? The Stanley tiger was the last one killed. Do you think that stopped other tigers from prowling through Hong Kong again? There's no reason to think the last tiger shot here was the last to set foot here."

"You're confusing me now. I had always assumed that the Stanley tiger was the last of a local population."

"Don't be silly, or daft, as your good father used to say to you. Tigers don't limit themselves to small, insignificant colonial outposts. They roam where they want, like ghost riders. I believe the subspecies shot at Stanley was a South China tiger. There's no subspecies called "Hong Kong tiger" indigenous to this poxy place. Go ask a zoologist."

"How the hell do you know so much about tigers?"

"I'm Indian, in case you haven't noticed. We are very learned, especially about tigers. Tigers think nothing of prowling 40 miles a day. They've always treated Hong Kong as an excursion point as they wandered somewhere between Fujian and Burma."

"Jagan, you were born in Kowloon, where the closest you would have come to a tiger was a Sham Shui Po alley cat fattened up on rats."

"Nonsense, Kennedy Town boy, even you might have been stalked by a South China tiger at some point as you rambled over those Pok Fu Lam hills, chasing pretty daughters of commissioners that you shouldn't have chased."

"It wasn't me who chased her, she was definitely the instigator, but let's stick to tigers. Jagan, you don't normally talk sense, but your tiger theory is more interesting than I thought it was going to be."

"Of course it's interesting, and Simon, the most interesting point is that it's an opportunity for us."

"How?"

"We're going to catch it, Simon, thus securing our place in history."

"Right, and I suppose Blind Wang is going to track it for us, and drunken Captain Falkirk is going to lead the charge."

"Listen, have you ever wondered why this hill right behind us is called Tiger Hill?"

"Well, usually it's about the shape, isn't it?"

"Does it look like a bloody tiger to you?"

"I haven't really thought about it to be honest."

"I think a tiger was caught on this hill once, so long ago that people forgot the event, but the name stuck."

"Well, there's Lion Hill and Elephant Hill. Did people catch a lion and an elephant too?"

"Don't be ridiculous, that's just shape. Tiger Hill is situated so that if a tiger got onto it, a village full of people could surround it, cut it off and close in on it at the top."

"Has it happened though?"

"Most likely did, or else how could the hill have got its name?"

It was at this point that everything changed. Their musings were shattered by a menacing cry.

"Long live the Nationalists. Die, Communist bastard!"

An explosion of gunfire then jolted Simon and Jagan from their seats as they grabbed their guns, sounded the alarm and sprinted down to the beach. Gongs and drums were banging from a junk now lit with flaming torches, the same boat that had drifted across the moonbeam, Nationalist flag at the helm. There was whooping and more gunshots into the air.

"Jagan, you take the south end, I'll get the north," Simon called across.

"Got you, Simon. Be careful, they look like pirates."

"Stop, police!" Simon shouted out at the boat.

Someone was starting an engine.

"A present for you Imperialist dogs. A Communist spy. Don't choke on the pork."

"This is your last warning. Stop, police!" Simon shouted.

"This is yours, mongrel," came the reply, with another round of gunfire above his head. Simon threw himself on the floor. The bullets triggered a rockfall and boulders were falling all around him.

"Mongrel? They know me. Do I know them?" Simon thought.

He scrambled up the beach, dodging rocks. He saw a figure on the sand. His hands were tied behind his back, he was blindfolded. It was an execution. Hot blood was gushing from his stomach and soaking into the sand.

"A man down!" Simon screamed out. "We need medical now!"

Above his head he finally heard cannons clink into action, and a blast into the dark where the Nationalists, or whatever they were, had already extinguished their torches of triumph and their chugging engine was pushing them out of range.

The man was still breathing as Simon took off his blindfold and looked at the extent of the injury. His chest, above the main gunshot wound, was carved with the Chinese character for "spy".

"I don't want to die," he said, squirming in agony, fat tears rolling down his skinny face. He had an accent that Simon felt he should recognise but he couldn't quite place.

"You won't. Hold on. Help is coming."

Simon had seen spilled guts before, when he had arrived at the site of a seaborne gun battle. An ashen-faced 17-year-old Tai Long Wan boy watched in horror then as his lifeblood drained from an obscene stomach wound. This chap wasn't going to make it either. The dying man knew it anyway. His tears were of regret, the knowledge that this was the end. He had tried and failed, he was alone, he would die. Simon held his head in his lap.

"Don't believe their lies. I only went to catch a tiger."

"What? Jagan! Where the hell are you?" Simon called out as the stranger died.

He lowered the man's head onto the sand, and moved off to look for his colleague.

Jagan was lying on the ground, blood spurting from his head. Rocks from the cliff above were all around him.

"Some warning shot," he said. "Those bastards need better training, the CIA haven't got a fucking clue."

"Are you OK? Jagan, it looks serious."

"Superficial," he said, and then passed out.

A deceptive calm resumed. For a moment the only sounds were the lapping of the waves, and the cry of a night heron crossing the bay.

Half a dozen constables came running on to the beach. Two police launches were started up to give chase. Officers carried Jagan up for triage before taking him to the clinic. Simon radioed to prepare for a possible helicopter evacuation. He sent a messenger to look for Falkirk. It was unlikely that the captain would be in a state to respond, but he needed to be told. A foot patrol headed into the village to investigate.

Simon and Patrick Leung, a cadet from Mui Wo, carried the corpse up to their building. It was a cool night, and the body could be kept in a cell for a few hours. Simon ordered that he should be cleaned up, and called for a photographer to take a picture of the man's wounds and his face.

News came back from the clinic that Jagan's head gash was indeed superficial. He was still unconscious but that made it easier to stitch him up. The doctor ordered the air evacuation to be stood down. Having dealt with those priorities, Simon came to the radio to report to Central what had happened.

He was just reaching for the mouthpiece when it rattled to life with an incoming alert. Simon picked it up immediately.

"This is Command, who are you?"

"Assistant Sub-Divisional Inspector Simon Lee, sir, deputy in charge tonight." He recognised the voice of Max Godber, a rising star in the force.

"Just had word from the Cousins Lee," Godber said, using police jargon for American secret services.

"I was just about to make a report."

"Our Cousins inform me that some Kuomintang hoodlums ferreted out a Commie spy and would deliver the blighter into our hands tonight."

"Yes sir, he was dead on arrival sir."

There was a pause.

And then a roar.

"Dead? What the blithering hell are you on about?"

"They brought him to the beach below the station and executed him with a round of gunfire. Jagan Singh was injured in a rockfall, after they threatened us by shooting up the cliff face while we were trying to make an arrest. By the time artillery kicked in, the shooters were out of range, sailing around Tiger Hill."

"And when exactly were you going to report that, sergeant?"

"Right now, sir," Simon retorted.

"What have you done about it?"

"The body is in one of our cells. We have photographed him and cleaned him up. A pangolin unit has gone over the hill to look for landing spots for the boat. Another patrol has gone to the village. Singh has been seen to, he was unconscious, but the doctor has cleared the need for evacuation."

Another pause. This one lasted a minute – a decade in a radio conversation.

"Sir?"

Another pause, then the resolution.

"Very well, Lee. As far as I can see, this is a simple matter. A spy has been killed, the murderers have scuttled away to some den, possibly in Macau, or even the mainland if there was some bluffing and shenanigans going on. Your man has been scratched but he's going to live. Open and shut case, there's nothing to cover. Where is Falkirk?"

"Well, this is only an hour old, sir, I think it's a bit early to wrap it up. In any case we don't know anything about the dead man. The killers said that he was a spy, that's all. We've sent out to find Falkirk."

"Lee, you mongrel, you've always lacked judgement. The Cousins tell me he is a spy, so that's good enough for me. I'm sending Wetherby out to wrap this up. Stand down your patrol units, the case is closed."

Mongrel again? Twice in one night was getting a bit much. "Shove it up your arse, sir," Lee very much wanted to say. Instead, through clenched teeth, he decided to use procedure as proxy for a shove up the arse.

"With due respect, sir, I'm not in a position to close the case. The only person who can legitimately do that tonight is Captain Falkirk as he is on duty tonight, sir."

"You are an arse, Lee. Wetherby will be empowered to override Falkirk when he arrives. I don't care how much of a war hero he is, this is a case for Central Command."

"Thank you, sir," Simon replied, making it sound as much like "shove it up your arse, sir," as he could.

Simon only noticed how much he was sweating once the call had finished. Golden Balls Godber, they called him. Had there ever been an officer so loved outside the force and yet treated so warily inside? They said Godber had access to any club in the city. He dined with governors, actresses, bishops and professors. He even dined with Xinhua on occasion. His wife was an English rose who joined him on the Repulse Bay golf course on Sunday mornings and had a better handicap than he did. Their two children were at the Peak School, on the tennis and cricket teams, and sang like angels in St John's Cathedral choir. Godber was the charming darling of post-war Hong Kong society. Yet within the force the man was treated with caution, and all the weathervanes instinctively knew that Godber was the man to keep on your side.

The carrot was that if you got inside the Godber clique, you would probably rise up nice and smooth, like a shopper on an escalator in the new-fangled Wing On department store. "Probably" was the best that could be said at the time, as Godber was still in the early stages of his career. He was in his twenties, just four years older than Simon. But it was obvious that he was going to climb high. He pulled all the right strings and kissed the right cheeks – any of the four that mattered, depending on the person to be flattered. The stick was not clearly articulated, it was vague, but there was a general understanding that if you got on the wrong side of him, he would probably hurt you, badly.

How the hell did the Cousins know about this so early? Simon wondered. Were they really running those Kuomintang thugs? It didn't seem to make sense. Of course it was well known that the American consulate was the biggest spy station in the world, but why orchestrate a bloody murder outside a colonial police station in sleepy Tai O?

The launch radioed a report that a burning junk was found near Sham Wat bay. Why burn the boat? Simon thought. Did they run out of fuel? Is that how competent the CIA-run Kuomintang are? It didn't seem too clever. But still, why burn it? Patrick Leung, who had gone on the search launch, said there were footprints that suggested about 10 people had scrambled off the vessel and headed into the bush. It looked like a local job.

There were also other prints, said Patrick, like big cat paws.

"Why are you telling me that, Leung?" a sleepy Lee asked irritably as the sky lightened with dawn's rosy fingertips.

"I heard you talking with Sergeant Singh earlier, sir, when I was just having a smoke outside as I couldn't sleep too well."

"Eavesdropping on your superiors, were you? You'll go far."

"I like the music you play at night, sir. Especially that song about the ghost-riding heroes."

"They're not heroes, Patrick. They're trapped."

"There were tiger prints on the beach, sir."

"Oh for God's sake, not you too, Leung. Get out of here, we've got a real murder on our hands. There's no time for Singh's fantasy talk, even Singh would admit that now. Hopefully the knock on the head will have bashed that tiger obsession out of him."

"Yes sir!"

2

You Ain't Nothing but a Hound Dog

It is difficult to say what really governed Tai O, but it was fair to assume that the traditional mix of Confucian ethics, Buddhist philosophy and Taoist reverence for universal mysteries played an influential role, much as it always has across China and its vast diaspora. Ideas of family order and social cohesion that were passed on from father to son, mother to daughter, would have helped to keep peace on the streets, on the waterways and in the home. Of course much has been made of the unique characteristics of Confucian-Buddhist societies, but for most people under its moral sphere the everyday principles that directed their dos and don'ts were broadly universal – basically conservative, somewhat clannish, somewhat communal common sense that could be found in all corners of the world.

As with any ethical code, there were frequent breaches of the Confucian-Buddhist facade from within and without. Within, boys did not always revere their fathers. Some openly challenged them. Girls did not always help with chores, and parents did not all place learning on the pedestal they were reputed to. Many were not as temperate as they claimed to be. From without, marauders raided villages, stole things, burned down houses, raped women – killed people. More often than not the gangsters and pirates that inflicted unprovoked violence were from nearby districts, themselves disciplined in a similar mix of Confucian learning, Buddhist mercy and Taoist wisdom.

The biggest breach of recent years was of course the invasion and occupation by Japan, another Confucian-Buddhist neighbour. The

Japanese unleashed a violent force across Hong Kong, of which Tai O felt a particular brunt for its strategic position on the edge of the Pearl River Delta. For many years before the invasion, Tai O people were already familiar with Japanese blockades and raids. During the occupation, people were executed in broad daylight, bodies lay in ditches or floated down waterways. There was a stench of death across the salt pans, the beaches and in the fields. The brutality of this occupation didn't stop Tai O gaining a special place in wartime Hong Kong history, by becoming one of the only places where significant territory was taken back from the Japanese. Mongoose Triads and other partisan guerrillas overran Japanese guards at the police station and held it for a couple of weeks, before dispersing with arms and ammunition from the station in the face of a massive retaliatory onslaught.

Other than the Japanese there was the notable invasion by Guangdong pirates in 1925, when around 60 bandits took over the streets of the village, raiding everything they could and holding hostages for ransom. These and other smaller raids that continued after the war were rightly seen as breaches of the norm, because the normal situation in Tai O was one of quiet industry, peace and family life. By the time representatives of the British colonial government turned up to "keep order" there were already shops on Wing On Street selling bamboo products, fishing tools, food and drink, live fish and cloth. There were six or seven shops that sold religious paraphernalia and all-important bits and pieces for worshipping the dead. There were Chinese pharmacies, a wine shop, a pawn shop, gold shops and three coffin shops. By the 1920s this cosmopolitan corner of China already had two hotels, and a decade later there was a regular ferry service that brought the place within a few hours of sailing to Kowloon on a good day, or about a day if winds were meagre. That left a people connected, yet separate, within reach, yet in practice independent. Tai O boatmen sailed to China or Macau as often as they sailed to Hong Kong, no matter how the political winds blew. And the people of the village hailed from Shenzhen, Guangzhou,

Guizhou, Foshan, Macau and other places across the mainland. Such was the mix, but the group that shaped the place more than any other were a people who ranked among the poorest and most marginalised of China. These were the Tanka seafarers who had been there for generations, and whose semi-waterborne stilt houses gave the place its characteristic architectural identity.

There are of course different theories about who exactly the Tanka are. The idea that they could simply be a marginalised caste – with no significant physical or racial difference from wealthier, luckier people – is not popular. There are always stories to explain how some people are different. One story is that the Tanka were the descendants of Mongolian guardsmen who were stationed in South China garrisons during the Yuan dynasty, when the wild tribal influence of Genghis Khan and his descendants had tamed itself by assuming the trappings of an Imperial Chinese dynasty. The Mongol overlords played the emperor game for a few generations, but no-one was convinced that the restless horsemen had become true Confucian rulers of the massive agrarian state. Rumour has it that they were finally kicked out by the founders of the Ming dynasty after a campaign of stealth and espionage aided by secret messages baked into mooncakes – a sweet, lardy, egg-yolk-laden confection so disgusting to the meat-eating northern savages that they would never go near them.

Once in power, the Ming issued an order to hunt down and slaughter the soldiers of the previous Mongol garrisons. But by the time of this order many a Mongol had intermarried and been absorbed peacefully into Cantonese society, and the imperial edict from Beijing was met with understandable reluctance and resistance. The instruction had been to "drive them into the sea," but local communities protected their friends and their in-laws, allowing these 'Tanka' to eke out a living on the shore, where they either lived on boats or half on land in stilt houses in the intertidal zones. The compromise allowed officials to report back faithfully that the Tanka had been "driven into the sea," while families carved out a niche on the maritime periphery of the Middle Kingdom.

Though they were saved from annihilation they were not spared prejudice, marginalisation and even hatred. They remained on the lowest rung of society. They were forbidden to live on land and forbidden to marry land-dwellers, though they didn't let that spoil their spectacular five-day waterborne wedding banquets. Their children were shunned by local schools and they handed down their own traditions through sea songs. Typically their songs lamented their outcast status.

When the Tanka built stilt houses on the intertidal shore they shared with mudskippers, they modelled their homes on boats. They drove pillars into the mud flats and raised a deck on stilts. They covered that over with a curved roof of bamboo strips, just like the top of one of their boats, and organised the inner compartments in the same way that their vessels were subdivided. The roof was held down by hemp guy ropes and retired fishing nets. Even their kitchen gods lived under curved roofs. Because of the curve, early dwellings tended to be on one level only, though later more Tanka adapted to design freedoms allowed by the land, and many learned to flatten their roofs and build additional storeys, though that would never be to everyone's taste. Sewage connection was an irrelevance when seawater slushed directly below their homes. Tides brought in life, tides took out the waste. Nothing could be more natural than to use nature's biggest cleansing and recycling organ. Who could imagine then that one day human waste could overwhelm the ocean.

Inland from these Tanka stilt-houses, the village grew with people from all around the region: traders, salt makers, industrialists, entrepreneurs and farmers. Fields around Tai O were worked by gentle buffalo that kids would jump onto on their way home from school. Village dogs lay sleeping in courtyards and on footpaths. Pigs, chickens and geese snuffled, pecked and waddled.

Tanka, Guangdonger and Hong Konger alike mostly lived their lives around the lunar calendar, marking time from New Year, through spring grave-sweeping, dragon-boating, hungry ghosts and Autumn moon festivals. These were huge events all around the Chinese diaspora, but Tai O had a few of its own unique ones, such as shamanistic rituals involving kung fu performers whose bodies would be possessed by spirits. One event was called the "Drunken Eight Angels," a ceremony that would last from morning to night. It involved young men chanting to induce possession by the Monkey King or some other god bearing messages from the heavens. Often participants would lose consciousness and would need to be revived with a bucketful of water. Women were banned from these events, though they had their own equivalent called the "Drunken Three Sisters-in-Law" that involved two participants holding the hands of a straw doll during a ritual that sought to "wake up" the effigy, to channel messages from the heavens.

Was Tai O backward, with its customs and superstitions that looked incongruous in the nuclear age? The past and its customs were a tangible presence – a living thing. Tradition, superstition and common sense merged in murky synthesis but the people of the village were always pragmatic. When they needed a seawall, they built one. While fish and salt provided good profits, they worked the waters and the sea beds. If they needed to cross a stream, they would make a crossing. When nylon became cheap and abundant, they abandoned their well-worn hemp nets and lines. If a trusty old buffalo died, there was always a villager who said, "Everything dies. Let life take its course."

They were always at the mercy of huge outside forces. Typhoons or fires could destroy hundreds of years of steady development, but so could imperial edicts, bandits, foreign invasions and colonisation. Most of all, there were huge economic ruptures around the world that could be felt in Tai O like the rumblings of an earthquake whose epicentre was far away. The two most important ruptures in Tai O were the shifting costs of production, labour, land and transport that priced their salt out of the market, and the coming collapse of the fishing industry. Against these forces was it irrational to seek the intention of the gods through possession by the Monkey King? No more so than relying on the expertise of random strangers from Hong Kong Island or London, who made claims to wisdom with no knowledge or experience to back them up.

Simon woke at noon after a few hours of deep sleep. He went down to the beach and saw a bandaged Jagan looking at blood-splattered rocks around the execution spot.

"You'll never believe what I just saw," Jagan said, without giving Simon a chance to check on his health.

"With you Jagan there's a chance it won't be true, especially after a knock like the one you took last night. You look more like a real Sikh every day, by the way. That bandage suits you."

"I just saw Mother Mary breach."

"Are you sure it was Mother Mary?"

"Yes, the notch on her dorsal was definitely in the upper half."

"Not sitting in the centre, as with Churchill?"

"No, upper half."

"Fair enough, I believe you. But that's not remarkable at all considering the fact that we see the pink dolphins every day."

"No, but she came out of the water with a sea snake in her mouth. Must have been a bloody four-footer."

"I've seen that before, and fair enough, that is quite a sight."

"More remarkable, Simon, was Sinbad."

"Sinbad? I haven't seen him for a while."

"I know. I think the kites have been giving him the runaround. Anyway, Sinbad had obviously already seen the snake from above 'cos he was well on his way down when Mother Mary came from nowhere and snatched it."

"Flipping heck. He must have been one grouchy raptor after that."

"Not at all, Simon. Well, not till later. Because instead of giving up the chase, the feisty bugger twisted his course a fraction and nabbed the snake from Mother. She tried to hold on but he yanked it out when she was adjusting her hold."

"Bravo. Victory for Sinbad."

"Not quite. I watched eagle and serpent rise up in union. The snake was writhing like the devil himself, with Sinbad fighting to quell each twist and turn with his lethal claws. Suddenly the snake's head lunged up and bit the bird. Sinbad lost his grip and snakey spiralled down. Sinbad tried to swoop back for a desperate air catch. Couldn't quite get it. Snake plopped into the water, and a split-second later Mother Mary snatched the poor beast and took a long deep dive. Sinbad, humiliated, flapped off over Keung Shan."

Simon took a few moments to digest what he had heard. Then he looked at Jagan, conceding, "OK, that's not a bad story."

Jagan nodded with satisfaction, rightfully lapping up the acknowledgement.

Simon looked back towards the hill, hoping to catch a glimpse of the white-bellied sea eagle, but all he saw was the odd egret winging across the bay. Then he looked down at the blood-covered rocks and the dark events of the night before came flooding back.

"So Jagan, you are OK, are you? What did the doctor say?"

"He's given me a clean bill of health, except for the eight stitches in my head, which will help to scare my enemies in the future, so those Kuomintang thugs did me a favour."

"If they were KMT."

"They were convincing enough with all that flag waving, gong banging and the usual Nationalist rabble-rousing."

"Sure. And they shouted back to us, do you remember?"

"A present for you Imperialist dogs. A Communist spy. Don't choke on the pork."

Jagan shrugged and flippantly declared: "Open and shut case then. A spy."

"Yep, that's what the 'grown-ups' are saying. Godber at least."

"God-botherer? Watch him suck some profit out of this one."

"He was tipped-off by the Spidermen and now he's sending Wetherby out to get the result he wants, which is to conclude that a Commie spy was killed by local activists." He was using Falkirk's preferred name for American spooks.

"Bloody Spidermen everywhere these days. But you're not sure, Simon?"

"No, I'm not sure. Of course he could be a spy, but I can honestly say I'm not sure."

Simon told Jagan the last words of the man. He admitted that it was not proof of anything, but there was something in the way the dying man spoke that pierced Simon's thoughts. Though, neither did the man deny being a spy. He just said: "Don't believe their lies." Who were they? No one believes the lies of the KMT yobbos. Most of them could hardly be called agents. They were a mixture of disgruntled officers of the old regime, former landlords with a grudge, half-witted fascist ideologues, and part-time rent-a-thugs who didn't care who paid them for their violence. You don't need a dying Communist spy to tell you not to "believe their lies." And the final part: "I only went to catch a tiger." Had Jagan been boring him with his theories too? Or was the tiger a person? Was this man an assassin? In which case, the simplest solution could indeed be that he was a Communist agent, on a mission to assassinate a big target, a tiger. Open and shut case. But those tears, the pain, the regret, his total isolation. They weren't political, not in any way Simon could understand.

They had walked back up the slope to the station when Cheung the photographer brought Simon the picture. A grim death mask. Simon always found it amazing how completely devoid of character a corpse became. Life leaves the body more quickly than the cells start breaking down. The need to see the body is the same as the need for proof of death. One look at a dead man's face is enough. There is no way you can mistake the corpse of your relative, friend or colleague, for the person you knew and loved. Of course it is an intense and upsetting reminder of that person, but it isn't that person. It is not much different from seeing the house that they lived in while they were alive.

Simon was nine years old when he last saw his dad alive. During the war Peggy kept telling him he was well, fighting tigers and defying the Japanese. She told Simon that there was a hill at Stanley where she could see the prisoners. She would go there unnoticed as some ragged noodle pedlar, and wave at Jack. That is what she told Simon. But then he didn't come back when the bony Japanese were marched out of town in shame, and half-starved Englishmen with weary faces took charge of the colony once again. Jack didn't make it. He had died a week before the end of the war, having lived in isolation for the last two years of his life after attempting to escape. Simon desperately wanted to see the corpse of his dead father, because, he thought, until he saw it he couldn't believe that it was true that he would never come back. But there wasn't a corpse and there wasn't a grave, not a real one. There was only absence and grief.

He looked at the picture in his hand. This is a dead man. He witnessed his death, though he didn't see his father's. At least this man's children, if he has any, would have a chance to see this picture and accept the fact. Though that wasn't the purpose of the picture. This picture proved that a crime had taken place. It would be the only lasting evidence that a man had been killed on the beach outside the police station the night before. A crime that he was beginning to fear his bosses might want to deny happening. It was also the first clue to start his investigation. Simon sent Cheung to get copies so they could start distributing the picture around the village.

Wetherby was on his way. He had the papers to override Falkirk, which in practice were the papers to override Simon. Where the hell was Falkirk? It didn't normally take this long for Simon to find Old

Typhoon, as the locals called him. Joycee's tobacconists was the first place to check, where he could usually be found in the company of Bad News Chu, the Shrimp Paste King, the Jap Devil and sometimes Ishmael Chalmers if he'd made the hike over from Pui O. Then there was the bar in the South China Hotel, and the unofficial smoking room at the back of Fook Min restaurant was another obvious site. There was also the Luncome massage house, and if that didn't work there was Old Lau's grocery store where fishermen and the Mongoose drank rice wine and beer in overlapping shifts that covered the 24 hours of the day, occasionally going out to check nets, collect debts and scout for business. None of these yielded results, and it had slipped Simon's mind that Falkirk could just as well have wandered over to his old pal Ishmael's beach hut.

Ishmael Chalmers was born in Whitby in 1884. He was a Nantucket apprentice by the turn of the century, and a seasoned whaling captain in the Pacific by the start of the First World War, though he knew little of it out in Tahiti where he settled for a decade. Between the wars he drifted to Hong Kong, which became a convenient base for his sporadic voyages. He spent a lot of time on the harbourfront drinking with old fishermen, Communist dockers and off-duty police like Falkirk and Jack White. He was retired by the time the Japanese shot their way into the colony to pen him up in Stanley Prison with Falkirk, White and other expats. Ishmael escaped with Falkirk, but instead of heading into China, as Falkirk did, he stayed with the guerrillas on Lantau and fought the Japanese alongside the Triads of Tai O, known locally as the Mongoose.

He fell in love with a fearless partisan during that time, a peglegged widow who led her own cell that included her three adult sons, and was affiliated with the Mongoose command. When the Japanese occupation ended, Ishmael moved over to Pui O with the widow Mui Mui, 'little sister', and her sons, and worked with them on their smuggling enterprises. The group did well on the kerosene run during the Korean War, and the sons built mansions in Kowloon, though Ishmael and Mui Mui stayed on the beach at Pui O where they liked it.

He was an old man now, he had seen it all, and mostly he was content to subsist on the bounty of the sea and land in the company of his wife. But the contacts he had made with the intelligence community during his guerrilla days still found him useful for his access to some of the more opaque sectors of Chinese society.

The morning after Falkirk had left, Ishmael received another visitor who had been monitoring radio waves from a highly-equipped listening post on a rickety old Chinese junk most people assumed belonged to a shell-shocked French fisherman from Indochina who had somehow drifted to Lantau at the end of the war and never returned to his patch across the South China Sea.

"Hello Z. What can I do for you today?" Ishmael asked with resignation.

"Hello Orca," Z replied cheerfully, dropping his French accent, and at close quarters looking every bit like the fresh-faced Birmingham University graduate that he was, even with his Karl Marx beard that worked well enough from 100 yards.

"There was a bit of chatter on the airwaves last night. You haven't seen your old pals from Tiger Hill recently, have you?"

The Mongoose would not have considered themselves to be Luddites, but neither did they see any use for electronic equipment, so they remained frustratingly invisible to the likes of technical wizards such as Z, although a good pair of binoculars would normally suffice to find them.

"Funnily enough I was just thinking about the Mongoose boys yesterday, though I haven't seen them for months," Ishmael lied without hesitation, recalling fondly the knees-up they had had on the boat the previous afternoon.

"How about Old Typhoon?"

"Old Typhoon? It's been a while."

"Who is that?" Mui Mui called out from inside, still tired after their raucous night with the windbag that was Old Typhoon.

"It's Z, dear, on Her Majesty's service. Do you want to come and say hello?"

"No I don't. Tell him to bugger off, will you."

"Sorry Z, do you mind buggering off? You're upsetting the wife."

"Of course, Orca. You do still have the radio I gave you, don't you? The one you can use to get in touch with me."

"Oh, yes, I expect so."

"Well, don't be shy of using it, eh? I do need to show something every now and again for that little retainer I arranged for you."

"Little is the word, Z. But don't worry, I'm always ready to call you," Ishmael said as he glanced to the side of the door at the hefty black box that was being utilised as a platform for Mui Mui's prize-winning bonsai trees.

Cheung returned from the printers shaking his head.

"Printer Lam won't take the picture. He's scared."

"What?"

"It's the fourth of October today and you're asking him to print a hundred handouts of a dead man's face. It's not going to happen, Sergeant Lee."

"Christ Almighty, what does he think is going to happen to him? Is he going to die for printing a dead man's face on a day that has a four in it?"

"Yes. That's what he thinks. He's going to die. That's how his cousin died in Tung Chung."

"Oh, what superstitious cobblers."

"No, it's true. The police there asked him to run up 45 printouts of a girl who'd been found dead in the woods. The machine jammed on 44 and he was so terrified that he hid in the print-machine room for two days. When they forced the door open he was dead. The doctor said he had choked on the type-setting he had chewed. But the printer is convinced. Don't mess with a four. I could always run up a few here on photographic paper."

"Well that's bloody expensive, but how many can you do?"

"I've got enough for about 14."

"Better stretch that to 15 if you can."

"Fifteen what?" came Falkirk's grizzly voice as he walked into the station.

"Captain Falkirk. Thank God you're here. There's been a murder," Jagan said.

"It's nothing to do with God, lad. I walked here by myself, God and I have been estranged for quite some time. Mind you, a night hike from Mui Wo under the moon and stars is almost a spiritual experience, especially when you stop by at Ishmael Chalmers' beach hut on the way and refresh yourself on his exceptional stock of whiskey. I have no idea where that man gets hold of such high-quality stock. Best not to ask too many questions, I always say. He sends his regards to you, Lee, by the way. So who's dead then?"

Falkirk listened intently to Simon's report. The hike had obviously sobered him up with good effect. Jagan could tell that the cogs were working in Falkirk's mind today.

"And Godber the gobshite wants it wrapped up, you say?"

"Yes sir, he is convinced that the man was a spy."

"Supposing he was a spy, does it not occur to Godber that a crime still took place in my jurisdiction? On my bloody watch?"

On his watch while he got drunk in Pui O, Simon thought, but stopped himself from saying.

"Does he not know that summary execution is against the law of this colony?" Falkirk's voice was rising to the pitch of an enraged Methodist minister.

"I think he will try to find some legal way to close the case. He is sending Wetherby to override you, sir."

This sent Falkirk into a rage as good as any they had seen before. Cheung thought Falkirk would hit Simon. Patrick Leung, watching from the side as he had a smoke, was convinced Falkirk would uproot some trees and throw them in the bay. Jagan was all ready to let off a cannon for the captain. When he calmed down enough to form coherent sentences he took Simon into the report room. He sat him at the desk in front of him, shooing out the onlookers, including a disappointed Jagan who nevertheless stood outside the open, barred windows, looking in. Predictably, Falkirk opened the trophy cabinet and brought out a bottle and glasses. He poured two, raised one to Simon's ritualistically held glass and both downed their drinks in one.

"Now, tell me why you don't think this man is a spy."

Simon retold the account, with annotations of his subjective judgements. He added the findings of the boat, the likelihood of locals involved.

"And what else?"

He was uneasy about the eagerness of Central to sweep it under the carpet. He also mentioned the Cousins and how they had tipped-off Central before Tai O had reported.

"So the Spidermen are involved. Nothing too surprising there."

"Spidermen" was Falkirk's personal jargon for Americans in general and American spooks specifically, depending on context.

Falkirk fell into silence, almost looked as if he had fallen asleep, then piped up.

"How old are you, Lee?"

"I'm 24, sir."

"With due respect, son, how did Jack White's half-caste boy get the deputy's job?"

In two years of being Falkirk's deputy, this was the first time he had asked Simon that obvious question.

"My uncle is Trevor McPherson. He has been a father to me ever since my dad died. Trevor was Jack's brother-in-law. The day before he retired, Trevor went to the Commissioner's office, locked the door and put the key in his pocket. Then he asked the boss why he hadn't replied to the letters he had sent about my contract. The boss pretended not to know anything about it. Trevor took out a full expat contract that we had already filled in the night before. He had got hold of it from the admin aunties with the usual tea money. He opened it up and told the Commissioner to sign it there and then or else he would cause an incident. The boss signed it."

"McPherson? Decent lad. Would have been with me in the jungle for sure if he'd have succeeded in escaping. Two years' solitary must have been a bastard, but at least he survived it. Then there was that wretched affair that got you banished here. McPherson must have been disappointed in you." That snippet of gossip had stuck with Falkirk.

Trevor had taken Simon for a hike the day before he left for Tai O. He said then that young men are fools and would always do stupid things, but fornicating with the Commissioner's daughter was probably the stupidest thing he'd heard of. Aunt Nancy wanted to give him a good hiding, but instead she told Simon to take care.

"He said there are always people wanting to see you fall flat on your face," Simon told Falkirk. "And that's true whether you're an honest hard-working Scot like him, a Tally-Ho English lord, or a Ching-Chong Chinaman."

"He's right about that, for sure. There is always some bastard sniping from a hideout. Your father Jack was a good man, Lee. Another trooper. Fact is we all were back then, when we had real enemies. For that I should thank the Jap Devil next time I see him at Joycee's. Now look at us, falling apart and rotten to the core, just ten years since the war. No proper enemy, just shadows and greed, and pomp and ceremony. In many parts of the empire we are the enemy now and the real troopers are jabbing at our bloated torso.

"Now listen Lee, Wetherby is a scumbag if ever I have seen one. Sycophantic to the core, but armed with papers he will be happy to snip my balls off. However, in a bureaucratic glitch that illustrates the stupidity of the nincompoops that write the rule book, this turd cannot take away my powers if I am not there to sign to that. So I'm going to do you a favour and offer you a strategy. Get digging on this case and find out as much about those local footprints as you can, before that arrogant cockroach from Central arrives. And when he does, you won't know where I am. Without my signature the case remains in our hands, the rest is up to you. Improvise as you like and see if you can hold out against those scheming bastards."

Simon was doubtful. Falkirk's great strategy to fight the strutting peacocks of Central was to disappear. It sounded mystical, a bit like the newfangled "Zen" that some of the expat recruits from English public schools liked to mention these days. But he could see the logic if he squinted his eyes enough. Of course, it gave Falkirk an excuse to disappear in an opium haze again, but this was not a man who ever made excuses for doing exactly what he wanted whenever he wanted. So maybe this was genuine strategy.

Jagan was still looking through the bars of the window, just three feet from Falkirk.

"Who is this Hindu, Lee?"

"Sergeant Jagan Singh, sir, my right-hand man."

"Ah, Singh, I didn't recognise you. Since when have you taken to wearing a turban? Is it a Gandhi thing? I expect you'll be sprouting a finely-curled moustachio next."

"No sir, this is a bandage. I was the one injured, sir, in the rockfall."

"Ah, fine job. Very brave Singh, carry on."

"Sir, I would just like to congratulate you on a fine and cunning strategy."

"Thank you Singh. Lee, give this man a drink, he's obviously a smart one. Down the hatch, boys, you've got work to do. And I have been informed from a good source that Bad News Chu has stumbled across a consignment of top-quality Russian vodka in a sampan from China. The Spidermen would be most upset that their trade embargoes on two sworn enemies have been squelched in a single deal by the criminal genius that is Bad News Chu. It is my duty as the top representative of the British Empire in this village to inspect that contraband personally. I may be some time."

"Sir, can you get me a bottle too? My dad loves the stuff," Singh said a little weakly.

"Get on with your work boys! Good Lord, a mongrel pariah and a brain-damaged Hindu, doesn't look good on paper. But let's see what results we get."

"Jagan, were you being sycophantic with the legendary Falkirk back there?" Simon probed as they patrolled the Shek Tsai Po lane that linked the station to the village.

"Oh come on, Lee, a bit of flattery doesn't do any harm. It's when you do it to someone you despise that it erodes your soul."

"Well, of course, if you were brown-nosing for a career-hike you'd know that Falkirk is a dead end."

"That's right Lee, dead as a T-Rex. And best of the lot."

"And that was the third 'mongrel' I had within 24 hours, what's going on? Has the United Nations called slap-a-mongrel day?"

"Falkirk is allowed, we all know he is a secret admirer of Mr Gandhi, Mr Orwell and Ho Chi Minh. In his filthy mouth, filthy words take on a different meaning. If any other English bastard called me a Hindu I would stab him with my dagger."

"Orwell hated mongrels."

Maria Chu walked up to Simon and slapped him in the face. She had the twins, Jeanie and Stevie, with her, and Madge was loping along a few steps behind, smoking a Chinese cigarette.

"What the hell were your boys doing dragging Danny out of his bed at 4 o'clock in the morning, waking up all my lot? Myself included. The only one that slept through it was dad of course."

The Shrimp Paste King's jaw dropped, as did his cigarette. Then he crumpled in laughter. They were right outside his pungent factory when she accosted Simon.

"Ouch. Oh. Hello Maria, nice to see you," Simon said, bent over rubbing his cheek, his eyes watering.

"No it's not. She slapped you," said Jeanie giggling.

Stevie wasn't sure if it was funny. He peered at Simon, concerned about the state of his hero.

Madge arrived at Maria's side, slipped her arm through Maria's and stared angrily at Simon. "Yeah, what did you do with my brother. Mongrel police?"

"Nothing Madge, Maria. We had to send a patrol into the village last night."

"What happened?" Maria asked.

"An incident."

"What incident? for God's sake."

"The twins... Maria."

"They're eight, they're not stupid. Just tell me what happened, because everyone in the village is talking about it but no one has a bloody clue what they are talking about. Someone says that the Commies killed a KMT. Another says the police executed a Commie. Another says that the CIA murdered a policeman by bashing him in the head. And then another wise-guy claims it was all just a rockfall. So just tell me what the hell is going on and why the hell we had to wake up at four in the bloody morning."

"OK. A man was murdered – execution style – on the beach outside the police station."

"Simon, has that been cleared?" Jagan asked nervously.

"Jagan, I'm clearing it now. It's no good having the whole village fuelling all their own fantasies up with the garbage they peddle each other."

"We don't know what it is about. And we are doing what we always do by asking around for any information we can get."

"Is that it? You're giving me the newspaper version I know, but what you've told me so far is true, is it?"

"Yes, Maria."

"Is Danny involved?"

"I know Danny, I know he is a good lad. I haven't got a clue who is involved. But you know as well as I do that he is spending an awful lot of time hanging around with people that he shouldn't hang around with. There is a very good chance that he can tell us something helpful."

"Well at least he hasn't joined the biggest Triad of all," Madge piped up, throwing a direct accusation at Simon.

"OK Madge, that will do," Maria came back.

The Shrimp Paste King was leaning leisurely against a barrel now, enjoying the show.

"Maria, I thought we had to go and help dad with those Russian boxes off the sampan?" Stevie interrupted.

"Don't worry Stevie, I'm going to help him with that," the SPK chimed in.

Maria held her hard stare at Simon for a few unnerving seconds. He knew that scrutinising, judgement-pending stare, and it was never comfortable to be on the receiving end. It lasted about 10 seconds but felt like an hour. Then she softened her face a tiny degree. Others wouldn't have seen the difference, but Simon knew it was enough to show judgement had been passed and he had been found not guilty for now, or at least there wasn't enough evidence to convict him yet. She turned around to walk away, and Madge did the same, flicking ash at Jagan's feet. Then Maria, as casually as she could manage, called out without looking back, "I'm making the kids some shrimp-paste fried rice tonight. There may be some spare if you're patrolling nearby at the right time. Either way, suit yourself."

Jagan and SPK looked at Simon, then at each other, and laughed.

"Ha ha ha, you're such a pussy in front of that girl. Simon, look at her father, this girl is Bad News," Jagan said.

SPK piped up, "She's soft on you though, Lee, mark my words. And I can personally guarantee the quality of the shrimp paste. Only the best."

"She has a funny way of showing it," Simon said, secretly pleased.

"You got the American radio on, SPK?" Jagan noticed.

"Yeah, I like this show. Strange music, but good politics. Anti-Commie."

"*Ain't Nothing but a Hound Dog*, by Big Mama Thornton," Jagan said.

"No, it's some boy called Elvis," SPK said.

"No no no, Big Mama Thornton. She does it best. She's a negress. Sergeant Lee, you ain't nothing but a mongrel."

"Madge's mongrel was quite a clever comment on the force as a whole, Jagan, it wasn't about me."

"It was still the fourth mongrel on the United Nations slap-a-hound-dog day, and the first real slap too."

"Come on, let's get to work. SPK, what do you know about this man?" Simon asked, holding out the picture.

SPK took a long suck on his cigarette.

Exhaled.

Took another long suck, head cocked, eyes focusing.

Nothing. Nope. No.

They walked on, not surprised and not convinced.

"Sinbad. South-southwest, altitude approx 600 feet," Jagan said.

"Got him," Simon replied.

3

FEVER

The first time Simon met Maria she had almost slapped him. It was only because he was a stranger that she held back. If she had known him, he would have got it then. It was about a month into Simon's banishment to Tai O. He liked being there, despite the fact that it was a confusing place. The worst thing about the Tai O posting wasn't necessarily that colleagues saw it as a career-killer, or the perceived rural hardship. It was leaving his mother Peggy alone, even if she was with good people like Uncle Trevor and Aunty Nancy. She was a widow in her early forties, her grown-up son now banished to the furthest spot he could go within Hong Kong territory. Peggy worried that Simon would have to eat stinking wind-dried seafood and strange fermented vegetables in that far off place, so she regularly sent him a cut of barbecued pork from his favourite cha siu stall in Kennedy Town. She would wrap it up in greaseproof paper, then wrap that in several pieces of newspaper, place it in an envelope and send it by post. Simon told Peggy that he could get cha siu pork in Tai O, but she insisted that he have the good stuff from Hong Kong Island.

He was about to tuck into Peggy's parcel as a late-night snack on duty when Maria appeared. The radio was on. Jagan was opening a bottle of beer. That wasn't quite the idyllic scene it might appear to be, because there was a disturbing presence in one of the two cells, both of which, the police proudly liked to tell visitors, normally remained empty. In one of those cells there was a man they had picked up on patrol, a pesky man they would rather not have had to lock up. Jagan was the first to spot him when they were out on their patrol at around midnight. He was perched on a rock, looking precarious. The tide was sloshing in and he was about a yard from solid land. They called out to him and he waved them off.

"Leave him," said Jagan, who had been stationed there about a month longer than Simon, and was ahead of him in beginning to tune in to the local wavelength. The man was facing the bay, trying to piss in the water. The wind, and all it carried, was coming back at him as the sea swirled around his ankles.

"How's he going to get off that rock?" Simon asked.

"He's probably done it a thousand times, forget him," Jagan urged.

"No, Jagan. He could easily topple over and smash his head. One rogue wave and he's out to sea."

"Fine, what do you care? Dolphin food. Come on, let's go."

But Simon wouldn't drop it. He hadn't done anything useful in the month he had been there, and now he saw an opportunity to make his mark on the community.

The man had finished his business and was wobbling precariously, trying to find his balance before making his move off the rock, back to dry land.

"I'm going to save this bastard," Simon said to Jagan as he waded into a foot of swirling ocean.

"Waddayawan?" the man shouted. "Bloody British polishbastards, mindyour own fushing bushinesh."

Simon thought the man was about to fall so he reached to grab him.

The man, who had done this a thousand times and wasn't about to fall, was alarmed at this young fanatic suddenly lashing out, so he instinctively stepped back onto the crest of a small wave and splashed backwards into the water. His body from head to toe was submerged into the foot-deep tide for a second before Simon grabbed his wrists and hauled him out.

"Wha? Fushingingabastard fushingfukkers. Whaddyawant you feckingturtlesfeckingeggs?" was the only thanks Simon got, as Jagan sadly shook his head. He was beginning to have doubts about this new deputy, seemingly mild from the outside, but a serious liability at random.

Impervious to reality, Simon gasped, "Did you see that? I saved him. He would have been a goner without me."

"Where is your house?" Simon asked. But there were two problems. Simon hadn't got used to the Tai O Tanka dialect, which this man was speaking with a slur. The other problem was, that even though this experienced drinker was quite used to getting home in robotic mode no matter how many drinks he had had, he wasn't used to trying to describe to a green policeman from Babylon the exact location of his stilt house within the warren of aquatic alleyways that made up Tai O. When he tried to explain, it came out as gibberish. Simon took this as proof that the old drunk was probably drunker than he had ever been before and was certainly incapable of getting home. He could not have been more wrong, as the old fellow was drunker only the night before, and as usual he got home without a hitch – though he couldn't explain the bruising on his lower left rib. Simon felt duty-bound to rescue this man from the perilous waterways of this village.

That is how Bad News Chu was laboriously and ungraciously escorted back to Hotel Tai O Station for the night, for his own good – protesting all the way – and locked into a lonely paranoid totalitarian dystopia where no-one could understand him in his own ancestral home. Jagan was somehow brainwashed into accepting that this was the only right course to take. They struggled, heaved, pushed and pulled. They helped him out of his soaking clothes, provided a prison smock and put him in a cell. Knowing there was no sense to be had from these sinister alien invaders, Bad News Chu put his head down and quickly dropped into a deep alcohol-assisted slumber.

Finally, things were settling for the night for Simon and Jagan. They tuned the radio, and got the beer out. Simon opened his meat parcel. All was looking good. Then a loud knocking, and a mad woman.

"Open up, you fucking numbskulls!" Such were the first words Simon ever heard Maria Chu utter.

He opened it and she burst in, followed by a younger woman.

She was gorgeous, and the younger was pretty too.

"Do you have any idea who you've got in that cell? That's my father, Bad News Chu. What the hell is he doing here?"

She looked about 22, the other one 18.

Jagan proffered an explanation: "He was having a wee on a rock."

"What? Is that a crime now? Are the Japs back? God knows they pissed wherever they wanted, but the wrong guy in the wrong place would be tortured to death. Is that what you goons are doing too?"

Her eyes, they shone like the stars on a moonless night over the Ling Ting ocean.

"No no no, it's not like that, Miss," Simon came back. "We were just trying to help him. The tide was coming in. We thought he might fall in."

"He did fall in by the look of it, which is unusual for him," she noted with disdain.

Her eyes sparkled brighter than stars, more like Jupiter or Mars. They burned through Simon's skull. She was the most beautiful girl he had seen in Tai O. Possibly even more beautiful than some of the wealthy stunners of Central that he used to fantasise about.

"Well, that was just when I was rescuing him, he fell in at that exact moment."

"He never fucking falls in. He was born on the fucking sea. His fucking father, my grandfather, was born on the fucking sea. How do you, fucking city boy, propose to save my family from the sea when we've been making a fucking living from it for 20 fucking generations? Fuckwit."

The younger girl lit a cigarette and handed it to the angry beauty in the stunned silence. She accepted it in her trembling fingers, sucked smoke deep into her lungs and exhaled slowly into Simon's face.

After a moment's pause a new song started on the customised radio. *Fever*, by Peggy Lee.

"Why is the police radio playing the Yankee music?" the younger one asked.

"That was me," Jagan said. "I'm good on the communications. This song is quite something. Listen. It's sung by a woman called Peggy Lee. I believe she is a beauty."

"My mother is called Peggy Lee," Simon heard himself say, realising immediately that he had dropped a ludicrous non-sequitur.

It threw Maria right out of her stride. She looked at Simon with a renewed focus. That was the first time he saw Maria's judgement-pending stare.

"What?" she said.

"This song. It's sung by this American called Peggy Lee, and the funny thing is that my Chinese mother is also called Peggy Lee."

"After her? She sounds like a prostitute." In the split second she heard herself say that, Maria regretted it. "I mean, you know, just the voice."

Her eyes softened a grade.

"I don't think it was after her, just a coincidence. My dad didn't listen to this stuff. He sang Irish songs, even though he had never been to Ireland."

"It's all Tanka sea shanties with this one here," Maria said, thumbing towards the numb bundle in the cell. She almost smiled, but not quite.

"Her real name is Lee Ka-yee, but my dad just called her Peggy. I don't think he thought about the combination of the first and last name."

"It's a good song," Maria said, "I've never heard anything like it. I like her. I didn't mean what I said before."

There was a pause as all four listened in silence.

"*Romeo loved Juliet*," Sally repeated quizzically.

"Shakespeare?" Maria suggested.

"Yup," said Jagan.

They tapped their feet quietly.

"How did you know your father was here?" Jagan asked.

"You were making such a racket when you passed Shrimp Paste King that he looked out of the window. He got worried when he saw you had arrested my dad, so he sent his son round to ours to warn me."

"It wasn't an arrest. Do you want some cha siu pork? It's from Kennedy Town."

Jagan was already pouring out two more beers.

"OK, but after that I'm taking my dad home."

"OK. So now I know your father's name and you know my mother's name. May I ask what your names are?"

"Maria."

"Sally."

"Simon."

"Jagan."

They tapped their feet.

"The British police give me fever, a bloody headache at least," Maria said.

"Tanka girls give me fever," Simon said, and left that hanging in what he thought was a subtle yet flirtatious manner, but was taken by the girls as plain rude.

"Why do you call him Bad News?" Jagan asked, addressing it more to the younger Sally than the hot-blooded Maria, thinking it was marginally safer.

"It's the first time you've come across him. Your uniforms got drenched in the sea, there are scratches on your arms, your supper is being disturbed by snores, and you've had a bawling from my sister. He's bad news, obviously," she replied.

They finished off the cha siu pork and their beers. Maria got up to leave. She took one look at the prison smock on her dad and asked what the hell he was going to go home in. After some dithering Simon and Jagan agreed there was no option but to lend Bad News a spare uniform. It was a decision they both regretted as it took a few weeks to recover that precious set of government property.

For those weeks, every time Bad News went for a drink at Joycee's, he proudly wore his new uniform. He got a lot of mileage out of recounting the tale of the Fascist Imperial Police that kidnapped him and forced him into recruitment as part of the puppet force. No one laughed harder at this than SPK who had that exact experience under the Japanese, though in his case it wasn't half as funny.

In the following weeks Simon did everything he could to orchestrate another encounter with Maria, but she had an uncanny knack for avoiding him. He would see her across the market square and she would be gone by the time he crossed over. He would catch her face at the end of the street, and there would be no sign of her by the time he had speed-walked to that end. Simon raised his rounds on the community meet-and-greet, regularly visiting stilt-house families, making friends along the way. The first time he found Maria's house his heartbeat quickened. Sally leaned over the balcony, flicking her cigarette ash into the wind that wafted across his dinghy.

"Is Maria there?" he called out.

"No. What's up?" came the reply.

"Nothing. Just saying hello to the neighbourhood."

"OK, hello."

"Right. Yes. So, how's your dad?"

"Fine. Thanks. How's your smiley sidekick Jagan?"

"Oh, good, good."

"OK."

"Can I come in?"

Sally disappeared inside for a minute and re-emerged, stifling a laugh, to give the go-ahead. Simon didn't have a plan, he was just following instinct as he climbed the ladder into Maria's family home.

Inside he was greeted by Sally, Danny, Madge, Jeanie and Stevie. They were all giggling.

"Hello everyone, I'm Simon, your community police officer," he started. The kids all burst out laughing. Simon left embarrassed within five minutes, having got no further in his quest to talk to Maria. After that there were a few other visits that went along similar lines and Simon gradually got to know the Chu family, except Maria, who normally hid when he came.

One day Danny came to the police station and said that Maria would be cooking crabs that he had caught, and would Simon like to come by for a portion that evening, along with his partner Jagan. Simon acted as cool as he could, which Danny read easily as unbridled enthusiasm, and the two police officers politely accepted. As Simon and Jagan were arriving at the stilt-house on a sampan ferried by a leather-skinned old lady, Bad News was on his way out to Joycee's to meet up for a "quick drink" with SPK and the Jap Devil. He greeted them like old friends and asked if they intended to arrest any other pillars of the community that evening. They laughed it off with good grace. Simon was relieved that Bad News had at least returned the uniform, finally.

At the meal, Maria acted as if Simon and Jagan were friends of the family, and it was perfectly normal for them to be dropping by on their beat, even though she had only officially met them once, six months earlier. With the twins, Madge, Sally and Danny there, it was of course impossible to be formal in any case as they all squatted around Maria's big wok with their little bamboo bowls. Of course it was perfectly natural that Maria acted familiarly with them, because she was familiar. On their previous visits to the house she had only been behind a rickety bamboo wall, sewing clothes, peeling garlic or doing her dad's accounts. She kept herself out of sight but listened intently to what the boys had to say for themselves, often laughing to herself at things they said that she thought were daft beyond belief. She knew of course that Danny looked up to them, and they talked to Danny without patronising him though he was still only a boy. She liked this about them and was glad of their influence, because Danny was spending far too much time with Salty Pang, the Dagger and, worst of all, Red, who made her shudder every time he appeared. She could also tell that Sally had a soft-spot for Jagan and she teased her mercilessly about that. Sally claimed Maria was completely wrong, but she was still young and not very good at hiding a crush. Maria, on the other hand was expert. She conveyed a brand of familiarity that was perfectly ambiguous, somewhere between totally platonic and slightly flirtatious. It had a dizzying effect on Simon at first, until he slowly began to read between the lines, and began to see that despite trying to hide it she was interested in how he spent his days, what he ate, who he talked with and how he dressed himself.

The meals with the family were fairly regular events, happening almost once a week without a formal fixture. Sometimes Bad News would be there, regaling the officers with smuggling tales that span the decades, the children egging their father on to recount the best episodes of Japanese ambushes, giant squid and contraband worth fortunes, encounters on the sea with generals, convicts on the run and drowned colleagues. But usually Bad News wasn't there because he would be out on the sea, or at Joycee's. Simon came to understand that Maria was the true head of the household. She was bringing up the twins, trying her best with troubled Madge, and had conceded independence to Sally and, only in recent months, to Danny who was determined to be a man, not a boy.

Simon and Maria began to spend time alone on walks over Tiger Hill, or round to nearby hamlets. He told her the story of his banishment, letting her know some of the details of his relationship with the

Commissioner's daughter, though she read between the lines for the parts he didn't spell out. She told him about Teddy Wang, who had asked her to marry him, before setting off to join United Nations troops as a British subject in the Korean War.

"What did you say?" Simon asked with some trepidation.

"I didn't say no," she replied, though she explained that things were not quite resolved when he went off to fight. That was two years earlier and he hadn't come back, even though fighting had ended a year earlier. She thought he was manning the re-established border between North and South Korea.

Teddy's leaving for war had coincided with Maria's mother's tuberculosis diagnosis. She was sick and bedridden for weeks, until Bad News told the family one day that a mysterious uncle that they had never heard of before had offered to pay for her treatment in a sanatorium over in Kennedy Town. They all wept, and waved her off from the Tai O pier, and Maria was left holding the hands of her four-year-old twin siblings, ten-year-old Madge, and the two teenagers, Danny and Sally.

Simon found out Teddy Wang had returned when he arrived at the house for a meal, expecting to take Maria out for an evening stroll afterwards. The kids were all subdued, and when he asked about Maria, Sally said curtly, "Gone to Cheung Chau to see Teddy."

"He's back," Danny said. "And if he slaps her once he'll have the Mongoose on him," he blurted angrily. Fifteen-year-old Danny had no such clout with the Mongoose at the time, but he was already beginning to run errands for the "big brothers" by then, buying the odd pack of cigarettes, passing on messages, delivering goods. Simon knew there had been abuse from Teddy. Maria had told him. It had been very rare, maybe three times in the two years he relentlessly pursued her, she said. She didn't make any excuses for him, but said there was much more to Teddy than that.

Simon got drunk that night, finally admitting to Jagan that he had fallen for Maria. Jagan laughed at him, saying it wasn't something that needed admitting. They were listening to American Forces Radio, and *Fever* came on for the first time since the night they had met Bad News, Maria and Sally.

"There's Peggy again," Jagan noted.

"Chicks were born to give you fever. She was right about that, I suppose," Simon said, telling Jagan that he was going to clear his head with a hike up Lantau Peak.

It took Simon two hours of hard trekking to rise up to Ngong Ping Monastery. It was a moonless night and there was little he could make out on his climb other than the path immediately in front. Incense wafted from the meditation hall. A bell was struck and dawn chants were beginning, the monks groaning and croaking like toads in the rain. As he climbed, he pieced together every conversation he had had with Maria. He was dealing with loss by fixating on detail. He had another hour on the steepest ascent of the hike that took him a thousand feet upwards inside of half a mile. He had started off confused. How could Maria go to stay with Teddy after everything that had happened between the two of them? Was there anything real about what had passed between them? Had it all been an illusion? Had he been wrong about Maria?

As he started seeing the lightening sky behind the peak, and felt his sweat pour in rivulets all around his body, he was beginning to come to terms with what had happened. He reached the top just in time to see the sun burst over the horizon a hundred miles out to sea, electrifying the world with brilliant shards of light. "Of course it was real," he said out loud. "I got to know a woman. I fell in love with her. And now she's gone. The sun rises, crosses the sea and sets at night. It will do the same tomorrow, the day after and for ever." He climbed down from the peak in cheerful mood, found his way back to the station and crashed onto his bunk.

He never quite regained that absolute certainty, but going back to it in the next few weeks helped him get through low points. Maria returned after three days. Simon didn't see the family for another two weeks until Danny came to see him.

"Are you upset about Maria?" Danny asked Simon.

"Yeah, I am, Danny. But I understand that Maria's got things to sort out," Simon said.

"You like her, don't you?" Danny asked.

"Of course I do, Danny. We're friends, me and Maria. Good friends."

"Right. Maria wondered if you wanted to come to dinner tonight. Dad caught lobsters."

Maria was unsurprisingly subdued at that first meal, though her natural confidence, humour and warmth inevitably bubbled through. Jagan did his best to dilute the tension by comically flirting with a compliant Sally. After the washing-up was done and Simon had had his smoke with Danny on the roof, Maria nodded to him, indicating that it was time for a private walk.

They strolled away from the submerged alleys and out along the coastline towards Tung Chung, and Maria told Simon that it was all over with Teddy Wang. Teddy wanted to marry right away, and for her to go with him to married quarters in Malaysia, where trouble was brewing among Communists. After that he would take her to Liverpool, he said, where he had family and good business prospects.

"Why didn't you go with him?" Simon asked.

"The twins. They need me," she said.

"But what about Teddy? Do you love him?"

"I did once. But not now," she said.

Simon desperately wanted to know why not now, but he knew she would never explain.

And so, that is how the second act of Simon's courtship with Maria started, though things moved more slowly this time, compared with the giddy first few weeks of act one.

One-and-a-half years later, after the blank they drew from SPK on the dead mainlander, Jagan and Simon waited a few minutes to let Maria, Madge and the twins get ahead without awkwardly having to follow in their footsteps.

"Simon, why haven't things progressed with you and Maria after all this time?" Jagan asked.

"What are you talking about?" he answered defensively.

"You know exactly what I'm talking about. The girl who gives you fever."

"Sinbad's winging over Keung Shan. He must have spotted something more interesting over at Shek Pik."

"He's probably looking for a mate."

They walked through the densely packed stilt-house neighbourhood along Shek Tsai Po, each waterborne home thriving with quiet activity. The shacks leaned into each other and creaked with the footsteps of all who lived inside and on open verandas. Even when half-built on land, they had rounded palm-thatched roofs echoing the shape of boat houses. Small children played in between the rickety stilts, chasing mudskippers and catching crabs. Old ladies sat and smoked roll-up cigarettes on lacquered platforms, spat out husks of sunflower seeds, and talked loudly in harsh tones. Men sat in groups on upturned boats and smoked tobacco in their three-foot bamboo bongs. They made predictions about the weather and tide, name-dropped legendary fishermen, Triads and village heads, and boasted of sea monsters they had seen. The odd opium smoker sat alone on a veranda staring at light and shade. Mothers with toddlers tied to their apron strings or babies on their back tended to charcoal stoves, as smoke wafted along alleys and mixed with the smell of fish and oysters, cooked, salted or fermented.

The market clamoured with sellers, labourers and buyers. A dozen people had gathered around two baby whale sharks laid out on the floor, each one plump and four feet long, the owner demanding hundreds for each. Two boys aged about six were falling about with laughter, daring each other to put his head in the mouth of one. Another crowd stared at a huge manta ray that spanned six feet, hoisted onto the side of a fence, dripping water and blood. A large octopus had climbed out of a bucket and was making its way over to a tray of crabs. Chickens and ducks clucked and quacked in tightly packed bamboo baskets next to caged civets and boxes of horseshoe bats. Soft-shelled turtles struggled to climb out of wooden bowls next to trays of little brown scorpions. Skinned pangolins were hanging blood-smudged from meat hooks, baskets of scales by the side.

"Is that legal?" Simon asked Jagan.

"Nope," he replied.

"What are we going to do about that?"

"Nothing. We're not the hawker police. We've got a murder inquiry on our hands."

"Yeah, but..."

"No. You have to pick your battles, Simon."

"We seem to be a very choosy police force."

"That's right, keep it choosy."

They posted a picture on one of the trees, with a handwritten message asking for information. Immediately there was a crowd of about 20 people, reading out loud, shaking their heads. Some wondered aloud what the world was coming to, some found it funny. Simon addressed them, saying they were looking for any information they could get on the man, or what had happened.

"He's a beggar, look at him."

"He's got the look of a pirate."

"Or a Yankee spy."

"A Jap."

"A Triad, I should think."

"Probably a worthless heroin smuggler."

"Definitely something wrong with him."

Then two men started to argue.

"He's a Commie for sure."

"No, a fascist KMT."

"You're a child-killing Commie bastard."

"You're a Nationalist rapist and you deserve to be chopped."

Simon and Jagan waded in, urging calm and warning against any rioting. The men were placated by others in the crowd who may have been sympathetic to one or the other, but had no stomach to see shops burned, looted and blood on the pavement again.

Simon and Jagan moved into the village square where a man dressed as the Monkey King was eating fire in front of the Kwun Tai temple. Two real simian assistants on chains walked among the gawkers begging for money. Nearby there were three leathery monks in threadbare Tibetan garb, with black sun-cracked faces that proved they were the real thing. They placed their wares in front of where they sat thumbing beads and twirling prayer wheels. They needed to sell the huge yak skull in front of them, along with the snow-leopard skin, in order to get enough money for the long walk back to the roof of the world. A line of children sat in front of the skull, mesmerised.

Simon and Jagan walked into the Rural Committee office where Jackson Tse sat at a desk piled with papers. Old Lau sat on a wooden bench on one side of the room and Salty Pang sat opposite Tse. The two policemen shook all their hands and offered cigarettes all around. All was quiet as five cigarettes were simultaneously lit, and then Simon said: "A man was murdered outside the police station last night."

"I know, I know. It's a terrible thing," Tse replied.

Jackson Tse was the head of the Rural Committee. He had a wind-chiselled face and a tough, sinewy body. A fisherman by trade, he was known as a hard man but was always civil. Stories abounded of his pre-war days, dodging the Japanese naval blockade to reach his favourite fishing grounds in the South China Sea where he hunted marlin, swordfish and great white sharks. He was widely respected as a genuine leader, with a good reputation for arbitration and dispute resolution. He helped to organise salt-smuggling boats during the American-imposed trade embargo, ensuring a lucrative delivery of the precious commodity to Chinese cities along the Guangdong coast. He was also known for leading the negotiations that brought the Yau Ma Tei ferry company to open a regular service linking Tai O to the rest of Hong Kong. He sat as easily with the colonial police as he did with Triad leaders, the grannies of the alleys and the girls at the Luncome. Simon got on with him, as did Falkirk and the Fox. Only Jagan was wary, detecting a well-hidden prejudice against Indians. It was so subtle that even Simon thought Jagan was being over-sensitive.

And though Jackson Tse was generally well liked and respected, there was a hint of malice about him, and some uncomfortable, unanswered questions. The biggest question was how he had survived the Japanese so well. Many had collaborated to a certain extent, it was a matter of survival. But the extent to which Tse had come off unscathed, possibly even richer than before the invasion, made some people, like SPK for example, somewhat wary. Was he selling people out as slaves to the Japanese? some had quietly asked. SPK had always suspected that it was Jackson who had betrayed him to the Japanese, just before the raid on his warehouse where they found grenades and guns for the East River guerrilla brigade. He was taken to the gasoline depot and tortured for two months before being forced into a Kempeitai uniform. This was an added torture as villagers assumed he had volunteered for the rice, and ostracised him. SPK always knew that Jackson Tse was a man who comfortably assumed the right to lead. In times of peace his instinct was to lead by pleasing everybody, often by greasing every palm and calling in favours in return. He was genuinely popular. But under pressure his survival instinct was sharp as razor blades and just as efficient, and SPK knew that.

Tse held Simon's elbow reassuringly and told him he was doing everything to find out what went on. He reassured Simon that if anyone in the Fishermen's Union or the Salt Workers Union was found to be involved they would be sent to the police immediately.

"I heard he was a Communist spy," Tse added.

"That's what his killers said," Simon replied.

"If he was a spy he might have deserved it. We don't want agents stirring up trouble here."

"Do you know who he was?" Simon asked, showing him a poster.

Tse looked carefully, then over to Salty Pang, who answered by stepping towards the picture. Pang scrutinised the image for a while and then shrugged.

"I don't recognise him. Why did they kill this man here?"

"That's what we're trying to understand," Jagan chimed in.

"We think that the killers got off their boat, burned it and came ashore near Sham Wat," he added.

"Could be Tung Chung Triads then?" Tse suggested.

"Or Tai O?" Simon said.

Salty Pang shrugged again. It was a well-known secret that he was at least a Red Pole enforcer for the Mongoose Triads – some said much higher up. He took hold of the handout again, looked at it with a theatrically furrowed brow and shook his head.

Simon had a sinking feeling that he would never know what went on in this village. He would never know if Salty Pang was really a Red Pole enforcer, an incense master, or even a mountain master – or even a member of the Mongoose at all. No one he could trust would tell him anything, least of all Jackson Tse who knew when to be vivacious and expansive, and when to shrug quietly. Old Lau would never tell anyone anything because he seemed every day to be lost deep inside a dark and warm opiate dream. Simon often wondered why the no-nonsense Jackson even tolerated this crusty old mystic in his office for hours at a time.

Of course people he couldn't trust would tell him all sorts. There would be random chicken-delivery men talking about the great men in the Mongoose they knew. "Salty Pang, he runs the show, I know that," one would say. Then there were boys in the Tai O Youth Soccer League that Simon sometimes refereed for. "Salty Pang is the toughest Triad, but you have to watch out for Old Lau, he is the real mountain master," one boy said. "No no no, it's Jackson himself, my dad told me that," another would say.

The most disturbing rumours were about the Fox. His real name was Ho Chun-ying, but most people did not know that. He had been at the Tai O police station before the Japanese, during the Japanese and since. He was 40 years old. He came from Mui Wo and of all the police at the station he knew the place the best, but he was Chinese, without any connection and not on track for promotions. Outside of the formal requirements of rank, the Fox hardly bothered to be civil to Simon or Jagan, though he was careful to butter up Falkirk at every opportunity. Shrimp farmers, ox-cart drivers, sedan-carrier girls and kitchen maids all dropped the odd hint: "The Fox is a Mongoose, he's an enforcer, he's a 'white paper fan', he's a vanguard operations manager." You name it, someone named him. There was no doubt he had something up his sleeve. Whether that was formal initiation or self-preserving calculation, something had got him the Rolex watch he wore on that sleeve, and rumoured ownership of flats in Wanchai, Kennedy Town and Kowloon.

Regardless of the misinformation and the lack of details, Simon did accept that Salty Pang was probably some kind of ranking Triad, and the Fox was more than likely bent. Old Lau and Jackson could however be anything. The biggest problem with any Triad-related rumour mill is that anyone who is telling you anything is by definition unqualified to know the truth. And anyone who knows anything interesting will always keep their mouths shut.

Jackson, Pang and Old Lau kept their mouths firmly shut for long enough to indicate that the conversation was over.

"Don't worry, Simon," Jackson said with a smile, "I'll put up your posters for you. Everyone in this village will see the handiwork of your printer and admire his skills, it is indeed a fine job that he did for you."

"Thank you, Jackson," Simon said, accepting that Jackson was quite deliberately missing the point of the poster.

"There is another thing I'd like to discuss with you, Simon, as you are here anyway," Jackson said. "Have you heard any rumours about a tiger?"

Jagan suddenly perked up.

"A tiger, yes I have, Jackson. You too?"

"Yes, from Blind Wang," he said, looking at Jagan for the first time in the conversation.

"Exactly," Jagan said with triumph to Simon.

Simon's eyeballs rolled up towards the ceiling. He wished he could wake up and find himself in a world where this annoying distraction had disappeared.

"Also Old Lau thinks he saw a tiger last week on his way over to his hut at Yi O."

Simon looked at Lau and he couldn't tell if he was conscious, but then he seemed to nod.

"What did you see?" Simon asked.

There was a long pause.

"I don't know, maybe a tiger. She roared loud enough," came the reply finally.

"Is he a good witness?" Simon asked Jackson.

"Well, at the moment he seems a little distant. Between you and I it's because of those anti-opium pills that he's taken to using recently. Seems like fantastic stuff as he hasn't smoked a pinch of the old O since he started on the pills. Of course there are side effects in that he can be a bit dreamy sometimes, but the point is that Old Lau isn't a liar so I think we can trust what he says. The boys are already making plans, Simon. We need to catch this thing and by golly, when it is caught there is going to be one hell of a festival."

"I heard that Old Lau shot a tiger when he was a boy. Is that right, Old Lau?" Jagan asked.

Lau suddenly looked alert, turned to face Jagan and nodded. "Yup. I shot a tiger in 1923 on the north side of Keung Shan. I nearly blew its shoulder off. It came at me in a rage, blood pouring down its side. I had one second to reload my rifle, take aim at its face and shoot. Its head exploded, which is a pity because I lost the best part of the trophy."

"What did you do with it?" Jagan asked.

"I put it on a boat and took it across the Pearl River during a typhoon to Guangzhou. We nearly sank four times, but I made it. The best prices were at Qingping market in those days. At the market there were already four tiger skins laid out when I got there. Mine was a bargain for some Manchurian skin collector who wanted it for coat trimmings, half the price with the head all shattered. But I got enough to buy opium for two years."

"Didn't you tell the authorities?" Simon asked naively, confused that this tiger didn't figure in the official tally of the last tigers killed in Hong Kong.

"What authorities?" Lau said, laughing along with Salty Pang.

"If you mean the Brits on Hong Kong Island, why would these old boys bother sailing out there to tell them about that?" Jackson said.

"The police station was here," Simon said.

Old Lau, Salty Pang and Jackson laughed as if Simon had deliberately cracked an absurd joke.

"Were there other tigers?"

"Yeah, every few years. We caught some, many disappeared. It's very difficult to hunt tigers. They killed us too. My uncle was killed, two children went missing one year, a salt worker one year..." Lau tailed off, seemingly shutting down again into the closed world of the anti-opium pills – otherwise known as heroin.

"We used to talk about the Beast of Tai O, a man-eater," Jackson said.

"Yes, there was definitely some devil around before the Japs came," Salty added. "And then they eclipsed all other beasts."

Jagan said to Jackson: "The authorities are very interested in tiger sightings now. Do let us know if you get any more information. We need to make sure people feel safe."

"Yes, of course, sergeant," Jackson said, reluctantly acknowledging Jagan's authority.

They stepped out into the market square, nearly treading on the scratty snow-leopard skin the Tibetan monks were trying to sell.

"These old boys, they don't half give me a fever, Jagan," Simon said. "They clam up at the first mention of the real investigation that matters, and then spread a web of intrigue about some fantasy beast of their own imagination. I mean, come on. He casually mentions four people killed by tigers in the Tai O area in recent decades. As if we wouldn't know about that?"

"Would we know it? I'm not sure. Anyway, it's time we took Maria up on the offer of that shrimp-paste fried rice. We should talk to Danny," Jagan said.

They walked to the Taichung crossing point and got a lift on a sampan punted by an old sea-hag with gold teeth, black deeply-scored fingers and a frayed top-knotted basket hat of the Tanka. Like many people active in Tai O and across Hong Kong she was a relic of the Qing dynasty, born well before the Brits had acquired the New Territories. She glided them past the stilts as families busily prepared their evening meals, tipping vegetable offcuts into the tidal lanes, holding up squawking chickens by their legs or rinsing rice in wooden buckets. Under one large two-storey house there were about six teenagers perched on the stilts, plotting their revenge on their old parents. Fish jumped out of the water and cattle egrets skimmed for easy pickings. A grey heron on the edge of a battered, sunken dinghy stared intently with its lethal stabbing beak poised. Some of the houses were whitewashed and lacquered, on firm straight stilts, instilling great confidence. Others were a rickety criss-cross of leaning beams, toppling walls and ragged fishnet hammocks, with chimneys thrusting at random angles from smoke-blackened kitchens. An old man stood on top of a shack and shouted at their gold-toothed Qing dynasty punter, throwing down a bag of sunflower seeds that she accepted with a barely perceptible nod.

Jagan pointed to Bad News Chu's ramshackle hut, where Sally sat on a veranda cutting Madge's hair, the twins Stevie and Jeanie watching Sally's handiwork. Maria could be seen squatting at the stove, stirring a large wok. Up above, Danny sat on the top roof, laughing with his partner in crime Spike, both of them dangling fishing lines into the water. Their punt-lady shouted up for Bad News and he came out with a big grin.

"Watch out, Danny, it's the Imperial Police. I'm going to Joycee's for a meeting with their boss, Old Typhoon. Oh I miss the days when I had my uniform."

The punt-lady burst into such a cackle of laughter that it set all the children off at her. Jagan took the two tied-up lobsters he had negotiated with the lady and the two policemen stepped out of the rocking boat, shaking hands with Bad News as he replaced them.

"Good luck, boys," he said, "We don't want nasty KMT executions around here. They can bloody well take their murderous politics back to the mainland."

"Thanks Bad News," Simon said, adding: "And you will of course tell us if you hear anything," without much hope in his voice.

"You'll be the first to know," he blatantly and cheerfully lied.

"Dad, don't be too late and don't forget you've got a crate of pineapples and mangos from Hainan at dawn," Maria shouted.

"Yes, captain. And you might need to say that again, louder, because I don't think Her Majesty's Marine Police quite caught that piece of intelligence," he called back, saluting her as the Tanka lady punted him between the stilts, wobbling and cackling. Simon and Jagan took the goading with their usual good grace. Everyone knew that it wasn't goading and that it was the actual plan, or something similar, but it was in everyone's interest to pretend that it was just teasing.

Jagan shrugged at Simon: "Choosy, that's what we are. It's fine."

They climbed onto the veranda and Maria gave Simon the judgement-pending look. Jagan saved him by thrusting the lobsters towards her. She accepted them with a nod and pointed to a vat of boiling water. He dunked them in, their clawing spiny legs slowing towards a dying halt as the flesh cooked inside the reddening shell. Then with the chopper on the board he expertly dug out the flesh from the rich thorax and abdomen, scraped out the soft brain and split the legs to chase down more white flesh. He piled the meat on the side of the board, then held the other side over the railing, pushing the broken shell parts into the water. Underneath, a shoal of small fish immediately rushed to the sinking carcass parts, cleaning up all the bits Jagan hadn't managed to hollow out. Maria took the lobster flesh from the board and tipped it into her wok, stirring it in with the greyish pink flecks of SPK's finest and most pungent. Simon's mouth was watering.

"Simon, Jagan, on the balcony! We've got a big one," Danny shouted down.

Simon looked up from the patio and saw him with Spike pulling on the line. A fish was on the end of it, thrashing for its life, flipping its tail violently as its head was yanked from the water.

"Grab it," Danny shouted as it came up to the railing.

Jagan handed Simon a bowl and he took the fish into it, squatted down and released the line. The fish struggled so much it nearly flipped out of the bowl but Simon kept hold of it long enough to hand it to Jagan, who knocked it dead with the blunt side of the chopper. Maria then took over, slitting it open, pushing its guts over the railing, causing yet another mass frenzy of small fish below. She scaled and filleted it within seconds, chopped it into small pieces and stirred it into the wok, placing the head carefully intact at the centre. By now Jagan, Simon, Danny, Spike, Sally, Madge, Jeanie and Stevie were all sitting, squatting, lounging or standing around Maria's wok with variously sized bowls, mugs, plates and lunch boxes – chopsticks poised.

After the meal, Sally served a round of tea to the older ones while Madge took the twins off to shower at the water pump. Simon asked Danny if he and Spike would come up on the roof to talk. Danny looked at Spike for a moment, then back at Simon with a big grin.

"Come on boys, up the ladder for a smoke."

Sally and Maria had already lit theirs as they squatted at the wash bowl, cleaning up their dinnerware. They were giggling, with Maria teasing Sally about the way she kept watching the handsome Jagan.

On the roof Simon and Jagan doled out the cigarettes.

"Lucky Strike again. Nice smokes. I get sick of the Chinese brands Bad News always picks up on the sea," Spike said innocently.

Simon showed the boys the picture of the dead man.

"Whoa, nice picture. Can we see the wounds?" Danny said.

"What wounds?" Simon asked, hoping to catch them out.

"I don't know!" Danny said with a nervous laugh. "Whatever killed him."

"I just wondered if someone might have said something."

"Oh yeah, everyone is talking about it. Liar Chou says he killed him himself with his chopper. Blind Wang said he witnessed it."

Spike fell about laughing.

"I watched him die," Simon said, jolting the boys.

Danny for a moment turned grey.

"We heard he was a spy," he offered by way of conciliation.

"That's what the killers said before they sprayed the rocks and caused a landslide that nearly killed me," Jagan said.

"Ouch, Jagan, you're going to have a mean scar when that bandage comes off," Danny cajoled while Spike sniggered again.

"Yes, and if I find out who did it, I'm going to put the miscreant behind bars," Jagan said with a smile that made him look slightly deranged.

"Have you seen this face before or not?" Simon asked.

Spike shook his head. Danny hesitated, then: "I can't say, Simon."

"What can't you say, Danny?"

Simon knew that it was a mistake to have this chat with Spike here too. If Danny was to give anything away, any hint or clue, he wouldn't be able to do it in the company of a sworn brother, even one as daft as Spike, not unless he was feeling particularly reckless.

"I can't say," he said with a shrug towards Spike and what looked to Jagan like a false snigger.

"Was he a spy?" Simon prodded.

"That's what you said, isn't it?" Danny said to Jagan.

"It's what you heard, isn't it?" Jagan came back.

"Yeah, that too. You know, people in the village, the usual yacking."

"But do you believe it?" Simon asked.

"I can't say."

Simon had been here before with Danny, and he knew he had pushed the questions as far as he could for the time being. Danny wanted to please, but he was caught between worlds. He knew when to clam up for self-preservation.

"When are you going to take my sister dancing in Mui Wo?" Danny threw in, trying to find a more enjoyable thread. This one was always good to tease Simon with.

"Your sister Maria is a fine lady. I like her very much, but it's not like that, as you know," Simon said, giving the usual spiel. "The newspaper version" as Maria would call it.

"Not like what?" Danny said, nudging Spike in the belly.

"Danny!" Maria's voice came from below. "You shut your mouth and go fill up the water barrel, you know it's your job."

"He was just looking after your interests, Maria!" Spike called down.

"You'd be better off looking after your own interests by helping your mate Danny get to that bloody water-stand now before they turn off the pumps!" she yelled back.

"Come on Spike, we'd better do it," Danny said, "Will that be all, officer?"

"Yes Danny, we'll talk later, OK."

"Adios Amigos," he said, copying something he had seen on movie night in the market square without knowing what it meant.

As the boys lugged the water barrel onto their small dinghy and unmoored it, Madge jumped in with them.

"Get back here, Madge!" Maria called out.

"Won't be long," she retorted, waving off her big sister without looking at her.

"Danny, keep her with you," Maria said.

He nodded and shrugged, clearly meaning he would try his best, but Madge was Madge, and this 15-year-old would go where she wanted no matter what her 17-year-old brother would do.

"Thanks for the rice, Maria," Simon said. "As usual it was delicious."

"Of course," said Maria with feigned coyness. "And if you find anything tastier you'd better report right back to me. I don't want some tart going around showing off with better fried rice."

"How's your mum?"

"The usual. Moaning about the sanatorium. She says half the inmates are mad. They just sit around smoking and gossiping all day, which is exactly what she does. She keeps sending messages asking me to bring the twins and some fresh food."

"I'm sure she's on the mend."

"Well, it's been four years. I should hope so. But I'm not too sure she wants to get better. She has a nice time at the TB clinic. All paid for by mystery Uncle Wang in Taiwan. It would be nice if we got some of that cash, it could help with food, shelter, schooling, you know, the basics. Mum has a nice quiet life. Her sister visits most days for gossip and chats. She doesn't have to work. No cooking. No cleaning. No kids around. Not a bad deal." She said this as she untangled nets for Bad News.

"I'll take you over on the police launch again when I get the chance," Simon said.

"Thanks Simon, but I'm not sure if I'll want to go. We'll see."

"We'd better be off, we need to have a chat with Madam Li."

"Fine. Might see you tomorrow. I told SPK I'd go and do his accounts if I can get away from the factory office for the afternoon."

They hailed another old Qing-dynasty crone and punted back to the Taichung crossing point.

"What does Danny know?" Simon asked Jagan.

"Something," he said.

4

NIGHT IN TUNISIA

The sun-baked middle-aged woman was digging in the garden, making the most of the dusk light. Two ragged children were helping her, collecting the potatoes she dug up and putting them in a box. She spoke to them in her jagged Shanghainese dialect and they giggled. Some people called Madam Li's house "The Hostel" because mainland refugees passed through there on their way to make their fortune in urban Hong Kong. A Tai O guest house was hardly the destination they were aiming for, but many found it a thankful stopping point on their risk-laden voyage into the unknown. It was a good place to take stock, rest, plan and gather useful intelligence on where to head, what to look for. For some it was a life saver. Thousands drowned on their illegal journey to Hong Kong, thousands more nearly drowned, and some of the lucky ones would drag themselves to Madam Li's, or be dumped there, where it was well known that they would receive food and shelter, and whenever possible some basic medical care.

Li had not set out to be a one-person charity. Her lodging was built as a commercial venture, but she was one of Hong Kong's luckier refugees in that she had a cushion of wealth that she had inherited from Shanghai industrialist parents. Originally she had thought of her place as a stopping point for the more comfortable travellers from China, running a lucrative and efficient hotel for those who could afford basic accommodation on their travels. But as the numbers crossing the Pearl River Delta swelled and their circumstances become more obviously desperate, Li found that she couldn't turn her back on the stream of human suffering that was washing up on her doorstep. She opened her doors wider. The private rooms became family rooms, then shared family rooms, then the house was divided between a wing for men and the rest of it for women and children.

There was a constant throughput of bedraggled mainlanders. Most only stayed for one or two nights, but many would find themselves putting off their forward journeys for a few days. Some ended up staying for weeks, helping Li run the place, including in her garden where she grew food for the hostel. There were vegetable gardens, chickens to tend to, eggs to collect and pigs to feed.

When this strange Shanghainese woman first hiked down from the monasteries, villagers were naturally curious about her, especially when she bought a plot of land outright with cash. Then she contracted a village architect and commissioned a large home. That's when the Mongoose took interest. They acted as go-betweens to organise labour and materials and skimmed what they could off the construction project. Once it was done they offered their services and protection in running the guest house, but Li, surprisingly and fearlessly turned them down. She promised to give her respects once a year in a lai see packet in a cabbage for the New Year's dragon dance, but that would be all. A bemused Mongoose leadership then tried out some trusty old intimidation tactics. Someone vandalised her water tank, but she got someone else to fix it. Another thug chopped down her papaya trees, she grew some more. The same happened to the banana grove, but they grew back even faster. When teenage hoodlums, including Danny Chu and his daft friend Spike, started drinking, smoking and causing a racket on her lawn she came out of the house with a hunting rifle, shot it into the air and told them to tell their stupid big brothers to stop hassling her.

Mongoose elders talked at Old Lau's grocery store.

"Who the hell is she?" Salty Pang asked.

"They say she is a shaman. She studied at the monastery," the Red Lieutenant reported.

They sent their colleague known as the Dagger to the monastery to find out about her. He came back shaking his head.

"There's nothing we can do," he said.

"She is a woman of independent means, and they say she has no greed at all, or fear."

"She's incorruptible," Pang said mostly to himself.

"What can we do?" the Dagger asked.

"Kill her?" asked Red.

"But why?" Pang asked him, genuinely perplexed.

"Why not?" said Red, nonplussed.

"Kill the chicken to frighten the monkeys," the Dagger said.

"She doesn't know anyone here. No one would miss her." Red said convincingly.

"But she hasn't messed with us," Pang said, almost disappointed.

They all nodded, sucking on their cigarettes.

Then the Dagger had a brainwave: "We'll just leave her to do what she wants, and that will show people not to mess with us. Because she hasn't messed around with us and we're letting her do what she wants. But if she had messed around with us we would have killed her with a thousand cuts. So it is only because we are letting her do what she wants, that she is doing exactly what she wants."

Salty Pang thought that was a reasonable idea, not genius as the Dagger seemed to think, but the most practical and wisest decision they could make.

Thus with one shot fired into the air for effect, Madam Li dealt with the Mongoose.

Salty Pang regretted his decision months later when he started to see the trail of refugees hobbling through her place. Such vulnerable people, such an opportunity to suck up profit. She must be exploiting them, he concluded. It was obvious that many, perhaps even most of the illegal immigrants or IIs wouldn't be able to pay their bills. What was going on? She must have been chasing up debts for high profits.

But how could she do that when she was growing potatoes all the time, or feeding chickens? Could it be that she was a Green Gang agent? They were the feared underworld allies of Chiang Kai-shek's corrupt Nationalists. They had been flushed down to Hong Kong by China's victorious Communists. She must have been taking II details and passing them on to Green Gang loan sharks in Kowloon and Hong Kong.

Thus assuming she already had a link to the underworld, Pang made one more attempt to get in on the game. He sent Red round to offer to pay all the II's fees, at a generous rate. In return they would have rights to chase up debts with them later. Madam Li was trying to be friendly towards Red over their cup of tea, but she found this difficult, because, of all the Mongoose that she had met, Red was the one that seriously disturbed her. He stared at her and said simply, with no embarrassment or hesitation. "All we want to do is to buy your peasants."

Not much flustered Madam Li, but something in the deadpan tone of the man in front of her shook her. She steeled herself, looked back into his cold eyes, and through gritted teeth spelled out her position. "Mr Red, I'm trying to help people here. It's not that I'm good, there just isn't any point in doing anything else. Compassion is all. Nothing else exists."

Red nodded, saying, "Madam Li, Let life take its course."

"Indeed," she said, puzzled by his quick capitulation.

Red wasn't one to waste time on hopeless causes, he walked away shaking his head. He knew a brick wall when he hit one. He took her simple and disarming frankness as a clear sign of stupidity. But her stupid wasn't the common type of stupid you could manipulate, it was the dull, unmoving stupidity of a brick wall.

"She's mad," he told Pang, "forget her."

Strangely enough, it was only when the Mongoose had completely given up on Madam Li, that Jackson Tse started his visits. He was polite and she was always welcoming. He would raise issues subtly every now and then, business registration, land use permits, marketing licenses, fishing boat registration. Fencing ordinance, slope inspection, rodent control. These issues innocently slipped into friendly chats, but Li ran rings around even the tricky Tse. She was always one step ahead of Tse, with impeccable paperwork immediately at hand. Tse saw that she was extremely cunning.

"She's mad," Pang told him, "forget her."

So Madam Li was an independent woman, not greedy and not needy. The fact was that her books were easily balanced by grateful former guests who generously paid back their debts when they were able to. Some she never heard from again, but plenty paid up when they could and some of those that became successful donated generous sums in recognition of her charitable intentions. Their contributions more than made up for the more numerous debt defaulters. The operation easily paid for itself without coercion or threat, something that amazed Pang when he finally accepted it.

Many in the police regarded Madam Li with a similar cynicism as the Mongoose had for her. Simon was among the distrusting, assuming that the sort of establishment that Li ran would have to be some type of exploitative racket. One of his theories was that she was probably in business with people-traffickers who brought IIs in for profit. Perhaps she drew a salary from them and provided a staging post on behalf of their network. She was certainly hostile enough whenever they were ordered by Central to raid the hostel. When that happened they would march purposefully along Shek Tsai Po, past SPK and the houses along the front, past the Hung Shing temple along the short stretch to Madam Li's hostel. By the time they got there the hostel would always be empty. The guests melted away on Tiger Hill. The Fox would be the most aggressive officer and Madam Li hated him. She would sit on her porch smoking and scowling and blatantly telling him that she would rather die than pay a bribe to the pathetic and corrupt Hong Kong police. The Fox would threaten to arrest her but Simon would have to intervene, even though he suspected Li was up to something.

It wouldn't have taken much effort to send a Pangolin patrol squad up Tiger Hill to flush out all the skulking IIs but Simon never bothered, knowing the whole thing was a farce anyway, as tens of thousands of IIs got to urban areas every month and supplied the territory's much needed labour. The ridiculous fact was that any time the police strolled past Madam Li's in the course of other business, they could easily see the packed house. Mainland families with little children shouting at each other in various dialects, women washing and hanging out old and tattered clothes, men talking earnestly under a cloud of mainland tobacco smoke. The place was a blatant refugee shelter.

But the whole of Tai O knew there was a different walk the police had when they were on an official raid. By keeping a few informants onside no-one in Tai O needed to be caught unawares whenever the Police were on a raid. Madam Li's secret was to run a network of observant and eager under-nine agents in strategic places. These kids could spot a police-raid march from a mile away and they could out-sprint any adult. They loved working for her because every piece of intelligence would earn them a delicious Shanghainese dumpling, otherwise known as xiao long bao.

If Madam Li wasn't an agent for people-traffickers, there was another possibility that Simon and Jagan discussed on many a night. She may well have been a Communist spy. There were rumours that she had contacts at the highest rungs of power in China, that she knew Mao, Zhou Enlai and veteran leaders of the Long March. She could have been running a safe-house right under their noses, processing a network of spies who wove their way in among genuine refugees. The hostel was a front for high-value agents who would be processed by Madam Li, a top spymaster whose renown, ranking and power would grow with each bottle of beer that Simon and Jagan had during their analysis.

Whatever the truth about her, dealing with Madam Li always put Simon on the back-foot because she was so utterly self-assured. So it was with some trepidation that he opened her gate and called out.

"Hello there Madam Li. Sorry to disturb you."

She looked up from her digging, and after a pause registered Simon and Jagan with a small nod. She told the little giggling Shanghainese kids to take the potatoes inside. As the two officers approached she reached for her cigarettes from her breast pocket and offered one each to the police, like she was a man. They lit-up in silence, took a breath in and exhaled.

"Yes?" she asked.

"There's been a murder," Jagan said.

"I know," she said.

"We are trying to find out who the murdered man was."

"OK," she said.

"Do you recognize this person?"

She took the photo and stared hard at the picture. She sucked on her cigarette and let the smoke exit slowly as she frowned in concentration.

Simon thought there was no need for such theatrics when it was obvious he would get the same old shrug from her that the others had given him. He looked at Jagan. Jagan shrugged back.

Madam Li looked at Simon then Jagan, looked down at the picture again and put on another show of deep thought.

Then she appeared to be mouthing different names, trying them for a fit.

"M....Mao? Mo?...Ma. Ma? That's it. Ma."

"Really?" said Simon.

"Yes. Ma...Xun. That was his name. Ma Xun."

"Who was he?" Jagan asked.

"A refugee," she said, with blatant disregard for their role as occasional refugee-patrol officers. It was obvious to her that this was a different matter.

"How do you know him?" he asked.

"He was sent to me by the fishermen after they had rescued him with his family 'near' the Chinese border."

It was an open secret that no fisherman from either side of the border took any notice of its existence, except when coastguards and marine police were visible.

"His family?"

"Yes, a wife who never spoke, and a little boy who clung to her all the time. They had all nearly died. One of the longest I've heard of people treading water until rescue. Ma told me it was about five hours until dawn. A miracle they had survived."

"How long did they stay with you?"

"Two nights, I think. Can't be sure. It was about three years ago."

"How many refugees come to stay here each month?" Simon asked.

"Who are you today Sergeant Lee? Refugee bounty-hunter or murder detective?"

"Always the same Madam Li. A Hong Kong Marine Police officer doing his duty."

"Well if you were doing the refugee-patrol march I would of course tell you that no refugees stayed in my business hotel. However, as you've got a more genuine walk today with a fair bit more humility than I see on those farcical missions, I think you're probably being more true to yourself on this occasion. So assuming you are trying to solve a murder, I'll let you know that I probably see about two or three hundred different faces a month."

Simon decided to ignore the blatant slur from this spy or Triad or whatever-woman. The main reason he decided to ignore it was that he didn't know what not ignoring it would entail.

"With so many faces Madam Li. It can't be easy to remember all their names."

"It isn't easy, and I probably do forget most of them Sergeant. But I remember this one and he's called Ma Xun."

"What do you know about him?"

"He was from Chiu Chau. His accent was obvious. He was in shock after their near-death encounter. He looked determined to make a go of things in Hong Kong."

"Chiu Chau?" Jagan and Simon both double-checked, eyebrows raised, expectant of a breakthrough.

"Yes. But not a sworn brother. You Imperial Police are so simple. Do you know that most Chiu Chau people are not connected to the Triads?"

"Yes, of course. But we would have to be stupid not to be aware of the shock waves the Chiu Chau Triads are creating here."

"Yes but he wasn't one. I could tell."

"How?" Jagan asked, genuinely curious.

"He didn't have the look."

"What look."

"The look of fear."

"Fear? I thought they were fearless."

"Individually they are terrified most of the time. Fear is the main control mechanism of their top-dogs. What else would it be? They don't have any ideology or vision for society. Their spurious "honourable" cause – the overthrow of the Qing dynasty – is long over and done with, even if it was ever relevant. So what's left? A racket, of course. Simple business. The stronger henchmen are kept in line with higher pay, but the lower ranks operate mostly on simple gut-fear. The Triads are the ultimate capitalist corporation. They practice the merciless exploitation of the working classes for the sake of profit. At least they are more honest than your banking corporations and exploitative employers who crush the weak with just as much ease as they do. Difference is that the Triads don't try to hide their violence, they flaunt it as an asset."

"Madam Li, are you a Communist?" Jagan asked, unable to stop himself.

"Sergeant Singh, are you an Imperialist?" she retorted.

Jagan failed to suppress a smile, despite himself.

"Very interesting. But how can we be sure that you are right Madam Li?" Simon asked, bringing the focus back on the task in hand.

"You can't, you stupid boy. I'm just telling you what I think."

Simon decided to ignore that one as well.

"The killers said he was a spy."

Madam Li tried to suppress a laugh, but failed to hide her derision. "Oh come on Sergeant. The Commies don't send spies with wife and kids in tow, leaving them to nearly drown in the PRD. No. Ma Xun was just another of the million desperados to have given up everything they had and risked their lives to get here for the small chance that they could survive and thrive. You know, even if the Commies do actually send over, say 10 spies a month to be generous, they would still be a tenth of one percent of the 10,000-a-month nobodies that drag themselves here by hook or by crook. Nice try on behalf of the killers, but there's about as much chance of Ma Xun being a spy as there is of me being one."

The final comment threw Simon and Jagan into a spin.

"Do you know where Ma went after here?" Jagan managed to ask.

"No I have no idea. The wife turned up about two years ago to pay off their bill. I saw her put some cash under a bowl on the garden table and leave quickly. I called after her but she never replied. It was the exact amount for two adults and a child to stay two nights."

"You're sure it was her?"

"I suppose I can't be too sure, not as sure as I am of the picture. But I remember at the time trying to recall which of the guests she had been, and the trace of that half-drowned family came to mind. That's probably the reason I recognise your death-mask picture."

Simon and Jagan looked at each other, Simon nodding slightly with a shrug.

"Do you know anything about what happened last night?" Jagan tried.

"Only the village gossip. Some said it must be the Green Gang. Others say it's the Mongoose trying to go up in the world. Still others said it was an official police execution."

"That's ridiculous," Simon said.

"Of course it is. But it's a good one. The police theory is that you boys executed your own informant."

"How terrible. Does no one understand how we operate?" Simon bemoaned.

"Probably not Sergeant Lee. People don't like dealing with complicated things. They like to label the world into simple entities, good and bad. And unfortunately, you boys fit the bad category."

Jagan was impressed by her frankness.

"By the way, what's the plan with the tiger?" she asked.

"What tiger?" Simon tested her.

"The one that Blind Wang saw and Dreamy Lau heard himself. Every man in the village claims he's going to be the one to get it. It'll kill them if I bagged it first. Ha."

"I don't think we'll be sending out any hunting parties until we get a better report than something Blind Wang and Dreamy Lau may or may not have seen or heard." Simon said.

"Oh, don't be fooled by Blind Wang, he sees very well for a man with no eyes," she said.

With that obscure comment Simon had had enough. They thanked her and left.

"She's mad. Forget her," Jagan said. "There's no way the men in this village would let Madam Li kill the tiger before they do."

"Yes why do they keep coming back to this bloody tiger? Anyway the ID is useful. He did have an accent that I couldn't place, and now that she's said Chiu Chau, I'm pretty sure that's what it was."

Sergeant Sebastian Wetherby was sitting at the reception office desk with his boots on the table. A sweaty gweilo sat in a chair opposite him pouring out two whiskeys from Falkirk's trophy cabinet. Neither of them got up when Simon and Jagan came into the room, they didn't offer a drink either, and no-one reached into their pockets to pass out cigarettes. It had taken Wetherby two days to get to Tai O from Central.

"What a bloody awful place this is," Wetherby said. "Two day's sailing with a stop-off in the cesspit that is Cheung Chau. Nothing but IIs, salt-making peasants, permanently-pissed smugglers and squirming mudskippers around here."

The sweaty gweilo guffawed at this as if it was the most original thing he had ever heard, when in fact it was a tired well-worn cliche that Simon had heard every time he talked to any Hong Konger outside of Tai O.

"Sergeant Simon Lee," he said, introducing himself to the fat middle-aged foreigner making himself comfortable in his office.

"Oh, right, very good. Barclay Harvestman, The Times. Old school friend of Wetherby's and partner in crime, I say," he said, cracking himself up. "Take no notice of Wetherby, old chap, he had a fine time in Cheung Chau at Madam Piaf's, ha ha. And we've both been admiring the beauties collecting mussels in the bay. Lovely tits when their drenched pyjamas stick to them, what!"

"Oh shut up, Harvestman," Wetherby said with a wink.

"Now Lee, I'm sure you know what we are here for. We've come to wrap up this mess with the sodding spy. I expect you'll be glad to off-load this on us."

"Sergeant Wetherby, may I ask why a man from the Times is with us?" Jagan asked.

"Who are you?" Wetherby asked, irritated.

"Corporal Jagan Singh, nice to see you Sergeant Wetherby. Again."

"Again?" He looked confused for a second, then dismissed the thought.

"Harvestman won't cause any trouble. He knows which side his bread is buttered."

"Frankly I was bored stiff in Central and when Wetherby told me he was heading down to sort you boys out, I jumped at the chance to hitch a lift," Harvestman volunteered.

"I doubt I'll get any story out of this, who cares about some anonymous spy being killed by thugs? But you never know, I might be able to score some feature about some illiterate stilt-house dwellers who swear their allegiance to the Queen. Or better still, I might be able to score a nice young, juicy fish scrubber for a night of debauchery for myself. What!" he said, slapping his thigh and almost falling off the chair with hilarity.

"Anyway Lee, the quicker the better. Just sign here," Wetherby said, without expecting Lee to read what he was signing.

Simon took the paper and read it over. There were two papers to sign. The first one was to hand over authority for the case to Central, and therefore Wetherby. The other part was a sworn affidavit that stated a Communist spy had been executed by unknown assailants. A statement that would effectively close the case. Simon passed the papers to Jagan and and shook his head.

"I can't sign the first one I'm afraid. I don't have the authority to," he said.

"It's alright. We've cleared that. Everybody in Central understands the special circumstances of Falkirk. Your signature will be adequate for this," Wetherby said.

"You might have cleared it in Central Sergeant but I'm afraid I haven't cleared it with Falkirk here. I answer to him."

"He can be overridden."

"Not without his acknowledgement of being overridden."

"For God's sakes, what's the matter with you man. If you're going to be like that we'll find the old bugger and make him sign it himself."

"Good luck with that," Jagan chipped in.

"Who asked you?" Wetherby shot out.

"I'm trying to help you Sergeant. I'm warning you that Captain Falkirk can be difficult to locate when you need him. He is a very busy man, as you can imagine of a man of such impeccable reputation."

"He has a reputation alright, but I doubt it's impeccable. I will find him if I need to, and I expect you to help me do that."

"Of course," said Simon, beginning to appreciate Falkirk's disappearing trick with renewed enthusiasm.

Over the past 48 hours Simon had become strangely intrigued by this case and he felt compelled to find out what the true story was. There was something in the evasiveness of the villagers that troubled him, and also the picture that Madam Li had painted of a family of desperate refugees. Most of all he couldn't forget the way the man had died in his arms, bitterly regretting the curtailment of his life. Simon had never witnessed a picture of such desperate loneliness, and he was haunted by the thought that his own father also died in such isolation. Had Simon been confident that the Hong Kong police would get to the bottom of this, he would not have minded handing over the case. But it was obvious from his conversation with Godber and with the attitude of Wetherby in front on him, that there was no interest in Central of finding out the truth. All they wanted was for the case to disappear, and the spy theory was the most convenient option for them. But protocol was the autocrat that imprisoned them all, so there was no choice but to help his superiors locate his immediate superior who had authority to sign over the case.

"Of course. We will do everything we can to help you find the Captain," Simon reassured Wetherby, knowing very well that Falkirk will not be found.

"Fine. Then be a good boy and sign the other one now so that we can get on with it and get the hell out of here before the damned Harvestman gets us all into trouble with some Triad's saucy slut of a daughter," Wetherby said.

"I say, that sounds rather tasty. What!" Harvestman nearly choked laughing.

Wetherby was holding out a pen at Simon, fully expecting total compliance. The possibility that Simon would not sign had not occurred to him once. He had not even asked himself the question "What if?" Simon had also expected that he would sign. He had tried for the past two days to get as much information as possible, but he didn't really imagine holding on to the case and seeing it through to the end. The grown-ups had made their intentions clear and it was unlikely that he could stand in the way of that.

But he looked at the pen in front of him and a thought began to dawn on him. Protocol was the autocrat that imprisoned them all. All of them. Not just the low lying coolie cadets, or the proud patrolling Indian officers, or the career-dead desk sergeants, but also the corporals and captains, and the commissioners. They were all imprisoned by protocol. And protocol demanded that for this case to be wrapped up, the main witness and duty officer at the scene of the crime must sign the affidavit. There was no doubt that the likes of Godber and Wetherby were more powerful men in the police force than Simon, but right now, for them to get their way, they depended on him to take the pen and sign.

Simon stared at the pen and didn't move a muscle.

"My God, what's happened to you. Have you gone into a trance or something?" Wetherby said, confused.

"The yoga master must have cast some spell on him. What!" Harvestman exclaimed, flicking his eyebrows towards Jagan.

Simon looked at Jagan to see if the racist jibe made any impact. Jagan's cheek muscles tensed as he gazed directly at Harvestman. What shocked Simon was, that for the first time, he realised that Jagan's stare wasn't just some mild contempt for what Harvestman had so casually tossed into the room, it was a hard and bitter hatred for the man himself. Harvestman was too busy laughing at his own wit to notice the murderous look coming back to him.

"Come on Lee, let's not waste any more time. This is getting even more tedious than I had expected."

Simon still didn't speak.

Sergeant Simon Lee was not a revolutionary. Except perhaps for a brief delusional period when he was about 17, Simon knew in his heart that he wasn't a man that would turn the world's power structures upside down. He had too strong a sense of absurdity about the world he found himself in to have a coherent plan to upset the order of things. With that came a sense of humour and the instinct to enjoy the good things in life, like decent conversations with friends, hikes over hills, swimming in streams, being with the girl of his dreams. He liked wildlife, beer, music and a good book. He was proud and he was loyal. What he didn't like were bullies, though he was aware that he was surrounded by them. His father, Jack White hated bullies, and his uncle Trevor McPherson hated bullies too. Both of them taught the young Simon to stand up to them and despise them. Those lessons hadn't turned him into an avenging hero who would stop the age-old ways of the world, but Simon generally stood his ground enough for bullies to mostly leave him alone. He now sensed an attempt at bullying.

Before this moment it hadn't occurred to Wetherby that he would have to bully Simon into signing. He took it for granted that Simon would sign. Now he found himself clumsily changing tactics, and resorting to well practised school-yard bullying tactics.

"What the hell are you talking about? Look at this prissy principled upstart," he spluttered at Simon.

"Sergeant, your friend, does he need to listen to this?" Simon said indicating towards Harvestman.

"Sod him Lee, just sign this or I'll have you suspended."

Harvestman looked delighted to be witnessing this insolence on the part of the half-caste sergeant he had heard so much about. Simon wanted to take the pen and stab it in Wetherby's arm. But he didn't need to. He had a revelation about power; the bullies were also imprisoned by protocol. He sensed how important it was for the arch-bullies in the force, namely the Godber squad, to get their version of the story established. Simon felt his heels digging in, as if they were controlled by a force outside of himself. Wetherby was helpless without his signature.

"This paper makes a factual statement that I do not agree with," he heard himself say.

"What could you possibly not agree with? The facts of the case have been established, you donkey," Wetherby said.

"Not at all sergeant. I can confirm that a man was murdered two days ago. I can also concur that his killing was carried out in a manner that appeared deliberately set up to look like an execution. Since then I have found out more about the man. He is called Ma Xun. He crossed illegally into Hong Kong waters three years ago with his wife and child, before their sampan sank and they all nearly drowned. The family stayed at Madam Li's guest house for two nights. They were from Chiu Chau. That's what I know about him, but I have no idea at all whether he was a spy."

"You seem to be extremely fussy today Lee. The damned killers said he was a spy didn't they?"

"It would be extremely naive to accept what the killers said as gospel."

"Don't patronise me you mongrel. We've also had it confirmed by the Cousins."

"I don't know anything about what the American secret service have to say about this incident as I am not in contact with them," he said, breaking a taboo by actually spelling out that "the Cousins" referred to the CIA.

"Godber told me the same, but that isn't something I can put on my affidavit. I cannot swear to the fact that the dead man was a spy, how would I know? You'll have to ask the Cousins to sign to that."

Wetherby looked stunned. He had not expected this at all. His instructions were to get the signatures and come back to Central to formally report the resolution of the case. They stared at each other and suddenly a gate to the past was flung open. They were both thinking about Jasmine.

Wetherby was the reason that Simon was in Tai O, though many in the force believed that it was because of Jasmine Thomas-Littleton. It was true that Simon and Jasmine were having an affair, but that would have easily gone on without any consequence, until Jasmine inevitably would have got bored of him. What brought it to a head was Wetherby's quiet word in the ear of Hugo Thomas-Littleton, father of Jasmine and deputy commissioner of the police. The short-lived affair had started when 25-year-old Jasmine, fresh back from postgraduate studies in fine art at the University of Edinburgh, went out of her way to stalk Simon at official police social functions to tease him and smile at him. The 22-year-old Simon, stationed at Kennedy Town at the time, was puzzled at first by her advances and then found himself flattered and eager to please. It was a big boost to his ego as he had always assumed gorgeous well-connected single women of the colony had no interest in him. His assumption was mostly accurate in normal circumstances. But Jasmine did what she wanted, and even though she was rock-solid establishment, she loved the idea of flaunting convention when she felt like it. She floated through the upper echelons of Hong Kong society with total ease, and her rebellious nature was just one of her attractions to the elite of the colony, a bonus added to her impeccable and ultimately respectable social standing.

Jasmine's sense of entitlement in Hong Kong was worn so completely and convincingly that she could never offend anyone with it. She was nothing but charm embodied. Any person who spent a short period of time with Jasmine became as convinced of her entitlements as she was herself. Her father took great pride in her ability to glide and sparkle in the company of the colony's political, business, and administrative elite, not to mention the culture vultures, academicians, theatricals and the sporting top-tier. She was as comfortable in the colony's old-school tribes – those who would hark back to Imperial triumphs before the war – as she was with the new young set who weren't afraid to discuss Mr Gandhi frankly and even express admiration for Marxism. She smoked French cigarettes, drove an American open-topped car and listened to something called bebop that no-one, especially in the police force, seemed to have heard of.

The first time she played Simon some bebop in her father's house he was bowled over. It was Charlie Parker's *Night in Tunisia*. He had never heard anything so exotic and exciting.

"Yes, Bird really captured the atmosphere of a night in Tunisia," Jasmine said, looking straight into his eyes and twirling her silky blond hair with the tips of her finely crafted fingers.

"Quite," he said, tingling with anticipation, though he hadn't yet admitted to his new special friend that he had never travelled further than Macau. It was because Hugo Thomas-Littleton had taken his "Queen" Mrs Thomas-Littleton to Macau for their 30th wedding anniversary that Jasmine had the house to herself.

"I know a place where you can see a bebop band. Do you want to come?" she asked.

"Yes, definitely," Simon said, trying to sound enthusiastic but hoping it would be later. He was certainly interested in that wild and fantastic music, even though it didn't quite grab you like rock and roll, but at that moment he was much more interested in Jasmine.

"But first, I wondered if you would like me to show you what a night in Tunisia is like," she said, pretending to be coy, as she stepped up towards him.

He nearly spilled his pina colada.

Simon wasn't a total fool. He knew that he wasn't in Jasmine's league, but he was helplessly drawn to the most sophisticated and exciting woman he had met. Despite that, he had quite a realistic view of how this miracle had happened to him. She pretty much spelled it out on their long walks into the country parks, where she knew all the secret paths and abandoned huts.

Simon was her holiday. He was a pre-emptive affair, a tryst with someone that she was never really meant to be with. He was good-looking enough, liked to enjoy himself, and quite rightly worshipped her. She first started flirting with him at police functions, because he was so unlike the boors that seemed to think her idea of a good time was to listen to a read-out of their curriculum vitae. Once they started seeing each other regularly she found that Simon, to his credit, still wouldn't spend any time detailing his triumphs and outlining his great ambitions. Nor would he discuss the failings of the colonial administration and everything that was going wrong with the empire, and tut and swear and say it was a "damned shame."

Instead he asked questions about life in Edinburgh and Tunisia. She knew that he knew she hadn't actually been to Tunisia but they both enjoyed maintaining the fiction. In the early days he told her stories about how his dad took him on patrols sometimes before the war, especially when he was on his favourite beat – a lap of interior Hong Kong Island once a fortnight to keep an eye on the country paths and new squatter camps. He would tell her about the birds, leopard cats and pangolin dens. He also told her about his mother and how he would help out at her uncle's noodle stall in Kennedy Town. Jasmine pointed out that there was a famous American singer called Peggy Lee, just like Simon's mum. To Jasmine all this was simple unpretentious living, nothing sophisticated, nothing clever, just an honest exchange of experiences. It was refreshing, even though after a while the conversation settled mostly on her, her breathtaking knowledge of art, her aspirations, her struggles to balance her modernity with her inherent conservatism, as well as her struggles with being so much in demand.

She accepted her destiny, that she would be married-off to some aspiring colonial of suitable ability and endowment. He would probably be charming and even fun if she was lucky, but he would almost certainly be self-centred, vain and narcissistic, because that was the trend among the most eligible of the set she had always socialised with in Hong Kong and at Edinburgh. His ambitions would rule the house that he would head. She would be a trophy, a precious one, and lovingly polished on a regular basis of course, but still a trophy first, then mother to his heirs. He might have had a smattering of culture drummed into him but his favourite expression of culture would probably be patriotic and misogynistic rugby songs, sang pissed at the top of his voice with thirty of his best mates. That and the Last Night of the Proms.

She could pick some kind of soft loser of course – possibly a dreamy second son of a banker – with an appreciation for bebop and genuine artistic knowledge. He would probably have plenty of money anyway and he might even treat her with the respect she deserved. But Jasmine didn't want to meet anyone with real artistic sensibilities, he might expose her as a fraud. The fact was, that while Jasmine's knowledge of art was as deep as you would expect from five years of studies at the best colleges, she secretly hated much of what she saw. Sometimes she woke up in the middle of the night and realised that most of the stuff she had gushed over in the past five years was a pile of meaningless garbage. It would have been to her credit if she had openly said so, but she was terrified that it was her that was at fault. She lived in fear of being exposed. The only person to whom she ever confessed this deep dark secret was Simon. When he casually nodded and said with certainty: "You're probably right Jasmine". She sadly took that as proof of his hopeless naivety, and that he would forever be an outsider, a cast-off of a colonial backwater.

And what if she got together with a kind man? What would she do with him? She never saw herself as kind. She was fun, vivacious, witty and clever, but kindness was not part of her constitution. Her mum was not kind. She was mean and narrow-minded. In any case it was well known that girls eventually marry their dads. And she knew her dad, a self-centred, vain and narcissistic bastard – not kind. She loved him and he loved her, as much as either of them could love anyone else, which was not much.

How long would the relationship with Simon have sustained her? He was never sure, but he had an idea that it would not last that much longer. She was so at ease with him that she openly discussed the merits of other men in the police for marriageability, or those that might be ripe for an affair, a real affair, not a pretend one like she was having with him. To her, the fact that she could talk about future prospects with Simon was proof of what a dear he was, an uncomplicated boy who understandably worshipped the ground she walked on. Simon on the other hand used to flinch at her calculating musings over the various merits of his better-connected colleagues, sometimes as they still lay half-naked in bed. He burned up with resentment whenever she started, and moved the conversation away from the topic as quickly as he could. What she saw as sweetness, he experienced as patience, a willingness to wait for her to shut up. But as he realised that his simmering jealousy was totally off her radar and that she was simply, even innocently, oblivious to his feelings, he slowly, without noticing, began to become free of the blinding delusions of love. After a while she stopped being amazing in his eyes, and to his own upsetting astonishment he admitted, while shaving one night before going to meet her, that she was actually rather boring. Perhaps the best thing about the end of their romance was that by being busted after six fun months it didn't quite have the opportunity to turn bad, even though the early signs of rot were just beginning to show.

The fall came one night when they were on their best behaviour, at a police charity function to raise money for orphans. Jasmine was on the arm of her esteemed father and she swanned about like royalty, bringing delight to all who were lucky enough to be touched by her presence. Hugo was doubly proud that night because as well as the event being an initiative of his – finely calculated to raise his own profile and to provide an opportunity to meet more of the territory's power elite – he also had the hottest girl in Hong Kong on his arm – his own daughter. His wife, "The Queen" was at home, having developed one of her inconveniently-timed headaches an hour before it was time to go out. She had started feeling unwell when she realised that Hugo was so obsessed by the attendance of the governor's family and some of the Shanghai tycoon clans that it became clear to her that it would be "one of those nights" when he'll fail to give her "a blind bit of notice." Hugo brushed off her rebuff by recruiting his daughter, who was glad of the excitement, and happy enough to see her secret lover who was duty-bound to attend.

Simon had unfortunately got stuck in a group of four officers, standing about nursing their beers, discussing once again the sad demise of the Empire. Wetherby was loudly talking about the achievements of his dear Daddy in World War II, and Simon was trying hard to understand how that fitted into the conversation. The whole discussion seemed to him like a series of non-sequiturs, only joined together by nodding and braying, and a vague underlying political philosophy that centred on the right of Britain to rule over any nation that was too stupid to manage its own affairs – which in their eyes seemed to mean anywhere hot. Thomas-Littleton, doing the rounds with Jasmine, politely gave each of the men in the group a one-second opportunity to present himself to her. Wetherby slinked up to her at his Winchester-best, taking the risqué French technique of a kiss on both cheeks, something that would have been scandalous and embarrassing for any British man over the age of twenty-five, but was seen as a mark of supreme modernity among well-educated younger adults. Jasmine took it without a flinch, saying:

"You are so forward for an Englishman, Captain Wetherby. Always my pleasure."

Hugo guffawed with a wink at Wetherby then reluctantly turned towards Simon.

"Good evening Miss Thomas-Littleton," Lee said with a stiff bow, thinking he was playing an admirably straight poker face.

"Good evening Captain Lee. You're also looking rather dishy tonight," she said with a mock curtsey, deliberately scandalously.

"Ho ho ho," Hugo put on, with none of the mirth he had a moment earlier.

"That's awfully kind of you Jasmine, and you are as radiant as ever," Lee returned, without a trace of formality and with a natural sincerity. It was a terrible slip, a scandalous first-name call in a formal official function. Jasmine's well-rehearsed hostess mask gave way to a genuine smile she failed to suppress, and she flushed just a touch while looking at Simon with unmistakable familiarity, her hand delicately touching his arm. Thomas-Littleton should have chastised Lee for this, but didn't because he had stopped listening after: "That's…" Neither did the others listen, except for Wetherby, whose jaw dropped. Jasmine quickly regained her professionalism and greeted the next eager hopeful. Hugo had immediately forgotten about Simon and was looking elsewhere for richer, more powerful people, and Wetherby realised he was in possession of a hand grenade.

He was seething too. Not that he had any claim over Jasmine, who only ever flirted with him in the same formulaic way she flirted with all the boys. But there wasn't a heterosexual police officer who didn't occasionally fantasise about her, and to a certain extent they would all be jealous of Simon's success. Sometimes Wetherby, drunk at the Duchess, would discuss her merits with Barclay Harvestman.

"A bit lippy for my taste. Rather likes to make a show of her own modernity."

"Talks too much about herself and her damned opinions in my opinion." Harvestman agreed.

"Thinks she can have any man."

"The tart. She can have me."

"I'm thinking of having a crack at her."

"She'll be more trouble than it's worth. She'll chew your balls off."

"I would see her as a career asset."

"If T-L approved."

"I can't see him turning me down. I've got damned fine credentials."

"Forget her, look at that Chinese virgin begging to be defrocked."

"Bags me first old boy."

Thus Wetherby had marked her down as a possible candidate to aid his advancement. His calculations were not far off the mark. Jasmine had listed him to Simon as a possible in her own plans. Winchester and Cambridge educated, upper-class home-counties stock with strong roots in London as well as good standing in Hong Kong through Jardines. An obvious officer-class recruitment, heading straight to the top. Could just as well stay in the police or sidestep into finance, whatever took his fancy. Good-looking, knows his literature, can do dinner-table art-talk, as much as she'd want from her husband and no more. Stalwart in the cricket club, on the field as well as inside the clubhouse. Member of the exclusive, secretive and mysterious Duchess club. All in all, a pretty good catch. His mentor Godber on the other hand, famously married to the sharpest, sportiest, most powerful wife in the colony – a woman Jasmine so admired – was clearly future affair material.

It was to Godber that Wetherby confided the following Monday. Godber had already been planning his affair with Jasmine, and he took the news badly.

"The disloyal bitch. Fornicating with a half-caste? What does she think this place is? Bloody Macau?" He virtually ordered Wetherby to tell Thomas-Littleton. Wetherby hadn't expected that. He didn't really know what to expect, he just knew that he could get Simon into trouble by letting the secret out. Bringing Simon down a peg or two was his main goal, a task made necessary by the fact that Simon Lee failed to act sufficiently grateful for being allowed to fraternise with true Englishmen, thanks to the legacy of his legendary uncle Trevor McPherson. Lee was an insolent Chinaman in a British uniform, the bastard son of a foolish recruit from among the homeland's far-northern peasantry.

Cowered by the prospect of being the messenger who will be shot for the scandalous news, Wetherby edged his way reluctantly to Thomas-Littleton's office.

"Ah, Wetherby, dammed good to see you. How's the cricket?"

"Splendid, Commissioner, splendid indeed."

"I saw those bloody Yanks playing that ghastly game 'baseball' in Victoria Park at the weekend. They looked like Neanderthals. Whacking the ball with a club like delinquents, huffing and puffing their way around the silly 'diamond'. Those oafs have no idea about true sport do they?"

"Not in the least. Sir."

"Overkill. That's all they know. Not sport. Plain overkill. Let's hope we'll never see a baseball ground in front of Legco where our cricket ground should always stand."

"Sir I need to talk to you about a delicate matter."

"Bloody hell, I don't like the sound of that."

"It's not good news I'm afraid."

"What? Spit it out man."

"It's your daughter."

"Jesus Christ what's the matter with her? Has she had an accident?"

"No no no, she's fine."

"You bloody idiot. Never do that to a father you clot. You have no idea do you? You dammed fool. What then?"

"Oh do forgive me. It's just that I noticed something at the ball. I believe she is having inappropriate relations, sir."

"What? Inappropriate relations? She's been to Edinburgh University for God's sake, do you think I'm an idiot? Have you never heard what goes on there at that bloody pagan Hogmanay? What the bloody hell are you? A boy scout?"

"Well sir, I thought you would want to know. It's Sergeant Lee, sir."

"Lee?"

"Simon Lee. Sir."

"The bastard son of Jack White? How do you know that?"

"I noticed the way they looked at each other on the night in question."

"You've got special powers of perception have you? We'll see about that. Now get out of here and don't talk to anyone about this private matter or else I'll be sending you back to Jardines."

When Hugo confronted Jasmine about it she didn't make any attempt to deny it. She defiantly asked him what he had to do with it.

"It is my duty to keep order in Her Majesty's colony and race-relations are a vital aspect of that order."

"Well you should thank me, Daddy, because I've been doing my bit for Anglo-Chinese relations with Simon."

"Don't be facetious. Frankly Jasmine you disappoint me. You are much more childish than I had realised. There are rules here that don't need to be spelled out in intelligent company, only imbeciles flaunt them, and you my dear have proved yourself to be an arch-imbecile. Of course it doesn't help that my predecessor caved in to that Scottish oaf and put this half-caste on a European contract. But that doesn't mean we should all go around acting as if he were one of us! You can't ignore the facts, child!"

To her eternal humiliation he confiscated her car keys and cheque book for a week, instructing their two drivers and his wife not to give her any lifts during that time. The Queen gleefully cooperated.

He returned to his office and issued a transfer for Simon Lee to Tai O indefinitely, with immediate effect. There was to be no appeal and he gave no explanation. By the time Simon was packing his locker, colleagues were coming past slapping him on his back calling him a dirty dog and a lucky bastard. In the 24 hours, he had he desperately tried to reach Jasmine, but she was hidden away. Soon he was on a boat to Tai O, a world so estranged from Hong Kong Island that it might as well have been a foreign land. The thick salty air battered his face as he leaned forward on deck, watching terns swoop and dive around the boat. He badly missed her company, her wit and her knowledge. He had learned a lot from her. He ached for her body. He had been in love with her for five-and-a-half of the six months they had been seeing each other. He realised he was lucky to have met her, he was also lucky that outside forces killed off their relationship, they didn't have to dismantle it themselves.

Jasmine cried for two days, grieving the loss of a person who had unexpectedly and unofficially become her best friend for a short while. Then she bathed, combed her hair, painted her face, went down to the living room where her parents reclined and said, "Daddy. You're right. I've been an utter fool. I won't do that again." He accepted her apology, formally forgave her, and returned the car keys. She went out to the Bebop club in Causeway Bay and sought out some bohemian company. She bitched hard about the Establishment, said she might kill her Daddy, and expressed admiration for the American beatnik poets. Then she went home and started plotting her campaign for the ever-so-suitable Wetherby, but she gave up on him after just three months because he was unbearably arrogant. She blamed Simon for making her intolerant to Wetherby's conceit. Before Simon she would not have noticed how much Wetherby loved Wetherby more than he would ever love her. Wetherby's pride was injured for about a day, but he was constitutionally incapable of processing a rejection. So he dismissed the aborted courtship as just another one of those bizarre experiences with women that he would never understand. She went on to plot her dangerous and hypothetical affair with Godber, but her plans were put on hold when a smooth talking American in General MacArthur sunglasses appeared on the scene.

Two years later, Simon and Wetherby were in Tai O looking at each other with a pen between them.

"Are you going to sign or not?" Wetherby asked.

"No," Simon said.

5

MAC THE KNIFE

The moon was out again, accompanied by the constant sound of soft breaking waves. Some splashes could have been a dolphin, it was too dark to see. A night heron squawked. Stray dogs across the bay at Yi O were barking. Silent sailing-junks slid past, what did they hold Simon wondered? Refugees, Nationalist gold, opium? The Fox had led Wetherby and Harvestman to the massage house, he promised them they would not be disappointed. Wetherby was still livid. He had been on the radio with Godber who said he was an idiot for not beating Lee into submission. There was nothing they could do until they got Falkirk's signature.

"Good show Simon. I never thought you had it in you," Jagan said.

"Why? I've got nothing to lose. We can't let twerps like that continue to believe that they have a God-given right to define reality."

"Yes. Their attitude to this murder is sheer incompetence, or worse."

"I saw how you took that yoga-mystic comment. I thought you were going to shoot that sweaty bigmouth."

"It's been done before Simon, right here."

"What are you talking about?"

"1918. Indian constable Teja Singh shot and killed his commander Sergeant Thomas Cecil Glendinning, right here in this room. He probably stood about where I was, and I would imagine that Glendinning was sitting where Harvestman was. I imagined that scene vividly today, down to the finest details of ruptured blood vessels and singed flesh."

"Why on earth would he have done that?"

"No-one knows I'm afraid, because he set fire to the station and committed suicide after holding Glendinning's wife and child hostage for some hours. You can see the bullet holes from the shooting in the iron window shutter right behind you."

Simon examined the rusty shutter and traced his finger into the nine bullet marks that indented the thick plate.

"Come to think of it, I do remember something about this in the force history classes during training, I didn't realise it happened here. The wife and child got away didn't they?"

"Yes they did. The wife dropped the baby down from the window and a Chinese constable caught her. Then she jumped out herself. I don't know what Singh was doing at that moment."

"He must have been a maniac."

"Funnily enough that's what the official report concluded because they couldn't think of any other possible explanation. Then – as a matter of coincidence – the colonial administration raised the salaries of the Indian police and extended certain privileges, such as letting them eat their lunch in the same canteen as the Europeans, though not at the same time. Nothing to do with Teja Singh of course. Glendinning was buried with full honours – a hero for managing to get himself shot by a subordinate."

"You're not suggesting your namesake had justification for killing an innocent man and holding his wife and child hostage are you?" Simon asked, perplexed.

"I don't know what the real circumstances were on that day in 1918. But I know enough about our history to believe that there could easily have been enough abuse and violence from an English sergeant to justify some act of revenge. How do we know that Glendinning was innocent? He could have been a sadistic slave-driver, he may have even beaten his wife on a regular basis. He may have been a murderer himself, or simply a common thief. He may have been a Satanist or a practitioner of bestiality. We don't know what he was like. But there are other sergeants, captains, lieutenants and commissioners we do know about who are at least some of those things, maybe even some that are all of them, and they deserve to be hanged if there was a court willing to try them."

"Gosh Jagan, I never knew you felt so strongly about the occasional rudeness of the idiots in Central."

"Oh it's not just our esteemed police colleagues Lee. This whole Hong Kong setup is a creaking pirate ship, strictly subdivided by race and fuelled by prejudice and exploitation. The likes of Harvestman and Wetherby still think they're the galleon owners, but their nasty attitude is a reflection that they subconsciously realize their days are numbered. They haven't quite admitted out loud that the real owners are simply letting them lease it a while before moving in to take back their claim."

"Oh God, you're not talking about Mr Mao and his brainwashed cronies are you? They're a mess."

"They are exactly who I am talking about. They are quite effective."

The US military radio was playing an old favourite by Satchmo. They both subconsciously sang along.

"Ya know when that shark bites with his teeth, babe, scarlet billows start to spread....now on the sidewalk lies a body just oozing life, eek and someone's sneaking round the corner. Could that someone be Mac the Knife?"

"What's it about?"

"Sounds like a Triad to me."

"Chiu Chau?"

"Well if the victim's Chiu Chau then Mac would have to be Green Gang or Mongoose?"

"Unless Madam Li was right and he wasn't a Chiu Chau Triad, just a civilian, and the Triads decided to kill him for impersonating a Triad with his Chiu Chau accent."

"That's just stupid. I dunno if the Mongoose are really up for it? When was the last Mongoose killing?"

"I heard they were ruthless before the Japs."

"That's a while ago, and under the Japs they were the main support for the East River Brigade guerrillas. They were war heroes as far as the villagers are concerned."

"Since then there's been a few fracases on the seas, but I think they've been mostly territorial disputes with Guangdong pirates. Remember the 17-year-old Tai Long Wan boy who was killed in a gun battle with pirates?"

"The poor sod, thought life would be exciting with the Mongoose, dead within a month of joining them."

"May be the grown-ups are right and he was a Commie spy?"

"They could be right. We just don't have any evidence. If they have it in Central they haven't shared it with us."

Patrick Leung burst in. He was breathless.

"A tiger. Over at Yi O."

"What are you talking about man?" Simon asked impatiently. Jagan was already reaching for their rifles.

"Dreamy Lau's been mauled."

"My God. Is he OK?" Simon reached for his hat and tied up his boot laces.

"They said he will survive, they've got him on a launch and are taking him across the bay to the clinic."

"I told you!" Jagan said, excited.

They put the station on alert, ran down the steps to the pier and jumped on a launch. Leung was about to get on.

"Hold your horses constable. We'll call for back-up if necessary, but at this stage, the two of us will be sufficient. We need to establish the damned facts before we know what to do next."

"Sir! I beg you. I have to see this tiger!"

Simon looked at Jagan who eagerly nodded back.

"Come on then, get on," he said starting up the motor.

They bounced over undulating waves as they powered at full-throttle to the clinic pier, leaving behind a spreading V of white foam. They quick marched along the pier and into the clinic, where a nurse ushered them to the ward where Dreamy Lau was lying fast asleep. He was bandaged at the neck and shoulders, two on his left arm and one on his thigh.

"He'll be alright," Dr Tu said.

"Was it really a tiger?" Simon asked.

"Well. I'm not an animal expert, but I would say it was some kind of wild animal attack. It could be the wild curs on the hills. I've petitioned the government many times about those packs. They used to eat corpses in the war you know."

"Were there any claw marks?" Jagan asked.

"There was a bloody mess I can tell you, but he was lucky that no major artery was cut, the bleeding could have been a lot worse. He would probably be dead if his wife hadn't come out banging pans and screaming bloody murder."

"Thank you Dr Tu, we'll go and see the wife." Simon said.

"I doubt he'll complain about the morphine we've pumped into him. How's your head Sergeant Singh?" the doctor checked.

"A bit sore Dr Tu, but I think it's healing up."

"Good man. It's just as well your skull seems to be made of granite, or I would have been picking bone fragments from your brain tissue with tweezers," he roared with laughter.

"Quite," said Jagan feeling rather upset.

The trio rushed out, along the pier and onto the boat. They weaved past moored sampans and large creaking vessels that stunk of fish and grease. Large mangy dogs barked at them from darkened decks. The soft light of oil lamps lit up the stilt houses lining the shore while the muffled murmurings of family life wafted out to the water. There were lights at the top of the village's tallest building, the watchtower where

Jackson, Salty Pang and their cronies sometimes played mahjong. As they passed the hostel Madam Li came rushing out with her hunting rifle in hand.

"Inspector Lee, please, I can help you."

"Oh no, not the Madam," he groaned to his companions. "We are fine Madam Li, we are just trying to find out what happened."

"I know what happened, it was a tiger. Trust me I am experienced."

"We know you are a very well-travelled woman Madam Li. But this should be left to the professionals." Simon said in his special-reserve maximum-patronisation tone that infuriated Madam Li.

"With due respect Inspector, have you ever killed a tiger?" she called out with clear and cutting scorn.

Simon flinched. "That's hardly the point woman. I know how to shoot my gun and that will do."

"I have killed tigers." Simon looked at Jagan and Leung, they were nodding at him.

"They say that she killed them on Mao's Long March. They were stalked by tigers that fattened up on corpses lining their route, people who were either picked off by KMT snipers or just dropped dead from disease and exhaustion. Once the beasts got a taste for human flesh they started actively hunting the stragglers," Leung explained.

"Madam Li volunteered for the tiger hunt and she gained the best reputation. The tigers learned quick that she was the one to avoid, but she stalked the man-eaters and finished them off," Jagan elaborated.

Simon had to make a quick decision. If even half of this was true she could be useful. He didn't have a clue what he was doing. They pulled up and let her on board.

"Thank you gentlemen," she nodded and stepped on.

"Why do you expect me to believe that you've killed tigers?" Simon probed, without much conviction.

"I don't care what you believe, but you'll be glad of my help if there's a tiger on the prowl. I saw the commotion when they brought Dreamy

Lau in. Chances are the tiger mistook him for a goat. Easily done in the dark, especially with a sinewy old ram like Lau. Or it might be injured and having trouble finding its normal supply of food."

"You don't think it's a man-eater?" Jagan asked as they pushed past the salt-plain wall.

Simon sensed that Jagan was trying to impress the Madam with his tiger knowledge.

"If she's a man-eater we would have known about it by now. The question is, will she become one from now?" Madam Li said.

"Why do you say 'She'?" Patrick asked, curious and hungry for tiger lore.

"Why the bloody hell not. It's either a he or a she, take your pick," she replied.

"What would its normal food be?" Simon asked. "If there was a tiger prowling around here don't you think we would have seen carcasses strewn around the place?"

"Not necessarily Inspector. Tigers are quite careful. Once they've killed, they'll drag the food off somewhere hidden where there's less chance another tiger or some crafty scavenger would ambush and steal its hard-won pickings. Then they'll eat up pretty much everything they can smash through with their monstrous jaws. There wouldn't be much left."

"If the tiger has been injured, what could have caused that?" Simon asked. As the boat neared Yi O where they could see lanterns in the dark, he was beginning to forget about his defensive scepticism and was drawn by genuine interest in Madam Li's answers.

"There are many hazards for a tiger. It could have fallen out of a tree and injured a limb, rolled down a cliff and bashed by rocks, Sergeant Singh. It may have been trapped in a farmers fence or hit by a motor bus. Or it could have been shot at by some scallywag Mongoose like Danny Chu or his daft friend Spike. Or, chances are it underestimated its prey and got what it deserved."

"What prey around here could possibly defend itself against a Tiger?" Simon asked. Patrick was drifting the motorboat slowly to the pier though none of it was available for a direct mooring. There were two other boats where there would have been space, so they had to park up against one.

"Looks like the Tai O gun club are here," Madam Li said, "This one's Jackson's boat, and that one there looks like your friend Bad News Chu's."

There was a third they hadn't noticed that had been dragged onto the beach. It had been rowed over by Bad News Chu's son Danny and his daft friend Spike.

"Bloody hell," Jagan said with anguish. "This is our tiger, we can't let those braggarts at it."

"To answer your question Inspector Lee. There are a few crazy creatures that could give a big cat some trouble. Mongoose for one, real mongoose, not pretend ones led by Salty Pang, are fierce, fast and not to be messed with. There are a number of snake species that wouldn't take a tiger attack lying down. Depending on the size of the tiger a big Burmese python coiled in a tree might contemplate a surprise attack by launching its huge mouth straight into the tiger's face, before coiling around its chest and limbs in a death-grip. A king cobra would be a fierce adversary and I wouldn't want to bet on the outcome. I'd expect tigers know that and would normally avoid them, but again, cases of mistaken identity can and do happen. Another contender could be a pig."

"Surely not? They are dull and docile," Simon said.

"Never underestimate the power of a wild boar," she warned, just as Falkirk roared over.

"Finally, here's the constabulary. Where've you been napping boys? There's action here."

"Captain Falkirk, Wetherby's desperately looking for you so he can relieve us of the murder case," Simon said quietly when he reached the old goat.

"He won't be coming this way to look for me. I gather the Fox is entertaining the two idiots at the massage parlour. They won't harm us tonight. Tonight we've got real police work to do. You've brought the rifles have you? Good evening Madam Li," Falkirk said, with a little too much respect, Simon thought.

Bad News, SPK and even the Jap Devil were all there, along with Jackson, Salty Pang, the Dagger, Red, Danny and Spike. There was a strong whiff of cigars and Chinese rice wine. Falkirk took command. "It's no good all of us blindly marching into the dark taking random pot shots at each other. We'll end up with a dozen dead hunters and one triumphant cat, happy to stockpile corpses for the lean months."

"Our main objective tonight," Madam Li interrupted, "Is to clear the area around Mrs Lau's farmland so that the poor lady can sleep in peace. We fan out, set up a few blazes and shoot some rounds into the air to let the beast know that she is unwelcome here. In the morning we can check for tracks. We won't be getting her tonight."

"She?" Falkirk and Danny Chu both questioned automatically.

"Why not?" Jagan challenged.

Falkirk shrugged.

Madam Li spoke with Dreamy Lau's weeping wife, reassuring her that Lau would recover. Mrs Lau took her over to the spot in their orchard where her husband was attacked and Madam Li searched the area with her typhoon lantern.

Simon went over to see.

"What are we looking for?" he asked.

"A clear paw print," the Madam replied, "Look you can see blood here and there's scrapings and scuffling. I don't think it was a pack of dogs. If it was we would see lots of dog prints all around, they are cowardly, they only act in packs. But the action is concentrated to this spot, it was one on one."

"What did the wife see?"

"Nothing. She heard Lau shouting for his life so she instinctively grabbed her pans and ran out of the house screaming like a banshee. By the time she reached him he was on his own, bleeding from his wounds and just repeating the word 'tiger' over and over."

Falkirk said he would take Danny and Spike up the trail that led from the scene. Simon had never seen Falkirk so happy at work.

"Be careful," Madam Li said, "It could be injured and that would be dangerous for you."

"I know," said Falkirk, too high on adrenaline to process the thought. Danny and Spike were already marching on, guns raised.

"Watch yourself Danny," Simon called out, suddenly a little protective of Maria's brother.

"You too Simon. I don't want to have to tell Maria you ended up as tiger bait," Danny called back, with Spike grinning by his side.

"No, Simon's right Danny. You need to watch yourself. Given the choice, a tiger would always prefer a nice salty piece of sea-cured Tai O beef to a pale half-cooked slab of city pork." Bad News laughed out.

"Madam Li, boys, will you join us for a drink before the great hunt?" Bad News asked.

"No thanks Bad News, I prefer to save the drinking for after we've caught the beast," she replied, quietly adding to her cell: "And none of you better even think about having one with those drunks or else you're off my team. And frankly I'd rate your chance of survival quite low if you weren't with me."

"Thanks for your offer Bad News, we'll have one with you over the tiger barbecue," Simon said.

"Suit yourself," Bad News said.

Red and the Dagger headed off over the top of Keung Shan, looking expectant.

Madam Li suggested that their group should take a launch round to Tai Long Wan and trek back via Fan Lau, expecting to meet up with Falkirk, Danny and Spike somewhere around there, and thus clearing the areas on the main trail where people lived. Bad News, Salty Pang, the Jap Devil and Jackson were already lighting a bonfire in the Laus' orchard, their rifles leaning together in a wigwam. SPK was opening a fresh bottle of rice wine, there was a crate with another five.

"That's them settled for the night then," Madam Li commented with a touch of scorn.

The four of them rounded the peninsula, bouncing on choppy waves and with little else to do Simon and Jagan teased out Madam Li's story while young Patrick piloted the boat past rocky outcrops. She let them in on some of her past, though she knew the full version would only leave them confused.

"Madam Li, is it true that you are a member of the Communist Party?" Simon asked stiffly, still not sure about her.

Wang Meili was born into a comfortable Shanghainese industrialist household. Her father owned a clothing factory that exported shirts to Taiwan and Hong Kong. She was a bright and rebellious student. Western people loved to romanticise her home town in the 1920s but she could never understand that. It was a city where Europeans – many of them shifty looking characters who looked as if they were fleeing some disgrace at home – came to seek their fortunes off the blood, sweat and tears of the Chinese peasantry who flocked there seeking stability, shelter and rice. Outside of the international enclaves – colonised and policed by foreigners – the badlands clustering the edge of Shanghai were a network of chaotic and violent shanty towns, lorded over by Triads who wanted to own the future and warlords who still believed they were living in the 19th century. Out there, brute force ruled a degraded society, where long-held village norms and protections were left behind in the search for a better life. In the shanty towns women stayed at home for fear of rape, children worked in brick-kilns and mines while their fathers eked a living off scraps that fell their way. Starvation haunted them all. While that reality bypassed the foreigners who fell in love with the "Orient" from a window seat at the Peace Hotel bar, the Chinese inside the city were only too well aware of the forces beyond the city walls that sent their tentacles slithering down dark and damp alleys and backstreets. Even those, like Meili, born into the relative comfort of the wealthy Shanghainese families, were well aware of the chaos massing outside and pulsating through the heart of their city. The place was a pressure cooker, cooking up two of the most potent forces of the 20th century – Nationalism and Communism.

It was a turbulent and indeed dangerous time to be a precocious teenager in Shanghai, but Meili wasn't left alone, as she found herself irresistibly drawn to the Communists. They attracted the brightest and most daring. They had a clear vision of the world and a strong ethical purpose. They were a dynamic and exciting force to her, with all the answers about the suffering that they were surrounded by. The Nationalists were xenophobic and corrupt. It never ceased to amaze Meili that a bunch of people so fond of talking about the "Nation" were so willing to grind down the very same people of that nation into the black dirt of Shanghai's streets. To her, Communism bridged anticolonialism with internationalism. It was obvious to her that Communism was the more progressive force. China should be free, but all Chinese should be free, and they were the natural allies of the people of all nations who sought to be free of the stranglehold of capitalists and imperialists. Communism was logical, humane and egalitarian. And just by coincidence, all the other 19-and-20-year-olds hanging about the Communist cells were the best-read, funniest and best-looking boys and girls of Shanghai. It was an easy choice for Meili.

"I was once," Madam Li told her easily-shocked audience of three young Hong Kong policemen. "But I left them."

"Why did you leave them?" Jagan asked.

Her parents could see it coming, they were worried, especially as they would be class enemies in her eyes as factory owners. But Meili wasn't dogmatic, she understood that her parents were trying to survive in a harsh world just like anybody else, only with them they got lucky. The factory was known for its good conditions, fair working hours and decent pay. They were never short of applicants who wanted to work there. On top of that they sponsored community projects such as maintenance for the local library and park. Meili had nothing against her parents, although that could get her into heated arguments with radicals in the group. One such fellow became her lover and then her husband in a ceremony that the Communists devised for themselves in rejection of corrupt Kuomintang administrators. His name was Deng Yingxiong, meaning hero, a name he lived up to in regular fights with KMT factions and nasty Green Gang henchmen. As the heat was turned up on the Shanghai Communists the revolutionary cells were forced underground and Deng led their faction with fierce and tactical skills. But one night in 1927 the Communists were all but decimated by the most vicious Green Gang onslaught there had ever been. The Green Gang's main line of business was heroin – marketed as anti-opium pills – but their leaders understood the economic value of politics and they made a deal with Chiang Kai-shek to clear the city of Communists in return for a guaranteed monopoly in anti-opium pills. It was an easy decision for the henchmen who gladly went on a murder spree. They shot, stabbed, hacked and tore through the city's warren of dark, twisted alleyways, chasing skinny Communists down stairwells to smash their brains in with bricks and hammers, or upwards on to roofs where they threw them off. That's how Deng went. He was thrown off the top of a five-storey residential block, terrified tenants desperately trying to stop their children from screaming out while Green Gang boots clobbered on the roof above, and bookish left-wingers begged for their lives. Meili and a small band of terrified survivors escaped through the labyrinth of backstreets and interconnected buildings that made up the city. They were hidden, fed and aided by left-wing sympathisers and apolitical humanitarians. Meili would not be back in Shanghai for another 18 years and she never saw her parents again.

A heartbroken Meili arrived bedraggled to the Jiangxi commune several years later where she met Mao Zedong, Zhou Enlai and other leaders of the Communist movement. She had been hardened by the events of April 12, 1927, that left her a widow at the age of 19, and the years spent in hiding in the Jiangxi countryside, unable to return to Shanghai where there was a bounty on her issued by the Greens. She moved through the ranks at Jiangxi as a cell leader of a group of 20 troops by the time the party made its decision to break through the KMT military cordon and march north. Its popular name as the Long March was rather an understatement. It was more like a long protracted slaughter. Eighty thousand Communists started out from various points, harrowed by KMT bullets and bombs, as well as disease and starvation, for more than a year, as they trudged thousands of miles north, traversing the lethal edge of the Tibetan plateau. Finally 5,000 survivors hobbled into Yan'an under the leadership of Mao Zedong who had consolidated his power over the party during the brutal death-march. Meili had seen how Mao eliminated his enemies and rivals over the year. She saw his ruthless ambition and the cult-like aura that surrounded him. She thought it strange and terrifying that she alone seemed to recognise that China's revolution was being led by a psychopath who had murdered his challengers and kept all others in a trance-like state under his total control. Any deviation from Mao's thought was a lethal flaw, especially among those who had attained leadership positions. Meili was having dangerous heretical thoughts every day during the last months of the march. She had already decided that as soon as they arrived at Yan'an she would escape.

"I wasn't too happy about how the Party was being led," she told Jagan.

"Is it true that you learned to kill tigers on the Long March?" Jagan asked.

She loved the stories of tigers stalking the March, but never heard about tigers during that time. Would tigers have stalked 80,000 people dying in their hundreds every day for a year? It's possible, she reasoned, there could have been a whole ecosystem following them from Jiangxi to to Shaanxi, wild dogs, bears, vultures, even pigs feasting on corpses, but the truth was that they never had any tiger stories on the run. The stories only appeared after it was all over. Meili's own experiences with tigers came afterwards when she escaped from Mao and the Red Army.

She slipped away in the early days of the Yan'an commune, an act that was easy to initiate, but left her alone and exposed once carried out. Where could she go? China was fragmented into violently conflicting territories of warlords, Nationalists, Communists, Japanese, and most of all, bandits. When a dozen Manchurian bandits approached her on the eastern edge of the Gobi desert late one summer's night they thought they had chanced upon easy pickings. They would take her horse, the old gun she appeared to hold, whatever ammunition she had, some saddle bags, textiles, whatever rice she carried, before dumping her corpse some place to remind villagers of the power of bandits. Before they had discussed their strategy two of their horses lay bleeding to death, one gang member had a broken femur, and the leader, Black Eagle, was on the ground with Meili's dagger poised at his neck. They understood too late that she was a battle-hardened guerrilla who was ready to kill for survival. Slowly, during a tedious and dehydrating stand-off over half a day under a burning sun they came to understand that she had no interest in killing their leader, but wanted only to survive. Black Eagle took the initiative and with her dagger pressed against his jugular, his beloved horse dead and crawling with flies, he offered her the opportunity to join his gang. Meili realised that her options were stark. She could either try to escape and be killed, or she could kill this man and then be killed by his henchmen, or she could see what happened if she agreed to join the gang, knowing that she could easily be stabbed in the back any time someone decided to have a crack. Thus she joined Black Eagle, became his lover, and part of a notorious bandit unit that did as much damage to the Japanese war machine in Manchuria as the Communist or KMT guerrilla troops ever did.

The Siberian tigers that prowled the forests were a larger breed than the South China variety and some would say more dangerous. Mostly they were cautious and shy, slinking in the shadows watching bandits at their camps, occasionally taking an opportunistic swipe at a lone woodcutter or deer hunter. But on three different occasions during the years she hid out in the forests it became clear that a man-eater was on the prowl.

"Tigers are normally shrewd and calculating and for that reason they generally do not hunt humans," Madam Li explained to her students, ignoring the question about the Long March.

"A single attack on a human could be a mistake, as I said earlier, the tiger could have thought Lau was a goat or a monkey. Or it could be totally opportunistic. There's a man, unarmed, alone. A swift attack would finish him off, a windfall. Another situation is that a tiger is under stress and unable to get the food it normally relies on. This could be the result of an injury making it slower than usual, or broken teeth. Maybe an infection is driving it mad.

Then there are the man-eaters, any one of the situations above could provide a tiger with its first taste of human flesh, but on rare occasions a tiger decides to make a habit of it and turns into a man-eater, a systematic hunter that uses all its intelligence to pick off human targets. Many attribute this to taste, but my belief is that it's a psychological breakthrough. They discover that it's a lot easier to hunt people than they had previously thought. They break through the barriers that society had erected to protect themselves. These barriers normally play a remarkable role, allowing us humans to master beasts that are bigger and stronger than ourselves, mainly by tricking wild animals into believing we are far more powerful than we are. Have you ever seen a pack of kites above your head circling and watching your every move? They could easily tear you to pieces and strip your bone of all flesh. But they never do that because they fear that we may use our magic to destroy them all. That we dominate nature by psychology and illusion is a remarkable feat I am sure, but the trouble with this is that when an occasional individual sees through our trickery, they can become very dangerous indeed. I believe this mental breakthrough is what happens to man-eating tigers, and I have also seen it happen to humans too.

Once the transformation happens society's illusions are reversed. The man-eater, previously intimidated by social norms and human myths, starts creating its own myth. It grows to become a giant, it becomes unreal and terrible, Godlike and invincible. Only a human who can see through this counter-illusion is able to kill a man-eater."

Simon noticed that she talked much more about the tigers than about the Communist party.

"Is it true that you killed three?" Jagan checked.

She paused.

Meili, who refused to believe the myth of the invincible man-eater, thought the first 'man-eater' was misnamed. She called it the 'woman-and-child-eater' because it never dared attack fully-grown men. Women washing clothes by the river, children playing at the edge of a village, a young girl hurriedly taking a shortcut through quiet woods, that's who the tiger went for. Meili followed Black Eagle as they tracked paw prints and cornered the tiger at the back of a cave, where, once it realised it had nowhere to escape, finally found the courage to attack armed adults, both of whom looked like men. She hit it squarely between the eyes before Black Eagle had a chance to pull his trigger, and instantly earned a reputation as a tiger killer. Black Eagle could have pretended it was his shot, but he proudly conceded that it was his woman who had made the kill. She was quicker and more accurate than him.

About ten months later there appeared a ferocious beast with a wild rage. It went on the rampage for about two weeks killing anything it could catch, including people, livestock and wildlife. Unusually, this animal left much of what it killed, only to kill again within a couple of days. It was truly evil, apparently killing only for the sake of killing. Black Eagle suggested Meili take charge of the hunt and she hand-picked half-a-dozen of the best shooters and led them towards their devilish quarry. They found a pig squealing, bleeding to death with a limb missing, its half-chewed flesh scattered nearby. She stalked the killer and caught its silhouette up on a ridge. One shot felled it. They ran to the carcass and found a bedraggled skinny cat that must once have been an enormous and splendid creature. There was an old Manchurian woodsman's arrow embedded through its neck, with sores around the entry and exit wounds. The neck was swollen with infection, while its body had wasted away. The tiger had been on a starvation-fuelled two-week rampage, driven madder with every kill when it discovered that no matter what he slaughtered he still couldn't swallow the prize.

Two years later, reports of a man-eater stalking the edge of a Japanese outpost in the far north was welcomed by Communists, KMT and bandits alike. A patriotic Chinese tiger eating Japs seemed too good to be true to Meili. But the rumours were confirmed for her when she received a credible message through a network of spies that the Japanese wanted to contract her to kill the beast. Meili instinctively thought about it but it was Black Eagle who pulled her up, and warned her that she would never live it down if she collaborated with the Japs. She thought that was fine talk coming from a bandit, but backed off anyway. Several weeks later the Japanese troops abandoned their rural camp and moved 100km south to set up in a city. Villagers literally worshipped their avenging tiger god, but not for long as they soon discovered that the man-eater could not give a hoot if its food was Japanese or Chinese. With the convenience of the Japanese camp gone, the animal, which had got used to human flesh and lost its fear of society, headed to nearby villages and started picking off any person it could pounce on unawares. This time Meili could accept the job with no qualms. It took three weeks of trekking, crossing back and fourth over the Russian and Chinese border. She finally had a clear shot of the animal that knew it was being stalked, as it ran for cover across no-man's land. She was sure she would have got it in the head, but it stepped on a mine and blew up. Singed tiger flesh rained all around her. Its head landed a few yards from her, the eyeballs on fire.

"I have killed two tigers," she said.

They arrived at Tai Long Wan. There was no pier there. Madam Li had her sandals tied around her neck and trousers rolled up as she directed Patrick as close to the shore as the boat could get. They splashed down and waded ashore, Patrick reluctantly seeing them off and chugging the boat back alone to Yi O, where at least he could get a drink with Bad News and Salty Pang and listen to their made-up stories of tiger hunting.

The village was mostly quiet at first, just the unmistakable clutter of mahjong tiles in stone cottages, but then there was a sudden, if not unexpected, explosion of dogs. Vicious curs, howling, growling and stepping towards the incomers. Pig Face Chan came roaring out, whipping mongrels out of the way, immediately recognising the Tai O contingent.

"Come in, come in, my word, what are you doing here, Inspector Lee, Inspector Singh?" he roared loud enough to make sure any contraband lying around the houses, whether that be bottles of diesel, liqueurs or tobacco could at least have a blanket thrown over them. Walking into the head-man's house there was an unmistakable whiff of diesel, red-faced men sat around a bottle of North Korean Shoju, and offered a round of Chinese cigarettes. There were boxes around the edge of the room and they all had blankets thrown over them.

People had got used to treating Madam Li like a man and she accepted her Chinese cigarette with smooth grace.

"We're looking for the tiger," she said.

Pig Face's eyebrows shot up.

"Fantastic. Boys get your guns. We've heard rumours, but mostly they seemed to come from Blind Wang, and who's going to believe him?"

"Dreamy Lau was mauled tonight," Simon said.

"How terrible. Is he dead?"

"No he survived. He's a tough old boy," Simon said.

"It's the opium, it makes him malleable," Pig Face said, so deadpan that there was no telling at all if he was trying to be funny or if he believed in the science.

"Malleable?" Simon checked.

"Yes, malleable. The drug makes you yield to forces. And by yielding you overcome evil. Just the same as what those monks teach upstairs, isn't it Madam?" Pig Face said, pointing vaguely towards Lantau Peak.

"In some ways, though some are over enthusiastic about yielding to evil. I believe the Abbot is a regular at the massage parlour," she said.

They all laughed knowingly.

"Well in any case, Lau is alive and we think we've got a tiger loose on Lantau," Simon said.

The village party took the mountain route over Keung Shan – ginger mountain – while Simon, Jagan and Madam Li took the main coastal path.

They worked their way through the dark, listening to owls, barking muntjacs and myriad night insects. Anything heavy that crashed through the undergrowth sent their hearts racing, but they conceded it was unlikely they'll meet the tiger face to face that night. Most of the heavier sounds came from wild pigs, leopard cats, muntjacs, porcupines and civet cats.

In silence they hiked on, and started drifting into their own thoughts. Simon remembered his pre-war hikes with his dad. Jack telling him all about the beasts of Hong Kong, and hikes he was going to take him on in Yorkshire. He said a cold hard wind chisels your face when you hike the hills overlooking Holmfirth, and kestrels hover over craggy fields waiting for a rabbit to wander too far from its bolthole. Black smoke rose from every valley crammed in between the hills, where thousands toiled to clothe the whole of India. Not me, said Jack, I'm never going to work in a mill, he told his own father before answering an advertisement in the newspaper for the Hong Kong police force. Jagan was thinking about Mr Gandhi and his refusal to wear British cloth. He also went back to his dad, in his big turban, drinking tea in Sham Shui Po, looking at the picture of the young Queen Elizabeth on the mantelpiece while he listened to the Proms on the wireless.

Madam Li was in Shanghai, 1945, picking through the ruins and rubble. A lynched Japanese soldier hung from a telegraph pole, his limbs were charred stumps. The city itself was a burned carcass. She conceded that she had been a child when she went on the run. 18 years had gone by and now she was a woman, a revolutionary, a bandit and tiger killer. At 37 she could have been a grandmother, but she knew she never would be. Their old home had been flattened, her parents died together on the same night. They found them in the ruined bomb shelter, a neighbour recounted, arms around each other, her mother still clutching a picture of Meili. It was an American bomb that killed them. She sat on the cracked stone steps that had led to their now obliterated front door and wept until dark.

The next day she visited the bank and claimed her inheritance. The Red Army were still some four years from Shanghai, but Meili had no doubt that they would come, and they too would be visiting the bank to claim what they saw as their inheritance. When Meili left the bandits she told Black Eagle that his acceptance of an offer by the KMT was a suicide note. She told him that China would be Communist within five years. He begged her with tears in his eyes to stay as his wife. She told him to stop robbing people, try to be a good man and not to join the KMT, keep his head down under the Communists. Then she kissed him on his forehead and walked out. The Red Army caught him a few weeks later and beheaded him.

She wired the cash over to her aunt in Hong Kong and telegraphed to say she was on her way. She hitch-hiked down the China coast on ferries, barges and fishing boats, with her gun always visible in case any sailor thought she was easy prey. They never touched her during the 10-month journey. She sailed into the harbour in 1946 on a sampan from Tung Ping Chau, climbed the stone steps of Ladder Street, and knocked on the door of a grand house on Wellington Street. Aunt Chau ushered her indoors, put her in the bath and scrubbed her back. She gave her a haircut and laid out the cocktail dress she used to wear when she was in her twenties. "We're going to a ball tonight," she said as she brushed Meili's hair. She stood up in her elegant dress and did a twirl for her Aunt. She was stunning. "I don't think we're going to have much trouble marrying you off to a good husband, even though you're old now, though we're going to have to put some fat on you," Aunt Chau said.

It was a beautiful dance hall just off Theatre Lane, the richest most powerful Chinese businessmen and women were there that night.

"Welcome to our city," a young tycoon in a tuxedo said to her in Shanghainese dialect, "may I ask your name?"

"I am Madam Li, a widow," she said.

A year later, and still ten years younger than her, he was the first of a string of powerful suitors to ask her to marry him. She turned them all down.

For about two years her life in Wellington Street was a string of parties. There were cocktail parties, teatime cake parties, morning coffees, dim sum breakfasts, racing night at Happy Valley, junk trips, cruise trips and Macau trips for gambling. There were plenty of other younger women of the correct marrying age on the scene, but Madam Li easily eclipsed them as soon as she entered a room. She commanded respect and had a chiselled beauty that none of the flowery maidens and needy husband-hunters could hope to compete with. Young bucks who couldn't see the ten to fifteen years she had on them did all they could to get her attention, as would old tycoons who genuinely appreciated her conversation. She played them all with no intention of getting trapped. There were earnest suitors wanting to marry her and bestow the easy respectability of tai-tai-hood, or others more worldly who made it clear they wanted to recruit her as a favoured concubine, a trade-off of respectability for the possibility of more power if she played her cards right. There was one overriding problem. She didn't like any of them. She didn't mind spending a bit of time just partying, after the Long March, the Yan'an commune and the life of an outlaw it was a welcomed break, like a sabbatical. She got on quite well with some of the tai-tais and concubines, but the men bored her. They were only interested in money and power. Money was a means to power, power was a means to money. It was a constant, meaningless treadmill. Sure, Black Eagle had been a money grabber, and vicious with it too, but he didn't think that the process of making money was an interesting topic of conversation. Instead he was passionate about horse riding, hunting and old folk ballads sung deep into the night around a bonfire. And he could tell the difference between a sparrowhawk and a goshawk from a quarter of a mile away. Deng, her first husband, thought he was going to change the world. She doubted he would have survived Mao's purges but he had vision, courage and compassion. He appreciated history, not as a boring recital of memorized quotes, but as a living trove of stories about real people in a changing and dangerous world. He also had the advantage of having been cut-down before the world could corrupt him.

Then there was the politics. Even though Madam Li had walked away from the Communist Party, she had deeply ingrained ideals about a fair society. Her parents were capitalists but they had a deep sense of social responsibility and civic society. They accepted the theory of taxation – in an ideal world they had yet to experience – as a fair way to redistribute wealth to correct some of the wilder tendencies of capitalism. These beliefs were deeply ingrained in Madam Li. In contrast, the post-war Hong Kong socialites were unrestrained free-market capitalists who never questioned the logic of a dog-eat-dog world. They made no secret of their wish to exploit poverty for maximum profit. She just didn't like these unpleasant people.

Besides, and perhaps most important of all, Madam Li would never be a kept woman.

She started turning down more and more invitations from idle playboys and would-be-sugar daddies. She also rejected a growing number of dim sum breakfasts, morning coffees and afternoon teas from the tai-tais and the concubines. Instead she went for long hikes in the Hong Kong countryside and started to realize that other than the odd feckless would-be-bandit that she could spot a mile off, she was in one of the safest places in the world. She started to experience a freedom that she had never had before and began to appreciate the good luck of being a single woman of independent means totally unhampered by societal constraints.

After a while she found herself increasingly drawn by the Buddhists of Lantau. She was attracted by their basic ideas about the transience of life, the illusions of society, the vastness of the universe, the search for stillness and the ability to stare into the abyss of nothingness and not be afraid.

These ideas thrilled her and that is why she gave up her freedom, to live and study with monks and nuns. But after a few months she noticed the rivalry and gossip among the trainees, then the vanity and self-importance of the teachers. Then she saw the physical and sexual abuse among the most revered, and finally the corruption and avarice of the most powerful and their love of the most powerful and most dangerous elements of society. She often spotted former suitors in company with head monks, Triad bosses and rising government ministers.

She climbed down the mountain, found Tai O, bought her piece of land and built her house. The refugees started arriving, the house became "The Hostel". Faces passed through, tired, scared faces, escaping old horrors, facing unknown futures. Faces like Ma.

They arrived at Fan Lau Fort. Falkirk, Danny and Spike were already there, Pig Face and his crew also just arrived. They pulled together some dead wood and piled it up in the middle of the Qing dynasty stone ruin. Falkirk opened his hip flask, Pig Face passed around the cigarettes, his crew scrambled down to shore to fish something edible out of the water. Simon wished they had got a muntjac at least on their hunt. He was hungry, though breakfast wouldn't be long. A faint glow behind Lantau Peak was struggling to break the night. A single owl hooted.

As soon as Madam Li took one swig of Falkirk's flask she thought of Ma again, and she remembered something.

She looked at Simon and said: "He called her Xiao Hu, Little Tiger. Your dead man, when he called out to his wife. What if she was the tiger that he went to catch?"

"That doesn't make sense," Simon said. "She was already with him."

"Yes, at the time I saw them, but what if he lost her?"

The Dagger and Red turned up. Red caught a rat by crushing its head with a perfectly-aimed rock. He skinned it with his knife and threw its flesh on the barbecue. He was absent-mindedly whistling *Mac the Knife* as the sun burst the sky above Lantau Peak. He fell asleep without eating any rat meat.

6

RAGS TO RICHES

"Xiao Hu! You have to live! Hold on Little Tiger. We're going to survive. Darwin! Hold on to my arm. Lift your head up. You're a trooper. You know that Darwin. You're a trooper. You need to be alert."

They were in the Pearl River Delta holding on to a floating bench that had been part of an overloaded sampan. The boat sank where the currents from China swirled and twisted against Hong Kong waters. Snakeheads in Macau had arranged passage for 250 people. They towed the cramped sampan out at midnight, easily slipping by the Macanese coastguards who were paid well to check the Chinese side of border after the clock struck twelve at the Guia fortress. The guides cut the rope at the border with Hong Kong, lit a flare and left the refugees drifting. The money they took from the immigrants more than covered the cost of the clapped out sampan that had already been condemned to the knackers yard.

The flare did no good. If any coastguard saw it they ignored it. When the boat began to sink there was wailing and crying. Some jumped overboard. Others went down with the vessel. Ma Xun instructed his wife and five-year-old child to jump as far from the boat as possible. They both begged him not to have to do it. He shouted at them: "Do you want to die? No. Then jump now." He pushed them first, then launched himself, and grabbed them both. He calmly instructed them to tread water. In the pitch black they could hear many others weeping at first, their numbers dwindling over the hours. Ma thought of sharks.

He would hear thrashing in the dark and couldn't tell if they were caused by a shark attack, or if they were the desperate last lunges of those trying to keep their heads above water. Xiao Hu got over her paralysis and helped Darwin keep his head above water.

Terrifying currents and eddies tried to separate them and suck them under, but they held together, tight enough not to lose each other, loose enough to be able to tread freely. They were saved by the bench that drifted into view. They grabbed it and held on. Xiao Hu wondered what happened to the others but she couldn't see or hear anyone else, only her family. For about five hours they clung to the floating bench. Ma shouting and cajoling his son and wife to hold on for life. Towards the end he was having to physically support both their heads above water and his own grip was slipping.

An old fishing boat cluttered into view like a ghost ship at dawn, with tangled ropes, lurching masts and torn nets dangling at all angles on all planes. Kites circling above like secret occult symbols. Bony fishermen at the front pointed towards them, they had been spotted. Ma nearly lost his grip in the agonising twenty minutes it took for the boat to arrive. Knowing rescue was imminent played dangerous tricks on his exhausted mind that wanted any excuse to let up and shut down. Xiao Hu and Darwin were quiet, struggling to keep their eyes open. He couldn't tell if the faint smile on Xiao Hu's beautiful face indicated that she knew rescue was on its way, or if she had resigned herself to her fate come what may.

A fisherman leaned from the deck and asked if they had any money. Ma felt a jolt of panic. Is this it? Is this what it has come to? Dog eat dog, shark attack shark. A despondent, hopeless Ma shook his head, his grip on life weakening by the second, his wife and son about to sink to the bottom of the delta. A rope ladder was thrown over the side, the fisherman clambered down as nimble as a sea-monkey and splashed into the water. He pushed the three of them to the side of the boat and pushed them up towards a dangling colleague who hoisted them up to the deck. They were given hot water, a bowl of rice and blankets, and were told that they'll have to wait on board until the day's fishing was done. Ma asked why they wanted to know about money when they rescued them in any case. The fisherman who asked shrugged and said: "You never know. I might have been lucky this time."

The fishermen brought them into port after dark and an apprentice guided them to Madam Li's house. The first thing they heard as they walked towards the door was a wireless playing *Rags to Riches*, and for a split second Ma felt like a millionaire.

Ma and Xiao Hu were in a daze for the first 24 hours, Darwin slept through most of that time. They kept themselves to themselves, politely accepting the credit that Madam Li offered them for two night's accommodation without making any arrangements for future payment. Madam Li didn't want to know anything about them other than what they wanted to talk about. Conversation didn't come easily to them anyway so it was a quiet time. Xiao Hu made Ma promise that they would pay back Madam Li as well as the fishermen that saved their lives.

"Is this a dream?" Ma asked. "Did we survive the crossing? Did sharks tear us apart?"

"No Ma, this is reality. We survived. You saved me. I owe you my life." Xiao Hu said. "I would have gone under, so would Darwin. You're now responsible for the rest of my life, you know that don't you?"

"It was Darwin, he saved us both. We lived because he needed us to live."

After the second night they pulled themselves together and set off to look up a contact they had at Shek Kip Mei squatter camp. They hiked a day and a night to the northern tip of Lantau Island, sleeping in a forest at night, drinking from streams and eating anything they could catch or pluck from the land. Ma used a spider web to catch three fat cicadas to Darwin's delight. He then plucked off the wings and legs and cooked them up on a small fire of twigs. It was a delicious meal. As they ate,

Xiao Hu and Ma told Darwin how they and their gang of village friends used to catch field mice by blocking off all but two ground-burrow exits, then syphoning water through one end and trapping the escapees at the other. They would skin and gut the mice, fry them up in sesame oil, and roll them in a cabbage leaf to eat with slices of raw garlic. Listening to their stories, Darwin thought they were on a fantastic holiday.

A battered old fisherman ferried them across the sea to Kowloon for free, telling them of his astonishment when he first met European horsemen on Lantau while he and his 16-year-old brother were hunting civet cats. His hotheaded younger brother wanted to slit the gweilos' throats and take their horses but he managed to talk the would-be assassin out of it. Nobody had bothered telling them that the Chinese government had signed Lantau over to the gweilos for a 99 year lease earlier that year. Twenty years later the same brother died of dysentery while digging trenches for gweilos in a country he never knew existed, for something called the "Great War."

"Be careful of the gweilos," the old man said as he dropped them near Tuenmen village. It was another day's walk from where the fisherman dropped them and they eventually reached the cluttered, pungent and creaking congestion of Shek Kip Mei squatter camp.

"You're in good company Ma," said their contact, an old primary school friend of Ma's who had got to Hong Kong a year earlier. "This place is run by the Catfish he said, using the popular name for the Chiu Chau triads. They'll sort you out for whatever you need and they'll find you work too. Obviously they charge a small service fee but you'll get a discount for being Chiu Chau yourself."

"But I'm not a brother," Ma pointed out.

"Doesn't matter. They always favour their own. I'm the same as you. Never joined them, it's not my style, but they still help out here and there, for a price, a fair price of course."

It was a dense and jumbled shanty town of creaking shacks and narrow dirt paths that looked to be in a state of anarchy, but the government marked out plots that new arrivals were able to claim through formal channels. They took a plot and with the help of Catfish-sourced building materials they built their own hut. Darwin soon found other children nearby and quickly fit into a vibrant and raucous street life. Xiao Hu's mother arrived with a group that paid Shenzhen snakeheads to show them a hole in the fence at Lok Ma Chau. She quickly took on babysitting duties while Ma and Xiao Hu worked long hours. Ma laboured on Chiu Chau-controlled construction sites. Xiao Hu worked in a plastic-flower factory for a while until she learned she could get twice as much money in bars. She had just switched jobs and was working late on Boxing Day when half of Shek Kip Mei's scrap-wood hovels were destroyed in a ferocious fire. Ma, Darwin and Xiao Hu's mother ran through the network of mud paths while flames leapt all around them. Darwin fell over when his heel was caught by the collapsing wall of a blazing house. He was momentarily stuck until Ma wrenched him free and threw him at Grandma just as the rest of the house toppled. Grandma couldn't reach Darwin as he disappeared in smoke and she was certain that Ma had died. In fact they were right at the edge of the fire and both escaped being engulfed in flames, though their injuries were serious. Ma had broken both his legs and he couldn't escape until rescuers dragged him from the wreckage. Darwin had lost consciousness from smoke inhalation. He needed immediate hospital treatment and was taken on the back of a tricycle with grandma running by the side holding his hand and making sure he didn't fall off. Ma was on the back of another tricycle, every bump on the road piercing him with pain. Father and son lay side by side on the ward, Darwin on a ventilator, kept sedated, Ma imprisoned in a pair of large casts from ankle to knee, and wires that suspended his legs. Grandma by the side of Darwin, whispering in his ear.

Xiao Hu ran onto the ward and threw herself at Darwin, sobbing, and then at Ma. The doctor came and told Xiao Hu that she would have to take them home as they need the beds, unless they were to take a private ward. She told the doctor they didn't have a home to go to as it had burned down in the fire, and the doctor said that was also true of everybody else there. She asked what would happen to Darwin if he was off the ventilator. He said that he couldn't say, he might live, or he might die. Then he took pity and told her that he can keep them for three days and nights but that would be the maximum he would be able to hold off the hospital bosses. After that she would need to find a way to pay for private treatment, or they will just have to chance it on the streets. She went off with Grandma and didn't come back for three days.

On the third day porters stretchered them to a different, quieter, slightly more spacious ward. Ma waited for the discharge and braced himself for being tipped out onto the street, him frozen rigid in a pair of pots, his son gasping for breath. The prognosis didn't look good. But no-one came to expel them. Instead a doctor visited on an evening round and recommended that Darwin could be taken off the ventilator in the morning. Two days later Xiao Hu came, showering Darwin with kisses, and with a stack of old books for Ma.

"Who is paying for this?" Ma asked.

"A friend. Don't worry. I'm taking care of it."

"How can I not worry about it."

"You need to fix yourself up. That's the most important thing. What did the doctor say about Darwin?"

"On the second day they said he would die. I told them he was a fighter and they did not believe it. But he has got stronger and now he is able to eat congee. I think it still hurts him to breathe but he is getting air into his chest."

"My poor Darwin, what have we done to you? First we nearly drown you, then burn you alive. I am so sorry." She started sobbing again.

After another two days the doctor congratulated Ma on having such a powerful and strong son. "This boy is destined to do great things Ma, there is no doubt about it. I can now say that I'm confident that he will eventually make a full recovery. He is very weak now and will need full medical care for another couple of months, but I think he will recover."

"What about me, doctor?"

"You'll need another three months in those pots. Then you'll be OK, though there is a chance that you'll walk with a limp for the rest of your life."

"Three months? Will I not be able to walk until then?"

"No of course not. But you shouldn't worry, everything is taken care of. Your wife has settled the bill and she says she has enough to keep paying for as long as it is needed."

"Where is she getting it from?"

"I don't know about that. It's none of my business to ask."

"It is my business."

The next time she came he quizzed her again.

"Xiao Hu. Tell me where this money is coming from? We don't have anything."

"I told you, a friend is helping me."

"We can't afford to get into debt."

"It's alright, Ma, I have made arrangements. I don't want to talk about it now," she said and a tear dropped down her trembling cheek.

He couldn't look at her. He was ashamed to be lying on his back for the second week, expecting to stay so for another two-and-a-half months. Meanwhile his wife brought in a regular income that had saved his and his son's life. He didn't want to think it through too deeply. Not yet.

"It was my responsibility to take care of you for the rest of my life," Ma said to Xiao Hu the next week.

"Well, you can't do that with two broken legs," she said, not looking at him.

Darwin played with a wooden truck she had brought him. For Ma she had found stacks of old comic-strip classics, *Outlaws of the Marsh, The Journey West*. They were ancient and frayed but she had quickly swooped on them when she saw an elderly man tip them out of a sack at the paper waste depot.

"Where is it coming from, Xiao Hu?" he asked.

"I'll see you next week. I've got a busy few days ahead at the restaurant," she said and quickly left.

He dreamed that night of seeing Xiao Hu standing under a street light on a corner. He came to her, lit her cigarette. Then he pleaded with her to come home. A car stopped and a door opened. She stepped into it. There was a man in the shadows inside. Ma shouted as loud as he could but no voice came out of him. The car drove off with his wife inside, he tried to run but he got nowhere.

He woke himself up shouting, then sensed relief when he realised he had been dreaming. But the next moment he felt as if he had been punched in the stomach. He was breathless when he finally admitted to himself that there was no other way that Xiao Hu was paying the hospital bills.

Though Grandma came every day with rice and to take Darwin for walks, Xiao Hu didn't come back for another three weeks. As soon as she saw his face she knew that he knew. She wouldn't take off her sunglasses or hat for the ten minutes she was there. She showered Darwin with affection and sweets. As she was leaving, without looking at Ma she pressed a folded note into his hand and walked away.

"My dearest Ma, you and Darwin will forever be the only real things in my life. The rest is an illusion. This hell we are living in is an illusion. Do not hate me – Xiao Hu."

He lay sleepless, knowing that without paying hospital bills they would have been tipped out on the street in the first week. Darwin would have died, there was no doubt. He would not have been able to do anything, except eat whatever food that Xiao Hu could have brought in. She saved Darwin's and his life by going out and earning money in the only way she could. And yet how could she do it? How could she sell her body?

The next visit from Xiao Hu was six weeks later when Ma had his leg pots cut off and Darwin was discharged. Xiao Hu was the life and soul, laughing and giggling, genuinely happy. She led the way on buses to the far end of Kennedy Town where she had managed to bag a squatter plot on a flattened piece of land that perched on the steep side of Mount Davis. There were already four walls and a corrugated-iron roof; inside, simple furniture and bedding that she had cobbled together from scraps here and there. Cats patrolled the lanes between the plots.

"Welcome home," she said with a smile. Grandma was there cooking up a pot of rice and cabbage with four chicken wings. For an hour over dinner they experienced contentment. They had a millionaire's view of Victoria Harbour that twinkled with junk lanterns as the sun dropped down to distant Lantau Island.

Finally, for the first time in two months Ma spoke to his wife.

"It's beautiful. Thank you," he said.

Xiao Hu kissed Darwin and told him to be a good boy, then put on a western dress. Ma had never seen her in western clothes before. She quickly left without a word and didn't return until dawn when she laid by the side of a sleepless Ma, alcohol on her breath. As soon as he saw light he was up and limping towards the city's construction sites.

Xiao Hu left for work in the afternoons and usually returned some time between midnight and dawn, though sometimes she wouldn't return for a few days and the interval of her absence gradually grew. In the end her returns became occasional visits and after two months Ma finally admitted to himself that she wasn't any longer actually living with them.

During this time Xiao Hu had advanced in the world of hookers, from street-girl to taxi-dancer, then hotel-lounge girl and finally recruitment to an elite secret club.

The Duchess was in some ways more exclusive than the most renowned clubs in the colony. It was there that the powerful people went to really relax after social duties in the top establishments such as the China Club or the Hong Kong Football Club. It was no place for the respectable elite who believed in the official propaganda on Hong Kong as a place for honest hard work. The Duchess was for the sharks who wanted to grasp what they could from the skewed economy of the place. The people who saw their mission in Hong Kong in purely financial terms.

It was the HQ for the sharpest police inspectors, the seediest of ministers, the craftiest civil servants and the most cut-throat capitalists. It was a British Institution and its ethos was elite naked ambition, with the general outlook of a public school rugby club mixed in with an underworld menace. All male, macho, hierarchical and imperialistic. The Chinese who were a part of it were among the most Anglicised of the Hong Kong and Shanghai elite. Their involvement would be through personal vetting, not in any formal way, but rigorous nevertheless. All the rules were unspoken. If you needed to have them spelled out to you, you didn't belong.

The girls that worked there were all whores, there was no ambiguity about that. But in a sense, the club was not primarily a brothel. The place was about power, celebrating it, furthering it, and abusing it. Sex was simply a by-product of that. To accommodate that there were private booths.

Occasionally there were guests who were not quite insiders, but had a good feel for the rugby-club mentality of the place. There were one or two Xinhua agents who the sharks were sometimes courting for business opportunity. The Xinhua contingent would be treated with an air of deference. Sometimes Harry Scroggins and other passable Spidermen would be there. Only the ones who clearly understand that this was no American frat house, but was very much an English gentleman's club.

The male bar staff were Catfish – the Chiu Chau police led by Johnny Tse having arranged that, knowing that these were the most powerful Triads in Hong Kong at the time, now that they had pushed the notorious Green Gang to the fringes. The police involved knew that having Chiu Chau staff would also help to keep out both KMT and Communist agents.

As Xiao Hu rose through the ranks at the club she became the most popular girl there, always busy, efficient and charming, despite the fact that the reason for staying in the business had shifted from saving her family to paying for her newly-acquired heroin habit. She had become a high-functioning addict. She had started off on anti-opium pills in the taxi-dance halls and had moved onto chasing the dragon at the Duchess. Heroin there was supplied by the Catfish barmen and it was also available for the club members. But the rules were clear and the drug was policed carefully. Anyone who turned into a junky nuisance was barred for life. The Duchess was neither a sex shop nor an opium den. Its real purpose being as a clubhouse for the colony's top predators.

Max Godber was a natural at the club. As he rose through the police ranks he became rich through his takings from gambling dens, opium dens, brothels, dance halls, smugglers, refugees, hawkers, illegal bars, unlicensed boatmen, fishermen, car drivers, doctors, dentists, you name it, he scalped it. Godber was a police genius. He could sniff out crime wherever he stood. But instead of stopping it, his first instinct was to check it for profitability. If he could squeeze something worthwhile out of it, he would take it. If he couldn't, he would crush it without mercy. And for that his reputation as a good cop grew beyond all expectations.

He was also media savvy and the force came to rely on him as the man to talk to the press, long before the role of Police Spokesperson had been invented. Through that he gained public recognition, and without yet reaching formal top ranks within the force he assumed the position of the public face of the police. Thus came the invitations from governors, banking heads, army chiefs, financiers, importers, exporters, movie makers, actresses, airline and shipping firms.

Max Godber was aligning his position as one of the most powerful people in the colony. But he was still young, and what really drove him was that in the class-ridden society that was Britain he wasn't a natural heir to power. He wasn't an aristocrat, as he so often dreamed of being. His father was an insurance salesman who worked hard and did well enough to send him to public school. Godber was privileged in the sense that he had never known hardship or the dread that hangs over you from impending hardship. His dad made sure that Max didn't need to worry about hardship. He brought up a son who had only ever known the privileges of comfort and security.

Max turned 18 in the last month of the war. He had trained enough to shoot a gun, but just before he had a chance to test his skills in a real battle, it was all over. He never fired a shot in the war, let alone had one aimed at him. But his colleagues in the Hong Kong police or anyone he met after the war would have been shocked to hear such a slur. In their eyes Max had been a monster in battle. They found that easy to believe, as Max was never shy of retelling his war stories with ever increasing detail.

The problem with Max was that being lucky was never enough. He had a huge sense of entitlement, it wasn't a chip on the shoulder, it was an instilled, undeniable expectation. And this fuelled his natural greed. He was a very greedy boy. He was greedy for power, success, fame, and most of all, cash.

Max's father was a caring, honest, hard-working man whose sole aim in adult life was to make sure his son suffered none of the deprivations, hardships and fear that had been present in his own upbringing. He succeeded beyond all expectations. Out of fondness and pride he used to call his son 'Tiger,' but Max hated it from a young age because it reminded him of his debt to his dad, so the name fell by the wayside as young Max grew up.

Godber was too young to rule the roost at the Duchess, but the tired old dogs that did saw it was inevitable that he would before too long. Godber himself saw it as his birthright. Hong Kong was a perfect hunting ground for a man like Godber, and the Duchess was by far his favourite haunt, and Xiao Hu – Little Tiger – was his favourite whore.

Ma struggled with low-paid labouring jobs, bringing home scraps when he could and trying to find time to spend with his son. He became a bitter and and angry man, raging against his own impotence. He had lost his true love. They had grown up together dodging Japanese swords and murderous KMT troops that rampaged through villages. They helped each other through the dark authoritarian rule of uneducated peasant Communists who robotically spouted the fundamentalist teachings of Mao. They supported each other mentally and physically until they thought their son Darwin was strong enough to risk the dangerous journey to Hong Kong.

On one of Xiao Hu's last visits he reminded her of the terrible night in the Pearl River when they vowed they would support each other. She cried and said that it was to do exactly that that she had gone to work in dance halls. Without her income they would have all starved to death. He said it was OK now, he could work, she could stop. But she cried harder, repeatedly saying it was impossible. After that she stopped visiting the shack, arranging instead to hand over cash to her mother once a month and to look at her boy from a distance without him seeing her.

Ma nearly fell apart. First denial, then grief and despair, and then a bitter, cruel anger. He hated Hong Kong, the British, the Communists, Nationalists, the Police, the Triads, and most of all the useless stupid victims exploited by all the predatory factions of the colony. He drank with what little he earned. He bought street hookers and took them down narrow, dirty alleys. He smoked opium and wished he could disappear, to anywhere, in any world. He was drowning again, barely treading water.

Then he noticed his son.

Skinny, dirty, lonely and afraid. The boy's grandmother stoically raising him in the absence of a heroin-addicted mother and a broken, self-destructing father. Ma forced himself to look at the situation and admit what was happening. He only had one life and this was it. He was destroying it, and dragging his own son down with him.

His son also only had one life and Ma could be a pillar in this life, or a noose around his boy's neck. He chose to become a pillar. He had no idea how to achieve it but he decided that he must try. There was nothing he could do about the world he found himself in, but he would try to see it for what it was, and to build something out of it.

He needed to work, earn and save money, be there for the boy, talk to him and make him believe it was going to be alright. Ma didn't know if it was going to be alright, but he wanted his boy to believe that it would be. He was still treading water in the violent, eddying currents of the Pearl River.

At the beginning his reconstruction didn't involve Xiao Hu. She was lost to him and mostly to Darwin, though her monthly cash contributions were a lifeline, especially during the period that Ma was breaking apart. But it slowly worked through his mind that Darwin's life would be better with his mother in it.

He was working on construction sites during the day, rushing home at lunch to see Darwin, rushing home at end of day to tell him stories before he slept. Once Darwin was asleep he would slip out of the shack to look for Xiao Hu. The more he searched for her, the more their life together came back to him. His thoughts always culminated in their life-and-death struggle in the Pearl River. It was also a frequent recurring dream that would often end with one or the other drowning – or Darwin. In the struggle there would be tenderness and love and a dedication to living. Sometimes he would wake up shouting: "I want to live!"

Ma quizzed the construction workers about prostitutes and what neighbourhood had the most, what kind of establishments there were. Most of these guys were two-dollar street-corner clientele, they knew little about the dance halls and sailor hotels, the kind of place Little Tiger would have to have been working at to bring home the regular amount she delivered. Even with little first-hand information from the coolies a picture started building up from the titbits of gossip and boasting that filtered down from the managers and the bosses and the suspected and would-be Triads. The picture pointed towards Wanchai and so at night Ma started snooping around there.

He noticed that Catfish controlled quite a few Wanchai establishments, though there seemed to be an uneasy balance of power between them and remnants of Shanghainese Green Gang. He started speaking to some of the Catfish who were friendly when they saw that he was also from Chiu Chau. He learned to talk with them more freely and gained the trust of one or two. Eventually he got word of a girl who seemed to fit the description of Xiao Hu.

The trouble was that she worked at the secret police club, or the "Blood Pipe" as the Chiu Chau boys called it, oblivious to the grandiose name of the Duchess its Anglophile clientele preferred. "Blood pipe" was slang for erection.

Ma followed instructions to find its location, accessed through a narrow staircase on Jaffe Road, but overlooking Lockhart Road from a balcony. He spent five nights watching people enter and leave until he finally saw Xiao Hu looking so beautiful he hardly recognised her. She was like some ice-queen, white-faced, chiselled and pristine. She walked with her arm through the arm of a gweilo. She was the epitome of glamour, the very picture of a woman who had made it from rags to riches.

7

THE LION SLEEPS TONIGHT

Dawn found most of the party sleeping off their rice wine and fish barbecue in the ruins of the Qing dynasty fort. The remnant of the night's fire smouldered as chickens from Fan Lau village pecked around for scraps, cautiously avoiding the slumbering tiger hunters.

Simon opened his eyes, looked up at the sky and saw Sinbad making a reconnaissance pass over their camp. He watched him disappear over the hill behind them, spiralling, diving and sweeping along contours. He wondered if Sinbad had seen the tiger.

By the time Madam Li woke up under the glaring sun there was no sign of the sea-eagle. Soon she woke the others and instigated a split force back to rejoin the Yi O contingent. Jagan, Simon, Danny and Spike took the coastal path while Madam Li and Falkirk went over the peak. Pig Face and his two sidekicks headed back to Tai Long Wan, explaining to Danny and Spike – with little regard to the police contingent – that they needed to get back quick to ship their consignment of diesel up to Dangan Island in Chinese waters.

At Yi O, Salty Pang, SPK, Bad News and Jackson were all sleeping around the embers of a fire when Simon and crew arrived. The Jap Devil was awake, alone with his easel and palette, painting the bay ahead, and Tiger Hill on the opposite side. Six empty bottles of rice wine were scattered among them.

"Some tiger hunters," Jagan said, while Danny and Spike tied the laces of Bad News and Jackson together.

When Madam Li and Falkirk came trampling down the mountain Simon asked if the hunt had been in vain.

"Not at all," Madam Li replied. "You have to understand that what we're doing is preventing a hunter from becoming a man-eater, by letting her know that we are not to be messed with. You may not have seen her in the night but you can take comfort in the thought that she was watching you. She would have considered springing you just as she had Old Lau, but she would have seen your guns, your gang, and your dangerous-looking, predatory demeanour. Now she will be reconsidering the consequences of ambushing a harmless-looking scrawny devil like Old Lau."

"Tigers are very smart beasts," the Jap Devil piped up without taking his eyes off his work.

"That's right. Never underestimate the intelligence of a tiger," Madam Li replied.

"It's all brawn, not brain," Danny said doubtfully.

"Danny, where do you think your brain and brawn come from?" Li asked.

"My dad, Bad News," he said, cracking himself up and throwing a flake of cow dung at his snoozing father's head.

"You and your dad got it from evolution my friend, just like the tiger. Trust me son, we're not that far removed from tigers and all mammals, we basically share the same anatomy, just packaged differently. Our brain isn't an exclusive property," the Jap Devil said, recalling his own hideous lessons in human anatomy.

"I don't understand. Are we the descendants of cats?" Spike implored.

"No. We are their cousins," the Jap Devil and Jagan said in unison and then laughed at each other.

Spike had a pained look on his face. All he could think was that he had four cousins and they all lived in Tung Chung, none of them were tigers. Then he looked at the Jap Devil's work and noticed that he had added ornate fortified watchtowers to his painting where none existed. There were balustrades and turrets, top-heavy curving roof tops and smoking cannons poking out of iron-plated gun holes. They had all noticed this curious trait of the Jap Devil, he would sometimes add things to his paintings that were not there. There was a huge old Korean gate over the Ting Ling harbour in one, another strange one showed a shrimp boat stuck with medical syringes, and one favourite of all the locals was of a beautiful mountain path where a wild boar wearing a Japanese military uniform walked alone, snuffling for truffles, he had explained.

"What are those towers doing there?" Spike innocently asked.

"Ah, these. These are the watchtowers of Kaiping. Have you ever been there?"

"No, are they really so beautiful?"

"Oh yes, normally, though not the last time I saw them."

"When did you see them Jap Devil?" Spike innocently asked.

"It's Mr Nagashima to you," Bad News piped up without opening his eyes, always amused by the naive questions Spike posed.

"Ah. Well it's a long story Spike," Taro Nagashima began. He gave Spike a vastly edited version, but he remembered his journey to the Kaiping towers well. He often played over scenes from his life as he sat fishing in his boat, or painting on the shore.

Taro was born in the Meiji era just before the start of the twentieth century. He was in the army by the age of 18, in 1917 when Japan was allied with Britain. Like many of his generation the army was first and foremost an economic choice for a man of humble background during tough and turbulent times. He also believed that the army was a force that contributed to the transformation of his country from a poverty stricken feudal backwater into a modern and progressive nation. He was proud of his smart uniform. His artistic talents were spotted early on and he was lucky enough to get recruited to compiling military records as an official army artist.

His early tours led him to document Japanese developments in Taiwan, Japan's first colony. It was a place where the relationship between the invading power and its subjects was relatively benign. That didn't make it free of atrocities, only less prone to them in comparison with other places Japan occupied later. Those conditions allowed a young recruit to keep his naive and systematically received views about development and racial destiny more or less intact as he went about with his charcoal and watercolours, documenting new railway depots and sanitation plants.

Korea was a different matter, where imperial arrogance, excess and violence was more difficult to hide. Cracks in his world-view began to form as he painted forced labourers in Japanese army coal mines and Korean men forced into Japanese militia uniforms. By the time he went to China he was a seasoned veteran, but even with his experience he wasn't prepared for the escalating brutality and the numbing war crimes of an army that was willingly marching over a cliff, and plunging into a sea of death.

Nagashima's job necessarily let him see the activities of his colleagues from the point of view of an outsider. As an artist he was forced to witness and record things that were taking place among other people. His colleagues failed to notice the drift that carried his mind away from the institution that fed, clothed and housed him. They all assumed he was one of them, a zombie of the Japanese war machine, totally committed to the Emperor, devoid of his own thoughts. It is precisely because they were zombies that they failed to read him and recognise a traitor within their ranks.

Nagashima's work took him to record the effects of chemical agents on Chinese peasants. He methodically drew the progress of anthrax on a village population and the foaming suffocation and seizures of women and children dosed with sarin gas. He documented the degrading nervous system of children fed mercury and the deformed newborns of women who had been given the same. He thought he had already seen the worst when he was ordered to accompany a unit to the invasion of Nanjing.

During the weeks he documented the aftermath of storming the city he failed to recognise his fellow countrymen as human beings. Here he saw the monstrous horror of war and the hopeless, eternal abyss of human evil. His fellow Japanese were engorged on total destruction, which saw its ultimate expression in violent rape, torture and murder. The only way he could get through the task was to work obsessively, like a robot. His goal was to record everything in minute detail, as clinically and as accurately as he could. The more professional he was the more he detached from his own panic.

Although he had not said anything to show it, he was now a total stranger to his countrymen, a traitor and a dangerous heretic, and he was terrified of being discovered. His worst crime was in an insight he had one night as he lay sleepless on his stinking bunk. He realised that there was only one man on the planet who could put a stop to Japan's murderous rampage, the country's act of willed insanity. The emperor of Japan knew for certain that the entire war was built on a lie. He was not a living god, he was a weak man who failed to stop his compatriots from turning themselves into wild subhuman lifeforms, and driving the nation and its neighbours to destruction.

Nagashima kept his mouth shut and went back to Manchuria to meet a general he sometimes suspected of harbouring similarly heretical thoughts.

"Come in, come in Nagashima. I was thinking about you. I need a new portrait my man," General Bando said as he welcomed the artist into his home. Nagashima sat down and told the general everything, finishing with: "The Emperor is a man, a most evil man."

General Bando didn't show alarm or anger, if anything there was a sign of relief on his face. He took his gun from his holster and put it on the table. Either of them could have reached it in a snatch at any time.

"You know Nagashima, it didn't take us long to gain a foothold on China. We were like some predatory mutant species of cockroach feasting on the rotten old flesh wounds of a gangrenous sleeping giant. I led a unit into Qingdao city and spotted a beautiful German town house there, built by a homesick brewery manager who wanted to recreate a piece of Bavaria in a strange land. I very much wanted that house, so I decided to have it. I got a squadron of army engineers to take the house apart brick by brick, each one carefully numbered, as were the wonderful blue porcelain roof tiles. I packed the whole lot into crates and shipped them to Tokyo where I commissioned army engineers to rebuild the mansion near Inokashira park. All expenses were met by the army, of course. I justified the whole thing by saying it was for the glory of the Emperor.

"But I'll let you in on a little secret. I never once thought of the Emperor while I rebuilt that house. The whole charade was to impress a geisha who was driving me nuts. I was besotted with her but nothing I could say would convince her to sleep with me. I thought I could have any geisha in Tokyo or Kyoto, but Harumi just wouldn't accept. So I built the house for her and invited her over. She slept with me, and accepted the keys. I went back to Qingdao.

"Next thing I heard was that the Emperor's cousin took a fancy to the 'Geisha in the German house,' as she was now known. I sent word back that she was my girl, but that seemed to make him want her even more. He was a well known imbecile and untouchable because of the godly status of his family. He moved in with her and there was nothing I could do. I learned from that that I'm an idiot, stupid, greedy and vain, and so are members of the royal family.

"But you see, this war, the Emperor didn't start it you know. We did, the generals. We did it because we could. You are right, the Emperor is certainly no god, just a grasping, self-aggrandising, grubby opportunist. But the war is the fault of all of us who egged it on and pushed it forward, each of us for our own purposes. Whether that be for gain, or to hide amongst peers and survive.

"The problem, Nagashima is that people like to think they do things for their beliefs. Sure you can dupe the dispossessed and the needy with faith, but the real driving forces are quite material. Martian anthropologists would see that clearly. Unlike us they will not hold personal belief to be a sacred mystery. They would cut through our efforts to mask reality. They will see that humans of whatever ideology, faith or race basically demand to be respected, take possession of things they like, eat well, fuck and go where they want. And if they find themselves in the driving seat of a war machine that gives them an endless supply of what they want, they'll keep driving the machine until it tips over a cliff. That's what we generals have gunned for in this war, taking our parasitical emperor along for the ride. The Emperor functions as our licence and passport.

"I heard the German house fell down in a small earthquake that didn't destroy any of the old wooden houses surrounding it. Turned out that the workmen had cheated me with cheap, low-grade cement. Harumi lost a leg, she went back to Kyushu to live with her parents. The imbecile royal was brain-damaged and never heard of since. There's a rumour that he was locked away in an institution on one of the islands of the inland sea."

Nagashima gave the general his drawings from Nanjing, walked out of the house half expecting to be shot in the back, and disappeared into the Manchurian forest. The next night General Bando studied the drawings in careful detail, each one signed and dated by Nagashima. He had sincerely believed at the time that he was drawing with strict objectivity, striving for realism, but the results were hideously distorted. The Japanese soldiers started as monstrous animals with pig snouts and blood-dripping tusks, and transformed progressively into more ghoulish apparitions. The shocking intensity of the images increased with each date until it reached delirious levels of insanity, the monsters and devils becoming abysmal and increasingly abstract forms. It was a work of breathtaking originality and power, a stunning collection, and utterly treasonous, a criminal act.

Bando finished his study at midnight, drained the last drop of sake, took the pictures into his Zen garden and burned them one by one. Then he knelt on the ground, prayed for mercy, drew his dagger from its sheath and pushed it into the left side of his abdomen, yanked it across to the right, turned it and pulled up with a violent force. He had decided to commit hara-kiri during the talk with Nagashima the previous night, which was surprisingly the first time he had admitted to himself that he too was a heretic with treasonous thoughts, and that it was better to go as his samurai ancestors would have, than to be humiliated in some kangaroo court by an ignorant self-important, pseudo-legal army lawyer, and be summarily executed.

Nagashima went underground and wandered through the chaos of China for years. He didn't speak much but when he had to he told people he was from the north-eastern region on the border with Korea. After stints as itinerant artist, casual labourer, jade miner, farmer and hunter, he eventually met an old travelling bee-keeper, who took his bees from Yunnan to Xinjiang and back each year on a circuit following various blossoming flower species, to create the best-grade honey in China. When old Deng finally died – in a tent pitched on an alpine meadow in Qinghai – he must have been in his late 90s. Nagashima took over the hives and continued the annual migration for several more years until he found himself caught up in a gun battle with a Japanese unit in southern China a week before the end of the war.

He was in Kaiping, Guangdong province, where beautiful 19th-century village towers had become strategic points in ongoing skirmishes between increasingly confident locals and desperate remnants of the Japanese army separated from their command. These units were on a suicide mission simply holding out, killing as many locals as they could before their own inevitable demise. The towers of Kaiping had been built by families whose relatives had gone abroad to toil for gold, in remote mines, in factories, in densely populated cities everywhere around the world. The migrants lived harsh, lonely lives, and sent back anything they scraped together, before dying as strangers in foreign lands. The families at home built upwards and embellished with ornate architectural flourishes. They fortified them with iron plates, bars and gun turrets. Their main concern had been Chinese bandits, but these fortresses later became hotly contested strategic positions against the Japanese.

Nagashima had been absorbed into a Kaiping defence squad made up of a mix of Nationalist and Communist partisans. They surrounded a tower where one Japanese private held out. It took them twelve hours to move up one floor, and two Chinese were dead. One was a father of two small children, the other had just married his sweetheart. The squad were enraged but their own tower was too good. Three hours later they had got to the sixth floor and another comrade lay bleeding on the fifth. There was still another floor left, it was midnight and there was a 19-year-old maniac in the building who was determined to kill as many people as possible before willingly dying himself.

Nagashima felt he had no choice. For the first time since he had talked with General Bando, he spoke Japanese. His fellow partisans were astonished and watched in silence as he walked up the stairwell, calling out his name, rank and number, place of birth, school and military-cadet college. He kept talking while climbing, giving the desperate fugitive a clear shot of his head and upper body as he rose. The private froze like a rabbit caught in an army camp spotlight, his face was a twisted mask of uncomprehending horror. "I've got something to tell you," Nagashima said sadly, wearily. "Your Emperor is a man, a weak, ridiculous man," and he shot him through the heart.

Nagashima's Chinese comrades sombrely tied him up and marched him to the woods. They asked him repeatedly if he was a spy. He simply denied it, there was nothing else to say. He didn't struggle. They made him dig a grave. Half of the group wanted to beat him to death, but the squad leader, Chen Ming, made all the other men leave, saying he would finish the job himself. Nagashima had stayed with Chen's family every year on his bee-keeping circuit. Chen had tears in his eyes as he raised his gun and shot bullets into the tree by Nagashima's side shouting: "Run my brother, run. And never come back you fucking Jap!"

He ran and hid for about another year then swam across the sea to enter Hong Kong on its eastern side at Sai Kung village, eventually drifting to Tai O over another eighteen months. Once there he decided to allow karma to take its course by dropping his expert northern-China-peasant act and presented himself simply and truthfully as a Japanese artist. He was shunned, reviled and hated. His shack was burned down twice, his boat frequently vandalised in the early years.

But slowly a handful of people started talking to him and Bad News and SPK gradually noticed he was a connoisseur of good boozing. While he mostly remained quiet, he was a listener and appreciator of a good story, and therefore good drinking company. They called him the Jap Devil and he gradually became absorbed into the tapestry at Joycee's tobacconists.

One night the Jap Devil woke up to find Red in his hut sitting by his bed, holding a knife and looking at him. Red's face was a picture of calm, almost with a faint smile. He felt a shiver run down through his body. After all the near misses he had had, he was now certain this was to be the end. Karma had finally come to settle his debts. He closed his eyes and entered a blackness that could have been death, sleep or concussion. He dreamed of a tiger that spoke, saying: "Everything dies. Let life take its course." When he next opened his eyes Red had gone, and neither of them ever mentioned to anyone what had happened that night.

On another occasion he had a visit from two British gentlemen who called themselves Mr Smith and Mr Jones. They were impeccably polite when they asked him to come for a ride in a navy launch. While it was not at all clear how they would have enforced it, he was left in no doubt that turning down their offer was not really an option, old boy. He was not surprised either when they apologised for being such a nuisance, but would he mind terribly slipping this silly old hood over his head like a good chap? Unwilling to be outdone by Englishmen he apologised himself for being so thoughtless as to forget to ask for the hood in the first place. Though he couldn't understand why they bothered, because it was clear which direction they were going in from the heat of the sun on the right side of his body, and the number of turns they made as they entered the Hei Ling Island harbour. He counted their steps from the pier and smelled a faint whiff of incense from the east, so he knew he was in Lai Chi hamlet, about a quarter of a mile from the Tin Hau temple. An iron door shut and he was at a traditional Chinese courtyard house, with customised high walls that gave wonderful views of the sky and the stars at night, but nothing else.

They held him for ten days and he was more than happy to help with their inquiries, though the process was slowed down by the fact that Mr Smith insisted on conducting the interviews in Korean. Nagashima had a working knowledge of the language but it was a laborious process to use it, and he kept telling Mr Smith that Japanese would be a lot easier. Smith politely insisted that they would stick with Korean as he was sure Nagashima had been sent by Pyongyang. Smith asked Nagashima his story twenty times, and every time he gave them the same account. Jones was always there politely taking notes. All the time they were very pleasant to him, making sure he never lacked for tea or sandwiches.

On the final night Jones switched to perfect Japanese and produced a crate of beer, apologising for not having done so earlier. All three of them became quite sozzled and had a jolly good laugh, even when Smith switched on the whirling tape recorder once again and Jones asked the same old questions in Japanese.

In the morning Smith dropped him off at Sha Lo Wan pier, reverting to perfect Korean with a wink, saying: "Let's keep this to ourselves, old boy. We'll be in touch."

"I joined the army, Spike, but it didn't suit me. So I ended up wandering around China and that's when I found the Kaiping towers," he said with a smile, and continued painting the bay.

Falkirk spoke up. "We've done all we can for now. As pleasurable as it is, there isn't any point in camping out here any longer, because for all we know the beast could have gone round to Tiger Hill by now, or up to Silver Mine Bay, or even left Lantau altogether. We'll have to regroup when we hear about the next sighting, and I hope to God it won't be another attack."

As they were setting off back to their boats Jagan noticed that SPK didn't have his usual fishing boat with him.

"Where's your boat?" he asked.

"Not here," SPK said quickly.

"That's unusual, isn't it?" Simon chipped in.

"Is it?" SPK asked.

"Oh, it's just that you know, the night of the murder, there was a burned-out boat over at Sham Wat. Obviously, we need to check that no-one had their boat stolen or anything on that night," Simon said.

"Oh, yes, yes, of course you need to check that. No problem with mine. I took my ancient wreck over to Tung Chung for repairs the day before. I swear that old junk fought the British in the Opium War," SPK said.

"That's good. You don't know of anyone who lost a boat do you?" Jagan checked.

SPK did a good show of deep thinking, then concluded predictably. "Nope."

Maria brought up some starfruit to the police station in the evening. She always came unannounced, saying she happened to be walking that way and thought she may as well come up to say hello. It was almost a weekly event and Simon had come to expect it, always prepared with clean glasses and a couple of bottles of beer.

Jagan was inside, his radio picking up on a special dedication to the "loyal and brave" Negro servicemen in the American forces. A scratched and ancient gramophone was wailing out a haunting and infectious rhythmic harmony. Simon and Maria, sitting on a bench outside could hear the melody.

"*The Lion Sleeps Tonight*," he nodded to her wisely.

"I thought it was a tiger you boys were hunting," she said, teasing.

"Not just boys, Madam Li too," he corrected: "She's the best tiger hunter of the lot."

"She's like a man. She smokes like one and drinks like one."

"You would hardly believe that from the stories Danny and Bad News came back with, they practically wrestled the big predator to submission, you'd think, listening to their accounts."

He poured her a glass of beer and they supped in silence for a few seconds as a perfectly round, blazing-orange sun dropped into the ocean to the sound of the undulating harmonies on the radio.

"Your friend and his sidekick asked me and Sally out for a horse-riding trip tomorrow. Over the hills for 'champagne, and cucumber sandwiches,'" she said laughing.

His stomach dropped.

"Oh God, he's awful, and that bloody Harvestman is even worse. I hope you put them in their place," he bluffed, not really believing that the fun-loving Maria was going to turn that one down, especially if she was egged-on by young Sally.

"Of course not. I have never had champagne or cucumber sandwiches, I may as well have the experience. Anyway, he didn't seem that bad," she said, testing his reaction.

"How did you meet them in the first place?"

"I saw them sweating in the village, eating noodles uncomfortably. I could tell they were city detectives and it was obvious they'd come about the murder so I asked them about it."

"What did Wetherby say?"

"He said it was top secret. He was sent by an important police chief to clear up some blunder. And then his chubby companion asked us if we wanted to go horse riding."

"Maria, truly, Wetherby is a pompous and arrogant fool, don't waste your time with him. And Harvestman is a horrible scoundrel. He is sly and he is nasty." he blurted, more irritable than he wished to sound.

"They were both charming to me. Why shouldn't I spend time with charming English gentlemen?" she asked, beginning to get annoyed with him.

"For starters Wetherby has no idea that there isn't a single person in Tai O who knows how to make cucumber sandwiches. He is so wrapped up in himself that he would find it inconceivable that there are no cucumber sandwiches in Tai O. And I can promise you that a man like Wetherby, who is used to being served on for every little need, has no idea how to make a cucumber sandwich, because he would never once have made any food for himself."

"I don't see why you have the right to tell me who to go horse riding with. It's not as if you have ever asked me yourself."

"Well, no, I know I don't have any right to tell you what to do. I'm just telling you the truth about him because you might not be able to see through his lies."

"What lies?"

"I told you. Cucumber sandwiches. And where is he going to get a horse anyway? He didn't come on a horse and he doesn't know this place. He doesn't know that Madam Li keeps the only horses of Tai O in a meadow five miles away. And there's no way she would lend hers to idiots like him and Harvestman."

"Simon, you seem to be quite fond of Madam Li these days. I thought you suspected her of being a Communist spy?"

"She's an interesting woman. I think probably not a Communist spy after all. But she's got enough intelligence to see through the likes of Wetherby and Harvestman."

He knew as soon as he had let that one go that it was below the belt. Maria was quite rightly sensitive to any suggestion that she, a stilt-house fishmonger and factory worker, whose formal education was stopped at the age of twelve because her father didn't have enough money and needed her around the house, was in any way lacking in intelligence. Simon knew all too well that she could outsmart any police officer in the force, or any university-educated socialite on Hong Kong Island.

He was under her judgement-pending stare, and he didn't expect the verdict to be favourable.

"Are you trying to say that it's because I'm not intelligent enough that I would end up going on a day-trip with Prince Wetherby and Lord Harvestman?"

He knew that whatever he said next was going to be wrong.

"Look. You know, I think you're smart. That's why I'm just telling you the truth. He's a liar and an idiot. He is self-serving and unpleasant."

"Don't patronise me, you pig. Your smarty-pants girlfriend in Central, Jasmine, she would have seen through him would she? Is that what you're trying to tell me?"

"Oh, no she's got nothing to do with it at all, and she isn't my girlfriend anyway. And as a matter of fact I don't believe she did see through Wetherby at all. She was silly enough to be impressed by his pretensions."

"She's only not your girlfriend because she dropped you like a hot potato when it got embarrassing for her to be with you, and then she had you banished to Tai O," Maria said pushing the knife in because she was angry.

"I'm pretty sure we wouldn't have lasted much longer if it hadn't been for her father getting wind of our relationship. To be perfectly frank, I did get to know her quite well and with that came the inevitability of finding out just how much in love with herself she was, which isn't a flattering thing at all."

"You bloody well did get to know her well enough," Maria said venting.

Simon was desperately looking for some way out of this conversation. The evening had started so perfectly with *The Lion Sleeps Tonight*, and the superb sunset that for a tiny passing moment wrapped the two of them in a thrilling warm glow.

"Another beer?" he suggested lamely.

"No thanks, there's no point sitting here arguing with you."

"I'm not arguing with you."

"Yes you are."

"No I'm not."

"Yes you are. I'm going. I need to get back to make sure the twins do their homework." And she left.

He punched the back of the bench in frustration and suppressed a scream of agony. And then remembered: "Clear up some blunder...", "What blunder?" he said out loud.

The next morning Wetherby came off the radio looking perturbed for a moment.

"I'm needed in Kowloon. Some kind of riot brewing," he said curtly to Simon who looked across and raised an eyebrow at a nonchalant Jagan.

"What riot?" Simon asked.

"I haven't the faintest. Some fracas between Commies and Fascists I expect. All as bad as each other as far as I'm concerned. Ranking officers are being called in, though obviously not low-ranking ones like yourself."

"What about the murder?"

"I expect Godber will find some way to wrap it up in Central. I wouldn't worry about it old chap. You can get back to your cabbage thefts and seaweed smuggling. That will suit you, eh?"

Wetherby had already told Godber that there was nothing to investigate as there were no substantial clues or sane witnesses. Harvestman had already filed his story as planned, and so, in the eyes of the world it was an open-and-shut case. As soon as the Governor reads it in the Times he'll be satisfied that there was nothing to add.

"I've got an investigation on Wetherby. I'll be sticking with it until a formal order comes through to inform me otherwise."

"You've always been strangely stubborn for a man with no clout, haven't you? Strange for a half-caste, usually much more subservient. Well do what you like, you'll be reined in soon enough. I've got more important affairs to worry about now, such as the security of this very colony."

"Why did you tell Maria Chu that you were here to clear up a blunder?"

Wetherby looked confused for a moment until he slowly joined the dots.

"That feisty fish-wench? She didn't half look tasty. At least she would do after a bath and a comb of the hair, eh?"

Simon smiled and visualised a satisfying right jab that would split the man's lip.

"What was the blunder you were referring to?"

"Did I refer to a blunder? I expect I meant that I was here to prevent blunders. Shame about the wench. I was going to treat her to more of a ride than she had bargained for. Though I suspect she knew it and relished that."

"I believe your superior is anxious to get you over to Kowloon as quickly as possible, sir. I shall arrange a launch for you," Jagan growled with unconcealed hostility.

Wetherby looked confused again for a moment, as if he couldn't remember why this funny chap was speaking to him.

"Frankly I'm glad to get away from this stink hole and the drunken sea-gypsies that inhabit it. Good luck chaps, you'll need a lot of it here."

He strolled out to the garden and spoke to Harvestman, who was sitting smoking. Harvestman appeared to punch the air in delight and the two strolled down to the pier.

Simon was almost shaking with rage. He was quite sure that Maria and Sally would have gone on that trip. What he didn't know was what would have happened when the sly, calculating Wetherby turned his full attention on Maria. Would she have thrown her lot in with a devil-may-care abandon? Would she have screamed in his face and scratched his eyeballs out? Would the bastard have raped her? Simon honestly didn't know how things would have turned out. An enormous sense of relief welled up in him as he came to realise that now he didn't need to be left guessing.

"What are you grinning at?" Jagan asked.

"Glad to see the back of them."

"I bet you're glad they're not taking Maria and Sally out for their horse ride."

"What were you doing listening to our conversation?"

"I wasn't trying to hear you, but you were raising your voices in your argument."

"It wasn't a bloody argument."

They were getting on to their launch to investigate the wreck at Sham Wat. They pulled away, bouncing on the choppy surf, salty ocean-spray sprinkling their faces as they rounded the mysterious monolithic General that guarded the harbour, a freak rock formation that inspired dread and awe in all sailors.

"You know Simon, the problem with you is that you believe in romantic love," Jagan said to fill the time.

"That's rubbish. Well, I mean, it's rubbish to say that what I think about that affects my acquaintance with Miss Chu."

"Miss Chu? Why Miss Chu all of a sudden? We always talk about Maria."

"And Sally."

"And Sally, but you only mention her because you think it disguises the number of times you bring up Maria."

"No I don't."

"You don't what?"

"Bring up Maria much."

"You do, because you've been in love with her for two years."

"Sinbad over Tiger Hill."

"Clocked him. See, your problem is that you think love and marriage are somehow relevant to each other. Take me. I've been betrothed to Sonja from Mongkok since we were both 12. It's been agreed by our families that we will marry when I finish my Tai O posting and get a good position in Kowloon. I'm not in love with her and I doubt she's in love with me. We have never been alone together. We don't have any pressure about romantic feelings, but what we do know is that our households are viable. Our families will help bring up the many children we will have. I'm looking forward to banging her in the marital bed, but in the meantime if I get horny and bang the wrong woman, no one is going to be upset."

"Bloody weird to me. Your prospective partner could be a nightmare. You might know the family formally but unless you've spent some time in private and intimate conversation you'll never know what she's really like until it's too late. Would you really want to spend the rest of your life sharing a household, meals, your bed, with someone you find out too late that you don't even like?"

"You and your fellow romantics regard your own judgement too highly. Subjective judgements are shaky at the best of times, but add infatuation and sexual desire and you're almost guaranteed a disaster. OK, we admit that there is an element of Russian roulette in our system, but that's a good thing because we enter into it with a lowered expectation. If it turns out to be a happy relationship it's a plus. If it doesn't it's not the end of the world. Your romantic love is also a game of Russian roulette. A random commitment made in a state of temporary insanity. Your odds are less favourable and the results more explosive. It's people like you who end up throwing themselves off cliffs and shooting your brains out. Crazy."

"Oh, stop your nonsense. Your Indian poets, singers and princes are full of epic love-yarns and infatuations. What about the Taj Mahal? The greatest symbol of India, a tribute to romantic love."

"The greatest folly on earth, a pretentious pile of garbage. What do you expect from pampered royals that know nothing of real life?"

"Anyway Jagan, what's with all this tradition in your house. I thought your dad was a secular Anglophile. Why has he followed the old customs and arranged a traditional betrothal for you?"

"He is British in his politics and certain random cultural trappings, like having tea and sandwiches at four o'clock and listening to the Queen's Speech on Christmas Day, but his personal beliefs are rooted in India, and increasingly so as he gets older."

"He used to be a firebrand, didn't he?"

"That was before the war changed him. I was only little at the time but I do remember him as a socialist, staunchly anti-imperialist and anti-British. He didn't hate Brits personally, but he was against the system. He drove for rich bankers and was close-ish to some of their families, though not nearly as close as some of them liked to think. They had no idea what he was like at home, shouting at the radio and railing against the goddamned British royal family."

Mohandra hated the British Broadcasting Corporation in those days. Desperate for news about real world events, he hated the way that radio freely mixed opinion, lies and rumour with their news reports, with everything heavily doused in imperialist rhetoric that achieved the contradictory duality of being both patronising and infantile at the same time. "They sound like sixth-form debating-society hopefuls, these so-called reporters," he would shout, pointing at the radio while Jagan's mother got on with the washing up. "A bunch of prefects trying to impress the headmaster."

In comparison to the moralistic and entitled tones of the British nationals, Mohandra found the aggressive anti-European and pro-Asian staccato of Japanese propaganda more attractive, and its basic premise just as plausible. He bought into the idea of the Pan-Asian Co-Prosperity Sphere. As tired Japanese troops eventually marched down Nathan Road on Christmas Day 1941, he didn't exactly welcome them with open arms, but he looked on with interest. While having a pang of concern about one or two western bosses he quite liked, he didn't dwell on their fate too long. "Yes, it is time for an Asian nation to take over," he quietly said to himself.

As Japanese soldiers with their Korean and Taiwanese conscripts settled into city patrols, Mohandra took the first affronts with a flinching stoicism, the inevitable chaos of war, he thought. There was the odd shove in a crowd, the occasional slap.

After some months they came for him, forced him onto the back of a truck before he had a chance to say goodbye to his wife or son, corralled him with other Indian workers – including friends from Kowloon – onto a barge that took them out to Lamma Island. There he spent three years in a quarry, contributing to the Co-Prosperity Sphere by breaking rocks for Japanese commanders.

Most of his friends died. He watched them waste away from starvation, fade from disease, and crushed in horrific accidents. Bodies would be dumped in the bay, and he would see kites, egrets and grey herons repeatedly dive to tear off rotting human flesh from carcasses.

In the final months he was assigned to the Kamikaze tunnels, the madcap idea of a deranged commander who somehow believed that even if Hong Kong fell to the Allies, a group of troglodyte Japanese could hold out on Lamma Island in a network of caves. One day he and two others who were forced to dig the granite with chisels noticed that the psychotic sergeant, who used to prod them and sometimes whip them from behind, hadn't appeared for half a day. They walked out of the tunnel to find his body on the beach, his mutilated head lying about three feet away where a stray dog was lapping up the blood. The war had ended.

After this experience Mohandra was a confirmed British imperialist. He put up a picture of the new Queen Elizabeth in his dining room when she was crowned in 1953, and the whole family had to drink tea from coronation mugs.

"When I started getting interested in Indian independence and the works of Mr Gandhi, politics became a taboo subject in the home. In any case, my dad talked less as the years went by, though he became more autocratic. He told me that I would be marrying Sonja. I was young enough to accept it without question, and old enough to get a stiffy when I thought about what she had under her sari. When it came to my career I did try to talk him out of enlisting me in the police. I told him I planned to be a zoologist. I also said that the imperialist police was institutionalised racism and that half the force saw it as an opportunity to steal. He just pointed to the application form and watched me as I filled it in."

A pod of pink dolphins appeared, led by Mother Mary and Churchill. They watched for a bit without talking, as the launch bounced on the surface and rounded the headland of Sham Wat bay. They saw parts of the charred and ruined boat sticking out of the water, "like the carcass of a whale that burned to death," Jagan said.

"How would a whale burn to death?" Simon laughed.

Jagan was thrown for a moment but collected his thoughts.

"There are two ways that a whale can burn to death," he said so confidently that it almost seemed like he wasn't making it up on the spot. "Have you never heard of spontaneous combustion?"

"No, is that something I should have learned in the engineering module at Police Academy?"

"No, it's when humans suddenly burst into flames because of some internal chemical process. A terrible way to go, but the point is, that if it can happen to humans, there's no reason that it can't happen to other mammals."

"A perfectly reasonable suggestion, but does it really happen to humans?"

"Yes. It's well documented. Although no-one has actually witnessed it happening."

"An interesting form of documentation. What's the other way?"

"Lightning strike. A direct hit to the skull makes the brain burst into flames."

"That's inconceivable."

"It's true. There's a story about Ishmael Chalmers, I've been told by the fishermen. He was shipwrecked off the coast of Madagascar in a terrible storm when a sperm whale came and towed him by the tail to safety in a bay. After he had delivered him, the whale was swimming away when a lightning bolt hit him right on the head. The skull exploded and flames leapt from his brain. He saw the carcass jump clear of the water several times as it was lifted by the force of exploding organs inside its body. They say that was the moment Ishmael finally lost his faith in God."

Simon wasn't really listening by then, he had heard too many improbable Ishmael Chalmers tales from his own father when he was a boy to take much notice of them now.

"What's that over there?" he said, bringing them back to their task.

"Looks like the sort of barrel SPK uses for his shrimp paste," Jagan said.

"Exactly."

They found some blocks of shrimp paste in a box, stamped with SPK's logo.

"So these either belonged to SPK or to a wholesaler he dealt with," Simon said.

The next find was a section of the hull that was relatively unaffected by the blaze, showing a turquoise-blue Plimsoll line. A diagnostic giveaway to any Tai O resident.

"Remember when SPK got that paint?"

"Yeah, he bought it off Bad News didn't he?"

"That's right. Last year. One tin only, in that hodgepodge consignment he traded with some fishing fleet from Hainan, wasn't it? What good is one tin of that? Jackson had asked him."

"Just enough for a handsome blue line around my hull. I'll be the only one with a line like that, he said."

"Very pleased with himself, he was, especially after he got Danny Chu and Spike to paint it for peanuts."

"Literally. The sack of peanuts he'd bought off Bad News in the same consignment."

"What the hell is it doing burned out in Sham Wat?"

They sailed back trying to make sense of what they had seen. SPK was one of the old rogues and blaggers that hung around at Joycee's, swapping tall tales and dirty jokes – drinking too much. He was lucky to survive torture and forced labour under the Japanese. He lost a sister and a brother during that time. His brother's body had washed up at Fan Lau, and his sister was never found, though it was suspected that hers had been among the skeletons found at the Chi Hing monastery. He seldom spoke about the horrors of war, always kept up a veneer of happy-go-lucky. Did he harbour secret bitter political thoughts? Did he equate the totalitarianism of the Chinese regime with Japan's atrocities? He never showed any political tendencies, never really took part in frequent political rows that ignited the drinking dens. But it now seemed undeniable that whoever killed Ma had brought him to the police-station beach on SPK's boat and then escaped as far as Sham Wat. SPK hadn't reported the boat stolen, but he said he had taken it to a boatyard in Tung Chung. Could someone have stolen it from there and carried out the execution?

"SPK? No, he isn't here," his wife said. "He's gone to Tung Chung to pick up his repaired boat, apparently."

"When will he be back?" Simon asked.

"No idea. He said it could take a day, or it could be a week. He's planning to stay with his cousin, the notorious drinker, layabout and part-time bird-trapper, so I expect it will be more like a week, leaving me to make the shrimp paste again. He calls himself the Shrimp Paste King, when really the work's done by the Shrimp Paste Queen. He should just be called Shrimp Paste Parasite."

On Jagan's suggestion they went to speak to Madam Li about her famous network of junior watchers, who always kept her one step ahead of police raids on her refugee camp. One of them may have seen SPK's boat leave the harbour. Simon wasn't convinced about the existence of the network but he didn't have much else to go on.

"Network of watchers? What rubbish are you talking about now?" she said, genuinely perplexed.

"The kids you pay to watch out for police raids so that your refugees can go hide in Tiger Hill," Simon suggested.

"Oh you boys love to invent intrigue and conspiracy don't you? Look, there's just a few kids here and there who like to earn the odd xiao long bao bun by providing some useful information for the community. It's not a network. But anyway, it's not illegal to keep an eye on the police you know. We'll never have an honest police force until we find ways to force you to let us watch everything you do."

"We just want your help," Simon pleaded.

"I'll see what I can do," she said, crossing her arms.

"Do any of your kids watch the harbour?"

"If it's the harbour you're interested in, you should of course talk to Tick Tock."

"Who is Tick Tock?"

"You don't know Tick Tock? He's the boy that sits on the seawall when he should be at school, always listing the boats going in and out, who's on them, what they've got. He's got boxes of notebooks. I know, because I buy notebooks for him. I started that after his mother complained that the boy had written on every scrap of paper they had in the house and was now starting on the doors and walls."

"Oh, he's the one who sometimes walks around the market square smacking his head and scaring the little kids, isn't he?" Jagan asked incredulous.

"Yes, that's Tick Tock. Rather alarming on first acquaintance, but a gentle soul at heart."

"He doesn't look like a very reliable informant," Simon hesitantly suggested.

"Go and look at his notebooks, you'll see what he's capable of."

It seemed like a simple enough task, but when they approached Tick Tock on the seawall and asked about his books he mumbled, growled, and rocked back and forth, eventually barking at them and running away.

Simon and Jagan went back to Madam Li and begged for help. She tutted with impatience and told them to do the hoeing she was in the middle of, while she went to do their jobs for them. She came back more than an hour later looking flustered.

"OK, that was a bit more complicated than I had expected. He said the Imperial Police had tricked me into working for them, which I couldn't argue with really. He thinks you want his notes so that you can do bad things to China and Chinese people. He thinks you'll probably create some kind of improved traffic and customs monitoring system to tax people more effectively. He said he knows how to do that but he would never tell the Queen's own Triads."

"You got all that from his grunts, growls and barking?" Simon said with accidental condescension that melted away when he began to digest the exquisite details of the boy's notes.

The information for the day of the execution was puzzling and disturbing.

SPK had taken his boat out on the afternoon of the killing, several hours before the fatal shots. On the boat with him were Salty Pang, the Dagger, Red, Danny Chu, Spike and five other known Mongoose, a mix of veterans and juniors. Simon remembered the busy deck of the boat he had caught a glimpse of that night. They looked like Mongoose on a mission.

"Is SPK a Mongoose?" Simon wondered.

"No, I don't think so," Jagan said, "He's polite enough to them but never hangs around any Mongoose drinking den or takes part in their big socials."

"No I don't think so either. SPK was a good support to me when the Mongoose were trying to muscle some extortion from my hotel."

"Then what was he doing with this lot that afternoon?"

"Didn't the Mongoose ship get wrecked in the typhoon?" Jagan recalled.

"That was two months ago. Are they that hard-up that they hadn't replaced it?" Simon asked.

"They must be. We haven't seen the replacement. You can imaging what kind of fanfare those fantasy pirates would have made of bringing a new boat into the harbour," Madam Li said.

"There would have been gunshots in the air, firecracker explosions, streaming flags, booming drums, roasted pigs, and a flotilla of ragamuffins who still worship the Mongoose, on little dinghies and makeshift rafts," she added.

"What's this 'M' next to some of the names?" Simon asked.

"That's Tick Tock's code for 'merry'. He always makes an assessment of seafarers' sobriety, just by how they are looking, standing, talking on deck. I think it's because they say his father was drunk when he slipped off a squid-boat and disappeared."

"So Salty and SPK were merry. What's this 'DD' next to the Dagger's name?"

"Dead Drunk. Tick Tock's second highest level on his drunk-scale, the highest being 'G' for 'goner' which can mean either unconscious or likely to die, he explained to me once."

"Salty and SPK merry. The Dagger dead drunk. Red presumably stone cold sober as usual. Nothing surprising there," Jagan said.

"So when did they come back?" Simon checked.

"They didn't," said Madam Li, who had already combed the list to check on that. "At least not during Tick Tock's watch, which usually lasts until a couple of hours after sundown."

"Well we know where his boat ended up, and just as strangely, SPK lied to us about his boat being in Tung Chung the day before that. It's not looking good for him, or his passengers," Simon summed up.

Simon and Jagan walked into Jackson's office to find him with a westerner they had never seen before.

"Harry Scroggins," he said, standing to greet them with a broad smile, his hand thrust forward. "American Chamber of Commerce."

Simon noticed that Jackson had a rare look of discomfort on his face, though he quickly wiped it off and offered the policemen cigarettes and a seat. Simon introduced himself and Jagan, and as politely as he could, inquired: "So what brings you to our remote outpost?"

"Trade," said Scroggins immediately. "Fantastic place you've got here. Fascinating heritage. Beautiful women," he said with a wink. "You'll have to excuse me, gentlemen, I need to be pushing off. Thank you Jackson, it has been most enlightening talking with you. I will call you," he said as he shook hands, put on his General MacArthur sunglasses, and quickly exited.

"Trade?" Simon double-checked.

"Trade," Jackson concluded with a shrug and a nod. "You know, fish, shrimp-paste, salt, that kind of thing."

"I didn't know Americans were interested in all that."

"They're interested in all sorts."

"Where's Salty Pang?" Simon asked.

"No idea. I haven't seen him since the tiger shoot," Jackson replied.

"What about Red and the Dagger?"

"Nope. I've no idea. They might have gone on one of their shark-fishing trips I guess. They shot a great white near the Philippines last year, do you remember that?"

"I remember them telling us they did, but we never actually saw it did we? They claimed they sold the carcass to Japanese fishermen on the high-seas. How's Old Lau?"

"Bearing up but not talking much sense. The morphine seems to be keeping him happy enough but I have a feeling we might never get the old Old Lau back."

"How old is he anyway?" Jagan asked.

"No-one knows, not even him, but he claims to have shot an Englishman during the Second Opium War. Ironic really, young Lau fighting for his right not to have opium sold to him, finishing his days a hundred years later as high as a kite."

"Yes, if it's true," Simon said.

"Do you know why SPK took out Salty, Dagger, Red, Danny, Spike and other 'associates' on the afternoon before the 'spy' was killed?"

Once again, the theatrical deep thought.

Salty Pang had been talking to Jackson, Old Lau, the Dagger and Red about Blind Wang and the tiger that afternoon when the line unofficially reserved for Mudskipper business rang. He issued a series of affirmations and grunts and came off the line.

"Three Eyes wants us in Cheung Chau. Not a great rate but sounds like some easy freelance work for the Turtles," he told the room, using the local nickname for the Green Gang. He positively swaggered to reach for his hat, expecting the other two Mongoose to follow. Everyone knew that Pang was looking for ways to strengthen his bonds with the Greens. He was concerned that since the Japanese war ended, the Mongoose had lost their steam and lost their status.

Everyone also knew that Three Eyes had led the mob that raided Tung Chung Fort a few years back and stolen half-a-dozen rifles, two boxes of ammunition, and set free a boar kept in the yard for the hated English policemen's Christmas dinner. The raid was carried out on horseback, on stolen animals from the Trappist Monastery. Even Catfish at Mui Wo admired Three Eyes for his style.

"How are you going to get there?" Jackson called after him.

"Shrimp Paste King," Salty said, Red striding after him, and the Dagger weaving a bit with a bottle of rice wine in one hand, his trusty rifle in the other.

Salty rounded up the crew and went to talk to SPK.

"I don't want to get mixed up in Mongoose business," he said at Joycee's where he was enjoying an afternoon tipple with the Jap Devil.

"Just a little escorting job, SPK. Nothing to worry about, and there'll be some pocket money in it for you," Salty said.

He reluctantly agreed that he could do with some pocket money and they were soon cutting through the surf, heading out around Fan Lau on a two-hour coastal cruise to Cheung Chau. The Dagger led the singing with his memory for epic Triad shanties. They included the yarn about fighting Qing dynasty salt-tax collectors, a renowned guerrilla ambush on a Japanese army unit, and the famed beauty of Macanese pearl divers. As he became drunker the ballads became less tuneful and the stories merged with one another to great hilarity. Danny and Spike were loving it, recalling that this was the sort of thing they joined the Mongoose for.

As they passed Pui O they were only half surprised to see an old man paddling towards them in a canoe waving a bottle of whiskey and shouting: "Call me Ishmael you miscreants and reprobates! Let me on board!"

He clambered on to everyone's approval and was soon singing duets with the Dagger.

"What's the occasion, Salty?"

"Nothing much, Shark Tooth," he said, reverting to his guerrilla handle. "Just a little job. A pick-up in Cheung Chau."

"Turtle?"

"Three Eyes."

"Be careful. Spidermen could be behind that."

"Have no fear Shark Tooth. Remember the Mongoose of Tiger Hill? We were invincible."

"I know brother. But take care. Three Eyes is one crazy bastard."

He dropped over the side, untethered the canoe and bounced back to shore on choppy waves to his one-legged wife.

Salty was nervous as soon as he saw Three Eyes and two powerful-looking sidekicks dragging a blindfolded and blood-encrusted prisoner on board. The earlier jollity among the Mongoose had evaporated, with all going quiet except the Dagger, who screamed orders at the prisoner and pushed him around.

"Calm down," shouted Salty. "We don't want any accidents."

"You need to dump him at the police-station beach," Three Eyes explained. "He is a Communist spy and you are delivering him to the imperialist pigs."

"No, no, I can't think. I didn't know they had," Jackson concluded to Simon and Jagan, who almost groaned in frustration.

"Please let Salty know that we would like to talk with him urgently, if you see him," Simon said.

"Of course, of course," Jackson said.

It seemed unlikely to yield any results but they headed out to Pang's house. They walked along the raised mound that cut through the salt pans where suntanned workers dotted the marshy landscape, raking white crystals in the glaring heat. Two grey herons perched at the edge of a marsh, pinching trapped fish. Pang's cottage was daubed in pitch with a tin roof on top. Chickens pecked around a small yard and a nasty-looking pair of curs came out to growl at them. The modest setup betrayed that while Salty Pang commanded a certain respect in the village, his Triad activities hadn't brought the riches he must have hoped for. Two boys were fixing a bike in the yard and Mrs Pang came out with a baby strapped to her back. She looked at them as if they were mad when they asked if she knew where Pang was, then laughed and went back inside.

"I suppose that's a 'no' then," Jagan shrugged as they turned back.

"What do you make of Scroggins?" Simon asked on their walk back.

"Smooth," Jagan said.

"A trader or a Spiderman?" Simon asked, using Falkirk's language.

"Who knows? Anyone who claims to know anything about the Spidermen is obviously not qualified to know anything..."

"...and anyone who knows anything knows enough not to say anything."

"Precisely."

"Just like the Triads."

"And just as ruthless in achieving their goals."

"What are the goals of the Spidermen in Hong Kong?"

"No idea. Restore Chiang Kai-shek?"

"If they are so bloody clever how come they haven't worked out that's not going to happen?"

"The boys on the ground must know it, but their Grand Elders back at home don't use their extensive resources to find out what the world out there is actually like. Instead they try to impose a strange vision of what the world should be like."

"I think the goal for the boys on the ground is to promote their business model."

"Yes, develop their trade."

Jagan froze and grabbed Simon's arm to stop him. Just ahead a king cobra had been caught by surprise and suddenly raised its front end to an attack position, with its hood fully flared. It was looking down at them. The policemen slowly backed off until the serpent eased itself down and slithered off the path with a plop into the water. They watched it swim expertly across the pool and called out to a couple of salt-workers nearby to watch out.

"That was a biggy," Simon said, his heart racing.

"Twelve-footer I'd say. Did you see how fat it was?"

"Like a python. Could have easily killed us."

"Yes, that's true, but it's a funny thing that you hardly hear of cobra attacks on people around here."

"No you don't. They seem to know that scaring us is as effective a defence as unleashing their arsenal."

It was low tide so they reached the Chus' stilt house by taking off their shoes and squelching through the mud. The house was quiet, the twins the only ones around. Stevie was trying to catch crabs under the stilts and Jeanie was drawing in a scrapbook that Joycee had given her.

"Where's Danny?" Simon asked.

"Gone fishing," Stevie answered. "He's going to catch a massive shark, bigger than a sampan."

"What about Maria?"

"Hospital," Jeanie said, "Madge is sick. What is 'Chasing the Dragon'?"

"She was up at the abandoned house with Spike's retarded brothers and their gang," Maria explained at the clinic, streaming with tears. Simon was still panting from his sprint. Jagan caught up on the ward. Sally had her arm around Maria.

"One of them came running up through the mud to ours and shouted that Madge won't wake up. We were lucky he came, the rest of them were lying about like zombies muttering about 'fantastic Turtle smack, the best in China.' The bloody idiots. They were oblivious to their little girlfriend dying a few feet from them, bits of scorched tin foil scattered around the floor."

"Is she OK?" Simon asked Dr Tang.

"They got her here just in time. She'll recover this time but she's got to change her ways or else she's going to have years of trouble. They must have come across a much purer batch than usual."

"What kind of monster gives this stuff to kids?" Maria implored.

"Where does she get the money for this stuff?" Jagan asked.

"I don't know," said Maria. "I fear the worst. She pinches stuff from me whenever she can. My clothes are locked in a chest now and we have to guard the kitchenware. But those things are just opportunistic grabs. I don't know how much she's using."

Dr Tang told Maria that there was nothing else she could do right now. They would keep Madge in overnight and he promised they wouldn't let her escape.

Maria and Sally, both looking exhausted, left with Simon and Jagan.

"Come and have some tea at the station," Simon said, "if you're not still mad with me about last night, that is."

"I was but I've lost my energy for that now," Maria said turning towards the station.

Sally said she wouldn't come, she'd go and tell Bad News about Madge. She knew she would find him at Joycee's as his fishing boat was in the harbour.

Twenty-four hours had passed since they had last sat on the bench watching the sun set. Maria had recovered a bit and the initial pot of tea had given way to beer.

"I don't know what to do about Madge," Maria said.

Neither did Simon. He didn't have a clue.

"I suppose you need to let her know you're there for her," he tried.

"Yes but that's making it easier for her isn't it? She knows we'll catch her whenever she falls. Maybe we should just let her fall?"

"I don't know what's best Maria."

"I don't either."

"What does Bad News say about it?"

"Nothing. Madge is his favourite. He refuses to see there's anything wrong. She's sometimes at Joycee's with him and he thinks that's great, when she should be at home doing her homework."

Simon didn't have any suggestions or words of wisdom. He just wanted to scoop Maria up and tell her it was all going to be alright, though he didn't know how it would be alright.

"You made me mad last night," she said.

"That's not what I meant to do," he offered.

"I hadn't made up my mind about going out with those two idiots."

"Would you have done then?"

"Maybe. I dunno, partly just to show you I can do what I want."

"Right. I'm sure you can."

"I can."

"I know."

"Good."

"So"

"So?"

"Do you want to stay with me tonight?"

"Maybe."

"OK."

Maria was quiet for a moment, and then a smile rose slowly on her sad face as she gently sang out the wails from the tune of the night before, leading into the the words: "*Hush my darling, don't fear my darling, the lion sleeps tonight.*"

And Simon kissed Maria. It was the first kiss after wanting her with every patch of his body and soul for two years and three months, since she first slapped him in the face. She responded with a force that he had never dared expect, and soon they were entwined in his quarters and he revelled in the good fortune to find that reality could be every bit as good as he had dreamt, though she abruptly stopped him as soon as he slipped his hand under her blouse.

8

GREAT BALLS OF FIRE

"I'm sorry I lied to you," Maria told Simon as she pulled away from him on his bed.

"Lied to me? Can't think what about. Don't worry about it, we can talk later," he murmured, not wanting to register the total change in her whole body.

"No, it was wrong," she said, turning away and brushing him off.

"What's the matter Maria?" he asked, concerned now.

"It's Danny. I should have told you about him. Not that he would have done anything himself. You know him. He isn't bad to people. But he might know something."

"Why?" he asked, drawn in, almost forgetting the crushing disappearance of the moment.

"I told you that he was hauled out of bed at four in the morning by your henchmen, which was true, but what I didn't tell you was that he only came home half an hour earlier."

"Did you speak to him?"

"Yes, he disturbed me. He was trying to be quiet but I could hear him shuffling about. I couldn't understand why he didn't just go to bed. I went out to the veranda and caught him crying."

"What? Danny, crying?" he checked, with surprise.

"Oh he tried to cover it up of course, pretending he was just rubbing dirt from his eyes, but I know what I saw and I know Danny. It wasn't that long ago since he cried when Sally stamped on a frog right in front of him. He's a softie at heart, though recently he has done a good job of covering that up with his happy-go-lucky act and his Mongoose swagger."

"So why was he crying?"

"He wouldn't tell me, and he denied he was anyway."

"Where had he been?"

"Business, he said, nothing very important."

"What did you think?"

"I was just worried. I felt that he was getting drawn into things that he can't handle. Then your bully boys burst in and for one moment I caught the look of fear on his face, but I was the only one who saw that. He had covered it up before the police took hold of him and replaced it with a cheeky defiance. I know it's wrong but I felt proud of him at that moment. My little Danny standing up against Hong Kong's biggest Triad."

"Well they didn't get anything out of him."

"I'm only telling you Simon because you've always been good to him and you'll try to get to the bottom of it without framing something on him. I can't trust any of your colleagues, except maybe Jagan because he's sweet on Sally."

"Where is he now? I need to talk to him."

"Shark fishing, he said, somewhere near the Philippines, like last time."

"Look, you didn't lie to me Maria," he said stroking her arm, hoping against hope that there might still be a chance of reviving the moment.

"No, I did, by deliberately not telling you important information that would help you with your case," she said, stiffening and moving her arm away.

That moment was definitely gone, he knew. He kissed her conclusively on her forehead.

"I'm exhausted Simon, do you mind if I sleep here?" she said, snuggling into the folds of his blanket.

"Not at all," he said, thinking he would deal with the looks from the housekeeper in the morning.

Quickly she was away, spinning into deep sleep, pursued in her dreams by the antics of Madge and Danny.

Simon lay there stiff as a ship's mast, watching her bosom rise and fall with her breathing. He tiptoed to the communal shower to relieve himself and returned relaxed to lie by her side, trying to piece it together. Danny's late return and tears. SPK's burned-out boat, and the full outing of the Mongoose – their disappearance. The Chiu Chau victim, a Communist spy, they said. The call from the Spidermen, Harry Scroggins from the American Chamber of Commerce. The victim nearly drowning, his child and wife 'Little Tiger.' It didn't' make much sense, and by the time he was drifting off, all of it had gone and he was instead hunting the Tiger, or it was hunting him. He wasn't sure which.

He woke up alone, disappointed at first but acknowledging that it wasn't surprising. Maria would have had to get back to fix up breakfast for the twins, and she had already told him that she would go to see Madge at the clinic as soon as possible. He wandered into the staff canteen and found Falkirk reading the *South China Morning Post*, the previous day's edition, as usual. Falkirk didn't operate on normal hours. He slept, woke, ate, drank, did what he wanted whenever he wanted. He didn't have much in terms of wealth or worldly goods, certainly not enough to retire on, but he was a man who had carved out his own freedom.

"Bloody bastard stiffed you," he growled at Simon who looked back questioningly.

Falkirk showed him the front page. The headline caught his eye: "Carnage in Sham Shui Po," but it was the smaller article that Falkirk was pointing at, illustrated by a grainy thumbnail picture of Ma's death mask that had obviously been taken from the posters they had produced in Tai O.

Communist Spy Captured and Killed by Angry Hong Kong Villagers
by Barclay Harvestman in Tai O, Hong Kong

Outraged villagers took the law into their own hands on Sunday when they caught an agent of Mao Zedong red-handed and meted out swift justice.

The man in question was a certain Chen Guanming and had been known to the authorities. He was suspected of laying explosives on the Canton-Hong Kong railway line, and according to sources in the police he was the mastermind in a series of kidnappings and other terrorist acts.

The Eurasian deputy superintendent at the Tai O Police Station, Inspector Simon Lee, said that there was no evidence to suggest the victim wasn't a Communist agent.

'It is not at all surprising that the villagers take matters into their own hands sometimes. They are frustrated by the number of atrocities carried out by Reds,' he told The Times.

Max Godber, head of operations at police HQ, said: 'We do not condone natives taking the law into their own hands. However we understand how feelings can sometimes take over. We urge all people of Hong Kong to abide by the law.'

Tai O is a sleepy backwater and home to simple fishermen, salt-farmers and pretty girls.

"What? I said nothing of the sort," Simon exclaimed. "I said there was no evidence that he was a spy, not the other way around. And the stuff about them taking things into their own hands, that's invented from scratch. I can't believe this."

"You'd better believe it, it says so here," Falkirk said provocatively.

"How can he just make up stuff like that?"

"He makes up the right stuff that the right people want him to. No wonder he has such an illustrious career. I've already had the call from Thomas-Littleton, congratulating us on wrapping up the case. I said we haven't, and he said: 'Yes you have, I've read it in the paper, so has the Governor, the Queen and the Prime Minister, so that's that,' he says. So I said to him: 'Do the Governor, the Queen and the PM know that the Spidermen are involved?' And he nearly choked to death. 'What are you talking about?' he screamed at me. So I told him: 'Your Godber received a call from a Spiderman about the prisoner, even before we had had a chance to report what had happened on the beach. Tipped him off, they did.' That shut him up."

"Harvestman knows very well that it wasn't Chen Guanming in any case. That terrorist was killed in a shoot-out at North Point six months ago. Harvestman was one of the journalists briefed about the incident and then told all reporting on it was embargoed, we got the internal memo remember?"

"I remember well. Apparently Godber authorized the use of Chen's name for this case, with the approval of T-L. He said it was a sensible expediency to help balance the books, whatever that means."

"We know that the dead man was called Ma Xun. He was washed up here with his wife and child after they all nearly drowned in the Pearl River. The only suggestions he was a spy came from his attackers, and what the Spidermen told Godber. Since when have we let the Spidermen solve our cases?"

"Could it be that Godber is working for the Spidermen? It wouldn't be the first time a colonial bobby was freelancing for the Cousins, usually for a bit of pocket money, say, to buy a house, or send a child to a good public school."

"I don't know Falkirk, but it's beginning to look clear that the shooting happened from SPK's boat and the Mongoose were all on it at the time."

"Including your girlfriend's brother, I presume?"

"She's not exactly my girlfriend sir, but yes, I think Danny was there and he probably knows something."

"You do realise of course that the powers that be are converging, to sweep this event under the carpet? Whatever it is that Danny knows, or did, doesn't necessarily need to be ferreted out."

"A man was killed and I have a feeling he was an innocent man. My dad told me that the real job of a policeman was to use the power of the state to protect the common man."

"Presumably you were about nine, Lee."

"Yes, just before the Japanese imprisoned him."

"A noble thing to tell a nine-year-old boy, but not very accurate I'm afraid. What makes you think that Ma was innocent? You said he was Chiu Chau. Could have been a Red-Pole enforcer for all we know, or he could indeed have been blowing up trains for the Commies – killing babies. Or he could have been a heroin pusher, enslaving the feeble-minded. We don't know."

"All true sir. But he died in my lap. He said 'Don't believe their lies. I only went to catch a tiger.' And I suppose I want to know what the hell he was talking about. Call it professional curiosity if you like."

"Professional curiosity? Makes a refreshing change. You do realise of course that the 'professionally incurious' are the ones most likely to flourish in their career? But fine by me if you want to travel the disappointing and lonely road of the dissenter, and good luck to you comrade. You've got another week to unmask the hideous lies of the vile Harvestman, as long as the cockroaches don't find some technicality to pull the paperwork out of our hands."

At that point the radio came to life: "All hands on deck in Kowloon. Middle-ranking officers from all district police stations are to report at Sham Shui Po HQ. Martial law is imposed and riot squads are deployed and armed. Army back-up is also deployed. A battle between KMT and Communist politicals has escalated. Triad elements are involved. Factions are using the breakdown in law and order to settle old scores."

Simon and Jagan were on the police launch within an hour, heading towards the dark heart of the colony, near to the streets that Ma Xun walked before events beyond his control entangled him and brought him to his death.

Ma used his connection with the Catfish to land a bar job at 'The Erection.' On his first shift Xiao Hu walked right past without a shred of recognition. When he called out her name she stared at him for a minute before she crumbled into utter confusion as she attempted to process what she saw. He reassured her it really was him, the man she clung to for life as they and their son all trod water in the Pearl River. She then seemed to succumb to him, as if she was in an opiate dream, smiling and kissing his hands, tears falling down her cheeks. Then she snapped out of it as reality came bearing down on her, and she knew for sure that she was in hell and he could only be an illusion. She looked at him horrified, asking only what the hell he was doing there and retreating into the dark recesses of the club.

Thus began Ma's slow process of trying to lure the Little Tiger back. He took every opportunity to try to convince her that he was no ghost, he was a flesh-and-blood human, and he was there just for her, he was there to bring her home. He kept this up each night, without letting the drama show to anyone else in the club. By day he worked the construction sites, seeing his son at the beginning and end of the day, just enough time to tell him stories of the Monkey King and the Outlaws of the Marsh.

The Duchess was a place of dark brooding power. Many a night was quiet and conspiratorial, bent police plotting with corrupt customs officials, builders passing envelopes of cash to grinning ministers, girls always at the side, ready to be beckoned. At the beginning, seeing Xiao Hu disappear into the booths with some swaggering gweilo was almost too much for him to take, and he would methodically visualise himself smashing a glass he was drying, taking a shard and driving it into the neck of the man she was with. But Ma steeled himself because he had a long-term plan. Once again he was treading water, determined to survive.

Yet, Xiao Hu wasn't ready to drop it all and come back to the hut. In her own eyes she was a fallen woman, cut off from a past reality when she dreamed of a happy future. She had made a pact with evil forces. Her son's life for hers. She had convinced herself so strongly of the irreversibility of her decision that the presence of Ma at the club made no sense other than as punishment or revenge. Every time she passed him he whispered: "Come home Xiao Hu. We are waiting for you."

"Darwin wants to show you the new words he has learned to write."

"Darwin has a new kung fu move he wants to demonstrate."

"Last night I dreamed of treading water."

She hardly believed he was real, and the truth was that her whole world was wrapped in a dreamlike blanket because she remained constantly high, regularly chasing the dragon between jobs. If she had been falling and stumbling or slumped in a drug-induced slumber she would have been kicked out of the place. The Duchess is not for losers. But Xiao Hu had a strong constitution, her professional conversation remained adequate and charming enough, even if inside she was a smouldering wreck.

With time, Ma's presence became more real, and memories would flood back. It then became more difficult to control her emotions, so she upped her heroin dose to push him back out of her world. Sometimes she would linger near Ma and listen to his whisperings. Despite her best efforts, he was beginning to break her down. The old self that she had killed off, buried, grieved for, was pulling on her, almost strangling her like the malicious spirit of the dead. Life was much easier without Ma at the Duchess and she hated him for this punishment.

Then the pull would overwhelm again. Occasionally she would get a vision of a future outside of hell. "We are going to the beach tomorrow Xiao Hu. We'll have a picnic. I've bought you swimwear." Ma would say and she would see the scene so clearly she could taste the salt in the sea breeze. She was swimming in the cool water, Darwin paddling by the shore, Ma lying on the sand, still handsome – her husband. It was as if they had been there yesterday, it was so clear. And she would then ache with a terrible longing, convinced that it could only ever be a dream, even though gradually those dream sequences became longer and the possibilities slowly became more real.

The truth was that there was a barrier so evil, dominating and crushing that it seemed impossible for any of those dreams to become real. Xiao Hu was in debt to the Catfish and the longer she stayed there the larger the debt became. The Catfish paid-up in cash every week for work done by the girls in the club. It wasn't a bad rate compared to other hotels and bars that she could have worked at. There was a set retainer to keep the select girls in house, and on top of that they were paid for each client serviced. She used this cash for modest daily needs, including rented space in a crowded Wanchai house that she shared with 12 other girls, two of whom had small children. What she didn't need she handed over to her mother at their secret monthly meetings. She would have had enough but the problem was the heroin. The Chiu Chau boys at the Erection had a system where all the heroin the girls took was cashless, with each purchase marked in a special ledger. The debt was payable when a girl wanted to leave and she couldn't leave until she had paid it all. It was a very effective way of achieving enslavement. Not all the girls were hooked but there was a strong culture for it at the Duchess so a good third of them were on it, as were a similar proportion of the male staff.

Ma Xun had worked out for himself how the system functioned and he sneaked a peek at the ledger one night – at great risk – to find out how much Xiao Hu owed. What he saw almost plunged him into despair. She was more than two-and-a-half thousand dollars in debt and he couldn't ever imagine how he would find money like that. He was treading water again, not knowing how to save his family.

On one of the quieter nights Conrad, the head barman, asked Ma why he hadn't been initiated. Ma said he didn't come from Triad stock. His family were artisans, blacksmiths. They had no interest in the underworld. Conrad laughed and said: "Look at this place, it's all underworld. This place was founded on the stuff that we do best, drugs and violence. If you want to survive here you need to be with a firm. Look at Godber and Wetherby, they are top-ranking enforcers of the biggest Triad in Hong Kong – the Imperial police. They are the most profitable, most efficient firm here. That's why we Chiu Chau boys respect them and like working with them."

"I know some police can be corrupt, but they're mainly here to keep order aren't they?" Ma offered without too much conviction.

"Keep order? Are you blind? Order only increases efficiency. The police regulate the traffic and they skim a hundred dollars from every driver that doesn't want to pay a four-hundred dollar fine. They pocket five-hundred dollars from every brothel, and the odd ten dollars from a street hooker. They take four-hundred dollars from a gambling den plus a hundred each from every punter there. A hawker without a license is worth twenty on each encounter and a motorbike with a broken light is another fifty. Order is great profit for the Queen's own Triads.

There are policemen in this club who can't find their shoes in the morning because the floor of their bedroom is covered in bank notes. That fat pig over there, Sergeant Fotherington, sent his wife and her sister on a world cruise for a year just so that he could have some peace. Do you think a police salary paid for that? No it didn't. It was Grandma

Ping who sells home-brew rice wine, and uncle Chu with his brain-damaged son who runs the gambling den behind Barber Todd's. Over there is Wang-bang-thank-you-ma'am-Yu, one of the highest-ranking Chinese police in the force. He owns two mansions in Taiwan. How did he pay for that? The one-legged mute who stands around the waterfront catching coolies for a swifty down the alley, she's a contributor at ten dollars a sighting.

These boys have more in common with us than you would ever imagine. And just like us they create myths and legends about their power and their right to feed off the weak. We have our old boys who come to believe the stories about the righteous mission to protect society and overthrow foreign overlords. They forget what brought them into the firm in the first place, and that is the same for every one of us. It's the fear of being left out in the cold, the thrill of being a gang member, and the power of earning good cash.

The old bosses forget those truths. Instead they peddle the hocus-pocus about ancestors and tradition. They organise lion dances and the festivals. Most importantly they organise the funerals, never forgetting of course to skim tax at every stage. People like me, we do the real work. We steal from the weak, sell drugs, service the highest bidder and we pocket what we can and send up the rest to the keepers of the myth, that's their pension.

It's the same with the Queen's Police. The boys we see are still more or less earning their keep. They collect their own bribes, use their own muscle to intimidate a hawker, recruit their own hookers to arrange a regular stipend. In effect they are our colleagues. But they also have their bosses. They are egged-on and supported by old high-priests who spin the myth of empire, destiny, and most of all, racial superiority. Everything they do here is underwritten by their own, and their masters' faith in racial superiority. We make up stories about clans, they have the Nation. How very much like us they are, though there is of course the difference in scale. We are sharks alright, maybe bull sharks, in which case the Turtles are tiger sharks. But the Queens own? I tell you they are the great whites, by far the most dangerous.

"You know, there is a world outside of all this," Ma suggested.

"Ha ha, you are a funny lad. Your life is hell. You toil for a construction Triad during the day, then you work here at night for the Queen's own Triads and your Catfish relatives, just to make ends meet so that your son can do the same when he has a son. You are a complete slave. You need to get real and join a firm. You need to accept reality."

"I'm not convinced that your world is reality Conrad."

"You have to accept human nature Ma. We are predators, it's inevitable that we hunt, or we're hunted."

"Technically we are highly-adaptive omnivores, which means we have options."

"What the heck are you talking about?"

"Have you ever heard of the ichneumon wasp?"

"The what?" Conrad spluttered, slightly annoyed to have his speech tripped up by a threateningly baffling question.

"It's a parasite. One of the two-thirds of animals that can't survive without exploiting other creatures."

"What's that got to do with anything?"

"Well my dad knew everything about animals and plants around our village. He was an expert. He used to say to me that ichneumon wasps were evil because they had no choice, but humans can choose whether to be parasitical or something they can be more proud of. There was nothing inevitable about how we chose to live our lives, he told me."

"What's so evil about these wasps then?"

"It's how they reproduce. When they lay their eggs they look for a nice fat caterpillar. Once they spot a suitable one, the female wasp pierces its side and pumps tiny eggs into its body. The eggs grow inside of the host and once they hatch, the newly-born wasp lava eat their way through the caterpillar's body. You would think that the host would just die, but here's the truly evil part of the ichneumon. They are genetically programmed to eat the victim from the inside out in such a way as to keep it alive for as long as possible. They instinctively keep vital organs intact until the last moments, so that their feed remains alive and fresh."

"There you are. This is nature Ma, you have to accept it."

"No, Conrad. The point is that this is nature for one species of insect that cannot choose. It is genetically hard-wired to exist as a truly abominable parasite. We're not."

"Oh come on. Don't tell me that we are hard-wired to live like bunny rabbits."

"No, not at all. Humans are adaptable. Opportunists for sure, but our hands, teeth and brains give us many options for choosing our place in the ecosystem. For us, all sorts of survival strategies are on offer. We can be the biggest predators on the planet, but we can also be the most cooperative species on Earth. We can live like parasitic ichneumon wasps if we want, but we can also choose other ways. We do have a choice."

"Good luck to you Ma on that. But seriously, in the meantime, until you find a non-evil crew to cooperate with, come and join us, the Catfish, we'll help you get on."

"Thanks Conrad, but it's not for me. Besides, I know you won't recruit a man of my age," Ma said – well into his late twenties.

"Yes, it's a pity, but I think it is too late for you," he thoughtfully concluded, looking genuinely sad about it.

Sham Shui Po was a battleground. Smoke rose from fire-gutted shops. Nathan Road was strewn with rocks, broken glass, scrap metal, and burning tires. Simon and Jagan stood in the front-line with helmets on, clutching batons and holding up shields. There were about 200 police in that line. Other lines dotted the smouldering neighbourhood, apparently in some strategic order, but none knew what the strategy was. Simon's eyes stung from the last round of tear-gas that had been fired at the rioters. It seemed like a good idea at the time but the officer who gave the order hadn't checked the wind direction. The acrid gas came straight back to them to make the police splutter and choke while the rioters first laughed and then charged with a roar. Simon estimated that were about a thousand fighting men, armed, enraged and charging, from behind a raining barrage of improvised missiles and Molotov cocktails. A colleague to his immediate right was hit by a screw driver that pierced his throat. He was carried off as blood spurted, his face ashen-white.

A gun-mounted army jeep screeched behind them and started firing over the heads of the front-line. The crowd panicked and retreated, some sprinting straight back down Nathan Road, others melting into side streets. Simon counted four bodies on the road. Two were struggling to get up, the other two were motionless, they looked like teenage boys. Slowly the retreaters regrouped, roaring with anger. When two or three came forward to help the fallen, the army jeep let off another round, downing one of the helpers and pushing the others back.

"We need to help the injured," Jagan said to the officer who had charge of their section. His real name was Robert Sharply, but the Geordie sergeant was better known as Mad Bob. That was how he normally introduced himself.

"Fuck 'em," he screamed. "Hold your fucking position wog, or you'll be up for fucking treason. I'll fucking shoot you me sen. Any other fucker wanna fuck with Mad Bob?"

There were skirmishes in all the side streets, not just attacks on the police, but full battles between Triads. There was a whole-scale re-assortment taking place of the power structures that regulated Hong Kong's streets, though in truth no-one really knew what was going on. The official version was that someone had torn down pro-Nationalist posters at a housing estate and this had triggered a series of vicious anti-Communist attacks, until it escalated to the complete breakdown of law and order in a three-square-mile area of Kowloon.

There was a commotion at the other end. It looked like a car was trying to push through the angry crowd. Soon it was completely stuck and the mob were rocking it from side to side. There was a sudden flash and it was engulfed in flames, as the panicked crowd pushed back from the danger. A door opened and a man struggled out, his hair and clothes on fire as he crumpled to the ground. Mad Bob raised the order to charge and the armed jeep roared into action, spluttering bullets from its turret. The mob scattered, leaving the burning car, and when Simon reached it he saw a body in the back, an unrecognisable face that had been burned off to reveal a charred jaw bone. They said later that she was the wife of the Norwegian consul.

Bullets were flying from alleyways along with broken bricks and beer bottles. Smoke from burning buildings engulfed the crowds and blanketed all in confusion. At one narrow electrical-repair workshop there was incongruous music blaring out from a powerful gramophone player. The shop on one side of it was on fire. Simon and Jagan both recognised *Great Balls of Fire* by Jerry Lee Lewis as they walked past the electrical shop in their full riot gear. It was full of people dressed like Rockers they had seen in a magazine, except these were Chinese. They were oblivious to the riot that surrounded them, gyrating with cigarettes and beer bottles in hand, combing their absurdly large quiffs.

In the smoke and confusion Simon lost Jagan and couldn't work out which direction he was supposed to move in or what the objectives were. He crouched behind a wall as lethal ammunition scorched past in all directions.

"Jagan! Where the hell are you?" he shouted out into the haze.

"Is that you, Simon?" a familiar voice called back from the other side of the wall. It wasn't Jagan.

"Yeah. Is that Danny?" he said, puzzled.

"It is. What are you doing here?" he asked.

"My job, Danny. What the hell are you doing? I thought you were shark fishing in the Philippines."

"Oh yeah, don't tell Maria you found me here. I'm doing my job, I suppose."

A bullet ricocheted off the top of the wall they were crouched either side of.

"Danny! You need to get the hell out of here. The police and the army are shooting live ammunition. This isn't a game."

"You too Simon, the Triads are shooting too."

"Go while you can."

"I know Simon, but I can't leave my brothers."

"Who are your brothers?"

"The Mongoose."

"The Mongoose are losers, Danny. They were lions against the Japanese, but that war is over. How the hell are the Mongoose mixed up in this?"

An orange ball of fire flashed into existence yards away from Simon and a split second later there was a boom as shards of glass splintered all around, and a sickening stench of scorched petroleum filled the air.

"Simon! Are you OK?" Danny shouted.

"Yeah, yeah, a bit scratched and possibly deaf for life, but I just heard you, so maybe not. You?"

"Yup, I'm okay. This isn't a good place to be," Danny said as another bullet ricocheted off the top of the wall.

"Stay put for now. It will all calm down," Simon said.

"Three Eyes called us in. He told us to lay into any Catfish we see."

"Who the hell is Three Eyes?"

"He's a Green Gang agent. We do the odd job for him." Danny said, surprising himself with how his tongue seemed loosened by the lethal chaos they were both trapped in. Then after a pause he added: "We owed him one after another job had gone wrong…"

"Why the hell are the Mongoose working for Greens?"

"I don't know Simon. It's Salty, he says the Mongoose have had it if we don't get more ambitious."

"Do you even know who the Greens are?"

"Yeah, yeah. They slaughtered Commies for Chiang Kai-shek. We've got a lot of respect for them."

"When?"

"When what?"

"When did they slaughter Commies for Chiang?"

"I dunno. A couple of years ago, I guess."

"Twenty-nine years ago Danny. Long before you were born."

"Really?"

"Yeah. And now they make a living by peddling heroin to fourteen-year-old girls like Madge."

Danny was silent, looking up at the sky where about fifty kites were wheeling over Sham Shui Po.

"They think there's a bush fire," he said.

"Who do?"

"The kites."

"Oh yeah. I can see them too. There's loads of them, watching us."

"Watching for rodents smoked out by the blaze."

"Seriously Danny, you need to get out before something tragic happens."

"Three Eyes said the Catfish had declared war on them in Wanchai, so the Greens are fighting back."

"You're on the wrong side Danny. I'll let you in on a secret. The Queen's own have pulled the plug on the Greens. They are on their way out."

Suddenly everything lit up and here was a huge explosion. Bricks and concrete chunks were dropping from the sky all around.

"Danny! Where are you?"

"I'm here. I'm OK. You?"

"Yeah fine. I've got to retreat. Mad Bob the commander is screaming blue murder."

"Me too. Three Eyes is yelling us back."

"Go, Danny."

"Simon, that man who died, he wasn't a spy you know."

"I didn't think so."

"He was just a barman at some pub in Wanchai called the Erection."

There was a burst of automatic gunfire. Chips of brick fell from the wall around Simon.

"Danny! Go!"

"Yeah. Look, it was an accident. The Dagger, he was drunk, he had no idea what he was doing."

"What did he do?"

A boom up above, and more machine gun fire.

"I've got to go. Three eyes is threatening to shoot us if we don't retreat."

"Same here with Mad Bob. Go! Promise me, for Maria!"

"You too. Stay clear of the Molotovs. For Maria."

For two more days Sham Shui Po smouldered. Bullets flew, violence flared. Camps were set up, then smashed and factions regrouped. Triads paid back old debts, took chunks out of each other. Snuffed out old rivals. The Greens were splintered by a Catfish alliance that had the tactical support of rogue police units. Three Eyes came to understand that their hold on Hong Kong had received a fatal blow, even if remnants of the group would survive for years in shady pockets of the territory. He realised then that their alliance with American agents was worthless and he started plotting his final deal with Scroggins.

The Mongoose were caught unawares after Three Eyes disappeared. They were ambushed by two dozen Catfish-affiliated Kowloon Triads, and a brawl ensued in which Danny was cut on the shoulder with a meat cleaver. They may have all been killed if a machine-gun-mounted army jeep hadn't turned down the street they were in, immediately firing off a round of bullets. The brawlers all scattered, leaving one body slumped in the street.

"Get up, Dagger!" Salty Pang screamed, but he was lifeless. The Mongoose regrouped and hid in a side alley where they could see the Dagger bleeding to death, while the jeep remained on guard at the top of the street. Pang led Simon, Spike and Red back into the middle of the street to pluck up the Dagger. The army shooter swivelled his turret and took aim at them, but didn't pull the trigger. The Dagger was already dead.

Fifty-nine people were killed during the Kowloon riots of 1956, hundreds were injured and whole neighbourhoods were trashed. The Mongoose headed back towards Tai O on a fishing boat, carrying the body of the Dagger in a makeshift coffin, their alliance with the Greens shattered. Three Eyes wasn't to be seen again.

9

SEVEN LONELY DAYS

Simon, Jagan and Patrick Leung were among a group of off-duty police drinking at a Sheung Wan dai pai dong after reinforcements were stood down in Kowloon. They were all relieved that it was over, and that the situation hadn't escalated further. For many of them too young to have fought in the war it was the most dangerous job of their policing career. Now it was over, they were all letting off steam. As the drink flowed, the atmosphere became more festive.

In that dai pai dong it was a mixed group of mostly middle-ranking officers, ranging from Simon as deputy superintendent, through Indian sergeants and Chinese corporals. Pent-up tensions of the past few days were dissolved by the fact that the danger had passed, and by the booze. A natural sense of camaraderie welled up and bonded the group of a dozen. Some between them were normally unfriendly or even hostile, but on this night animosity melted and they were a united band. They were proud of what they had been through, even though they didn't understand the forces at work that caused the violence to erupt.

"It was basically a Triad war, the settling of old scores," said one.

"Not at all. It was fundamentally an ideological struggle," another insisted.

"Ideological? That's utter garbage. It was totally cynical, all manipulated by Mao to consolidate his power in Beijing."

"Nothing of the sort. A CIA plot to undermine Britain's control over Hong Kong."

"Don't be so naive. It was orchestrated by a secret cabal of retired army officers who harbour fascist sympathies. Their aim is to impose martial law in perpetuity."

"Nah. Trade union power struggle. Simple as that."

There were as many theories as there were men drinking. More if you kept in mind the tendency for each theorist to invent a new one whenever inspiration struck.

The postmortem was hitting its liveliest best when Wetherby stumbled across the dai pai dong that spilled onto the pavement. He was with Mad Bob, Dickie Anderson – one of Wetherby's bland Cambridge sidekicks – and Arthur Miller, a surprisingly self-effacing and open-minded old Etonian, and good friend of Simon's from his Central days. They were moving between pubs, and as hammered as the dai pai dong gang.

"Boys! What are you all doing at this bloody tip?" Wetherby exclaimed. Despite the rudeness of the comment and its insulting connotations, this was in fact Wetherby at his tipsy, amenable best.

There were chants of "Drink! drink! drink!" from the sitters as the two groups greeted each other with handshakes, slaps and uncharacteristic bear-hugs. Jagan had not forgotten the racist threats Mad Bob had made to him a few days earlier, but Mad Bob didn't have a clue which smiley wog he was slapping on the back. Places were set for the newcomers as fresh glasses were filled from the countless bottles strewn across the table. They all downed one and Wetherby immediately stood up shouting: "My round!" waving a wad of cash at the owner who eagerly fetched another 10 bottles of beer.

Even Simon greeted Wetherby with a warmth he had never imagined he could have mustered. For one moment the two of them shook hands and all the rivalry, resentment and contempt was absent. There was a genuine meeting of two individuals who held each other at a respectful distance with a mutual acceptance. They would never understand each other, but for that moment there was respect. Neither of them dwelt on it, and it lasted precisely one moment. No more.

More familiar was Simon's greeting of his old friend who had been out commanding the police post at Tai Po for as long as Simon had been in Tai O.

"King Arthur! How's the trekking in Tai Po?" Simon asked, remembering their hikes all over Hong Kong Island.

"Not bad, not bad, my old friend. Tai Mo Shan is a fantastic climb. And how's the hunt in Tai O?"

"More exciting than you'd imagine. We were on the trail of a tiger last week!"

"Oh nonsense!" Wetherby piped up, triggering an hour of rowdy arguments about the existence of tigers in Hong Kong.

Eventually Wetherby enforced everyone's attention with chopstick taps on a bowl, and in an uncharacteristic and almost certainly miscalculated move, invited the whole company to the Duchess as his guests. Bland Dickie immediately looked uncomfortable and started to mutter some protest about the unsuitability of that idea, but no-one was listening to him. Mad Bob, who had been boasting to an increasingly uncomfortable subgroup of Chinese officers about the dozen or so rioters he claimed to have shot himself, roared with laughter at Wetherby's suggestion, "Godber would fucking skin you alive, man!"

Wetherby, unfazed and steaming drunk by now, claimed it would be fine. The grown-ups were on a special invite to the Governor's residence that night to celebrate the victory of law and order over anarchy.

Arthur tutted and raised his eyebrows: "Oh God, that bloody place," he said, more with resigned acceptance of the inevitable than with any intent to oppose the move. He wasn't a member but had been there on invitation a couple of times. He wasn't particularly impressed with the place but he had never noticed anything particularly egregious. It was all a bit like an Etonian house, he had thought on previous visits.

Simon had heard about it of course, but he had never been invited so he was curious.

"Shall we?" Arthur said to Simon and Jagan.

"Why not?" they both shrugged.

Six of the Chinese officers declined the offer with good-humoured slaps and additional toasts after which Wetherby's foursome, plus Simon, Jagan, Patrick, two other Sikh officers Vikram and Naresh and two young, very drunk, Chinese officers piled into taxis.

The inside of the Duchess was mayhem. Though the place was not exclusively a police club, this night was very much a police night. It was packed with drunk officers shouting, slapping, downing drinks and chanting.

"We are the Queen's! We are the Queen's! We are the Queen's! Come on, come on, come on boys. We are the Queen's!"

"Gosh, that's inventive," Arthur said to Simon in a familiar tone that Simon used to call "maximus sarcasticus" in their hiking days.

The truth was that Simon, Jagan, Patrick, Vikram and Naresh were secretly intimidated on arrival. This looked like the kind of crowd that could suddenly turn their attentions on them and lynch them. But it helped that they had arrived already well on the way to inebriation, and the first couple of whiskey shots in the club helped to further ease the transition. They weren't the only non-Anglos there, but the small group of other Chinese and Sikh officers already there were obviously comfortably Anglicised and rugby-tested. All except Johnny Tse, who was the life and soul of the party but remained very much the Chiu Chau boy.

Wetherby was grand with his generosity, lapping up an imagined kudos he was earning by showing his powerful connections. His guests thought he was a boor but they didn't mind enjoying the drink and the exclusive experience.

A group of girls sat chatting, nursing their drinks in the corner, laughing at the antics of Johnny Boy who was demonstrating kung fu moves on a table to the chants of English captains. One of the girls caught Simon's attention. She was looking at him but turned away as soon as he caught her eye. He wondered what her story was, but remembered Maria with a warm drunken glow, and expected he would never know that pretty girl's story. Then he saw Scroggins at another table nursing a whiskey, talking to Harvestman who was laughing constantly.

"What the fuck is so funny all the time?" Simon wondered into his pint, swirling the beer into a whirlpool. Then he wondered why Scroggins was there.

There was some pasty-skinned flabby-bodied gweilo standing on a table now, showing his bare arse and chanting "We are the Queen's! We are the Queen's!"

"Remember him?" Simon nudged Jagan.

"Eh? Never seen this hairy arsehole before," Jagan said, breaking off from the chant he was punching out.

"No, over there. Opposite side."

"Harvestman? Yeah total prick," he said.

"No, the other one."

"I dunno," he said, curious now and staggering towards him.

"What you doing?" Simon asked, a bit alarmed.

"Gonna order a whiskey at the bar, and I'm gonna listen to what he's talking about and see if I can remember who the fuck he is. OK?"

"Do what you like," Simon said.

A few minutes later he returned with a round of whiskeys.

"Wasn't he that one that was at Jackson's?"

"I think so. What's he doing here?"

"Just told Harvestman he's waiting for Godber. He's obviously a member, why shouldn't he be here?"

"Suppose so. Anyway," he said, changing the subject. "Why didn't the other Chinese boys come along? That wasn't very friendly of them."

"They said they wouldn't be welcomed here."

Simon looked at the full-moon party going on across the room and saw the two Chinese youngsters that did come with them dancing on the table with the pasty-bottomed one, and taking it in turns to slap his arse, to the hilarity of the braying crowd.

"They seem to be doing alright," he said.

"The others said the only Chinese police that came to the Erection were the boys with good contacts with Johnny Tse and the Chiu Chau brotherhood."

"The Erection? What the hell kind of name is that?"

"It's what all the Chinese boys call this place."

Simon's drink-addled brain fumbled in the dark to remember when he had heard that name. Then the voice of Danny Chu came to mind: "He was a barman at the Erection."

"Ma Xun used to work here," he said to Jagan, who looked back at him through a hazy fog of uncertainty. He was just beginning to remember who Ma Xun was, when Scroggins came over with a satchel under one arm and three whiskeys in his hands, all smooth and friendly.

"Welcome to Wanchai," he said, sliding into an empty seat without spilling a drop, his bag awkwardly landing near Jagan's feet.

"Thank you Mr Scroggins, what a surprise," Simon said.

"Oh I'm quite a regular here. Helps to keep up contacts for a commercial man like myself."

"Indeed," Simon said, drunk and not really knowing what else to say.

"Did you know the barman here?" he heard himself asking without a plan.

"Oh, you mean the man who died?" Scroggins said without a hitch.

"Yeah, the one that was killed."

"Yes, of course I knew him, as far as you ever know a barman at your regular."

"They said he was a spy."

"You never know who is these days."

"This would be a tough place for a spy to operate," Jagan suggested, looking around at the buffoonery surrounding them.

"Tedious, I'd imagine," Scroggins said.

The room was spinning a bit. Simon was not concentrating too well. He found his gaze drifting easily towards Xiao Hu.

"You like the Little Tiger do you?" Scroggins asked.

"Little tiger?"

"Yes, Xiao Hu."

"Ma said he only went to fetch a tiger."

Scroggins tensed up, surprised that Ma had said anything.

"What else did Ma say?"

"Don't believe their lies."

"Don't believe whose lies?"

"Theirs," Simon said, giggling a bit and shrugging his shoulders.

"That's it?"

"That's it. Then he was dead."

Simon remembered something. "Your friend over there wrote a pack of lies about the killing. Said the dead man was Chen Guanming." Harvestman was talking to Wetherby at this point, clearly finding his conversation hilarious too.

"He works for the British press, they have no scruples," Scroggins dismissed.

A waiter whispered in Wetherby's ear. He suddenly crossed the room and hissed: "Fuck. Get out. Godber and Fotherington are coming up the stairwell, must have got bored of the Governor's place."

Simon was annoyed. "For God's sake, I thought we were your guests."

"You were, now you're not. There's a back way out. Follow the waiter."

As they shuffled past the girls' table Simon looked at Xiao Hu and asked: "Where's Ma?"

She looked confused, glazed over, then shook her head: "I don't, I don't know." She looked utterly lost.

"Get lost, creep," Queen Bet said.

It had all started several weeks earlier. Max Godber and Fotherington were discussing economics. "Who's dealing the most heroin in Wanchai?" Godber asked.

"It's still the Green Gang. We're getting the best squeeze from them."

"How come the Catfish haven't taken over?"

"Well they're not a pushover. The Greens still have the technological edge. Most of the heroin labs are run by pupils of the one-armed master from Shanghai. In the balance, the chemists that learn from him tend to be loyal to the Greens, though people in the heroin business are not so well known for the strength of their loyalty of course. The product from the one-armed master, branded 'Green Turtle Smack', is still considered the best stuff in Hong Kong, which by implication is probably the best in the world."

Godber looked around to check if any nosy parker was listening, composed himself, then launched the most ambitious scheme of his career to date.

"Fotherington, we have access to a regular supply of raw opium. It's been a slow and patient campaign on my part, but I've finally got a chap I can trust at customs who says it's easy to diddle the books to offload confiscated contraband. They're all at it anyway but none have their own chemists to turn it into heroin for them, the stuff that matters. They're just earning peanuts for their risk. My plan is to use that to build up our own supply chain of branded, high quality smack, and of course, that means Green Turtle Smack."

Fotherington giggled.

"My God, you're serious aren't you?"

"Listen Fotherington, it's ridiculous that all we make from H is pocket money."

Godber was unusually frank because they had just imbibed a rare line of cocaine – a drug considered an unfashionable relic of the 1930s in polite society, but loved by a small group of dedicated hedonists. It was fresh from a cargo ship that had crossed the sea from Panama.

"We need to get deeper into the heroin business or we'll never make any real money. After all, we control the streets of Wanchai right? We're the ones providing a nice stable society where people can trade and make money, but the ones reaping all the profits are a bunch of thugs from Shanghai, and the Catfish. How can that be right? So, fine, the Chiu Chau are our partners, but it's time to take over the Green Gang operations. It's time there was some justice around here."

Fotherington had also just imbibed a line of the exotic stuff and he was rather euphoric.

"I say Godber, you're a positive genius. How shall we take over the Turtles? Kill them all?" he laughed like a maniac.

"No that would be insanely risky. We use the Catfish. We give them the green light to drive out the Turtles. At the same time we raid their weakened infrastructure, take control of the labs and sell Green Turtle Smack to Catfish." Godber felt his plans landing fully-formed and crystal clear from his brain to his tongue, the cocaine was helping him work it all out.

"Steady on, old boy. The Greens, as you know, have got the protection of the Cousins. They won't be a pushover. If they had been they would never have gained the foothold they had."

"Yes and I would wager that Green Turtle heroin tax is finding its way into the pockets of many a Cousin. But the CIA mavericks dealing in the heroin economy can never reveal that of course, especially to their bosses. That's where that idiot Wetherby's even stupider sidekick Harvestman comes in handy. We help him prepare a story for the Times that exposes Green Gang-CIA collusion. Something that would shock the bible-bashing elders at Langley off their rocking chairs. The story is held, waiting for 'fact checking' and we tell the boys on the ground that if there's any intervention in a strictly local power struggle, the world, and their bosses, will likely hear about their cosy relationship with some of China's most ruthless murderers."

"Wow. Are you effectively declaring war on the Cousins here in Wanchai?"

"No, stupid. The Catfish are moving in on the Greens. It's a silly local matter that has nothing to do with the broader wellbeing of the colony."

"This is insane, Godber. We will never get away with it. There would be a bounty on our heads."

"Your problem is that you're too scared of the Cousins. Trust me, they are not infallible. They are powerful, and yes, you could say they are brutal, but they have their blind spots and they don't work as a coherent entity. Look at their whole operation here. A hundred and fifteen staff members in the biggest US consulate in the world and of them at least a hundred are spies on full pay, and they still haven't worked out that they are backing the wrong horse in China! I mean, for God's sake, who in their right mind thinks that Chiang Kai-shek is going to take back China?

"How does that happen? I'll tell you how it happens. It happens because the Cousins are blinded by their own self-belief. These boys pride themselves in the idea that they are 'realists' but they are so far up their own arses that they can't see that the rest of the world see them as fanatics. So the automatons on the front-lines go around trying to fit the world into the fucked-up vision held by their doolally bosses back home. That translates, in the real world, into vicious goons on the ground protecting Green Gang assassins, giving them cash, maps, champagne, and plenty of smack, all in the name of making the delusions of their elders a reality. If the bosses found out the kind of dirty tricks their prodigies were up to in the field, they would call them back, pretending to be outraged that their own peaceful vision of the world was interpreted by such misguided gung-ho brutality. The Cousins, in summary, are a schizophrenic entity. And that's proof enough to know that they are not infallible."

"You're mad. And how are we going to get the Catfish to bite?"

"Easy. Their pride would not let them turn down the opportunity. They're as greedy as we are, and the market demands that someone provides the service that the Greens are providing now."

"How are we going to hold on to our newly gained position in the supply chain? Surely the Catfish would want to take over the labs for themselves. What's the point of only taking over the retail if the Greens are going to be knocked out?"

"Fotherington. You're forgetting something. We are the police. Our job is to keep order. Any rotten Chiu Chau found taking part in Triad activities, especially near Green Turtle heroin labs will be arrested and possibly deported into the arms of Communist authorities. Her Majesty's Police will not tolerate illegal activities."

This was almost too much for them as they fell about in their armchairs, cackling like maniacs.

"We need recruits," Godber went on. "We'll need Wang-bang-thank-you-ma'am-Yu on board to organise raids on the Green Gang labs. He'll need to get a team together that thinks it's on an official top-secret mission, and then he has to scrub the record clean so that it never happened. We'll give that lot a generous one-off payment and make sure they have no inkling of the big picture. Johnny Boy Tse is going to be indispensable for coordination with the Catfish, so he'll need to be kept on a retainer. We'll need Wetherby too."

Fotherington raised his eyebrows, already nervous about the number involved.

Godber explained.

"The good thing about Wetherby is that he desperately wants to play with the grown-ups. Like a well-trained police dog he offers total loyalty with his tongue hanging out."

"What do we need him for?"

"Foreman, Fotherington. Johnny Boy is too unpredictable to leave in charge of operations. There's the danger that he would try to take over the scheme for himself. He's mad enough to think about it. So Wetherby is our representative, and we have no contact with anyone else. You understand Fotherington that we are embarking on a venture at a much higher risk than routine tax collection? The difference this time is that instead of scraping up the usual chicken feed, we reap decent returns as befitting buccaneers who sacrifice themselves to tropical hellholes for the sake of profit."

"Most audacious, Godber. I congratulate you."

"One more thing, Fotherington. We need a delivery boy who takes the O from the waste disposal unit, delivers it to the labs, picks up the H, delivers to Chiu Chau retailers, and most importantly, collects the cash."

"A crucial role, taken at great risk, yet needs to be trusted."

"Quite. I have a person in mind. I have been watching him closely for the past few weeks."

"Who the devil is it? Not that scoundrel Barclay Harvestman I hope."

"Not that bloody fool. It's the barman here. He's been working here for the past six weeks. The chap over there. Ma's his name."

"The quiet one? Can't say I've taken much notice of him, I'm afraid."

"Exactly. He's an innocuous bugger. I've been watching him. He's not a Brother, I checked with Johnny Boy. He's competent and he's sharp as hell, you can tell by the way he works the bar. And he's got a secret and that's how we'll get him."

"What secret?"

"I'm not sure. Something to do with one of our star performers, the Little Tiger. He's obsessed with her. His eyes follow her every move. Every time she goes off to service one of the boys he looks as if he's going to shoot himself in the head."

Fotherington laughed out loud at this.

"But why would Catfish buy from our man? They've got their own suppliers."

"Two reasons. One is that it's a supplier's market. I'm telling you, this drug is a businessman's dream. The more the chemists produce, the more the demand grows. It's truly wondrous. If the Catfish expand their retail, they'll need more producers. They'll have to buy what they can get.

"The second reason will be contractual. When Johnny puts this offer on the Catfish table they will be dripping with gratitude. Everyone knows that the Turtles are history. Their nasty reputation is mostly rooted in their massacre of Commies in 1927. What an investment that was! They've reaped nearly 30 years of profits from that brilliant move. Of course many of them were caught, tortured and killed by the Commies later, but the survivors exported the brand to Hong Kong and dined off it for a good few years. They thought they would be ruling this place within a few years but they underestimated the local boys, and of course their Catfish rivals.

"Now their operations are scattered around the territory and other Triads are taking bites out of them whenever possible. While the Greens fragmented, the Chiu Chau, on the other hand, made some very sensible moves. Not only did they ally themselves with us operationally, but they sent new recruits to join the Queen's own! Now the Greens hold on to operations in Wanchai, as one of their last remaining retail strongholds. The Catfish have lusted over the Green's share here for years. The only reason they haven't kicked the Greens out of the district is because of Thomas-Littleton's befuddled, hand-me-down doctrine that it's better to have rivals counter-balancing each other here.

"'We British rule the world by keeping the brown people fighting each other,' the daft old fool loves to say. I'm now saying: 'Sod that'. We kick the old cutthroats out and deal one-on-one with the trusty Catfish. They'll be bloody grateful for the opportunity, and in return for the favour we're giving them, we tell them that every Green Gang business that they take over will be supplied by us and us only. If they don't like that there's no deal."

"I'm beginning to get a picture of where I'm going to come in on this."

"That's right Fotherington, you're the old master here. I'm recruiting you to deal with Thomas-Littleton. You have to make him reverse his divide and rule policy for Wanchai and you must do that while making the idiot believe it was his own idea in the first place. You also need to make sure he has no idea bout this scheme. We'll be finished if that nincompoop gets involved. Not only would he be unscrupulously greedy, he won't be able to handle it. He'll get us caught and we'll all hang, because taxing drug pedlars is one thing, while actually supplying heroin to dealers is a new low even for the Queen's own."

"Well of course it has its precedents. The British government only gave up its lucrative opium monopoly 10 years ago, thanks to the badgering of the do-gooder bible-thumping Americans."

"Those interfering bastards with their anti-opium crusades are the cause for all this heroin. There are still old duffers here who can't go half a day without one of those 'anti-opium' pills, and they don't realise that they are heroin addicts."

"I can see what's needed here Godber. I'll bring the boss in for a night of debauchery next week. Might help to make sure the top girls are working on that night."

"A bit of O might also help relax the mood, I'd say."

"Ah yes, he'll like a little treat like that, we'll have some on standby in case it's needed to tip the balance."

"Johnny Tse should be coming later tonight. I'll brief him, he's going to love it. He'll be the only other chap who'll know the role Ma's going to play, and he needs to guarantee protection for Ma from the more aggressive Chiu Chau foot soldiers. Ma will become police property and the Catfish will not harm a hair on his head. After briefing Tse I will deal with Wetherby. Ma hands the cash to Tse, Tse takes his cut, hands it to Wetherby. Wetherby deposits it in the account of a newly created drug rehabilitation charity. I pat him on the head and give him a biscuit. We get rich."

Two nights later Fotherington called Ma over and asked him to check a side booth where he thought he had left a box of cigars. Ma strode across, cursing the lazy fat bastard, slightly confused at the unusual request. He walked into the booth to find his wife buttoning up her shirt and Godber doing up his belt, cigar in his mouth. Ma turned straight around and tried to step out but Godber had his wrist.

"Hold it, son."

Murder was the thing on Ma's mind. But his brain told him that if he took any steps in that direction he would be crushed and ground into the dust of Hong Kong. All trace of him would disappear. By simply being in this colony Ma was already lying on the ground with a boot stamped on his face. He just didn't know if it would be for ever.

Godber also knew about that boot as he guided Ma back into the booth. It was understanding the boot that gave Godber the supreme confidence of treating Ma as his own property – as his slave. Xiao Hu quickly escaped, thinking only of the logistics of going into another booth, taking out the powder from her pouch, opening up a neatly folded piece of foil, rolling up a ten dollar bill, crumbling the powder, and lighting a match below the foil. She would then watch the heroin bubble up, and inhale the vapour as deeply into her lungs as she could.

Jagan, Simon and Patrick found themselves in a random rowdy bar. Vikram and Naresh had had enough and headed home to their wives. The bar was full of sailors, traders, random drunks and taxi-girls. There were Cockneys, Geordies, Yorkshiremen, Scousers, Paddies, Jocks, Frogs, Germans, Welshmen, Texans, Yanks and Canadians. There were Jamaicans, Mumbaikers and even a delegation of Fijian administrators.

Simon wobbled his way to the urinals and learned the name of the place from the signs there, the Red Parrot.

"Great place, this," he said out loud to no one in particular as he pissed in a bucket.

"Was better when it was the Green Parrot," came a slurred response from an Irishman next to him.

"Used to be run by the Greens then. The nights were wilder, the women were more generous. Now it's the Catfish, they're not as fun as the Greens. Rumour has it that they took over the place after a tip-off that the pigs would turn a blind eye."

"Who are you?" Simon asked.

"Me? I'm just a drunk from Galway, and maybe a bit of a junky," he said laughing to himself.

"How do you know all this?"

"I dunno. It's what people say. Who knows why people say what they say?" he said, fumbling to do up his fly. "Do you want some tip-top smack? One thing that didn't change is the quality of the H here. Top-grade Green Turtle Smack, the connoisseurs swear by it. I myself am a connoisseur of some experience, and I personally vouch for it. There's only one chap can make Green Turtle and that's the one-armed master from Shanghai, they say," he was pretty much talking to himself by this point, giggling a bit. "Don't let the staff know I'm offering this stuff though, they'll kill me. They killed the last bloke," he broke off laughing.

When Simon got back to Jagan he was sitting with a sullen-looking stranger.

"Simon, meet Bob. Bob Lomax. He's an artist," Jagan shouted over the tune.

"Hello Bob. What do you paint?" Simon asked.

"Wimmin," he slurred. Tick Tock would have given him a 'G' for goner.

"He was just telling me that he lives over at Nam Kok," Jagan said, mouthing, "with the whores," with a big grin on his face.

"Yesh," Bob said. "I love Shuzee, you see. This song is our song," he choked through tears.

"*Seven Lonely Days*," Jagan said knowingly.

"I've had seven lonely days and nights because of that American bastard who took Shuzee away," Bob said, breaking down into a messy puddle of misery.

Suddenly Simon was starving.

"Noodles," he declared.

"No shanks," Bob sobbed.

"Not me," Jagan said, smiling.

"Noodles and I'm going home," Simon said.

"Not me," Jagan repeated. "I'm going to Nam Kok. I'm going to have to help Bob get home."

Patrick had already disappeared.

"Suit yourself," Simon said, and walked out into Lockhart Road, turning a corner at random.

He had no idea where a noodle shop was but his feet kept him marching obsessively on. He wandered away from the bar strip and into a residential block that became quieter with every step he took. The drunk quarter faded to a vague memory, a blurred dream that became more muted and more absurd as he pulled away slowly towards the fringes of Wanchai. There was the occasional person shuffling home. A woman dressed like a movie star, a weaving man in a shabby suit, cats on the hunt, their fat prey waddling along the side of a wall.

He reached the Pak Tai temple that marked the edge of Wanchai with its ornate curving roofs. Its doors were wide open and a thick tarry smoke bellowed out from the main hall, faint orange spots in the dark showing the tips of huge incense coils that dangled from the rafters. The angry eye-popping faces of the gods stared from within, and though the drunk Simon leaned in for a few curious seconds he didn't like to stare at their menacing, challenging faces for too long. At the back of the temple a narrow path rose up and away from the last houses of the built-up neighbourhood. Insects buzzed collectively like an electric transformer in the forest. An owl hooted from an upper branch in the invisible distance. As he entered the pitch black, ghostly faces appeared before him and voices came to life in his head.

He saw the face of Ma, fading, as life itself oozed out of his spilled guts. "Don't believe their lies. I only went to catch a tiger." The sound of Godber's voice came to life: "Lee, you mongrel, you've always lacked judgement." Simon suddenly felt a strong presence in the dark wood. The image of Godber loomed large, then the voice of Wetherby: "I expect Godber will find some way of wrapping it up." He could hear shuffling in the trees, behind him, ahead of him. Was he being stalked? Where was Godber? "Lee, you mongrel." The tension was too much for him. Simon turned around at random and shouted at the top of his voice. "Shut up Godber, you gobshite bastard. What do you know about my fucking judgement?" Creatures all around crashed through the undergrowth in panic. Birds flapped in terror, squawking, shaking branches, tearing leaves. "What monster has the night evoked?" piglets grunted to one another, while a sow seriously contemplated a thunderous charge, until dismissing the 'monster' as another lost Wanchai drunk. And the voice of Danny Chu came echoing back: "He was just a barman in some pub called the Erection." The owl hooted. It was always the same distance away from him, no matter what direction he walked in. What direction am I going in? North, south? West? Left, right? Is this a path? Yes, it's a path. Is it a pig path, a dog path or a human path? Then the face of Maria. "She hit me like a slap in the face," he said out loud and then giggled. "You can't use an actual event as a metaphor for the event," he repeated two or three times, remembering his father trying to help with a school essay, before the Japanese took him and left him to die. Maria's voice tuned in, "I caught him crying...Business, he said, nothing important..." Bullets ricocheted. An orange ball of fire exploded. "Go Danny, Go! Promise me, for Maria."

"You too. Stay clear of the Molotovs. For Maria."

Simon was tired, he wanted to lie down, but he wanted to think, and to think he had to walk. "It's Salty, he wants to get involved in bigger things," Danny's voice came back, "...it was an accident. The Dagger, he was dead drunk..."

"What did he do?"

"Did I say blunder?" came Wetherby's voice. The owl hooted again, still the same distance away. "I expect I meant I came to prevent blunders."

"Three Eyes said the Catfish had declared war on them in Wanchai."

"We owed him one after another job had gone wrong...," echoed Danny's voice.

"Was it another job for Three Eyes?" Simon said out loud. He nearly tripped on a rock. The rock uncurled itself and lumbered off. "Pangolin!" Simon shouted out. "That's a hundred dollars creeping away. Come back!"

Then Scroggins' face. "Smooth," Jagan said.

Is he a Spiderman?

"What else did he say?" Scroggins had asked. He looked panicked. Why did he want to know?

"That's it?" He wanted to make sure.

"The Cousins called," the voice of Godber. How did they know? He was a spy. That's why they knew. Ma was a spy. The Spidermen were tracking him. They contracted the Greens to kill him and the Greens sold the job to the Mongoose. That's what happened.

Madam Li was laughing at him. "Spy? He's about as likely to be a spy as I am!" She's a spy, right?

"Don't believe their lies. I only went to catch a tiger." Ma's face appeared in the tree branches. He was alone when he died, except with Simon, but that was alone because Simon was a stranger. What about his dad? Was he alone when he died? Was Uncle Trevor or Aunt May nearby? Did he remember Peggy Lee? Why didn't he live?

"You like the Little Tiger do you?"

"Scroggins, you smarmy Yank bastard!" Simon shouted at the top of his voice. Birds, bats, every beast that could, scattered. Here came a monster, a deranged primate.

"Fuck off, creep." Who was that? Queen Elizabeth, that's what Jagan said. The bitch.

The owl. The fucking owl was still the same distance away, hooting like a machine, but with no rhythm. Hoot! one two three Hoot! one two three four five Hoot! one two three four five six seven Hoot! one two Hoot! Where was the rhythm? The fucking rhythm?

And the voice of Wetherby: "You're quite stubborn for a Eurasian with no clout, usually so subservient."

Simon climbed a tree to look at the stars, scraping his shin against bark and drawing blood. Jupiter or Mars was up there, sparkling with a force that outshone outer-galactic suns. He looked across the tree tops at the black night and bellowed at the top of his voice. "To hell with you Wetherby, you arrogant stupid man."

Then he came down and walked on. The path was descending now, he had crossed over the hump. Gravity worked for him, pulling him forward. I should have gone to see Peggy instead of going drinking with the boys, he thought to himself as he calmed down.

All was quiet at the edge of Aberdeen. There were just a few cats, rats, the odd baby crying for a feed, bats that fluttered near lamps in the centre of the village. The harbour was more active. Fishermen were huddled, having their breakfasts, or their suppers, it was never clear. The beers could have been to mark the end of a shift or to warm up for a new one. An old crone wandered up: "Sampan?" She flashed her gold teeth. "Lamma?"

"Mui Wo?" he said. She told him to sit and wait at a shack, where a strange sound leaked out. He recognised a tune he had heard earlier in the night, now being played on a traditional erhu, but the rhythm coming from two accompanying guitars seemed turned inside out. He walked in to find an exotic-looking Chinese man in a pork pie hat, a smiling black man in a sailor suit, and a weathered, stony-faced Aberdeen fisherman holding the erhu.

"Whappen Mon, the name's Clive, Clive Chan from Kingston, Jamaica."

The sampan lady opened a beer for Simon. It had been about three hours since his last drink. The sky was lightening, some tea would have been better, he thought, but he took it anyway.

"Nice to meet you, Clive. I'm Simon Lee. That's *Seven Lonely Days* you chaps were playing, isn't it?"

"Yah man. But we turn it into ska, because that's how we take nice songs from the radio and make them better Mon," he said, laughing out loud.

"I didn't know there were Chinese Jamaicans," Simon said, not even sure if he could point to Jamaica on a map.

"Didn't you? There are Chinese everywhere man. My Pa sailed out from Kaiping to the Caribbean with hundreds of coolies. Now he sent me back to Aberdeen 'cos I've been running around with dem rude-boys too much. They said go stay with Uncle Big Squid in Aberdeen, he'll teach you how to be a real Chinaman. But they have no idea that every day when Big Squid finishes fishing, all he wants to do is drink beer and play the blues on his erhu. He's a rude-boy too, an old Chinese rude-boy! Ain't that right Uncle?" Clive said, slapping Big Squid on the thigh.

"And this here is my cousin from Alabama. His humongous aircraft carrier came in from Guam yesterday, and he escaped AWOL for a few days just to come see me and Big Squid, and play his guitar in peace without them nasty Babylonian dictators telling him to clean the deck all day. Didn't you Nestor?"

"Sure did," Nestor said, beaming. "I'll go back for a floggin' tomorrow, or the day after, but it'll be worth it."

Simon then remembered that he was supposed to be at a roll call this morning in Central, before the reserve riot squad were to be dismissed and sent back to their stations. He too was AWOL.

"Sod them," he said to himself, and to Nestor.

One of Nestor's duties on the ship was to DJ for the American Forces Radio, a fact that delighted Simon when he learned it.

"I thought you sounded familiar. I've heard you before, I'm sure of it."

"You probably have, brother. You like blues and rock'n'roll?"

"Of course I do."

"You like jazz too?"

"Yup. All of it."

"I tell you what man, I'll do you a dedication when I next broadcast. What's your girl called?"

"Well, I, er. I'm not sure if I've got a girl to be honest," he spluttered.

"What're you talking about man? You've got a girl, I know you have. Come on man, what's her name?"

"Oh, ehm, well Maria maybe?"

"Maria? I like that name. I can tell you're smitten bro."

"Oh, it's not like that. We're just friends really."

"Yeah, whatever man. I'm gonna shout you and your sweet girl out. Just you listen out bro. I'll have a real special tune for you."

Big Squid then nodded and launched into a blues riff that the guitarists immediately picked up and accompanied, with Clive flipping the rhythm around into a ska beat.

The sun rose to cast hundreds of red and green fishing boats in a slowly intensifying glow, as Simon's sampan weaved through the harbour. A large ocean-battered vessel came gliding in, suntanned sailors busy on deck, and a huge shark strapped to the mast, a bloodied trophy of their hunt. The sampan slipped past it and exited to the Lamma Channel. It was an exceptionally calm sea that glistened silver and rippled like mercury in the brilliant morning sun. Simon wanted desperately to enjoy the beautiful ride, but he felt the irresistible force of sleep sucking him into the deep, where he stalked a tiger. He felt close, but the tiger always remained the same distance away, like that ludicrous hooting owl.

10

Bye Bye Blackbird

"Nice girl, that. Why do you always stare at her?" Godber asked Ma without mercy.

Ma didn't speak. He looked at some imagined focal point between them. He couldn't trust himself to move a muscle. His only thought was on how he would kill Godber, if he were to kill him. He imagined a gun, and his brains blowing out, or smashing him in the face with a brick. Perhaps stabbing him with a screwdriver would be effective, but where? In the heart? Or in the neck? Another possibility could be to throw kerosene in his face and set it on fire. Would it smell? How long would his screams last? Would he hear body fluids boiling?

Godber wasn't prepared for the hostile silence. He was used to deference at the Duchess. The Chiu Chau barmen were known to be ruthless, but they knew how to behave inside the club. If it wasn't for the special mission Godber had for him, he'd be out on his arse by now. The truth was that Godber was deeply unnerved by Ma's dark insubordination.

Ma pictured a scene. A man on a beach, blindfolded, hands tied behind his back. A cold-blooded execution. The man bleeding out on the sand.

Godber pulled himself together: "I know why you were looking at the Brothers' special accounts ledger. You want to buy her out, don't you? The Little Tiger."

Until Queen Elizabeth had told him about the ledger, Godber had never heard of it. He had contracted her to spy on Ma and report back anything she found. Queen Bet was head of the girls and solid in loyalty, but he offered good financial incentive to ensure the quality of her intelligence. When she told him about the book, and Ma's interest in it, he knew it was significant. He stumped up a large sum to get Queen Bet to smuggle it out to him. She was afraid to do it, but a combination of loyalty and money gave her the courage she needed to bring the ledger out to him one night when drunks sang rugby songs in the bar. Godber quickly guessed the entries were heroin debts and he was amazed at the size of Xiao Hu's. She covered it up well. Queen Bet explained the rest. This is all outstanding debt, she told him. None of the girls that chase the dragon are free to go until they have paid up, and the longer they stay, the higher the debt gets.

"Such an evil drug," Godber said with feeling, and not a trace of irony. He took note of the latest entry for Xiao Hu, 2,740 dollars.

"I've got a job for you," he said to Ma. "It's worth 2,740 dollars."

Ma was jolted by the significance of the figure. Godber delighted in his direct hit.

"The job involves regular round-trips, from picking up government waste, to collecting manufactured goods, delivering to Wanchai, collecting cash. It's a top-secret mission. Are you the man for the job?"

Ma knew there was only one product that would generate the kind of money Godber claimed to offer, the same product that his wife was enslaved to.

"How long would it take me to earn 2,740 dollars?"

"You should be able to do it in about two years."

"I'll need more than that by then."

"Add another year and I expect you should clear it."

It was a ridiculous offer, utterly meaningless. Xiao Hu could be dead by then, or Ma. He didn't have three years. The fact that Godber thought this could even tempt Ma was testimony to the level of contempt Godber held him in.

Godber thought he had him.

"You'll never speak about it to anyone. You will never speak to me about it again. You will have protection."

"What if I refuse?"

"Then you'll walk away from the best business opportunity you'll have in your life, and you won't have a job at the Duchess."

Ma was trapped. The only options worse than being a police-Triad drug mule were to carry on as he was or abandon Xiao Hu all together. She had saved his life, and their son's life. He had no plan of his own. He was racked with guilt every time he whispered to her that he would get her out, because he had no idea how to do it. Xiao Hu had studiously avoided him at the start, but in recent weeks he could sense that her resolve was weakening. She lingered close to him just a bit longer. Occasionally her eyes met his. She was still in there somewhere, and she was waiting to see how he was going to save her.

He had to acknowledge that it was an offer he couldn't refuse. It was ludicrous and demeaning, but still he couldn't refuse it. Hatred boiled in his veins and he plotted his revenge. Finally he shrugged his shoulders to show he was interested. Godber filled him in on the details.

Wetherby had looked overjoyed when Godber called him over to his table, just as Fotherington said he was leaving to chase a whore down at the Nam Kok.

"What's wrong with our own tarts?" Godber called after him.

"Nothing. I just fancy a bit of the rough stuff sometimes," he said, walking away.

Wetherby laughed knowingly even though he had no idea if the Nam Kok totty was rougher than what he could find at the Duchess. He made a note to himself to do some research.

Godber told Wetherby to sit, and he explained that he planned to put him on a top-secret mission. Wetherby would open a private bank account in the name of a new secret charity, the Saint Paul's Charitable Drug Rehabilitation Fund. Its purpose was to collect anonymous donations to help young people who had fallen victim to vicious and addictive drugs. Godber winked at Wetherby to make sure it was clear that this was of course a front. He needed Wetherby to believe he was part of the inner circle without letting him anywhere near it. There was no way that Wetherby could be trusted with full knowledge of the scheme. He wouldn't even know any other person involved except Johnny Boy.

Johnny Boy would give Wetherby regular bundles of cash, left at a drop-off point that would change each time and stipulated by a coded note inside the envelope. Wetherby would take this and bank it in a safe-deposit box to which only he and Godber had the key. He would be paid a small amount each week for the legwork, but he came cheap because of his eagerness to work with the big boys. He thought he was getting a nice bit of pocket money for an easy job when in fact his sole purpose was to be a buffer for Godber, who wanted to cover himself as best as he could. Godber was aware that even the corrupt and kleptocratic Hong Kong Police would not accept its officers becoming involved in the production and distribution of heroin. Wetherby had no idea what the source of the cash was, he assumed it was the usual mixed takings from the street, and therefore quite legitimate.

Simon knocked on the cottage door of his old friend on the beach at Pui O.

"Call me Ishmael!" the old man greeted him, as he always did.

"How goes it?"

"Not so good," Simon replied.

"What troubles you, lad?"

"The Mongoose, Ishmael. I think they've got caught up in something."

"Salty's been looking for something to get his teeth into. Those boys don't have much to do between wars."

"Would they kill a Communist spy for profit?"

"Not sure. We all worked with Commies against the Japs. Good men they were. Brave and principled. Salty would have died for Communist comrades back then, but who knows how things stand now. People do strange things during peace time."

"Have you seen them recently?"

"Aye, the whole band of them sailed by. I paddled out to join them for a drink. They were in fine fettle, especially the Dagger, pissed as a jellyfish he was. Singing his head off."

"Bit of a loose cannon, the Dagger."

"Always has been. Bit of a liability sometimes in them hills with the Japs, nearly gave the game away on many an occasion with his potshots. He never did learn to shoot well."

"Where were they heading?"

"Cheung Chau. Said they were on a job for Three Eyes."

"Who is Three Eyes?"

"He's a Green Gang enforcer. A bit of a psychopath. Also freelanced for the Japanese during the war, and then the Spidermen since. I told Salty to be careful but he's convinced he can handle him."

"They were in Sham Shui Po for Three Eyes and the Greens. Backing the wrong side. Said they owed Three Eyes for some other job that had gone wrong. The Greens melted away and I don't know what became of the Mongoose. I'm worried for Danny."

"Danny's making his own choices now Simon, you're not responsible for him."

"Have you ever heard of the Duchess?"

"The Duchess? Sounds like a pub. I can't say I know it."

"How about the Erection?"

"Erection, oh yes. Mui Mui's boys used to talk about that bar. Said it was the best place to meet bent coppers. They were always trying to get an introduction there but said the Catfish kept a tight control. Wanchai, isn't it?"

"Yes. I was there last night. Nest of vipers, that's for sure. Its real name is the Duchess. It's full of bent coppers, bent civil servants, bent businessmen. Probably bent vicars and bent firemen too."

"I thought all you coppers were bent," Ishmael teased.

"Oh don't start that again. We're not all bent," Simon said wearily.

"Hah, I know that. Falkirk's told me about your deluded ways. Says you've got refreshingly naive ideals that'll probably be crushed out of you in a few years' time."

"Gosh, that's cheering."

"Though of course you're not above knocking-off the boss's daughter, eh?"

"Ah, leave it out Ishmael!"

"He-he, you do remind me of your dad sometimes."

"He used to tell me about the old mariner he'd go drinking with down at the Kennedy Town docks. My favourite story was about a sperm whale you chased down the Namibian coast. You finally caught it after nine harpoons had been implanted, and the monster dragged your dinghy on the old 'Nantucket sleighride' for two whole days. Then you strapped it up and butchered the carcass..."

"Only to find a live giant squid that came out of the stomach, flailing and demented..."

"And you wrestled it to the deck, finally stabbing it with your dagger."

"And then I sliced the bugger up."

"And you found a whale's eye in its stomach, bigger than the eye of the whale that the squid came out of!"

"Ha ha ha. I remember it like it was yesterday!"

"Even when I was nine I knew my dad was pulling my leg."

"Was he though?"

Mui Mui came in with steaming garlic prawns, clams in chilli sauce and a big crab that Ishmael had caught that afternoon.

Simon slept under the stars that night in a hammock outside the beach hut, then hiked over the hills for six hours back to Tai O. Refreshed and stimulated, he walked into the reception office to find Falkirk with a strange gweilo woman.

"Aha, the detective returns. Have fun banging heads together in Kowloon?"

"It was chaos out there. Madness."

"You missed your roll call. I got a call, took a tongue-lashing on your behalf. I told them to check the whorehouses of Wanchai and to get off my back."

"Sod them."

"Sod 'em."

The gweilo woman obviously got sick of waiting for an introduction and stood up with her hand thrust forward. "Jane O'Connor. South China Morning Post. Were you boys there to keep the peace or to help the Catfish rout the Greens?" she said in broad Australian, with a bright grin on her face.

Simon mumbled something bland about doing their best, and, obviously bored, she got straight down to business. She slapped a copy of the Post with the Chen Guanming report on the desk and pointed to the thumbnail. "That's not Chen, is it? I know about the bloody embargo, and even though I wasn't deemed important enough to be invited to the briefing with the likes of that bloody galah Harvestman, I saw the memo with his picture attached. That picture was enough to explain why the one-eared Chen was called the bloody Van Gogh Terrorist. This boy here clearly has two ears, no?"

Simon opened a filing cabinet and placed one of the original prints in front of her.

"Yup, that's him. Ma Xun. So the bastards killed him."

"What bastards?" Simon asked.

"That's what I want to know."

"How did you know him?"

"I hardly did, to be honest. He doorstepped me. I'd noticed a shifty-looking Chinese fellah watching me enter the office the day before. Next day I had a boozy lunch with the editor, self-aggrandising prick that he is, and when I left the bar I noticed that some bastard was tailing me. He wasn't bad, 'cos every time I turned around he was casually inspecting the back of his hand or straining his neck to see something across the road. I did two laps of Victoria Park to be certain he was still with me and then sat on a bench to wait for him to introduce himself.

"He came and sat beside me, putting a copy of the SCMP between us. He had it folded open on an article I'd written a few weeks earlier about a bent copper being caught with his hands in the till and getting sent to jail. He said, 'Are you Jane O'Connor?' pointing to my byline. I says to him: 'That's me. Who are you?' Then he tells me he's a barman and he's got a story about police corruption. I says to him: 'Look here mate, we all know about police corruption but I can't write a bloody story on every bobby taking kickbacks based on something I hear in a pub, or on a park bench. How did you find me anyway?' And he says I was the only woman going in and out of the building that didn't look like a secretary or a cleaner, and I thought, OK he's not daft. So I told him: 'Look, that story you're pointing at, I could only write that one 'cos Max Godber gave it to me at some boring dinner party.' Sold it to me to be precise, 'cos no-one is better than Godber at wringing out the most profit from a task – multitasking, the business editor calls it. The main reason he gave it to me was that he wanted rid of some pesky junior who wasn't playing by his rules.

"In any case, I says to the fellah, Ma Xun, if you haven't guessed, why are you coming to the SCMP, why not the Chinese press, the pro-Commie papers will love your story. He says, 'I want everyone to know my story including the Queen and Governor,' that's why he needed it in English. He was right about that, 'cos although the Governor pretends to monitor the Chinese press, he only reads the odd story his aides can be bothered to highlight for him, and only then if he thinks someone's going to test him later. Also, Ma said he had a teacher at school who taught him about civil liberties and the independent press. So I says, sorry to break your heart sweetie, but the reality is always a long way from the ideal. I told him Pom journalists are as corrupt and co-opted as any other around the world. Luckily however, I says, I happen to be Australian.

"So then the bombshell. He says Max Godber is setting up a supply and distribution network for Green Turtle Smack. Ha ha ha, I says, c'mon son that's horseshit right? And he says no it's not. Says Godber's orchestrating a takeover of Green Gang businesses in Wanchai for the Catfish and then he's gonna supply the new Chiu Chau premises with Green Turtle. You're mad, I says and asks him how the hell he knows that. And he says, I know 'cos I'm going to be the courier, for the opium, the heroin and the cash. I says how the hell did you get that position, did Godber advertise for it in the classifieds? And he says he's a barman at the Duchess, and it begins to start sounding almost plausible. If this is true, I says, you're risking your life. And he says he's got nothing, he's a slave, and his son will be too unless the world becomes a better place, and that can only happen when people stop being enslaved to tyrants, but to do that we have to first expose the tyrants and strip them of their respectability.

"Pretty impressive, I thought. So I says to him, OK Ma, just supposing, as unlikely as it seems, that you are telling the truth, how the hell do you expect me to believe any of this? And he says it's all gonna start with the Catfish takeover of Turtle properties in Wanchai. If that happens, you'll know I'm telling the truth. Then he tells me where he lives, where he worked during the daytime, when he went to the Duchess. He told me of the one other bent copper he knew was involved, John Tse. And he says if I want the story just start tailing him and snap him with whoever he's talking with.

"As you can imagine, I put his name down in the 'lunatic column' of my notepad and thought: 'Shame that's probably a pile of garbage, would have been a good story.'

"Then hey presto, two days later his predictions come true. The Catfish who'd traded side-by-side with Greens for the past few years in Wanchai suddenly turned on their rivals, beating the crap out of them and burning down their bars. The cops helpfully stood idly by and let it all happen. Even the Green Parrot gets smashed up and reopens a few days later as the Red Parrot, courtesy of the new Catfish affiliated staff."

"Why do you say 'even' the Green Parrot?" Simon asked.

"Cos it's Wanchai's best kept secret that the bar's under special patronage of a Yankee spook. It's a money-laundering outpost for his special operations."

"Do you believe those rumours?" Falkirk asked. "I neither believe nor disbelieve them. I'd say it's possible because they definitely need dirty money for their own dirty work, but I can't say I've got any evidence."

"Who's the spook?" Simon asked, knowing what the answer was going to be.

"Chap called Scroggins. Very smooth chap. Charms the pants off everybody."

"So did you tail Ma?"

"I tried to, but it wasn't easy. The only vaguely useful shots I got were these." She took out some photographs. "Here he is picking up a sack of garbage where the customs haul of contraband are known to be disposed of. Then this one shows him entering the no-go area at the Kai Tak squat, but that doesn't prove anything. After we got these he disappeared. These help to corroborate his story but there's no way I can get a story out of that lot. Not that the SCMP would have gone with it anyway. I really don't know what I could have done with it."

"So you're expecting us to help you complete the story?" Simon asked.

"I don't know what I'm expecting, but I needed to come here to try to understand what happened. Call it professional curiosity if you like."

Falkirk's eyes went to the ceiling as he muttered: "Oh lord, not another one."

Simon talked her through what he knew, and the different threads of the story almost seemed to come together.

A few days after Godber had had his talk with Wetherby, Fotherington brought Thomas-Littleton into the club. T-L had been there before, but as Chief of Police it was an unspoken rule that he shouldn't hold membership of the place, with its carefully fostered image of mystery and menace. The truth was that T-L wasn't in any case natural material for the club. He might have had his hands on a number of grubby extortion rackets, but he didn't quite have the killer instinct and fluid mind required to be on the inside track at the Duchess. The sharks at the Duchess found it relatively easy to handle the pompous, vain commander, to flatter him when it suited, but to keep him at arm's length from the real action. T-L was so lacking in self-awareness that he failed to see the incongruity of a man of his rank taking pride in an invite to the Duchess. He was very pleased with himself.

Fotherington ordered two pints of India Pale Ale and two double Glenfiddichs to set the mood. They talked about the form of the police rugby squad and the coming visit of the Singapore Police team. They plotted how they would get the B team to take out the visitors the night before the big match and keep them out for a night of hard drinking and tarts. The next morning the A team would walk on to the pitch fresh as a daisy and slaughter the Singaporeans.

The second two pints of IPA and two more double scotches arrived just as T-L slurped up the last drop of his first pint. This time they discussed the merits of Queen Bet and Xiao Hu, and both agreed that Xiao Hu was the superior model, despite Queen Bet's status as head girl.

"Good filly. Give you a cracking ride every time," T-L said knowingly, despite the fact that he had never seen her before, and for all his other vices whoring wasn't a habit of his.

The third set of drinks arrived and they moved on to the activities of the Cousins.

"Bloody heavy-handed these days," T-L said.

"Desperate to score some points, justify their enormous budget," said Fotherington.

"They seem to think that they can regain China by infiltrating every socialist theatre group and student committee."

"I heard there's a Harvard graduate that poses as a retarded imbecile, just to gather information on the Christian volunteers that aid the handicapped."

"No doubt. They see Commie agents wherever they look. I had that smarmy Texan genius Harry Scroggins ingratiating himself with my wayward daughter the other day at some senseless social event. God knows what rank he is but he's like a cartoon secret agent. The poor bastard should at least take off his MacArthur sunglasses every now and then, for God's sake."

"Did she like him then?"

"Oh God, who knows with that daughter of mine. I don't know where she gets it from. She's nothing like her mother. She still doesn't think she did anything inappropriate in getting mixed up with that half-caste mongrel. Anyway, she came home tipsy and told me straight away: 'Daddy it's hilarious. Harry thinks you're a lefty!' The bloody cheek of it, I should have the boy flogged."

"He's obsessed, that Scroggins. I don't know why we even entertain him at the Duchess, other than just to keep an eye on him. Godber seems to think it's better to keep some of them close to our chest, and I suppose he's right. He's certainly not much fun I can tell you. He drinks coffee most of the time, slamming the occasional shot before going into a room with one of the girls. I imagine he thinks he's watching us, but

I assure you, we're the ones watching him. We make the venue available for some of his dark arts. Only him, mind, we don't want the place taken over by earnest God-bothering Yankee agents."

Two more pints of IPA arrived with two chasers.

"Down the hatch," proffered Fotherington.

"Aye, better in than out."

"T-L, what do you think about these bloody hooligan attacks we've had around here recently?"

"Yes, I've seen the reports. Seems like some hotheads are getting restless. Unless the attacks are random."

"Meat cleaver attacks don't tend to be random, boss. Let's face it, carrying one down a dark Wanchai alley implies intent."

"Quite."

In fact John Tse had already let word out that the Queen's own may not necessarily get too involved if the Catfish took the initiative to upset the balance of power on Lockhart Road and Jaffe Road. They responded immediately with selective attacks on Green Gang members involved in heroin distribution. Three murders in two weeks was a high count, with a fourth victim left paralysed.

"I expect that you might have already started reviewing our policy in the district, T-L."

"Quite, quite. I'm always looking for ways to take the initiative," he said without a clue what his initiative would be.

"Indeed. I'm sure you too have noticed that the Green Gang are a spent force. That's why young Catfish are targeting them. Easy prey to notch up credibility as the up-and-coming foot soldiers jostle for position."

"Damned Chiu Chau. Should have wiped them out years ago and left the Greens to do for us what they did for Chiang Kai-shek."

Fotherington took a second to digest this. T-L was meandering down the wrong track. How could he be so stupid as to not realise that the

Queen's own had been in bed with the Catfish for years. Didn't he have any idea how Johnny Boy got his influence?

"You are dead right boss, dead right. We should have crushed the Chiu Chau ten years ago. But if you don't mind me saying so, your predecessor – and I knew him well – wasn't quite the visionary that you are. To be fair to him we were in disarray after the war of course. We didn't know which of the ungrateful bastards in the force had been collaborators, and which were going to murder us in our beds. It took a few years to build us back up. And then the Greens came in like a damned typhoon, destroying everything in their path."

"Machine guns, street battles, bombings, bank heists. My God, it took a fair few floggings and hangings to teach those savages some manners."

"Exactly. I mean, by golly, every other man in Hong Kong seemed to be a bloody Triad, they outnumbered us fifty to one, we needed some help and the Chiu Chau were quite handy. The Wanchai balance of power was perhaps an expediency that was necessary at the time."

"Bloody genius, I'd say," T-L chipped in, reversing his earlier judgement.

"But I wonder why it is that things keep changing, T-L. Isn't life a funny old thing?"

"Damned slippery that's what it is. You think you've got it by the scruff of its neck, turns out you're just holding on to it by its toe."

"I heard a rumour that you were thinking about pulling the plug on the Greens, and might I say how astounded I was with your audacity. And then it struck me how brilliant your move was."

T-L took a deep swig of his IPA and tried to recall what could have possibly triggered such a thought, because he couldn't remember having it. Then he remembered Jasmine teasing him about Harry Scroggins, saying he had great contacts in the Greens. Not that he had told her, but it was all over the socialite rumour mill.

"It's about time we wiped out those bloody thugs," had been his irritated response. She must have leaked it. She loved being in possession of high-quality intelligence. Most of all she loved disseminating it.

"Yes, well, I have been reviewing our options," he cautiously said.

"But the balance of power is sacred, right?" Fotherington timidly suggested.

"Not when one side no longer has the strength to hold up its end of the bargain."

"You wouldn't be suggesting that we let Catfish take over in Wanchai?"

"Why not?"

"Well I suppose they could be a stabilising influence, and it will be easier for us to deal with just one set of hooligans."

"They'd be a stabilising influence."

"You're right."

"And it would be easier to deal with just one."

"That's logical."

"I've made up my mind."

"That's very wise sir."

The fifth round arrived. Conversation moved on to reports of recent tiger sightings, and whether such wild cats had ever lived in Hong Kong. T-L said it was impossible that they had ever even visited the place. He assumed that the stuffed head mounted over the entrance to Central Police Station at the police HQ had been shipped over from India. All the talk about sightings and shootings in the past was just tittle-tattle among the feeble-minded.

Godber came over with three whiskeys in his hands.

"Gentlemen, this looks like the kind of table I like being on," he said.

"We're having a very interesting chat, Godber, and I'm afraid your rank doesn't qualify you for the privilege of hearing any of it."

"That's quite right. And don't you try telling me there's any bloody tigers in this damned place. It doesn't have any of the magic of India. That's where tigers belong, you see," T-L piped up.

"I wouldn't have said anything of the sort sir. This is surely a place just for mongrels, macaques and greedy pigs."

"That's correct. By the way Godber, you'll be hearing it through official classified channels tomorrow but I may as well tell you myself now, I've decided to move things along a bit in this district. It's about time those Green thugs were kicked out. They're finished anyway."

"Surely not, sir. What would the Cousins say?"

"I don't give a damn about Harry Scroggins and his tennis-playing, bible-bashing boy scouts. What the hell do they think they're doing soiling their hands with grubby criminals like that anyway?" T-L roared to the amusement of the others.

"Well, there's rumours that business with the Greens provides a convenient source of covert revenue," Godber said, suppressing the volume of the conversation.

"Wouldn't put it past them. Anyway, I don't give a hoot. It's time to clean this place up."

Jagan and Patrick Cheung turned up in the report room. Jagan looked at Simon with a faint flicker of relief and then admonished him, saying: "You missed the roll call two days ago."

"Sod 'em," Falkirk said. "You well?"

They both reported good health and fine adventures in Kowloon and said they'd made their way back via Cheung Chau. They introduced themselves to Jane. Jagan brought out an envelope and said to Simon and Falkirk: "I need to talk to you about this."

"What is it?" Simon asked.

"Pictures. Very interesting ones."

"Of?"

"Ma Xun, and others."

"How did you get them?"

Jagan looked uncomfortable, indicating Jane. Falkirk said it would be alright. Jane had some helpful contributions to make to the case.

"OK, so I was drunk, but when you pointed out Scroggins to me in the Erection – sorry – the Duchess, I went over to eavesdrop on him. God knows why but it was the first thing I thought of doing."

"Oh yes, I remember that, I was a bit surprised."

"Well it was worthwhile because I heard him say to that oaf Harvestman: 'Where the hell is Godber, man, I thought you said he would be here.' And Harvestman says, 'Steady on, my man, why are you so anxious to see him anyway.' And Scroggins replied that he had some important pictures to show him. That had got me interested in the first place, and then Scroggins came over to talk to us, all smooth and generous, remember?"

"Yeah, yeah, and a bit leery, I thought."

"I noticed that when you told him poor old Ma had been speaking as he lay there dying on the beach, Scroggins looked alarmed. For the first time his unflappable facade flapped. Did you notice?"

"Yes, that did strike me as odd," Simon said.

"Right. He recovered quickly enough but then there was the confusion as we were unceremoniously kicked out of the back door. That's when I noticed the envelope peeking out of Scroggins' bag. It was a moment of madness really but I made a grab for it."

"Ha," Falkirk interjected, "I think that's what the spooks call 'tradecraft'!"

"Gosh, you didn't say anything to me about it."

"Yeah, well, I was just sober enough to realise that we were far too drunk to discuss it or even look at the contents. So I shoved it into my bag and forgot about it until I woke up on the floor of a hotel room. Fully clothed, I'll have you know, though surrounded by rather rude paintings of women, and my bag under the empty bed next to me. God knows what I was doing there. Turned out to be the room of some chap called Lomax, though he'd slept elsewhere, but anyway, there I was, body and belongings intact."

"My goodness. I'm impressed with the professionalism of our forces," Jane said with a smile on her face.

"Oh yes, Mrs O'Connor. We always know when we are too drunk to examine evidence."

"Ms O'Connor is impressed, Captain," she said, enunciating 'Ms' with pedagogic clarity. "So come on, Corporal Singh, spill the beans," she added, unable to hold back.

He took the pictures out and placed them in sets on the table. They were a series of dated, timestamped images. Jane recognised Ma in them immediately, and whistled her appreciation for the quality of the work.

"Hats off to Scroggins' boys, they're obviously much better at snooping than the SCMP."

The first set showed the same place that Jane had snapped, but from a different, clearer angle. Ma was picking up rubbish from a government waste depot in Kennedy Town. There were five of these pictures on five consecutive days, all around the same time of day. The next pictures were of Ma emerging from the no-go area of the Kai Tak squatter camp, also about the same time of each day. The next set showed him exiting the Red Parrot every day. Then a series of pictures that were inconsistent, from various angles and sometimes not very well focused. It was of John Tse at the bar of the Duchess.

"What's happening here?" Falkirk said.

"Look carefully. Ma is handing Tse a packet of cigarettes in all of them. Now this next set shows Tse dropping off envelopes in different locations. Here he is at St John's Cathedral. This one's at Star Ferry, this one up on Bowen Road. Note the times inscribed, and then look at this set. Wetherby at St John's ten minutes later, Wetherby at Star Ferry 12 minutes later, Wetherby on Bowen Road, seven minutes after Tse. And then the final set, all of Wetherby making regular visits to the offices of private bank Barings."

"Wow. That's Ma's story corroborated. But where's Godber?" Jane said.

"Nothing on Godber here, I'm afraid."

"This is crazy. The police running a heroin supply? And if that junky I spoke to in the toilet of the Red Parrot was right, we're talking about Green Turtle Smack here, the best in Hong Kong. I can't believe it," Simon said.

"Doesn't surprise me," Falkirk said. "They're happy to skim tax off the dealers. It's only logical to get more involved in the supply chain if they can."

"But none of this explains why Ma is now dead," Simon said, exasperated.

"He was a key asset to the scheme," Jagan said.

"Who'd want him out of the way then?" Falkirk thought out loud.

"Scroggins," Jane and Simon both concluded.

"But he wouldn't kill him though, would he?" Simon immediately asked.

"Scroggins is a snake, that's for sure," Jane said. "But he isn't an idiot. And as ruthless as his firm is, I don't think they randomly assassinate dirt-poor nobodies."

"Though of course millions die as collateral damage," Falkirk said.

They all jumped when they heard gunshots and explosions outside. Then there were trumpets and drums. Jagan looked out of the window and reported a flotilla of fishing boats decked out in full ceremonial regalia of flags and pennants flapping in the breeze. The lead boat looked brand new. All four of them stood outside of the police station now, watching the maritime display as more guns and cannons shot out, clearly in ritual display and not anger as they had first feared.

"For God's sake, where are they shooting those bloody things. Don't they know that what goes up must come down," Falkirk said.

"It's a funeral. They're in white," Jagan observed.

"There's SPK at the helm of the new boat. And Salty, Red, Danny and Spike. Looks like a Mongoose event," Simon said, secretly relieved to see Danny, who he hadn't heard from since they parted under a hail of bullets and chipped brickwork.

"Who's dead?" Falkirk asked.

They went down to the shore and saw clumps of people lining the Shek Tsai Po path. There was a coffin on the deck of SPK's lead boat. Simon saw Bad News and called across to him.

"Who is it?" he asked. "It's the Dagger," he said shaking his head. "Killed by one of your colleagues in Sham Shui Po, I heard."

They stood in silence as the boat chugged past with thick plumes of incense bellowing at the head and foot of the huge coffin. Simon saw Maria down the path with Sally, Madge and the twins. He surprised himself with a quickening of the heartbeat. He hadn't had too much time to think about her during the chaos of the last few days. He made his way through the gawping crowd towards her.

On the night that it all kicked off, John Tse had nodded to his trustworthy Chiu Chau contact, and expectation immediately rippled through the Wanchai brotherhood. He had laid out the terms clearly. Make it quick, clean and effective. Once the Greens are gone a new courier would appear. If they lay one finger on him the deal is over, all Chiu Chau privileges with the Queen's own will be null and void. The courier will deliver top-quality Green Turtle Smack at market rate.

At the same time that the storm was brewing in Wanchai, Wang-bang-thank-you-ma'am-Yu was on a one-shot job for Johnny Boy Tse at the Chai Wan squatter camp. He was leading a special squad of well-paid 'volunteers' to take apart a Green Gang heroin lab that they had long left to its own devices in a no-go area. A group of Catfish prize fighters also turned up at the edges of the camp shortly after the police had arrived, and in an unusual move marched right into into the Green Gang-controlled squat, bashing the skulls of any rival members who couldn't sense the direction the wind was blowing in. As the police eventually melted away, the Catfish took the lead. They smashed their way into the heart of the heroin factory, found the notorious one-armed master from Shanghai and bundled him away with them, warning Greens not even to think about following.

Back in Wanchai the assault on Green Gang businesses was well underway as Harry Scroggins strode through the once-familiar streets in a state of mind that moved from confusion, to shock and then rage. Windows were smashed, bar entrances stoved in, furniture slashed to bits. Three premises were on fire in Lockhart Road and another three on Jaffe Road had been trashed completely. In one of the locked establishments four staff members were being beaten unconscious by men wearing face masks. Two bodies bled in alleys. Firemen stood around, waiting to be paid to do their jobs, but no-one dared to cough up.

"What the hell is going on? There's some kind of territorial war happening out there," Scroggins thundered at Godber as he burst into the lounge in the Duchess.

Godber was sitting calmly with a cigar in one hand, a brandy in the other, content, like a man without a care.

"What are you talking about?" he asked, amused at Scroggins' panic.

"Triads man, everywhere!"

"Oh God. Don't get involved. I expect it's some ridiculous face thing. Someone's thug didn't say 'how do you do?' to someone else's goon, and now they are in a huff. Something like that, I should think."

"No. They are targeting Green Gang businesses. It's quite specific," Scroggins said, not mentioning that even more specifically it was his Green Parrot bar that he was most concerned about, last seen with its door hanging off its hinges and a Catfish delinquent throwing a beer bottle through a window.

"Leave it to them, that's what I say. There are 250,000 Triads in this town. They outnumber us by more than ten to one. We can't possibly get rid of them, but they know the rules. Leave the citizens alone and they can do what they like to each other."

"My God, that's a disgrace."

"Well it's better than getting them to do your dirty work for you..."

"What are you implying, Godber?"

"I've been talking to Barclay Harvestman of the Times. He's pitching a most interesting story to his editor, he says."

"What about?"

"Well come on Scroggins, I thought you boys knew everything. Why do you need me to tell you?"

Not 100 yards from the back door of the Duchess a 16-year-old Green Gang recruit was chased into a side alley where he was ambushed by a waiting Chiu Chau youth wing, mostly two years younger than him. His screams gurgled on blood, choked and fell silent quickly, as seven choppers hacked him from every angle. He didn't suffer long – though his parents who had never had any Triad involvement would live with gaping wounds for the rest of their lives.

"I have no idea what you are talking about," Scroggins said.

"Harvestman's apparently had some interesting chats with a Green Gang hitman who claims to have made good money freelancing for you chaps."

"I doubt that the Times would accept stories made up by street hoodlums."

"He's got details of an interesting kidnapping job back in September. A Bank of China executive, you might recall. I do because we had orders from higher up not to interfere. I remember being particularly surprised as the order came before the kidnapping had happened. Turned out of course that the 'kidnapping' was quite a jolly affair and the man taken was safely whisked off to Taiwan where he is now a chief banker for Chiang Kai-shek. Isn't that right?"

"I don't know. Why would I know?"

"Of course maybe it was the kind of job that you boys should have been proud of, but there was a hitch wasn't there?"

"Was there?"

"A small matter of collateral damage. The two dead bodyguards were bad enough, but the Sikh policeman, a colleague of mine, really was going too far. Unfortunately he wasn't of high enough rank to have been given the order to stay clear of the Bank of China that day. So there he is, a man of exemplary record, he sees a commotion on his beat, goes to investigate, is dead in seconds after being shot in the head by a kidnapper who was hired by your team, Scroggins."

"I still can't imagine the Times running this on the word of a thug."

"There were six of us in the force privileged with the instructions to turn a blind eye to what would happen. I for one would never squeal of course. I understand the forces of history. I know that you boys are the real bosses now. But one of us retired six months ago. He was a bitter, headstrong man, rather fond of drink, with a good war record. He was proud of his record, but technically the poor Sikh who was killed by your thug was under his watch. He ought to have found some way to have kept the constable away from the scene, but you can't control everything can you? Now despite the drink and this niggling regret, he would never have been a talker except for one of your pesky preachers.

"The damned fool got into a panic when he retired because he had nothing to do but to sit around with his chatterbox wife all day. Have you met her? Never stops talking. Enough to drive anyone mad. So he's walking around Victoria Park one evening, avoiding going home, and wondering where it had all gone wrong. Along comes this clean-cut Oklahoma boy in white-shirt and tie, name-badge on his chest, shiny black shoes on his feet, talking about sin, divine mercy and God's mission on earth. He got him on the first take. Our man was smitten and kneeling on the ground, praying to the Lord and dedicating his life there and then. You see, you need to be careful about the forces you unleash, 'cos you can't always control them. CIA-sponsored evangelists in particular have a tendency to unlock a creative and insistent power from within.

"In the coming weeks our man was seen at Methodist meeting houses all round town, taking a fondness for a roving – and therefore the most damaging – style of preaching. He spoke wildly at witnessing sessions, denouncing the Devil's work. In particular his own actions as a former colonial policeman, with a special anecdote about the Sikh constable he had let down. It was through this itinerant babbling that Harvestman got wind of the story and he went sniffing around the Greens until he found a fellow who corroborated the details and added a touch of gold. I must admit your payment method via top-grade heroin is pure genius. Harvestman has got himself a nice little scoop, don't you think?"

"Jeez Godber, you're right, it's a good story. Pity it's bullshit man. I can't imagine the editor of the Times wasting his time mulling that over for long."

"Oh, Harvestman's done his homework pretty well, Scroggins. He's checked all the dates, times, movement of officers. It all fits well. He's just waiting for the next visible action that shows your favour for the Greens. You know that the story of the Greens and their murky alliance with Chiang Kai-shek is popular fodder for the self-declared intelligentsia that reads the Times."

"Our favour for the Greens?"

"Yes and their main produce of course. For example, if your boys took sides in the fight going on outside these doors right now, that would probably complete the story for Harvestman just nicely."

"And supposing we didn't?"

"I'm almost certain that the editor would spike it. Let's face it, it's almost too good to be true, and the sources that he's got do seem a tad wobbly on close inspection."

"I'm just wondering who's behind the routing of the Greens here?"

"Nature taking it's course I would say. Let's face it Scroggins, the Greens are a spent force, and anyone caught doing business with them should really be ashamed of themselves."

"I'm kind of surprised that you're so taken with this stupid story and it makes me wonder what you're up to."

For a split second they saw each other clearly, past their respective everyday facades. They both sensed something significant was at stake, and no number of bluffs, euphemisms or proxies could hide the simple fact that there was a power struggle going on between them, though Scroggins was still in the dark about the exact details of Godber's scheme.

For a moment Godber flinched within. What if this all explodes in his face? Will his own greed drive him to destruction? He had a momentary glimpse of the abyss. It didn't last long, however, and he quickly regained his inner composure. He remembered that winning was a gift that his dad had earned for him. It was his right, and his destiny to come out on top. Besides, the two of them were not designed to attack each other. They would never brawl or bawl each other out, they would always fight their battles through proxies.

"Relax Scroggins, have a drink on me," Godber said with a magnanimity that annoyed Scroggins for having come from Godber first, though he quickly recovered, like a true professional.

"Sure Godber. After all, we are on the same side, right?"

"Precisely. We're the unsung heroes on the frontlines of a global war on a scale never seen before," Godber reeled off, just as he had reeled off every other profitable oath all his life.

"We are comrades in a struggle between tyranny and freedom," Scroggins said in all sincerity.

"It all boils down to a battle between right and wrong, Scroggins."

"You know, Godber, you're not far wrong. And one of the things about being on the frontline, is that you sometimes have to do things in a way that the bosses back home could never understand from the comfort of their situation room. You and I understand that when you fight for a righteous cause you might sometimes have to fight dirty."

Godber looked at Scroggins amazed, humbled and admiring of the faith of the man in front of him, though he himself had never found a doctrine more righteous than self-enrichment. Scroggins looked back at Godber with admiration for his extremely convincing performance as a natural-born liar. He had never been more certain that Godber had the morality of a thieving jackdaw, though he still couldn't work out what was his part in the night's events.

"I'll drink to that," Godber said.

"I will too. God bless you," Scroggins said.

The remarkable fact was that they each sincerely believed in the righteousness of their respective and divergent causes. No amount of bullying, backstabbing, extortion, racism, whoring, trafficking, thieving or killing would ever dislodge their beliefs from their minds.

Scroggins drank up and immediately went to find out what was really going on in Wanchai that night. It was only midnight as he walked down Lockhart Road but most shutters were down, except at known Catfish bars, which were packed with thuggish men who were celebrating. One bar had a contingent of British sailors, who sounded to Scroggins' trained ears like northerners. They were obviously oblivious to the territorial war they had stumbled into, and probably thinking that this was a normal night in Wanchai. At the crossroads with Fleming Road there was a car on fire. It was parked at an angle in the road, all its doors open. Around the corner Scroggins saw the only police vehicle in the area, an armoured personnel carrier. He indicated to the driver that he wanted a chat with the officer in charge, went round the back and banged on the iron door which swung open to show a team of eight, smoking Chinese cigarettes and playing cards.

"Johnny Boy, what's going on?" he said, using the familiarity of the Duchess. His man Tony was third to the left from Johnny Tse. Their momentary glance, imperceptible to anyone else, was enough to clock and acknowledge each other.

"I need to know what's happening here," he said looking at John Tse but addressing Tony. "It looks like the Catfish are hounding out the Greens," he continued.

"It's hard to tell," said Tse. "Our main objective it to make sure it doesn't spill over, and to protect the lives of innocents."

"I thought your main job was to keep law and order?"

"We look at the big picture," Tse said with a big grin on his face.

Two hours later Tony dropped a cigarette carton into a rubbish bin at the Kowloon terminal of the Star Ferry. Scroggins appeared five minutes later, quickly fished out the box and put it in his pocket. He took it to a small bar on Ashley Road that he had never been to, ordered a whiskey that he didn't touch, opened the box, took out a cigarette, lit it and unfolded a piece of paper he had taken out with the cigarette.

JT made it clear not to touch Catfish all night. One man beaten in an alley visible from van position. No order to move. Catfish seen moving into Green premises. Followed JT after end of shift. He visited Catfish installed in the Green Parrot. Ends.

Scroggins was seething. The Green Parrot was his pet project, he had diverted a lot of operational expenses into the place. It was an important liaison point and a clandestine cash-cow. It was covert, not in the ordinary sense of being a something that the Agency denied, but in the sense that the grown-ups at Langley knew nothing about it. This was the pet project of Scroggins and his cell, an elite core of dedicated operatives who knew better than the bosses what the bosses wanted and needed. That being the case he had no higher power to appeal to, to crush the balls of Keystone Cops who were trampling all over his work.

It was a rare, clean, clear night as he crossed back over the harbour towards Wanchai on the Star Ferry. He could see smoke rising from parts of the pleasure district and some fire engines cluttering along the harbourfront towards the battle zone, presumably paid off now that the Greens had been routed, and Catfish would be wanting to salvage properties that can be saved. The red star on the Bank of China building glared across the channel they sailed in, and Scroggins spat down into the black water. "What the hell is going on?" he yelled out in frustration, under cover of the labouring boat engine and the frothing waves just three feet down from where he leaned over the railing.

He walked into the Captain's Bar at the Mandarin where two or three old soaks murmured over their silver tankards. The old bar head gave him a slight nod and passed him the phone across the bar. Scroggins rang a number, let it ring three times and put the handset down, rang it again, let it ring once, and put the handset down. "Drat," he said and walked out, slipping a piece of paper under a beermat with the words: *Full watch on PC JT. Immediate.* The barman took the phone and the mat back.

One hour later, Barclay Harvestman walked into a small flat on the fifth floor of a block in Aberdeen Street.

"What's this about a story you're pitching to the Times?" Scroggins demanded of him.

"Ah. Hilarious load of nonsense that Wetherby started prattling on about in the last few days," he chuckled.

"Did you write it?" Scroggins asked, more menacingly than usual.

"I did a draft mock-up for him. It was never going to get published."

"What did he say about it?"

"He just asked me to do it, as a favour. He supplied the details. Have to admit, rather a good story on the face of it. Damned shame we can't publish it if you ask me, what with your boys keeping tabs on our rather flamboyant proprietor."

"Why didn't the Queen's own stop the Catfish in Wanchai tonight?"

"I haven't the faintest, old boy. Scouts' honour."

"Jeez Harvestman, lucky for you we keep you on a retainer rather than pay you for the quality of your information, eh?"

"Well you don't pay me much at all for keeping you abreast of my countrymen and being on call for meetings at all hours, like tonight when I was entertaining a particularly talented young lady."

"Know by any chance why Johnny Boy visited the Green Parrot?" he asked halfheartedly.

"Gosh, I didn't know he had."

"You're useless. Go back to bed."

Scroggins went back to the Captain's Bar where the same bar head looked at him through flat, opium-glazed eyes and nodded. He handed him a bourbon with a note under the beermat.

Watchers report police raid at Chai Wan squat at 9pm. Cleared out Green H lab. Chiu Chau Catfish appeared soon after police left. Chased out Greens resisting. Possible 10 or 12 hackings, including three deaths. One-armed master abducted. No record of police operation at HQ. Ends.

"Wanchai and Chai Wan at the same time. The master of the Green Turtle brand," he muttered under his breath, with an excruciating look on his exhausted face.

"Well I'll be damned," he said out loud, as the penny dropped. "A straight-up commercial takeover."

The Queen's own had dismantled his carefully constructed operation. The one that he had set up for the sake of humanity, for the war against tyranny. They did this for simple straight-up profit, to take over Green Turtle production and retail. "The greedy bastards!" he roared out too loudly, burning up with anger and barely able to control himself. He wasn't much of a drinker, as others at the Duchess complained of him, but he knocked back the bourbon and immediately ordered another. He was on the warpath, indignant that his countrymen had saved these limey asses in the real war, just to be paid back like this.

The sun was coming up. He headed up to a small flat on the seventh floor of a Sai Ying Pun block. Two men were lying on a sofa, heads, arms and legs covered in bloodied bandages.

"What's Uncle Sam going to do about this then?" said his contact, Three Eyes, gesturing at his ailing colleagues. He was a leery looking rogue with rough, sunburned skin, stubble on his face and wild hair, but he was much more calculating and steady than his alarming looks implied. Scroggins had never worked out why he was called Three Eyes.

"It looks like the Queen's own have pulled the plug on your Wanchai operations with the help of their Catfish partners," he said to Three Eyes.

"So what's the plan then?"

"There isn't one right now. Give me a foil of Green Turtle will you. I need to think."

Three Eyes handed him a line on a foil and passed him a match. Scroggins had his rolled-up ten-dollar note ready, held the match underneath and sucked greedily.

"You better come up with a good one."

"I will," said Scroggins, falling back in the armchair into a warm glow, where for an hour or so he was on a blissful break from the car-crash that his life resembled that night.

For the next four days Scroggins waited for word from the JT watchers. He finally got a note at the Mandarin.

JT met a barman from the Erection in the afternoon. Not Catfish, the one called Ma.

Scroggins scrolled through his mind. The quiet watcher, never got a drink wrong. Can handle three or four orders in one go, shouted at from any part of the lounge, each arrives as quick as the other, calculates the bill in his head. Faultless. Damn. Why didn't I recruit him?

JT and Ma go to Kennedy Town government depot. Pick up sack.
Cross harbour to Kai Tak squat. Ma leaves car alone. Reaches squat
newly-occupied by the one-armed chemist from Shanghai. Emerges
10 minutes later. Picked up by JT.

Scroggins headed immediately to pick up Three Eyes. They parked
at a point where the service entrance to the Duchess was visible and
waited. As expected, Ma walked in at 9:20 to start his 9:30 shift.

"That's him," Scroggins said. "You'll need about two or three of your
best watchers for the next two weeks. Professionals who know what
needs to be snapped and what can be dropped. No thugs."

"Usual price," Three Eyes said.

"$10 bag of Green Turtle Smack per day," Scroggins confirmed.

Ma's pattern quickly emerged. Mid-afternoon start from his Kennedy
Town squat after helping Darwin with his homework, sometimes
kicking a ball with him. Pick up at the government waste disposal unit.
Tram through Western, Sheung Wan and Central. Walk to Star Ferry.
Weave through Kowloon East to Kai Tak squat by 7pm. To the new lab
in the no-go area. Emerge 20 minutes later and walk on to Hung Hom,
cross the harbour to Wanchai. Service entrance to the establishment
formerly known as the Green Parrot, now named the Red Parrot and
run by Catfish. Then out and walk two blocks and into the Duchess to
appear at the bar at 9:30pm.

Once the daily routine outside the club had been established,
Scroggins drew on his best trade-craft to watch and record events inside
the club. John Tse would come in around 10pm and call Ma over for a
drink and a packet of cigarettes. It would always be Ma, and always a
new pack of cigarettes. Easy. There's the takings. What Scroggins tried
desperately to work out was who else was involved. Godber had to be,
or else why the blackmail on the night of the takeover? But he was good.
There was no sign from him. No obvious contact with Ma, nor Tse. No
obvious avoidance either.

Next was a close watch on Tse whenever he wasn't inside the Duchess. No pattern emerged, he was erratic. Was he too erratic? Hard to tell, he was an erratic character. Was he hoarding the cash in his house? Hopefully not, or else the only thing Scroggins could hope to bust would be a one-man operation by John Tse. If he wasn't hoarding the cash there had to be another person involved, whose movements would make sense of Tse's. Scroggins was running through his stockpile of $10 Green Turtle smack too quickly for his comfort. He went back to the Mandarin after the Duchess closed one night. He called Harvestman. Three rings. Receiver down. One more ring and a quick hike to the safe house on Aberdeen Street.

"Tally ho. Business for me?" Harvestman walked in, a little breathless.

"Who's been talking to Tse recently?"

"Everybody talks to Johnny Boy. You can't go to the Duchess and not talk to him. He is the life and soul of every party there. Last night he beat Fotherington in a five-pint speed-drinking competition. A new Scottish recruit was passed out under the table, and one of Johnny Boy's Chiu Chau boys was puking in the corner. Johnny Boy was the last man standing, and then he's still on the beat at 6am on the dot for the morning shift. You can't avoid a man like that. He is everywhere."

"What about Godber? What's he got going with Tse these days?"

"Nothing unusual I'd say, maybe the odd bit of cockfighting and porno."

"What about drugs?"

"Can't say anything comes to mind. The usual tax collection I would expect, once the old Wanchai reshuffle has settled into place. You're not still sore about that, are you, old boy?"

"How about the fool Wetherby?" he asked, ignoring the question that dug into the heart of his obsession.

"Nothing special. Except, come to think of it, he did say something a bit strange about Johnny Tse the other day."

"Finally, are we getting somewhere?"

"'That Johnny Boy is the bane of my life' he said. 'He's got ants in his pants and now I've got blisters on my feet.' 'What the bloody hell are you talking about?' I said. We were of course, pissed as newts, and he says something like: 'I'm not allowed to tell you, it's a top secret,' and of course we pissed ourselves laughing."

"And you're only just telling me that?" Scroggins asked, incredulous.

"Oh come on, this is ridiculous. I mean he was drunk as a skunk. There was no rhyme or reason to anything he said."

"No, probably not," Scroggins said, putting on his coat and walking out of the flat without saying goodbye.

"You're welcome. I hope that's helpful to you, you damned-rude American bastard," Harvestman said to himself, staring into the space where Scroggins had been and feeling sore for not even getting a bourbon out of this meeting.

The spotters were on Wetherby the next day and it wasn't long until a pattern began to emerge in relation to Tse's movements. One day Tse would make a quick visit to St John's Cathedral. Five minutes later Wetherby would be passing by. Another day a walk through Victoria Park with Wetherby strolling through quickly from another direction. Then a casual amble through the Star Ferry terminal, or a visit to a public toilet, a browse through a bookshop. It wasn't difficult to crack once they were watching the two of them. From there it was a matter of time before seeing Wetherby's more-or-less regular visits to a private bank in Central.

So did the Queen's own turn a blind eye to the Catfish takeover of Wanchai just for Wetherby's own profit? That was impossible. Godber. He had to be involved. He was the sharpest shark of the lot. Scroggins turned up at the Sai Ying Pun flat and said: "Come on."

"Finally," said Three Eyes. "What's the plan?"

"We're bringing in the courier."

Three Eyes and two henchmen watched Ma pick up his opium stash and walk through Kennedy Town. They ran round a block to wait for him as he approached a narrow alley cluttered with boxes of dried shark fin, crates of gecko carcasses, and other objects of trade in the desiccated food and medicine market. They grabbed him and threw him onto a sack of caterpillar fungus just arrived from Tibet via Canton. A canvas bag was thrown over his head and his limbs were tied behind his back within seconds, leaving him helpless and disorientated. He felt a knife point pressing into his back and he recognised the Shanghainese accents of the Green troopers instructing him to walk.

A short car ride brought him to the Kennedy Town docks where they bundled him to the end of the pier, down steps to the water's edge and pushed him into a sampan that he couldn't see. Forty minutes later, somewhere in the Lamma Channel, he heard a radio playing western music on the junk he was transferred to.

The American agent on the boat kept his instructions mostly to gestures, pointing and eyebrow movements, to avoid giving himself away as a gweilo. The only words he spoke were monosyllabic orders barked out in perfect Chinese with a hint of a Beijing accent. Three Eyes knew what was required and he always enjoyed working on these special missions with Scroggins. The table was already prepared, slightly higher at one end and sloping down to the other. Ma's feet were tied down to the higher end with a belt, his head down at the lower end.

Earlier Scroggins had described the process to Three Eyes.

"A little trick we taught the French Foreign Legion in Indochina," he said, "it's a wonderful way of inducing terror in your subject without doing much real damage."

Before Ma had any chance to say anything a wet towel was pressed against his nose and mouth, and a bucket of water was tipped over his face. He was overwhelmed by a dreadful sense that he was drowning. He gasped in panic at the drenched cloth in a desperate bid to extract air, but he only managed to seal his airways more completely. His chest burned in exploding pain as he tried to flail his arms in terror, only to discover that they had been strapped down too. He was drowning right there on the table, and the moment before he blacked out the cloth was lifted, allowing him to immediately suck air down through his chest, into his stomach, through his toe tips to the depth of his being.

"What do you want?" he shouted, livid, contemptuous of the stupidity of his hosts. "Just ask me," he spat out in the moment before the wet cloth slammed back onto his face and another bucket of salty sea water was thrown over his head.

He had flashbacks to the Pearl River. Where was Darwin? Xiao Hu? He was drowning, it was an obscenity. The cloth came off, a burst of air, Three Eyes pulling up the face mask to grin down at him. "Who set you up as a heroin courier?"

"Godber," he screamed without hesitation. "Motherfucking Godber. Go kill him. I don't give a fuck."

That was quick, thought Scroggins. Too quick, who's he hiding? He nodded to Three Eyes who slapped the wet towel down again and threw the water over him. Ma was back in the Pearl River calling out to Xiao Hu and Darwin. He was urging them to hold on, to live. "You have to live!" he screamed at them. He was treading water. I can survive this, he thought to himself. Airways opened.

"Who else?"

"No-one, just Tse, that's all I know."

Ma noticed the tune on the radio – *"Pack up all my care and woe, here I go, lying low, bye-bye blackbird..."*

Another nod from Scroggins and Ma was drowning again. He blacked out and floated somewhere. He wondered if he was going to hell.

"I don't want to go to hell," he said.

"bye bye blackbird..."

But then he realised that nothing could possibly be worse than the hell that humanity inflicted on itself. He was already in hell. All the worst terrors humans could ever invent or dream of were already a reality in the world he lived in, in the one real world that all humans shared. He was living out some of the worst, he had been walking through hell for months. Nothing could possibly be worse than life itself.

Then he had a vision of a leaf flittering through a bright sunlit sky, constantly turning over its dark and light side, the two opposite sides of the leaf facets of each other. And in the same instant he understood that the happiest moments of his own life were the pinnacles of human happiness. The joy of running down a hill trying to catch a butterfly. The first friendship he had at school. The praise he received from his father for his perfect score in kung fu. Secretly making love with Xiao Hu in a wood behind their village. The triumph of a successful bear hunt in the mountain forest on a winter's night. The birth of his son. The relief of his family being alive after their ordeal in the sea. Sharing stories as they hiked over Lantau, full of hope for their new life.

Did he have enough of these experiences? No. Did the bad outweigh the good? Yes. But heaven and hell, he had lived them both. He had lived. But it wasn't anywhere near enough. He wanted to live more, he wanted to live longer, he was greedy for life.

Scroggins began to feel nervous, as Ma had been unconscious for a minute that felt much longer. Suddenly Ma's eyes opened wide and crazed and he gasped desperately for his life, an act of will that both alarmed and reassured Scroggins.

"No one here can love and understand me, oh what hard-luck stories they all hand me..."

"What about Wetherby?" Three Eyes read out from his script.
"No idea."
The towel and bucket came down again.

"Nope, still no idea, except he's an idiot."

"How about Thomas-Littleton?"

"Never heard anything. I doubt it, far too stupid."

"You'd better make my bed, and light the light, I'll arrive late tonight..."

Three Eyes was just about to slam the towel on his face again when Scroggins raised his arm to stop.

"Blackbird, bye-bye, goodbye..."

Scroggins calculated that they had got about as much out of him as they could, which boiled down to the fact that Godber was involved. Johnny Tse he knew about, Wetherby, he knew more than Ma. T-L was inconclusive, though Ma's assessment seemed reasonable. At the back of his mind Scroggins realised that he probably could have got these answers without his 'water-based enhanced interrogation contraption,' but that wasn't really the point. Scroggins most of all wanted to impress Three Eyes, not for any strategic reason, simply to impress him with his own prowess.

As a middle-class bookworm from a comfortable American suburb, Scroggins had always been fascinated by underworld characters who refused to bow to the polite and restrained conventions of respectable conformists. He idolised pirates, smugglers and gangsters. Until he started real-life operations in the agency, all his idols were fictional characters. Once he started meeting real life versions he thought he was living out his wildest dreams. He secretly hero-worshipped Three Eyes, though he hid it well, and was constantly looking for ways to impress him, and for that, the 'water contraption' was certainly worthwhile.

A psychologist at Langley had made a small footnote on Scroggins' file that he had an infantile fascination for the underworld and he was slightly at risk of going rogue, but his handlers crunched the scores into their algorithm and were satisfied that Scroggins fit their scientifically-calculated maverick quotient for that year's Asia operatives.

When Scroggins set up the Green Parrot without his handlers knowing about it, he justified that as part of his mission to keep the all-important Green Gang onside and close. To those he couldn't avoid telling, it was a covert means to an authorised end. Privately however, Scroggins saw it as part of an alternative reality, where he was a player on the tough streets of Wanchai. He was the fantasy boss of a Chinese Triad.

Scroggins took immense personal pride in the Green Parrot, and this was the real reason he needed to teach Godber a lesson. The British police officer who really did act like a gangster needed a kick up the ass from his American rival. Godber needed to be taught a lesson he would never forget, he needed to be taught never to mess with the Cousins again, especially with Agent Harry Scroggins. It was time for a showdown.

"Three Eyes. Ma is a Communist spy," Scroggins said.

"No, no, he's a pawn, Scroggins," Three Eyes retorted.

"No Three Eyes, he's working for Mao. That's why he came to Hong Kong."

"Mao? He is a good man."

"What are you talking about? You're part of Chiang Kai-shek's warrior guard! You can't be praising Mao."

"Chiang, Mao, all the same. Two powerful generals, both love China. I love both."

Scroggins was finding this all too confusing. He had to shake himself out of such a baffling distraction.

"Your politics, Three Eyes, is as baffling as it is irrelevant right now. What we need to do is to establish that Ma is a Communist spy."

"Whatever boss. What do you want me to do?"

"There's a beach outside Tai O Police Station at Lantau. You know Tai O?"

"Tai O? Mudskippers and crazy pirates. I love it."

"Take him to the beach, with the Nationalist flag hoisted at the front of the boat. Blindfold him and stage a fake execution, shouting out: 'Long live the Nationalists! Death to the Communist Spy'. Shoot the rocks above his head, maybe some rocks fall and injure him, the main thing is to scare the shit out of him."

"Fake? Why not kill him?"

"No. I want him to live to tell the story of the water contraption, the danger of messing with the wrong people. He is more useful as a warning."

"That's it?"

"That's it. Except one thing."

Three Eyes went back up to the deck where Ma was still strapped on the board. He put the bag back over Ma's head so that he wouldn't see Scroggins, who stood at one side with a sharp knife and proceeded to show off his calligraphic skills by carving the Chinese word for 'Spy' onto his chest. Ma screamed out, believing this to be his final moment. Searing pain shot through him as the blade cut through his flesh.

Scroggins flagged a passing sampan and left the junk heading towards Lantau.

Three Eyes made a slight diversion towards Cheung Chau port once Scroggins was nearly out of sight. He calculated that his profit would be slightly higher if he subcontracted the job and kept the fuel stipend Scroggins had left for the return trip to Tai O. He knew the Tai O Mongoose were keen to pick up freelance work, usually at a good bargain as they were always looking for opportunities to play with the big boys. He moored at the harbour and borrowed the phone at the local office of a Triad group that had a wavering old acquaintance with the Greens. And though he didn't know the name of the tune, Three

Eyes found himself whistling *Bye Bye Blackbird* as he waited for the Mongoose to arrive.

11

RING OF FIRE

The whole village turned out for the Dagger's 'homecoming.' It was seven days since he had died, so this night was the welcoming home of his soul. The Dagger had been left on the steps of the Kwan Tai temple as a baby and had lived in rented accommodation all his adult life, so the market square was the home his soul was returning to. He had no known relatives, he was brought up in the village orphanage and had never married. His mother could well have been one of the old crones sitting around the edge of the square chewing sunflower seeds, or could have been a passing Cantonese traveller, or Pekinese, Shanghainese, Mongolian, Korean or Japanese, for all anyone knew. The Mongoose were the closest thing he had to a family.

A duck on a piece of string was walked into the square to bring the Dagger's spirit home, and soon it was plucked, gutted and roasted. The square was lit up by big flaming torches. A wooden statue at the head of the coffin had a face skilfully carved to resemble the Dagger, with his pirate's ponytail, and in his hands his hunting rifle. The coffin was bedecked with white flowers and a solemn-faced photo of the Dagger. His seemed to be the only solemn face in the market square, with everyone else enjoying the chance to catch up with one another. There were giggles and heckling as Red recited the ancient question and answer riddles, the answers to which the Dagger would need to know before being admitted to live with the elite seafarers of the heavens, or 'ghost riders in the sky' as Jagan whispered to Simon.

"Which fish puts its fin in the air?" Red asked.

"The shark puts its fin in the air!" the crowd replied, with the children shouting the loudest.

"Who hides in the mud?"

"Moray and snake eels hide in the mud!"

"Which fish likes to shoot?"

"Long Tom likes to shoot."

Salty, Red and Jackson were smoking cigars, the two Mongoose recounting to Jackson tales of heroism and triumph at the Sham Shui Po riots. Old grannies were yakking about the past, some remembering the young Dagger who always did the funniest moves in the lion dance and had an unpredictable temperament. Danny, Spike and two or three other young Mongoose smoked and played dice games loudly. Trumpeters, symbol-smashers and drummers kept up their mournful yet clanging dirges from the land of the dead.

Simon, Jagan, Patrick, Maria, Sally and Madge sat eating dumplings at one of the makeshift tables that dotted the square. Falkirk, Madam Li and Jane O'Connor were on another. Ishmael Chalmers and his wife Mui Mui were also there. They had sailed over from Pui O as soon as they had heard the news. Two of Mui Mui's sons had come over from Kowloon with wealthy-looking wives in tow. They had driven to the Sham Wat road and been carried over the hills by the sedan girls.

Towards the end of the square, the Monkey King performer was entertaining awed children with fire-eating and juggling, while his chained pet primate did somersaults in front of him. The twins Jeanie and Stevie were among the children who giggled, clapped and clambered over each other at the front. Some dared to creep forward to try to pull the monkey's tail, though the animal clearly lacked a sense of humour and irritably swiped back at any child that got too near. At the opposite side of the square the sun-crusted vagabond Tibetans were now selling a bear skin, twirling their prayer wheels and reciting a more exotic chant than that of the more familiar tones wafting out of the Kwan Tai temple.

Bad News, SPK, the Jap Devil and a few others from Joycee's bar were sitting on one table enjoying a bottle of Bulgarian raki that had mysteriously arrived in a crate from Macau that morning. They talked about the Dagger's exploits during the war. The prevailing view on the Mongoose during that time was that they were heroes. The Dagger had led the legendary attack on the Tai O police station, side-by-side with Salty and Red, when they successfully routed the Japanese and held the station for two weeks. When Japanese reinforcements returned with enough firepower to bomb the station deep into the ground, the guerrillas quickly melted into Tiger Hill and disappeared, leaving the shell of a building stripped of all arms and assets and its communications destroyed.

As was often the case at large gatherings the evil of the Japanese resurfaced in conversation. Danny, who had been struggling with events his Mongoose career was imposing on him, felt a burning curiosity towards the Jap Devil.

"Does it not bother you to live here in Tai O?" he couldn't stop himself asking.

"Well I suppose I had to live somewhere," he replied with amusement.

"No but, you know, this is your enemy's land isn't it? Here you have to listen to these horrible stories about the things your countrymen did."

"Well, for starters, you boys aren't my enemy. I have no quarrel with any Chinese person, except that bastard who stole my fishing boat last year," he said with a chuckle.

"But do you hate Japan? Is that why you prefer to live with us?" Danny went on.

"Well Danny, do you love your mother?"

"Of course I do."

"I loved my mother too, when she was alive. She was a courageous woman and she taught me to love the beauty that surrounds us. She gave me life, and she was Japanese. So was my dad who taught me that kindness was a force to be reckoned with. So no, I don't hate Japan, I love it."

"But it was wrong, wasn't it? What the Japanese did?"

The Jap Devil laughed with incredulity, as others did with him.

"What? You mean killing and maiming civilians? Slaughtering babies? Enslavement? Rape? Forced suicide? Brainwashing? Human vivisection? Were these wrong? Let me think, what would mum and dad have said? Evil. Definitely evil."

"But why are the Japanese so evil?" Danny said, simply echoing what he had heard all his life.

"Are we especially evil? We were then, yes. But I'm not sure if we are in general. At that time there was a military and political entity that was clearly evil. People became evil, they chose to do evil things. But it wasn't the first time in history that such an unimaginable monster rose from among people who started off doing what they told themselves was good, right and inevitable."

"There are all sorts of evil aren't there?" piped up Ishmael. "There are the evil works of an evil empire, that's for sure. Who knows why that happens when it happens, but I don't think that evil is the exclusive property of one nation. Mr Darwin would postulate that all our behaviours would have evolved in nature. Have you ever seen orcas, Mr Nagashima?"

"Much to my regret I've never had the pleasure," the Jap Devil answered.

"Beautiful animals. They are intelligent, sociable, they cooperate. They are capable of empathy too. I've seen them grieve a lost calf and console a heartbroken mother. I saw them down in the Southern Ocean where ice floes threatened to sink our boat. One time we were lost in the dark and almost certain to be sunk, when a group of orcas appeared by our side, and went to the front of our ship. They steered us out of danger. They are good.

"They are evil too. They hunt in packs to isolate seals and tear them apart. They need to to survive, you can't begrudge them that. But they don't need to torture an orphan by tossing it repeatedly in the air until all its bones are broken while still alive, and then tear chunks out of its flesh as its screams die down. I've seen a pod of juvenile males do that. How can that be anything but evil? What was curious to me was that there seemed to be one leader of the pack that was the most active in the killing, almost visibly taking pleasure. In human terms I wondered if such an individual would be labelled a so-called psychopath. The others on the team looked more hesitant at the beginning. But by the end they were just as enthusiastically joining in.

"I don't believe in angels and devils and religious hocus-pocus, but you only need to open your eyes to see that evil exists. Some people like doing evil, maybe there's something in their brain that makes them addicted to it. Then there are others who have different goals, like getting rich or winning admiration, but they don't mind committing evil to reach those goals. Then there are just accidents and natural disasters, they don't come from any evil intention but the results can be more horrific than anything an evil mastermind could have dreamed up. When it comes to sheer numbers, though, I would say that two types of evil affect us more commonly than any other. That's the evil done by people who think they are doing good, and evil carried out by ordinary people following orders."

"My God, what's all this morbid talk?" Bad News roared. "Don't give Ishmael or the Jap Devil any more of that Bulgarian raki, it's reserved for the Tanka! And no more of anything to that nosy parker son of mine. What do you think this is? A bloody funeral?"

The table erupted in laughter and glasses clinked. Danny laughed along too, a bit embarrassed to be caught out being so earnest, but privately he continued to think about Ma Xun, wondering what kind of evil had killed him.

Suddenly there was pandemonium as Blind Wang came storming into the square shouting "Tiger! Tiger! Tiger!" Men, as well as Madam Li and Mui Mui, jumped to their feet and surrounded him. "It came leaping out of the sea, clambered up the bank and chased a muntjac into the bushes. My God, it's huge!"

Many of the men had their rifles with them. Jackson handed out a cache of guns from the Committee Office, as Simon, Jagan and Falkirk noted with alarm the extent of their arsenal. Danny and Spike were at the head of the line. Jackson raised his arm and called for attention. "We can cut this beast off, as long as he's on Tiger Hill. Everyone grab a flaming torch, we need to approach it as a closing ring of fire. We have to be organised, or he'll slip past us."

With their torches they split into groups to cover every path that went up the hill. The police contingent headed back to the station to approach from the far north-western end. Madam Li led another group via the Hung Shing temple. Salty Pang and his boys went in the opposite direction, along the back street towards the Yeung Hau temple, in the area the beast was first seen in by Blind Wang. Jackson followed the same direction, leading a group that went along the coastal path as far as it could and then climbed up steeply towards the summit.

All the monks, including the Tibetan visitors also sprang to action, grabbing guns while chanting for Buddha's mercy. Adolescent kids tried to join but the smaller ones were pulled back. Maria rounded up their brood along with other kids of parents worried that their stilt houses might prove too flimsy for a rampant tiger. She herded them into the schoolhouse near the fish market. Ishmael and Mui Mui stood up together for the hunt, but Mui Mui scolded her husband saying he was too old for the job. After a brief argument Ishmael stood down, muttering and grumbling, while Mui Mui grabbed a Rural Committee gun and caught up with Madam Li's contingent, telling her she needed someone who knew Tiger Hill as well as she did. Mui Mui's sons looked eager to go, but their tai-tai wives clung to their arms in terror. As soon as Mui Mui had disappeared, Ishmael grabbed a flaming torch and headed in the opposite direction to join Salty's crew. This gave the sons the excuse they needed to prise their wives off their arms and join the hunt to escort their elderly stepdad. They had their own pistols. Jane O'Connor took pity on the tai-tais and guided them towards the schoolhouse. Once the ladies were safely in the care of Maria she headed off towards Madam Li's unit, Maria shouting after her: "Where are you going? You don't have a gun," and Jane shouting back, "I'm a journalist, damn it. I don't need a bloody gun, I've got a pen."

No-one knew how Tiger Hill had gained its name. Some said if you squinted at it from exactly the right spot it almost resembled a tiger. Others said the grasses growing on the sides looked stripy. But the villagers were now certain that destiny was about to be fulfilled. This would be the place where they would catch the tiger, because surely there was no escape. It was technically an island, surrounded easily by the villagers within 20 minutes, connected to mainland Lantau only at the bottleneck of the village. The tiger had swum the 20-metre neck of water near the Yeung Hau temple to get onto the hill, but now that it was there, the beast had trapped itself. It was exactly as Jagan had envisioned it. There was great excitement among the hunters, though Jagan and some of the other early advocates of the hunt were a bit saddened that the glory of the killing would have to be shared by all, including the sceptics and opportunists who had never showed any interest in the hunt until now that the animal was trapped.

The sub-groups reached the hill through their respective approaches and then fanned out. A line of flaming torches slowly tightened towards the centre of the hill, the western edge guarded by a steep descent into the sea. For two hours they crept forward. Some were lucky, easily advancing over a grassy bank, others had gnarly bushes and tricky rocks to contend with. As the line converged, communications became more possible among the main leaders of the hunt, Salty, Jackson, Madam Li and Old Typhoon. They could let each other know what was happening by passing messages along the lines, though inevitably, as with Chinese whispers there were misunderstandings and garbled instructions. "Hold back at the west" became "Advance to the west." "Commotion at the knoll" turned to "Silence at the knoll."

Simon began to wonder if their earlier confidence was hasty when he realised how chaotic it was in the unevenly-torchlit dark, with each move executed as an improvisation. But as they converged there was a huge and terrifying roar that erupted from ahead, confirming the fact that a real tiger was right there on the hill and was becoming agitated by a tightening ring of fire. There was a palpable shock of excitement through the hunters. Some tingled with anticipation while others wished they were back at the schoolhouse. Salty and Mui Mui, though apart from each other, were both remembering the same occasion, when guerrillas closed in on a Japanese commander they had managed to separate from his unit and stalked him to the top of the hill. It was Red who had sniped the kill shot on that occasion. Salty had been annoyed that Red had jumped his command, but couldn't complain about the result.

Madam Li turned to her group and told them to be meticulously vigilant. "You're in as much danger as the tiger is right now," she warned.

Falkirk had a flashback to the mountains of Yunnan, when he and his group of a dozen prison escapees were being stalked by three tigers. The Brothers, they called them. For ten days the cats had followed them. They would look behind to see one on a rock, another crossing a stream, a third visible through tall grasses only by its upheld tail. The first of their party was taken when exhausted; he had fallen behind as they climbed through a forest towards the Tibetan plateau. Another was dragged from his own tent, the tigers clearly having spotted that he was sleeping alone that night. It was the first night he had done so, having volunteered to take himself away from the others because of a fever he had. Falkirk eventually got the leader of the pack by dropping behind and hiding in a tree branch for half a day. The remaining two, seemingly out of habit and not knowing what else to do, continued following the troop for a couple of days, but then lost heart without their leader and slunk off.

Finally the circle converged at the top of Tiger Hill, an orange noose of fire. In the centre there prowled a silhouette, now roaring with alarming frequency. The front line of the circle was not for the faint-hearted, which was a pity for them as there was only a front line.

"Hold still everyone, this is a lethal situation. We can't all just let our guns off or we're going to kill each other," Madam Li said, without once taking the tiger out of her gunsight.

"We need one shooter," Jackson called out. "Who's the best shot?"

Several voices called out at once. "Red."

Salty confirmed it, "Red has never missed a shot. Isn't that right, Red?"

"Can't say never, but certainly popped a few Japs in my time," he replied.

"Not bad with sprinting muntjacs through a forest either," Salty embellished.

So it was agreed that Red would kill the tiger. Those who stood behind the beast in relation to Red nervously tried to shuffle out of the sightline.

The tiger was magnificent, with its huge head and lethal fangs that glowed in the orange hue of the torchlight. It took nerves of steel for all in the circle to hold their position in the face of such savage power. Mui Mui looked across and saw that her mad mariner husband was there, supported on each side by her sons. She admitted to herself it was inevitable. The police group held one side of the circle, Falkirk, Simon, Jagan and Patrick in one line. Also present were the Fox and other constabularies. Salty was side-by-side with Red as he so often had been over the decades. Not far away were Bad News, the Jap Devil and SPK, all slightly sozzled and gently swaying. The beast loped left to right on its huge clawed pads. Simon could make out kites in the sky above, wheeling, transfixed by the drama below them. Red was locked on, waiting for the perfect moment for a faultless, clean kill.

Suddenly the tiger made a decisive move. Perhaps it had seen a strategic opening, perhaps it was running at random, but whatever the rationale it was running at full power towards the east, directly towards Danny. Salty shouted the order to shoot, just like he used to in their guerrilla days. Red, composed, centred his well-worn rifle at the animal's massive head, now about ten yards from Danny, who had a split second to see the predator leap into the air and lunge towards him.

"This is it," he thought, not clear in his own mind if he meant for himself or the tiger.

The action almost froze in Red's mind as he processed his own thoughts. Time to pull the trigger, he knew, but then it struck him that he had never seen a man mauled to death by a tiger and he was gripped by an overwhelming urge to witness an awesome moment of truth. He had nothing against Danny, but perhaps it was nature's turn to express its full force when man had already done so much to tyrannise the world. Everything dies. Let life take its course. In a split second he made a minute adjustment of his stance, aiming at Jupiter up in the night sky, or was it Mars? he wondered, distracted, as the bullet scorched over the leaping predator's head.

The tiger continued on the trajectory it had set for itself and cleared the space where Danny's face had been by an inch, though Danny's head had already hit the ground as he instinctively threw himself down. To the others who stood transfixed, it was an utterly confusing moment. Most believed Danny had been swatted by the tiger, though some thought he had been hit by the bullet. As soon as Madam Li snapped out of the collective and momentary trance she realised that the tiger had cleared the circle and was running for its life towards the village. She raised a thunderous war cry and charged after it, drawing with her around a dozen of the hunters who leapt into action. The chasers would keep going for the rest of the night, crossing water at Yeung Hau temple and pursuing the cat northwards on Lantau Island, but they would never get it. The moment it flew over Danny's head would be the last true sighting of a tiger on Lantau, though no-one who wasn't at the Dagger's funeral would ever believe that there had been one at all.

Bad News rushed to his son, who was lying on the ground with his eyes closed.

"Talk to me Danny, are you OK, boy?" he called out.

Danny himself wasn't sure if he had been hit by a thousand pounds of tiger or a bullet. To test his condition he opened one eye and then the other. He saw the ring of faces around him, his father, Simon, Jagan, SPK, the Jap Devil and others, all familiar to him.

"Erm, nothing hurts," he said. "A bit confused, anyone know what happened?"

"Red missed, and so did the tiger by the look of it. Can you stand up?" Jagan said.

He got up. Four people examined him as he insisted: "I'm OK, I'm OK, I'm fine," and they didn't find a scratch on him. When he was given the all-clear there was a cheer and everyone instinctively knew it was all over. Bad News gave Danny something that almost resembled a hug saying: "Good, good, all good. Come on son, we'll go and reclaim that Bulgarian raki."

"I think I'm alright for the moment Dad. I'm in the mood to enjoy the stars for a bit."

"Suit yourself lad. The main thing is that you're intact, unharmed and OK. I'll drink to that," he said, eager to get back to the square.

"Me too," SPK said, as salutation to the accidental and non-achieving hero of the night.

Red came over and said: "Well. Looks like I'm not a perfect shot after all."

"No one's perfect," Danny tried to joke, though he couldn't quite raise a laugh so close to the event that nearly killed him. Red shrugged nonchalantly and wandered down the hill with the others.

Danny sat down and looked up at the night sky, which became clearer once most of the flaming torches had disappeared.

"Is that Mars or Jupiter?" he wondered out loud.

"Maybe Mars," Simon suggested, without any reason to put forward one or the other.

"Jupiter," Jagan said, with a certainty that discouraged dissent, though he kept his doubts to himself.

"Ring of fire. That should be a song," Jagan said after a pause, thinking of the scene on the mountain with the trapped tiger in the middle.

"Why?" Danny asked.

"It's poetic. Like song titles should be."

"So, are you like a frustrated poet and musician in the uniform of a policeman?" Danny teased.

"Don't forget zoologist, and stargazer all of a sudden tonight," Simon chipped in, handing out the cigarettes.

Jagan laughed at this but he gently put the spotlight back on Danny. "How about you Danny? What's your true calling while you take on the form of a Mongoose Triad?"

"Oh I dunno. Maybe fisherman, like my dad. I wish we had gone shark fishing rather than street fighting in Sham Shui Po."

"Your dad is so good at fishing that he can hook a crate of Bulgarian raki from the South China Sea!" Jagan said, triggering a laugh between them all.

They were the last three on the hill, lying back, smoking their cigarettes and enjoying the calm. When Jagan finished his, he said he would go and catch up with the chasers. Something told him that they had missed the last chance to get the tiger, but he needed to be certain.

"That was close," Simon said.

"Yeah. I thought I'd had it, or the tiger at least. I didn't think we'd both get away with it."

"The Dagger got away with it, didn't he?"

"What do you mean?" Danny asked, knowing exactly what he meant.

"He killed Ma Xun, didn't he? Drunk as a skunk."

"It was an accident."

"You said."

"We were supposed to just scare him, and leave him for you boys to pick up. I think he was some kind of a message for someone. We didn't know anything about the reasons. The Dagger was too far gone to understand the instructions. We shouldn't have let him have a gun at all, though it would have been quite tricky disarming him in that state."

"Do you know who Three Eyes works for?"

"I dunno, Yank agents? He gave us the KMT flag to put on the front of the boat and told us to shout out Nationalist slogans. Who does he work for?"

"I don't know to be honest, but possibly the Yanks."

"Ma said a Yank carved his chest. Said the guy didn't say much, but by the few words he uttered he got the impression it was someone who thought himself to be a good Chinese speaker, though to Ma it was obvious – a Yank."

"What did you get paid?"

"Salty got a bag of Green Turtle Smack. We all got a small cut. Didn't amount to much to be honest. Spike sold mine on for me. I got about a dollar."

Simon thought it best not to tell Danny right now about Madge's near-death experience with the stuff, but he knew that once he told Maria it would get back to him.

There was a pause as they both appreciated the constellation that Jupiter or Mars was traversing – and the Chinese cigarettes they were smoking.

"Danny, the Mongoose..."

"I know, I know. Losers."

"Yeah."

"Yeah."

They walked down, in silence at first, then in increasing animation as they recounted their own experiences on the tiger hunt.

"You don't want us to finish him off then?" Salty Pang had asked Three Eyes back at Cheung Chau on the day of Ma's death. He was trying to sound as casual as possible but he was already regretting their involvement.

"No. He just needs scaring. You stage a mock execution and shoot above his head. The stupid English police will shit their pants, run down from their cosy police house, and you're already halfway around Tiger Hill."

"Easy," Salty said, relieved.

"Yeah," said the Dagger, "we'll finish him off for you."

"No you don't. Is this man stupid?" Three Eyes asked Salty with menace.

"No, no, no we don't!" shouted Salty, "I apologise for my associate. He's just got a very stupid sense of humour. We understand clearly what we need to do."

They sailed back through the dark with their captive cargo. The outline of Lantau was stark and clear against the moonlit sky, the ridge pushing up into the mound of Sunset Peak then dropping sharply before its second rise to majestic Lantau Peak. Here and there faint lights indicated small fishing villages that dotted the coast. Pui O twinkled where Ishmael had joined them for a drink on the ride out, then village mongrels were barking at the tiny hamlet of Cheung Sha followed by three miles of yellow beach down to Tong Fuk where someone had lit a bonfire. They rounded the Deer's Head and Shek Mun hill and glided past the Soko Islands, where pink dolphins swam ahead of them, illuminated by the moonlight.

Danny was left in charge of their captive on deck, while the rest of them went below to pass the time playing cards. He lit a cigarette and passed it to his charge.

"Are you going to kill me?" Ma asked.

"Nah, that's just all talk. This is just business Mister, nothing personal. Don't worry, I know the mongrel pig at the police station. He's OK. He'll treat you fair. Are you really a Communist spy?"

"A Communist spy? That's a new one. I might have considered the position had they offered me a job, but not even a friendly chat or a cup of tea with Xinhua since I arrived in Hong Kong. Almost feels as if they don't want to know me. Back in my home village, all they wanted from me was slave labour. Maybe I'm too ambitious, but I thought there's got to be a better way of life than that. I didn't want my son to grow up in their clutches. So we escaped the bloody Communists, and now you're calling me their agent."

The Dagger was shouting loudest in the card game below deck, topping up his intoxication with regular pulls from a bottle of Beijing Er Gou Tou that had arrived in a consignment of contraband that morning.

"So why did they catch you and carve your chest?"

"I was doing some dirty work for one group of dirty scoundrels and that upset some lunatics from another set of scoundrels and they tortured me for information I would have given up for free, and I guess they then sold me on to you."

"I see."

"No, you don't.

"No, I don't."

"It was a gweilo that carved my chest. He tried to say 'hold him' in Cantonese, but his accent was obvious."

"Are you a member of the Catfish?" Danny asked, recognising his Chiu Chau accent.

"No. I don't have time for Communists and I don't have time for Catfish either. Running around with the Catfish is a loser's game. I know them well, I know how they operate. They think they are players, and that they are winning, but they don't have a clue what they're doing, or why. They don't know who they can trust or who their friends are. When some of them get rich they are surprised that they are just as enslaved as they were before, and they don't know what to do with their wealth. The average Catfish really has no idea what he's fighting for and he spends most of his time running scared."

"You sound like Madam Li. You would like her."

"I know her. I stayed in her house. She's a good woman."

A pair of terns flashed by, close enough to show their black caps and wing tips on their white bodies. SPK at the wheel had a line dangling out of the pilot's window, hoping to snag a squid in the boat light.

"Why did you get involved?"

"I went to catch a tiger," Ma replied.

"A tiger? We have one here. We're going to catch it," Danny said, animated.

"It's not easy, son, and very dangerous. You can get yourself killed trying. My tiger was in a bar called the Erection. You ever heard of it? I was the barman there."

Danny laughed at the name but didn't have time to find out why it was called that, as the boat arrived outside Tai O Police Station.

Salty ordered Red to take Ma across on the dinghy to shore. Ma showed no resistance. He wasn't afraid of the Mongoose, he saw the difference between these subcontracted country bumpkins and the nasty operatives that kidnapped and tortured him.

"Back in Tai O," he thought, "back with the people who saved my life." He felt comfortable there.

Red tied his hands and feet together and tightened his blindfold. He told him to stand still on the beach and wait. They would raise the alarm and the stupid English police would run down to get him.

They lit up the torches on the boat and gunners took position as drummers poised for the order. This was theatre, they were proud performers. Salty told the shooters to aim for the cliff, making sure they set their sights high enough to avoid an accident. He yelled out the signal so loud that Danny and Spike nearly leapt into the air.

"Long live the Nationalists! Die, Communist bastard!"

A thunderous volley was released. The drummers and gong-bangers beat their instruments with all their power.

Ma flew back, then slumped down. Danny was confused.

"That looked realistic," he said.

Then the Dagger, swaying, pumped his fist into the air: "We got the bastard!" he shouted and shot another round into the sky.

Salty realised with horror what had happened.

"You fucking fucking fucking stupid fucking idiot," he hissed.

"Get this boat moving right now!" he hissed at SPK.

Danny heard the police station alarm ring out and the silhouettes of Simon and Jagan rushing down to the beach. He wanted to call out and say there had been a terrible mistake.

"Stop, police!" shouted Simon.

"A present for you Imperialist dogs. A Communist spy. Don't choke on the pork," Red shouted out on script.

"This is your last warning. Stop, police!" Simon replied.

"This is yours, you mongrel," shouted the Dagger off-script, before shooting at the cliff above Simon and Jagan's head and single-handedly triggering a rockfall.

SPK rammed the boat into full throttle and pulled away around Tiger Hill. Spike was the first to break the silence: "Did you see him fly back and go down?"

Red looked at the Dagger: "Someone shot him."

"Yeah, I think it was me!" the Dagger said, still not understanding that he might have done something terribly wrong.

Danny looked at Salty, who was deep in thought with his head between his legs.

"Where are we going?" Danny said.

"Tung Chung," said Salty. "We'll stay there for a couple of days. That will be our alibi."

"No we won't," SPK said. "No fuel."

Salty started shouting at the Dagger and pummelling him with punches and slaps. The Dagger, bewildered, nearly hit back, then sensed he had better not and retreated into a corner, confused and muttering.

"Fuck. Burn the boat. SPK, I'll get the Rural Committee to loan the money to Dagger, he'll pay for your new boat and he'll pay back the committee for the rest of his life, though at this rate he may not have many days left."

They landed at Sham Wat and scattered through the bush after syphoning the remaining fuel from the tank, splashing it across the boat and setting it ablaze. Once on land it was every man for himself, except the Dagger who was effectively Salty's prisoner. They were sworn to secrecy.

Red was the only person who knew that it wasn't the Dagger who had killed Ma. He had never missed a target in his life. He had killed many times before, mostly the Japs during the occupation, but he'd already notched up a few before then. He did miss the Japs though, because they were such great cover for his killings. Before that, he took cover in the myth of the Beast. His kills were mostly random, some may have had a vague vendetta attached to the act, but Red mostly killed for the hell of it. SPK's sister was one of his. He'd found her walking near the monastery one night. He didn't plan it, he just saw it as a great opportunity.

He felt bad, in theory, when he realised that had been the second time he had badly hurt SPK. The first had been his tip-off to the Japs that SPK was letting his warehouse be used as a storage depot for weapons bound for guerrillas. His main reason for that tip-off was curiosity. He wanted to see what the Japs would do to SPK. It might seem strange that he, a guerrilla fighter, would tell the Japs about a stash of contraband weapons, but not to Red who lusted for murder and saw war as sport and the ultimate expression of life. He thought they would kill SPK, and was surprised that they left it at torture and forced recruitment into their own hated police troops. He had nothing against SPK, or anyone in particular. He wasn't a particularly emotional person, just curious.

He never killed children, he didn't think that was right. But when a 17-year-old joins the Triads, he's an adult, right? That was when he killed the Tai Long Wan recruit in crossfire with the pirates. He'd already killed two pirates in that shoot-out, but where was the challenge in that? Instead he wondered if he could murder one of his own in broad daylight and get away with it. A gunfight gives great cover. The boy's guts spilled all over the deck, and Red found that particularly interesting. It was fascinating to see the emotions going through a person who, realising the extent of his injuries, gradually comprehends the inescapable truth that he will die.

So it was with Ma, a stomach shot, it couldn't be any other. The Dagger was a clear liability that night, Salty should never have brought him on, but Salty was like that, loyal to a fault. Red had tingled with excitement as he tied up Ma on the beach. It took all his self-control not to tell Ma what he was going to do, but then again if Red didn't have immense self-control he would not have had such an illustrious career. It was a shame he could never reveal how creative and prolific he had been over the years. It was all for science, of course, or knowledge, or something. Everything dies. Let life take its course.

12

In Other Words

"This is a most interesting report, Simon. Let's go over your conclusions," Falkirk said.

"Certainly sir. One: The deceased is Ma Xun, believed to have entered Hong Kong illegally from mainland China three years ago with wife and child. Two: Ma Xun was known to officers of the Imperial Police who frequented a private members' club in Wanchai known as the Duchess. Three: It is believed that Ma was an illegal drug courier for corrupt police officers John Tse and Sebastian Wetherby, as the anonymously donated photographs show. It is recommended that these two officers are immediately put under surveillance. Four: It is possible Tse and Wetherby were colluding with other corrupt officers as the scale of their operation would suggest cooperation would have been necessary. The significance of the timing of their operation after the Chiu Chau takeover of Green Gang establishments in Wanchai should be investigated. Five: The American secret services knew that Ma would be delivered to Tai O on the night that he died, although it is possible that they thought he would be alive. Inspector Max Godber called Tai O Police Station on the night of the murder, before local staff had had the opportunity to report to Central. Six: It is believed that American agent Harry Scroggins may be able to shed light on the event. There are several leads that suggest his involvement with the bar formerly called the Green Parrot, which was ransacked in the Chiu Chau takeover, and re-branded the Red Parrot, and which became the venue that Ma supplied heroin to before his death. Scroggins was also seen visiting Tai O Rural Committee the day after after the killing, for unknown reasons.

Seven: It is believed that the killing of Ma took place in the hands of local Lantau Island secret society members. As there is community-wide silence of Triad activities it is impossible to ascertain the exact details of the death. It is believed that a Green Gang member known as Three Eyes contracted the local group. Ends."

"You are sure you want to go through with this?" Falkirk checked.

"Yes sir. This is the best report I can give based on evidence. There's more I can say if you want me to give my opinion, but in the meantime the report presents the facts. Most of them in any case."

"But you know that this isn't going to go down well with powerful people in Central."

"Sir, one of my favourite moments in policing has been hearing you tell a superior, who was clearly in the wrong: 'Shove it up your arse.' I'm good with this report sir, if you are."

"I did have the advantage of being a war hero, Simon. But all credit to you. You won't last long, but I'm proud of you. It is a shame that we can't make the link to Godber more strongly, but this is going to send the peacocks squawking in panic. I wish I could be there to see T-L's face when he reads it."

Falkirk brought down the rubber stamp on the cover of the report and marked it with the word: "Unsolved." There were four copies, the official one for Thomas-Littleton, one for their own safe in Tai O, one to be leaked to the Governor, and one for Jane O'Connor.

Jane, having already had her tiger story spiked, had said that there was no way the full story of Ma Xun could get published now, though she may one day in the future be able to write a book about it.

A few days later Thomas-Littleton had just finished reading the report when he put the papers down, took his glasses off, sighed deeply, lifted the report up and hurled it into the waste paper basket, right on top of the tiger report that came from the same mob of unruly pariahs at the Tai O station. "Tigers, heroin rackets, spies tipping-off police. What a load of old cobblers," he said to himself just as the phone rang. It was Sir Mark Johnson, the Governor.

"I've just seen a report on the Tai O murder. It's an outrage."

"Oh really? We've just had the official report delivered to us an hour ago," T-L said, perturbed and defensive.

"It's the same one, I can reassure you. It's been leaked to me," Johnson spelled out.

"That's rather irregular," T-L said, taken aback and not too sure where this was leading.

"It is indeed. I can only imagine that someone must have been concerned that you might have overlooked the report. You would never bury a report of such importance, would you?" Johnson asked accusingly.

T-L took a look at the rubbish bin.

"Certainly not. Of course the report is rather shoddy at best, containing some serious allegations. It's definitely misleading on some issues. We need to clear up some inconsistencies. I'll need to investigate the author."

"Nonsense, Thomas-Littleton. It looks impeccable to me. I will be dispatching a copy to the colonial office and I'll be meeting with the American consul to discuss the involvement of their spooks. I expect you to conduct a thorough inquiry. That will be all," he said and rang off.

T-L stared out of the window for a moment, envying the kites that soared so freely over the harbour. Then he called Godber to bring him in for an immediate meeting.

"Bit of a tell-tale tit, this Simon Lee, isn't he?" Godber said through clenched teeth after reading the report in front of T-L. As he read through it, he made constant calculations about which parts to accept as fact, what to use for his own advantage, what to cast doubt on, and what he could tear apart. His overall aim was to put together a comprehensive plan to annihilate the upstart Simon Lee.

"I mean, Godber, this link between Ma, Wetherby and Tse. Is it credible?"

Godber looked at the photos. They were difficult to explain away. Wetherby and Tse were expendable, that is what he hired them for.

"I have no idea, sir. You never know how greedy people can get these days."

"Now that the Governor has seen this piece of excrement, we are going to have to put Wetherby and Tse on surveillance, you realise. If this goes any deeper we could be in a lot of trouble."

"Leave it to me sir. I'll watch them like a hawk, and once we've got what we can from them, if we find that they have indeed been running a racket, we'll get rid of them. For now I'm just trying to understand how these pictures came into existence. All taken before the killing by the look of it. They are very professional."

"Yes, including these from inside the Duchess. Do you have any idea who could possibly have taken these images from the Duchess?" T-L implored, genuinely baffled.

Godber had no doubt that it was Scroggins. It was inconceivable that it could be anyone else.

"I have no idea. It's shocking," Godber said to T-L, making his own plans about what to do with Scroggins.

"Well I don't know if it is connected but there is the delicate matter of the call you received from the Cousins before you got a report from Tai O."

"I'm afraid that's an example of the worryingly muddled thinking in this report. I made no mention of a call from the Cousins and simply made a routine call to Tai O to check up on the post. I am willing to testify to that in court."

"I thought as much. That bloody Simon Lee is a troublemaker."

Godber was thinking about how Lee had got into the skirts of T-L's daughter Jasmine, and he had still not managed to bed the notoriously modern woman. He was filled with raging jealousy.

"The bastard needs to be taught a lesson," he said, almost to himself as much as to T-L.

"You're right, Godber. The problem is that he's half-caste, you see. You can never rely on a mongrel."

"No loyalty. That's their problem."

"And low ethics. You see, when thoroughbreds mate outside of their line, their offspring tend to revert to a wilder, more primitive form of the species. Stick to your own race when it comes to breeding, Godber, or else you'll end up with freaks like Lee."

"Very true sir. Leave Wetherby and Tse to me. You can trust me, you know," he said, making plans for how he would eventually mate with T-L's certified thoroughbred daughter.

"I know."

Two weeks later an internal memo was sent around to all police stations. John Tse had been exposed as a Communist spy and was deported to the mainland. Wetherby was caught stealing from the St Paul's Charitable Drug Rehabilitation Fund and had been transferred to a rural post in Borneo. Simon Lee was under investigation for incompetence and had been suspended. Godber's thorough investigation had found Tse and Wetherby had acted alone and no other officers were involved in their scheme. Unmentioned in the report was the fact that the original scheme continued to run with barely a hiccup caused by Ma's death, with stand-ins for Tse and Wetherby, and Ma's former role taken by a very competent Catfish brother from the Duchess called Conrad.

When Simon knocked on the front door of the house in Kennedy Town, Aunt Nancy greeted him with a big hug, calling out to Peggy to come quick. Sensing urgency in Nancy's voice, Peggy rushed from the back of the house and stood face to face with Simon for the first time in two years, though she was confused for a moment as all she saw was Jack White, back from the dead. Then she broke into a wide grin, took her son into her embrace and began clucking around him, worried that he looked so thin. She sat him down on a stool in the kitchen and talked at him while she prepared a big meal. At one point Simon was packed off to the *cha siu* man for a piece of his legendary barbecued pork. She also prepared noodles in a broth, the broth that her uncle was famous for when he had his street stall, where low-ranking police would come hankering for a taste, including Jack, who soon started appearing not just for the broth but for Peggy.

Uncle Trevor came in from an afternoon of fishing on his new dinghy and roared with delight at seeing his nephew. "Tiger!" he shouted, calling Simon by the name that only he ever used for him. He had two sizeable fish and a crab that he thought would last for the next couple of days, but he immediately threw into the meal as a contribution to the welcome dinner. He then turned around and went back to the store to fetch bottles of stout. Over the meal Simon recounted the story of the murder, the corruption, and the village Triads. He was worried that Trevor would be disappointed that he got himself suspended, but Trevor dismissed his concerns: "Sod them," he said. "There's a lot of stinky bastards in the force, always has been. It's more important that you keep your dignity intact than worrying about approval from these creeps."

Then it was time to launch into the tale of the Beast of Tai O, and that kept them going over several bottles of beer. Peggy, slightly bemused by the tiger story, said she had heard Simon had a girlfriend. Simon was a bit surprised that she might have heard about Maria, but was secretly quite pleased. He said he wasn't exactly sure how things stood, but he hoped that maybe the next time he returned home he might be able to bring Maria with him. He felt slightly guilty saying this, knowing that Maria had never agreed such a thing and that he didn't have any clue whether she would accept such an invitation in any case. Aunt Nancy then piped up: "Well I hope she's not a dirty slut like that bloody superintendent's daughter was." Simon was a bit taken aback by the vehemence of her sudden interjection, but also pleasantly surprised that she had forgotten her original stance on the incident when she blamed him.

The call came through from Falkirk two days later. "The investigation is over, Lee. I have no idea how this happened but it seems like you've been cleared of all charges and you're to be formally commended for busting Wetherby and Tse. You're required to attend a reception at the Governor's house on Sunday. They want to give you a medal for God's sake. Don't get carried away son, they're all vipers and they're all in it for themselves. Be on your guard."

If the meal on Simon's first night had looked like a feast, Saturday night at Trevor and Nancy's was a banquet fit for a national hero. Peggy had gone to the market in the morning to source a prize grouper and the best king prawns. Her noodle soup was on slow cook all afternoon to create the top-grade broth. Trevor had gone to Shek O early as he had heard the retired police in the village had shot a juvenile boar in the night. He came back with a leg. Aunt Nancy baked her speciality, an apple pie, and homemade custard.

At the meal Trevor had forgotten his anti-Establishment stance of a couple of nights earlier and now sang the praises of the top ranks in the force and the Governor. Simon was relieved about the the latest development as it indicated that he may not necessarily remain a pariah forever among the officers in the force, but he did find it strange that he had so quickly been promoted from the scrapheap to the ranks of the decorated.

"Good show, old chap," Sir Mark Johnson said, warmly shaking T-L's hand.

"Good result, good result, Johnno," he replied, using the name Johnson was known by when the two of them were on the Oxford rowing team together. None of the tension of their last phone call was present, every bit of animosity had dissolved when the powers that be put the two of them on the same, winning side.

"It was the Colonial Office," Johnno confided. "They've been getting a lot of flack from lefty do-gooders recently. Hounded for so-called 'human rights abuses,' and whatnot, whatever they are. Quite extraordinary. And busybodies banging on about newfangled concepts such as 'transparency' and 'governance'. My God, what a bunch of tosspots these are. Grammar-school educated killjoys, sickeningly worthy civil servants and Trotskyite academics, no doubt, not forgetting their pals from deepest darkest Africa at the UN, and uppity Indians quoting mad Gandhi. Right here in Hong Kong, would you believe that there are small tribes of religious maniacs from backward hamlets in West Yorkshire, Wales and Essex who live in tin-shack squats with illegal immigrants. They teach them to believe the bible literally, which is fine by me as long as they stick to floods, plagues, Lucifer, and water into wine. But other more subversive stuff like God making man in his own image, and loving your neighbour and whatnot, seems to get picked up by the more radical elements that start causing trouble."

"I know the type. Annoying persistent lunatics. Think they have a direct line to God Almighty, always surrounded by adoring Chinese followers. No respect for authority. My God, you should deport the fools. The peasants from China can be driven back into the arms of the Chairman, and the nut-jobs from Wales can go back to the pits!"

"Well, it's not as simple as that, you see. You would think that such unhinged specimens would be illiterate, but it turns out they love to write letters. Prolific, some of them are, and awfully fond of describing corruption, bribery, abuse and whatnot in every minute detail. They write to MPs, colonial secretaries, newspapers, mayors, governors. Terrible interfering simpletons, scribbling away, thinking they're going to change the bloody world. Immensely boring people. Anyway, all that nonsense has a way of insinuating itself into the corridors of power. All you need is one smart alec at some ministry to pick up a catchy idea from the letters and start brandishing it as his own to further his career. Suddenly you get a whole load of busybodies, from fresh-faced graduates who never fought in the war, to middle-aged has-beens looking for a cause to jump on, all versed in issues of 'human rights'. So just when the Colonial Office was looking for a contribution from Hong Kong to prove our commitment to 'governance' and 'transparency,' I find myself holding a juicy document, that for the price of a couple of easy scalps, offers an honest colonial bobby an opportunity for a transparent police force to do some spring-cleaning, and a chance for a vigilant Governor to flex his muscle without hurting anybody. Everyone's a winner."

"Sounds about right Johnno, and I dare say a decade or so in Borneo will do the young Wetherby a world of good, and rotten Johnny Tse can get lost in China."

"So Godber is clean then?" Johnson checked, losing a bit of the confidence he had just been riding on.

"Squeaky. And what about the Cousins?"

"Who knows about them? Their right hand doesn't seem to know what the left hand is doing. And quite frankly neither hand is known for honesty with the rightful colonial government of this bloody cesspit."

Not long after that day, Sir Mark Johnson was recalled to London for demotion to a desk job. A member of the new breed of accountants at the Colonial Office, a fresh-faced Cambridge graduate who had read a lot of French philosophy and American 'beat' poetry while he was studying economics, easily unravelled huge discrepancies in Johnson's expenses to the order of hundreds of thousands of pounds. Johnson stuck with the desk job for about six months and then disappeared with his family – to South Africa, most people believed.

The string quartet was playing a familiar tune, though Simon couldn't quite put his finger on it. Then he saw Jane O'Connor with a cocktail in her hand, mouthing the words of the song.

"Fly me to the moon, and let me play among the stars..."

"Welcome kiddo," she said, kissing him on both cheeks in the continental style with which he was totally uncomfortable. To Simon's surprise and momentary confusion she was with Madam Li, who was almost unrecognisable in a cocktail dress instead of the usual farming attire she walked around in at Tai O.

"Gosh. It's nice to see you, Madam Li. I never thought I'd see you here," Simon spluttered clumsily.

"Why ever not? I know you see me as a tiger-hunting potato farmer, but I have swanned about on these lawns more times than you would imagine. Appearances can be deceiving, Simon. There are at least three men dressed as penguins here who proposed marriage to me a decade ago," she said with a chuckle.

"I used to call her Madam Butterfly back then, fluttering from one flower to another," Jane revealed.

"Oh yes, and we used to call you Calamity Jane, I seem to recall, for all the scrapes you got yourself into," Madam Li replied.

"None of which I failed to extricate myself from politely..." Jane dangled.

"Yes, yes indeed. I do beg your pardon Madam Li. I didn't mean anything by my surprise," Simon said sheepishly.

"You are duly pardoned. And may I take this opportunity to congratulate you for earning the inaugural Police Ethics Award," Madam Li said with mock formality.

"Yup. Well done mate. You did good nailing Wetherby and Tse, even though the crimes they've been publicly accused of have got nothing to do with what you described in your report. Personally I think they should be behind bars, but I suppose the powers that be think that red China and Borneo respectively are just as bad. They might have a point."

"What happened to the tiger story, by the way, Ms O'Connor. I've been looking forward to reading the account in the Post."

"Oh, don't bring that up, Simon, it's a sore point. The bloody editor spiked it. Said it was utterly implausible. There are no tigers in Hong Kong, he says, the last one was killed in 1942."

"Did you tell him you saw it yourself?"

"I sure did, and that I had a quote from the police station chief. But he still wouldn't have it. Says no one would believe it. He says he knows what happens at these village wakes, everyone gets hammered on moonshine, all sorts of regrettable things take place, like hallucinations and collective hysteria. Where's the picture? he says. Wouldn't budge, the old bastard. Some people just don't recognise a good story when they see one."

"You would have thought the editor of a newspaper would," Madam Li suggested.

"Oh, you'd be surprised," Jane said with exasperation. "The most successful editors are the ones that willingly deliver what their masters expect, not the ones that have a genuine nose for a good story."

Simon froze as he saw Jasmine striding across the lawn with Harry Scroggins on her arm, heading directly towards him.

"Simon, darling. So well done. I'm proud of you, baby," she said almost warmly, but mostly for the audience of onlookers and hangers-on. She also gave him the continental air-kiss, her lips not touching skin at all – an utterly pointless gesture.

"Nice to see you Jasmine, I hope you're keeping well," Simon said politely. A vision of her dancing naked to jazz music flashed across his mind, but he quickly put the distracting memory away to focus on the present.

"I'm good, Simon, you know the scene, one party after another. All gets to be a bit of a bore after a while, but I can't complain. In any case, Harry's keeping me entertained these days with his conspiracy theories. You've met Harry, haven't you?"

Scroggins, true to form, was professionally smooth with a double handshake and an unflinching smile. There was no way of telling whether he knew he had been named in Simon's report.

Alongside Simon, other upstanding members of the community were honoured by the Governor that day. A fireman who had saved half a dozen children after their flimsy classroom collapsed in a landslide, a bomb disposal expert whose arm had been ripped off by an American bomb found in Nathan Road, a tax collector who had blown the whistle on his bribe-taking boss. Beside the governor were Thomas-Littleton and Max Godber, the public face of the Hong Kong Police, standing in line shaking hands with the heroes of the day.

"Let me see what spring is like on Jupiter and Mars…"

When Simon reached the podium, Godber warmly shook his hand and congratulated him. Then he tightened his grip on Simon's hand to make it a painful vice-like hold, pulled his ear close to his mouth and hissed through gritted teeth: "Watch your back, cunt. You're a dead man walking."

For a split second Simon was at a loss for a response, then he thought about the medal hanging around his neck and he realised that, for one day at least, he had earned hero status, just as Falkirk's wartime stories had done for him. So he pulled Godber back close, held him in an intimate embrace and whispered back: "Shove it up your arse, sir. Shove it up your arse." Godber was utterly flabbergasted but when they pulled away from each other, both had a grin as wide as the other's.

Hours later, Godber and Scroggins clinked their glasses at a subdued Duchess.

"No hard feelings eh?" Godber said.

"All water under the bridge, old pal," Scroggins replied. "Though next time you have a business proposal, just come and talk to me before setting off a goddamned turf war, will you?"

"Oh, I knew you'd understand. It was a bit of a gamble, but hey, where would the world be without the risk-takers, eh?"

"Listen, I think the customers would also be happy that the name reverts to Green Parrot."

"All the same to me, as long as the Greens don't return, as agreed."

"Well, as we discussed, if we can cooperate in Wanchai, I believe there's no limit to how far we can go."

Scroggins had observed with admiration how smoothly the Green Turtle operation sprang back into action after the death of Ma. He realised then that the brain behind the scheme was very determined, and once his photographs had emerged in the reports, he felt confident that it was a matter of time before the architect identified himself. So Scroggins showed no surprise at all when Godber approached him on the Governor's lawn towards the end of the award ceremony and invited him for a chat at the Duchess.

Over drinks it quickly transpired that they had a mutual admiration for each other's aims and methods. Scroggins said he was impressed with the scope of the takeover and operation. Godber admitted that Scroggins' fine work in unravelling the scheme usefully exposed flaws that needed to be fixed. It was clear to both of them that teaming up would be more beneficial than being in competition. The photographic surveillance at the Duchess was a sore point for Godber, however, and he stiffly requested that Scroggins refrain from carrying out any spying inside the club in the future. Scroggins told Godber that he had come to the club with the pictures to confront him in private but they had been stolen by a British policeman.

"What can I say? Not one of my team, I can assure you. I don't work with idiots who don't know which side their bread is buttered. But here's the deal, Scroggins. If we are going to work together on project Green Turtle, you're going to have to turn over your mole."

Scroggins had anticipated this and already made up his mind. Tony was reliable and very cost-effective as he was on the local rate. Harvestman on the other hand was an expensive buffoon, a useless spy and a liability. And in any case, he would be redundant once Scroggins had a direct line to Godber.

"What will you do with him?"

"Prison. That's the penalty for espionage I'm afraid, and it doesn't matter if he was spying for the good guys, he was spying and that's that."

"Very well. Let's shake on that. Hong Kong today, New York tomorrow, right?"

"Oh yes, I can see how Green Turtle Smack would go down well in New York."

"It is a shame about the collateral damage of course," Scroggins said, with a rare pang of guilt about Ma.

"Oh, don't worry, Harvestman deserves everything he gets, and Borneo will do Wetherby good. Johnny Boy is the type of chap who thrives wherever he is – assuming they don't execute him, of course."

Conrad turned out to be an excellent replacement for Ma on the Green Turtle job. He gradually increased his own shares in the operation and expanded it to greater profits, all the while patiently edging out Godber and Scroggins – so slowly that they didn't notice it happening. It wasn't just the courier job that Conrad took over from Ma. He also inherited his concerns for Xiao Hu, eventually acquiring enough wealth to take over her debt at the Duchess, marry her and move her into his home along with Darwin and her mother. Xiao Hu gave up her job at the Duchess and successfully brought her heroin habit under control. There was enough money around for her to live comfortably as a tai-tai, going from dim sum breakfasts to lunch buffets, afternoon teas and wine bars in the evening, a never-ending treadmill fuelled by gossip and the need to be seen and recognised. The monotony of it was threatening to drive her back to drugs, but a chance meeting with Madam Li near the ferry pier in Kowloon set her off in a new direction.

It was Madam Li who had recognised Xiao Hu, asking why she never stopped to say hello the time she snuck back to pay off her bill all those years ago. After they got talking, Madam Li invited the glamorous-looking tai-tai to visit Tai O and see how the refugee operation had expanded.

Her first visit brought back her own memories of arrival, her fear and exhaustion, but also the wonder she felt at being alive, and the hope she and Ma shared for their future. The years that followed were hell, and yet she was immensely grateful to the simple support that Madam Li had given them by providing an accepting and hospitable shelter when they first set foot on Hong Kong soil. Xiao Hu returned twice within six months, helping out where she could with catering, gardening and – most importantly – by talking with the new arrivals who turned up, frightened and exhausted, just like she had. Before long she was a regular visitor and volunteer, and once she started studying laws, policies and administrative procedures she became a prominent and respected campaigner for refugee rights. It was work that her now gentrified husband fully supported her in.

Darwin grew up with vivid memories of the father he lost when he was nine years old, the same age Simon had been when his father died. He remembered him as always happy, and always telling stories. He had no idea of the kind of hell Ma was living in during that period, a side of his life that Conrad and Xiao Hu explained when he was old enough to understand. In their house Ma Xun was a hero of similar stature to the Outlaws of the Marsh or the Monkey King. Xiao Hu never hid the fact that – once she emerged from her opiate fog – she had never ceased loving him. Conrad told Darwin that Ma was the best man at the Duchess, by far.

When Darwin was 16 he was packed off to a posh school in England called Winchester to study for something called A-levels. He flew through them and went off to study law at Durham University. After that, he went down to London for a couple of years, discovering things about the country that his parents would never believe, such as the crippling psychological straitjacket of class that they all wore, the parochialism of the people there, and their unhealthy obsession with the weather. He then went overland across Europe, through the Middle East, and stopped for six months in Kabul, generally accepted at the time as the best party town on the overland route. Eventually he made his way over the Pamirs, through Xinjiang and Tibet, making the hair-raising dip into deep Yunnanese gorges where old peasants in hamlets still remembered Old Typhoon who had killed a tiger. When he hit urban China he disguised himself as a mute peasant, and eventually made it back to Hong Kong the same way that he had attempted it with his parents when he was six years old, on an old boat, fixed through a snakehead – though this time it didn't sink.

Back in Hong Kong his first task was to help his stepfather launder the millions he had made from the Golden Triangle during the Vietnam War. Conrad told Darwin frankly that he had no pride in the source of his wealth, he simply did what he had to do.

"Your dad told me about his dad, your granddad. You know he was obsessed with animals for some reason, right? A funny thing for a blacksmith, I thought. But he told Ma that about two-thirds of lifeforms were parasites. Living off the products of the other third. Interesting enough he said, well worth studying, but he said it's better to aspire to be like the other third, isn't it? I laughed at your dad then, thought he was too naive to survive. But that had nothing to do with it, he was unlucky, that's all. So now I'm done with the two-thirds, I'm moving over to the one-third."

"But Conrad, what are you going to do? You only know the way of the Catfish."

"I'm done with the Catfish. My money's going into underwear, Darwin. Everyone needs underwear, right? It's useful."

Thus Darwin helped Conrad make his investment into garment factories in the New Territories. But all that was to come years later.

Simon Lee sailed back to Tai O the day after the award ceremony at the Governor's house. He had a mild hangover after a final night of noodles and beers with Peggy, Nancy and Trevor, but the boat trip was pleasant, with favourable winds that brought him to Tai O bay in the evening, as egrets flew in from the rocky shore to marshy roosts inland. Falkirk, Jagan and Patrick Cheung came to greet him at the pier when they saw the ferry sailing in. They were there to shake his hand and congratulate him, but mostly they wanted to look at the medal and see if it had any real gold on it.

"It's yours too, Jagan. We cracked this case together," Simon said.

"Well, you didn't actually crack it. The case was officially unsolved," Falkirk corrected him. "Though you did a good job of uncovering some stinky shenanigans by the likes of Wetherby."

"That's right Simon, you didn't get the medal for solving the murder. You got it for the report you wrote. There is no way I would have written that report. The medal was for that, and it's all yours."

Maria had been short-tempered and sharp-tongued for a couple of weeks while Simon had disappeared to Hong Kong Island, though anyone who said that it was because of his absence got bawled out and told to stop being infantile. It was always slightly nerve-wracking to goad her, but Sally and Madge found the risks were worthwhile for the mirth it brought them to see their idol brought down to the level of ordinary mortals. That evening Bad News had slipped into the conversation that he saw Simon arrive back on the ferry from Kowloon. Outwardly, Maria showed no reaction. She carried on wringing out the washing until it was all done. Then she lit a cigarette and looked across the murky bay water from their veranda. Sally and Madge were preparing to go down to Joycee's to earn some pocket money collecting glasses and washing up. Bad News was already there by then, with SPK and the Jap Devil. Jeanie and Stevie were practising calligraphy with ink and brush. Danny and Spike were on the roof getting their fishing lines ready for the incoming tide. She had about two minutes to get out if she wanted to reach shore without the help of an old crone to punt her across, and if there was an old crone to do that, the old girl would doubtless needle her for gossip until she let slip that she was rushing to the police station because she couldn't wait to see the returning deputy. That wouldn't do. So Maria made a run for it.

She hit the market and found a stall selling exotic-looking things from the Philippines.

"Your dad brought this stuff in this morning," stallholder Chan told Maria. "Said he met some Mindanao boys in good spirits, happy to offload some rarities for a decent price."

There were two live fruit bats, three crocodiles and a couple of odd-looking eagles. Maria spotted a strange dwarf-like monkey, or a monkey-like dwarf, she couldn't tell.

"What's that?" she asked.

"I don't know. Some kind of fairy I think. They say it's called a 'tarsier' and lives in some place called the Chocolate Mountains."

The minute primate had huge eyes and a slow-moving head, but every now and then it made lightning strikes on locusts that were infesting its cage, eating them messily with sharp teeth, as wings and legs wriggled from its mouth.

She recovered from her distraction and spotted some delicious looking mangoes, a more natural type of thing to happen to be carrying than a fairy-like dwarfish simian, as she happened to walk past the police station for no reason at all.

When she arrived, Patrick and Jagan politely pretended that she had come to chat to them as much as she had come for Simon, but as usual they subtly withdrew, leaving Simon on the bench with Maria, looking across the Lin Ting Ocean as the sun sank towards the horizon.

"I heard you got a medal," Maria said.

"Yup. They decided I did good, though I still don't know why they did."

"You're so cynical. Maybe they just thought you did good."

"How's your mum?" Simon said, changing the subject.

"Oh, the same. Still waiting for the all clear, she says. In the meantime seeming to enjoy her quiet days without little kids or big kids to worry about, no meals to cook, no washing to do."

"I've got the police launch tomorrow. We can visit if you like."

"Maybe. Did you see your mum?" she asked.

"Yeah. She made noodles and asked about girls."

"What did you say?" she asked, tensing slightly.

"Nothing much, just that there might be someone I liked."

"Who?"

Jagan, surprisingly, interrupted them through the window.

"Hey, the American DJ just said he's going to dedicate a song to a Tai O policeman!"

They came over to the window just in time to hear a smooth announcer say: "OK now, all you boys of the American Forces, I just want you to know that I met an off-duty policeman from Lantau down on the Aberdeen docks, and he told me how much he digs our radio show. So let's hear it for Simon Lee. Simon, I hope you're out there listening tonight 'cos this is for you and your gal. It's time for you to do some straight talking, brother."

The sweet introduction to *In Other Words* came through the speaker as Simon, Jagan and Maria cheered.

Jagan kept the window open for them as the couple retreated to their bench, the blazing sun dropping into the ocean so vividly that Simon almost expected to hear the water hissing and see steam rising.

"Let me see what spring is like on Jupiter and Mars..."

"What does that mean?" Maria asked.

Sinbad cut across the bay in front of them, his white belly lit up by the afterglow of the sunken sun.

"In other words, hold my hand, in other words, darling, kiss me."

"Oh," said Maria, blushing a bit – putting her hand on his.

EXPLORE ASIA WITH BLACKSMITH BOOKS

From retailers around the world or from *www.blacksmithbooks.com*